D.E.

YOUNG MRS. SAVAGE

Born in Edinburgh in 1892, Dorothy Emily Stevenson came from a distinguished Scottish family, her father being David Alan Stevenson, the lighthouse engineer, first cousin to Robert Louis Stevenson.

In 1916 she married Major James Reid Peploe (nephew to the artist Samuel Peploe). After the First World War they lived near Glasgow and brought up two sons and a daughter. Dorothy wrote her first novel in the 1920's, and by the 1930's was a prolific bestseller, ultimately selling more than seven million books in her career. Among her many bestselling novels was the series featuring the popular "Mrs. Tim", the wife of a British Army officer. The author often returned to Scotland and Scottish themes in her romantic, witty and well-observed novels.

During the Second World War Dorothy Stevenson moved with her husband to Moffat in Scotland. It was here that most of her subsequent works were written. D.E. Stevenson died in Moffat in 1973.

NOVELS BY D.E. STEVENSON
Available from Dean Street Press

Mrs. Tim Carries on (1941)

Mrs. Tim Gets a Job (1947)

Mrs. Tim Flies Home (1952)

Smouldering Fire (1935)

Spring Magic (1942)

Vittoria Cottage (1949)

Music in the Hills (1950)

Winter and Rough Weather (1951)

The Fair Miss Fortune (written c. 1938, first published 2011)

Green Money (1939, aka *The Green Money*)

The English Air (1940)

Kate Hardy (1947)

Young Mrs. Savage (1948)

Five Windows (1953)

Charlotte Fairlie (1954, aka *The Enchanted Isle*, aka *Blow the Wind Southerly*)

The Tall Stranger (1957)

Anna and Her Daughters (1958)

The Musgraves (1960)

The Blue Sapphire (1963)

(A complete D.E. Stevenson bibliography is included at the end of this book.)

D.E. STEVENSON

YOUNG MRS. SAVAGE

DEAN STREET PRESS

A Furrowed Middlebrow Book

FM77

Published by Dean Street Press 2022

First published in 1947 by Collins

Cover by DSP

ISBN 978 1 915014 42 9

www.deanstreetpress.co.uk

THE children were playing in the garden. Polly and Christine were wheeling their dolls' prams up and down the path and talking earnestly. Their heads were close together, nodding as they talked. Dinah would have loved to know what they were saying, but of course she would never know. The twins had climbed into the oak-tree and were intent upon the somewhat complicated business of rigging up a small platform amongst the branches. Dinah could hear their voices from the window of her bedroom. (She had just finished making her bed.) Mark's voice, rather gruff, even at six years old, and Nigel's light and charming. No two children could possibly have been more unlike than Dinah's twins. "Pass the nails." Mark was saying. "There now!—you've dropped the hammer, Nigel." Little boys were much less mysterious than little girls. In the far corner of the garden stood the pram with its tussore canopy and, glancing over in that direction, Dinah could see the rounded blue bulge of Margy's back. The voices of the others at play never wakened Margy; she was used to noise.

The two little girls walked to the end of the path and turned. Dinah sat down on the window-seat and watched them. It was good for Polly to have Christine to play with; Christine lived next door and, being an only child, she was more often to be found in the little Savages' garden than in her own. Sometimes she and Polly fell out, but their quarrels passed like thunder-clouds, leaving the sky clearer than before.

They had stopped beneath the window now, and Dinah could hear what they were saying.

"Sit up, Rose!" said Polly crossly. "Do try to sit up and look intelligent. Don't *slump* on your pillow."

(But she never heard *me* speak like that, thought Dinah, appalled.)

"You must make allowances, Mrs. Fitzgerald," remarked Christine in an affected voice, "Rose hasn't got a father, you see."

"That doesn't matter," retorted Polly as she arranged the pillows and shook her unfortunate child until its eyes rattled in its head. "Fathers are no good at bringing up children. They only make them naughty. I have lots of money to give her presents with, myself."

The children moved away and Dinah was left to reflect upon her daughter's words; they provided food for reflection. She hardly

2 | D.E. STEVENSON

knew whether to be glad or sorry that Polly had such a poor opinion of fathers. In one way it was quite horrifying, of course; but in another way it was comforting since it showed that Polly felt no lack of paternal influence in her own life. Polly was the only one who had any recollection of her father. The twins were too young to remember him, and Margy had never seen him for he had been killed before she was born: killed, not in the war (which, somehow, would have seemed less tragic and unnecessary) but in a flying accident when the war was over and Dinah had ceased to live in constant apprehension of his death.

Dinah sighed. She was tired. Sitting down at the window had been a mistake, for it was when you sat down that you realised how tired you were (she had noticed this phenomenon before); not that you had much time to sit down with a house to look after and four children to feed and clothe. Four children . . . but it wasn't too many, thought Dinah hastily. She wouldn't for worlds have surrendered any one of them, of course. Sometimes she wished she could stick up a large notice saying: "FOUR CHILDREN ARE NOT TOO MANY," so that people wouldn't pity her. It was hateful to be pitied. It was hateful when people said to one another behind her back, "Yes, she's a widow with four children. Poor girl, isn't it sad?" Dinah always knew when they were saying that, because it made her hot all over; "widow" was such a horrid word. Widow! It sounded all droopy like a weeping-willow tree.

Dinah's reflections were interrupted by the arrival of her next-door neighbour (Christine's mother, of course) who had entered the house unperceived and was shouting for her. Dinah had a sort of feeling that the shouts had been going on for several minutes when at last they reached her consciousness. She leapt to her feet and ran downstairs and found Irene Barnard in the hall.

"My dear, where *were* you!" exclaimed Irene. "I thought you had *vanished.* I've been shouting for *hours!*"

"I was thinking," admitted Dinah.

"You shouldn't think," declared Irene. "I *never* do. It makes wrinkles on your forehead. Besides, I never have time to think except when I'm in bed."

"Something started me off," explained Dinah. "As a matter of fact, it was the children talking . . . something Polly said."

They went into the sitting-room, which was full of sunshine, and Irene produced a little parcel from behind her back and pressed it into Dinah's hands.

"I remembered," she said, smiling. "Many happy returns, and may we always live next door to one another!"

"Irene! how kind!"

"It's pretty, isn't it?" continued Irene (as Dinah tore off the wrapping and discovered a jumper, hand-knitted in soft blue wool). "I won't say I don't think it's a nice present because it would be a silly thing to say . . . and of course if I didn't think it was nice I wouldn't give it to you."

"Coupons!" exclaimed Dinah. "Oh, Irene!"

"I mean," continued Irene, returning her friend's kiss with affection, "I mean I can't stand people who give you something and say it's nothing, or that they bought it for themselves and are only giving it to you because it doesn't suit *them*. I feel like telling them to give it to the Jumble Sale. I bought that jumper for you because it's your colour and I knew you'd look sweet in it with your fair skin and blue eyes; in fact, the moment I saw it I said 'Dinah' straight off."

Dinah agreed rapturously that of course that made the gift twice as valuable; and, stripping off her old brown jumper then and there, she put on the blue one and examined herself in the mirror.

"Perfect!" declared Irene. "I knew it would be, and it is!"

"Perfect!" agreed Dinah.

"Now tell me all," said Irene with a sigh. "Tell me about your brother. Is he coming to-night?"

Dinah nodded. "Yes, isn't it marvellous! Almost too good to be true! I haven't seen Dan for nearly seven years—it was before the twins were born—and we haven't had a birthday together since we were thirteen, and now we're twenty-eight!" Irene settled herself upon the sofa. "Tell me about it," she said. "I've got a hundred things to do at home (I haven't even finished making the beds because I was in such a hurry to see you) but thank goodness I don't *worry* about household chores and they always seem to get done sooner or later . . . so tell me all about it."

"About what?" asked Dinah, as she hastily reviewed her own housekeeping arrangements and decided that she could spare twenty minutes or so to devote to the entertainment of her friend.

"About the thirteen-year-old birthday, of course."

"Oh, that!" smiled Dinah. "That's an old story. Dan was sent home from his prep. school because of an outbreak of whooping-cough, and I had had measles and was growing too fast, so I was at home too. I was taller than Dan—it was the first and last and only time—and Dan was annoyed about it. He insisted that we should measure ourselves once a week. I remember that as if it were yesterday. We aren't a bit alike, you know. Nobody would think we were twins. Dan is dark with wavy hair and brown eyes—frightfully good-looking—every one used to say he was like mother. She died when we were born."

Irene knew this (she knew quite a lot about Dinah) but to-day for the first time she realised what it would be like to have no mother, never to have known your mother at all.

"Dreadfully sad!" said Irene with a little thoughtful sigh.

"I suppose it was, but Dan and I didn't know it was sad. We had Father . . . and Nannie. Nannie was a splendid person; she was plump and comfortable and we adored her. She was strict, of course, but very good to us in her dry Scots way. She called us the 'Dees' (Daniel and Dinah), or sometimes if we were naughty she called us 'the De'ils.' We rather liked it. The house was a dear old rambling house close to the sea, and we spent all our waking hours on the shore. It was a lovely place for children."

"The thirteen-year-old birthday," murmured Irene.

"I know. I'm coming to that. Dan and I had a gorgeous time those holidays, we enjoyed them all the more because they were stolen holidays—not ordinary ones—and because for the first time in our lives we discovered our freedom. Father was a doctor, as you know, and much too busy to keep an eye on us, and Nannie had become a sort of cook-housekeeper by that time. So we were absolutely free to do as we liked, and we made the most of it, I assure you. We climbed the rocks and paddled and bathed, and we went out with the fishermen and helped to bring in the lobster pots. We fished off the rocks and went for picnics; we were even allowed to go down to the harbour in the evening all by ourselves and listen to the pierrots. It was wonderful. Looking back, it seems like the golden age; no worries, no troubles, just happiness and blue skies all the time. I remember our birthday lunch. We had salmon and strawberries and cream—heavenly food!

Nannie made us a cake with our names written on it in pink icing, and thirteen blue candles."

"What has become of Nannie?" Irene asked, for she and Henry' often worried about the friendlessness of Dinah. She seemed so completely on her own with no relations except her sailor brother. Dinah was attractive—and sociable by nature—but she was far too busy to cultivate friends in Nettleham. Irene and Henry Barnard were her only real friends, and although they were devoted to her they felt a certain uneasy sense of responsibility on her behalf.

"What has become of Nannie?" echoed Dinah. "Nothing, really. I mean she still lives at Seatown in the old house. She writes to me sometimes (though she isn't much of a hand at correspondence), and as a matter of fact, she sent me a cake this morning, with our names written on it in pink icing, but no blue candles, of course. You see, when Father died he left Nannie the house and any of the furniture we didn't want; so Nannie married the butcher (who had wanted to marry her for years) and settled down comfortably. She lets rooms in the summer and makes quite a good thing of it. Seatown is quite near Edinburgh (it's convenient for Edinburgh business men) and Nannie is an excellent cook, so people go back to her year after year for their summer holidays."

"How long is it since you saw her?" Irene wanted to know.

Dinah made a rapid calculation. "We were seventeen when Father died, so that makes it eleven years. Dan was in the Navy by that time, and I was leaving school. We had arranged that I was to go home and live with Father, but instead of that—which would have been lovely—I had to go and live with an aunt in Glasgow who didn't want me at all. Then when the war started, I went into the Wrens and met Gilbert . . ." She hesitated, and added with a little smile, "So that's the story of my life."

Irene would have liked to know more, for she had an insatiable thirst for information about people in whom she was interested. For instance, what had Dinah done with herself in Glasgow living with the aunt who didn't want her? How unutterably dreary it must have been! No wonder Dinah had fallen rapidly and completely in love with Gilbert Savage, who looked like a Greek god and behaved like a Don Juan! It was curious and very interesting (thought Irene) how little bits of information put together made a picture of a person and her background . . . just like those frightful jigsaws which Christine adored, and which, however much one despised them, one was forced to complete, thereby wasting hours of precious time. The analogy was not exact, of course, if you followed it to the end, for the puzzle of Dinah's personality was worth completing and not a waste of time.

The Barnards had lived next door to Dinah for nine years; they had arrived at Nettleham at the same time. Irene and Dinah were "brides," so they had a good deal in common from the very beginning, and from the very beginning they had liked each other immensely. Dinah's husband was a naval officer, so she did not see very much of him. Irene's husband was on the Stock Exchange and travelled to London daily. The war brought little change, except increased anxiety to both young wives; but Irene realised how much worse it was for Dinah who bore this anxiety alone. Polly and Christine were born within a month of one another. Their mothers had wanted sons, but they agreed that little girls were delightful . . . and how nice it would be for them to play together when they were bigger! It was fun to compare notes about the babies, to exchange patterns for small garments and recipes for diet. It was not so much fun when the sirens went oft in the middle of the night, and the babies had to be carried out to the blast-proof shelter which the two families shared. After a bit, the twins arrived upon the scene, and there were four babies to be cared for in the blast-proof shelter. Looking back, Irene wondered how they had managed, how they had survived the misery and terror of those nights. Night after night of bombs raining down upon Nettleham; Henry walking among the blazing ruins of the town in his warden's uniform; every one worn out and irritable with sleeplessness and strain. Wonderful what you can bear if you have to, thought Irene, but, of course, it has left its mark. Nobody who came through *that* can ever be quite the same.

"I must go," said Irene at last. "I really must. Would you like to bring Dan to dinner to-morrow night? Henry said to ask you, but don't come if you would rather have him all to yourself."

"Lovely!" nodded Dinah. "Of course we'll come. I want you to meet Dan. It seems all wrong and quite ridiculous that you've never met him."

"Commander Bell—is that what we call him? I shall *never* remember. Perhaps if I go to bed saying it over and over it might help."

"Call him Dan, of course. Everybody calls him Dan. Anyway he's only a Lieutenant-Commander and won't be that much longer. He's getting out of the Navy any minute now."

"Has he got a job?" asked Irene, rising to go.

"Only a temporary one, I'm afraid. It's in a shipping company at Leith."

"Leith!" echoed Irene in horrified accents.

Dinah laughed. She was aware that Irene thought England was the only civilised portion of the British Isles.

"Leith!" repeated Irene. "Couldn't he get a job in London or Southampton or somewhere? Why must he go and bury himself at the North Pole?"

But Dinah would not rise. "Go home and make your bed," said Dinah, laughing. "It's a disgrace to any self-respecting Englishwoman to have unmade beds in her house at this hour of the morning."

"Yes, isn't it?" agreed Irene. "It's frightful. I meant to pop in for a few moments and I've stayed nearly half an hour—wasting your time." She was on the doorstep now, and was really on the point of departure, but Dinah could not let her go on that note.

"Nonsense!" exclaimed Dinah. "You never waste my time. You're as good as a bottle, Irene."

"What on earth does that mean?"

"Difficult to explain," said Dinah thoughtfully. "A bottle is short for a bottle of medicine, of course (the medicine given you by the doctor to cure you of your ills), and of course all Father's patients clamoured for a bottle no matter what was wrong with them, even if they had housemaid's knee. So when Father said: 'You're as good as a bottle' there was a joke within a joke, and his eyes used to twinkle when he said it. Father believed in fresh air and exercise and soap and water, but he had to give his patients bottles to keep them quiet. And of course," added Dinah with a little smile, "of course, I've spoilt the whole thing by explaining it. One always does."

2

THE children had been put to bed early. Dinah slipped into a blue silk frock, brushed her hair vigorously, made up her lips and powdered her nose. She looked at herself in the mirror somewhat anxiously, for seven years was a long time and she did not want Dan to be disappointed. She was pale of course (because she was always so tired), but fortunately one could remedy pallor quite easily , . . Yes, that was better.

Dinah ran downstairs to put the finishing touches to the birthday supper. She would have liked to give Dan salmon and strawberries and cream—thick, rich cream and lashings of it—but as that was impossible she had done the best she could. The haddock with its creamy, cheese sauce was in the oven, browning nicely; the salad bowl was full of crisp, green lettuce and tomatoes; the coffee was ready; there was a trifle made with sponge cakes, strawberries and evaporated milk. Dinah spent a few minutes decorating the trifle. It looked quite nice. Unfortunately it would not taste as nice as it looked.

The table in the dining-room was set. The silver lamp stood in the middle, flanked by Nannie's cake. The silver shone and the glasses sparkled, Dinah had seen to that. She was still standing, admiring the effect of her handiwork, when she heard the "chuff-chuff" of Dan's ancient car. She rushed out of the house to meet him.

"So brown and beautiful!" cried Dinah, flinging herself into his arms and hugging him. "So *much* better-looking than me! It isn't fair!"

"Darling donkey!" exclaimed Dan, kissing her fondly.

"Just as silly as ever! Let me look at you properly . . . much too thin and pale in spite of all that red stuff on your cheeks."

"Isn't this fun?"

"Isn't it? Wasn't I clever to manage it? Are the brats in bed?"

"Yes, and you're not to go *near* them to-night. You'll see quite enough of them to-morrow."

"Our night, isn't it?" smiled Dan.

"Nobody else's!" replied Dinah.

They went into the house, arm-in-arm, talking and laughing and teasing one another. There was no strain at all; it was just as if they had met last month instead of having been separated for seven years. Dan had brought a large silk square for Dinah, with sheaves of golden corn all over it and blue cornflowers to match her eyes. It was a lovely thing, Dinah thought, much nicer than the silver-grey pullover which she had knitted for him.

"I wish it were nicer," said Dinah, looking at it, distastefully.,

"It couldn't be nicer," declared Dan.

The fact was Dinah had taken so long to make the pullover that she was bored with it, bored to death with the pattern and the colour. There were mistakes in the knitting (a dropped stitch beneath the arm-hole which had had to be carefully darned, and here and there a flaw in the pattern) for it is difficult, if not impossible, to concentrate upon a complicated pattern when you are surrounded by chattering children; or, alternatively, late at night when your eyes are almost closing with drowsiness. Dinah had intended to point out the flaws to Dan—it was her nature to be completely frank—but, remembering what Irene had said about the blue jumper, she decided to hold her tongue. Dan would never notice the flaws; nobody would notice unless they examined the garment closely, and Dan might take more pleasure in his pullover if he thought it perfect. Such was her reasoning.

In addition to the scarf Dan had brought a bottle of white wine and a small jar of caviare—these were his contributions to the feast— and soon they were ready to begin.

Dan poured out the wine. "Here's to us!" he said, raising his glass.

"Wha's like us!" responded Dinah.

They touched glasses and drank quite solemnly, for the occasion was solemn. Seven years had passed—seven years of war and peril and horror unimaginable—and here they were again, united.

"We're still the Dees," said Dinah, voicing the thought.

"Still the Dees," agreed Dan, gravely.

But they could not stay solemn for long, and soon Dan was saying: "D'you remember our tenth birthday, Di? It was before I went to boarding-school. Father gave us bicycles and we spent all day learning to ride them on the sands. You were better at it than I was—you got your balance at once—it was dreadfully galling."

"You were better than I was at everything else," said Dinah quickly. "You were better at rowing and jumping and climbing rocks—and much better at swimming. How I longed to be a boy! D'you remember, Dan?" She paused and looked at him.

"Yes, of course, I do," said Dan, smiling.

The incident which the Dees remembered so well had taken place during the summer holidays. The Dees were eight years old, and as full of innocent mischief as a pair of puppies. One day they were sent for by their father and appeared before him in his surgery, looking somewhat scared. There was nothing very serious on their consciences, but you never knew . . . sometimes grown-ups took a grave view of activities which seemed comparatively harmless.

"You're getting big," said Dr. Bell, looking at them over the top of his spectacles. "You're eight years old. Dan is too old for Miss Thomson's school, so I've entered him for Mr. Ferguson's. He will start there next term."

"And me, too?" said Dinah confidently.

"It's a boys' school," explained Dr. Bell, and left it at that.

"You mean we shan't be together!" cried the Dees in horror-stricken tones.

"You can't be together," said Dr. Bell. "I'm sorry about it, but it's impossible. Dinah can go on at Miss Thomson's in the meantime, but Dan must go to a boys' school. Boys and girls go to different schools—you know that, don't you? And that reminds me, Nannie is going to move you into the two little front rooms so you'll each have a room of your own instead of sleeping in the nursery. You'll like that, won't you?" added Dr. Bell, hopefully.

They didn't like it at all.

"Well, anyway, that's what is to be," continued Dr. Bell. "Nannie and I have talked it over, and it's all decided."

"Couldn't we stay as we are?" asked Dan.

"Have we been *dreadfully* naughty?" asked Dinah.

"It isn't a punishment; it's because Dinah is a girl."

The Dees filed out of the surgery and closed the door.

"It isn't a punishment," said Dan, in bewildered tones.

"It's worse!" declared Dinah. "It's the worst thing that has ever happened to us. That's what it is."

"You can't help being a girl," said Dan, trying to comfort her.

"No," said Dinah. "No, but I wonder. Dan, listen to me."

It was an idea which had burst upon Dinah suddenly in the mysterious manner of inspiration. She explained it to Dan and they talked it over all day, talked about it as they sat on a rock and dangled their feet in the sea, talked about it as they put their shoes on and trailed home to tea. Nannie found them unusually subdued that evening. She had known that the new arrangements would upset them considerably, and she was surprised at their apparent resignation; she had expected arguments and tears. They were unusually willing to go to bed that night, unusually eager to see the last of her. She had a feeling that there was something up, and she lingered, hoping they would tell her; but nothing was said, and at last she went away.

When Nannie had gone the Dees got out of their beds and knelt down side by side on the floor. It had been agreed that Dan was to be the spokesman—he was half an hour older than Dinah—but the prayer was a composite effort and had entailed a great deal of thought.

"Please God," said Dan; "please God, you promised in the prayer book that when two or three people are gathered together You would grant their request, so please listen to Dinah and me. There are just two of us but that ought to be enough. Dinah wants to be a boy so that she can go to school with me and do all the things boys do . . . and I want her to be a boy. So that's our request, and we hope You will grant it. Amen."

"Amen," said Dinah, loudly.

They got back into bed and lay down.

"When will it happen?" asked Dinah, in a voice that trembled slightly.

"Not till it's dark," replied Dan, firmly. "Everything *important* happens in the middle of the night—things like babies coming, and Santa Claus—you know that, Di."

"Yes," said Dinah, meekly.

They turned over and snuggled down, but it was a long time before they went to sleep.

"I remember the whole affair as though it had happened last week," said Dan, smiling at Dinah across the lamplit table.

"I was frightfully scared," said Dinah, thoughtfully. "So scared that it was almost a relief when I woke in the morning and found it hadn't come off."

"I was thankful! I didn't want you to be different—not really. I just felt I had to back you up because being a girl must be so rotten. Afterwards, when the miracle didn't happen, I had an uneasy feeling it was my fault because I hadn't wanted it with my whole heart."

"Silly little donkeys, weren't we?"

"Not really. The prayer book says distinctly, 'When two or three are gathered together in Thy name, Thou wilt grant their request.'"

"Yes, I know," agreed Dinah. "But I don't think people should have their requests granted if it would do them harm. That's why the prayer goes on to say, 'as may be most expedient for them.' It wouldn't have been very expedient for me," she continued, with a little smile, "and think of Father's feelings—and Nannie's! It's like this, Dan; I love the children dearly, but I wouldn't give them a young tiger as a pet, however much they wanted it . . . as a matter of fact they were extremely anxious to have a baby tiger (they saw one at the Zoo) and Mark assured me that it would cause no trouble in the house, he would keep it in a rabbit hutch and look after it most carefully."

The Dees laughed over that, and then were silent.

Dan was worried about Dinah. She was pale and much too thin. Of course she had had an awful life, thought Dan. Everything had gone wrong; Gilbert had been crazy to let her have so many children. Gilbert ought to have had more consideration; he ought to have taken more care of her; he ought to have waited . . . but, of course, Gilbert had never waited for any one or anything; he had never looked beyond the present moment; he had always done as he liked and been a law unto himself, confident and carefree, full of gaiety and easy charm.

"Do you ever hear from Gilbert's parents?" asked Dan, at last.

"Gilbert's parents! No, of course not."

"It seems a pity."

"Dan!" cried Dinah. "You know quite well what happened. You *know* how they behaved. He went to Harrogate to see them and tell them about me—that we wanted to marry each other—and they were simply horrible to him about it. They ordered him out of the house. We never heard from them again. There was some other girl they wanted him to marry—you know all that!"

"All right, all right!" said Dan. "No need to go up in the air. I was just asking, that's all. It happened so long ago I thought they might have come round."

"Why should they? If they didn't come round when Gilbert was alive, why should they come round now? I don't worry my head about them."

Dan said no more. Personally, he thought the Savages should be asked to contribute to the education of their grandsons, and he could not believe they would refuse to do so if properly approached; but obviously it was no use suggesting this to Dinah.

Dinah's thoughts had taken another line. "It's been pretty hard going," she said at last; "but I've managed to pull through, and to tell you the truth, I've never been so utterly and completely miserable as I was when Father died."

Dan nodded. It was his low-water mark, too. Dark shadows are blacker than jet to the seventeen-year-old child.

"Never," repeated Dinah, thoughtfully. "It seemed the end of everything. There wasn't a single bright spot. I got back from school and Father was dead and Nannie was going about the house with her eyes so red and swollen that she could hardly see—and you arrived looking like a ghost."

"I was sick all the way from Portsmouth," said Dan. "I can't think why, because I'm never sick in trains . . . must have eaten something, I suppose."

"People came with letters," continued Dinah. "People came and wept on the doorstep. Flowers came—flowers and flowers and flowers—will you ever forget the flowers? The whole house was full of them, we didn't know what to do with them; do you remember, Dan?"

Dan remembered. He remembered Aunt Teena's arrival—the aunt from Glasgow whom they had never seen before—and how she had made everything a thousand times worse by trying to take control of everything and getting on the wrong side of Nannie and insisting that Di must go and live with her in Glasgow instead of staying on at Craigie Lodge with Nannie, which had been the obvious thing for Di to do.

"I don't know why Aunt Teena took you to Glasgow," said Dan at last.

"She did it to score off Nannie, of course—she was furious with Nannie about the will—but afterwards she was sorry, and all she wanted was to get rid of me. Oh, dear! It was a miserable time. I can hardly bear to think of it."

"Well, don't let's," suggested Dan, very sensibly. "Let's think of something cheerful instead. I've got a plan."

This was an old Dee-saying, and hearing it again Dinah looked up and smiled. "You've got a plan?"

"Yes, rather a marvellous plan—at least, I think it's marvellous. The plan is for you to bring the children to Seatown for the whole of August."

"You must be mad!" exclaimed Dinah, in amazement. "Why? Nannie would love to have you at Craigie Lodge. It would be a rest for you, wouldn't it? I could easily run down and spend week-ends with you."

"Nannie couldn't possibly have us!"

Dan smiled. "She can. I went down and saw her. It *was* odd seeing Nannie and the dear old house again. The people who were coming to her for August have cancelled their rooms. I took them for you."

"Dan!"

"Provisionally, of course. It was a sudden idea. Nannie had got the letter that very morning, and was busy wiring out an advertisement for the rooms. I just suddenly thought of you, and how lovely it would be. It's the way things happen, Di! Nice things always happen like that; they fall from the skies."

"I couldn't *think* of it!"

"Please," said Dan, earnestly. "*Please* think of it. And don't forget the children. They would love the sea and the sands, wouldn't they?"

"I couldn't!" repeated Dinah; but this time she said the words without conviction, for already she had begun to envisage herself and the children at Craigie Lodge. She thought of Nannie. How lovely to see Nannie again! How lovely to be free from household cares! How lovely to smell the sea and watch it rolling in—waves tipped with frills of foam—to burst with a swishing sound against the rocks! Already she saw herself sitting on the golden sands with Margy beside her on a rug, while Polly and the little boys paddled and sailed boats or searched for crabs amongst the tangled brown seaweed. She would take their milk and biscuits with her and give them their "elevenses" on the shore. They would stroll back to Craigie Lodge at dinner-time . . . and dinner would be ready waiting for them.

Dan was silent, watching her face; he was a very wise young man.

"How could I?" said Dinah, with a sigh. "Think of that long journey!"

"Well, if you can't, you can't," said Dan regretfully. "I'm disappointed, of course; I was looking forward to long week-ends at Seatown, visiting our old haunts and that. Nannie will be sorry, too. She was asking all about the children. I had better write to her to-night. She'll let the rooms quite easily."

"Leave it till the morning . . ." began Dinah, and then she caught his eye and burst out laughing. "You demon!" she cried. "You know quite well we shall go! I can't resist it! Nannie, and the dear old house, and the sea, and no cooking for a whole month!"

"And me for week-ends," Dan reminded her.

They had finished their supper by this time, so they washed the dishes together (which was a cheerful business, quite different from washing dishes alone) and then they went into the drawing-room and sat by the window, watching the twilight fall. They were still playing the old game of "Do you remember?" for birthdays are occasions when one is tempted to look backward down the years and, once started, it is difficult to stop; one incident leads to another in the easiest way imaginable.

"D'you remember our cameras?" Dan inquired. "That must have been our eleventh birthday, Di. What appalling pictures we took!"

"It was a hit or a miss. We didn't understand the first thing about those cameras. I remember hiding in the sandhills and taking a photograph of Malcolm Armstrong riding along the shore."

"Malcolm Armstrong!" exclaimed Dan. "Goodness, how long ago that seems. We thought he was marvellous."

"So he was!" cried Dinah. "He *was* marvellous. Tall and strong and handsome and good at everything, especially good at golf. D'you remember the East of Scotland Amateur Championship?"

"We walked round and watched every shot and held our thumbs when he putted."

"And he won!" added Dinah. "I shall never forget the thrill."

Dan was still worried about Dinah. In a way she was wonderful (gay and sparkling and intuitive, his very own Di and the best company in the world) but there was an odd sort of tension in her. She was restless. He comforted himself with the idea that she was tired, and that the month at Seatown would set her up. Sea air was what she needed.

It was late when they went to bed. Dinah accompanied her guest to his room as a hostess should.

"I hope you'll be comfy," said Dinah, anxiously.

"I'm sure I shall," declared Dan.

Dinah turned at the door and smiled. "Good night," she said. "Do you remember how Nannie always said, 'Now then, away off to sleep! It'll be another day in the morning'?"

3

DINAH couldn't sleep. She was over-tired and over-excited. Dan's coming had stirred up happy memories, but now she was remembering unhappy things. Talking about Gilbert had upset her—how silly that was! She rose and drank a glass of water and composed herself, breathing deeply through her nose which was supposed to induce sleep. But this didn't help at all. She was all "het up" as Nannie would have said and the memories kept crowding in, miserable memories which she had tried vainly to forget.

Dinah had been nineteen when she met Gilbert Savage. They had fallen madly in love with one another in the first five minutes of their acquaintance. It was elemental—dynamic—it was like thunder and lightning. They met and loved one another and were married in less than a month. Their honeymoon was short but rapturous, for Gilbert was the most delightful companion, gay and carefree and full of life. Dinah knew she was the luckiest girl in all the world. The only flaw in her happiness was the fact that Gilbert was in the Navy, which meant that they could not see as much of one another as they would have liked, but of course Dinah had known that all along, so she was sensible about it—or tried to be sensible—and when he went to sea she settled down at Nettleham and waited for him to come back.

It was a curiously unrestful life, so Dinah found. She was either wildly excited at the prospect of seeing Gilbert or sunk in gloom when his leave was over and he had gone. Her life was totally different from that of her friend, Irene Barnard, whose husband was with her all the time; and as the years went by Dinah began to realise that her relations with Gilbert were different from the relations of other husbands and wives. She loved Gilbert—of course she loved him—but he was not a part of her life, as Henry was part of Irene's life and Hugh Starkie a part of Joan's. Even his leaves became less rapturous, for the children never showed to good advantage when Gilbert was there. She found herself acting the part of buffer between Gilbert and his children—easing the shocks and trying to keep things smooth.

Dinah saw Gilbert only at long intervals when he was on leave, and his leaves were not a part of everyday life, but were periods of stress and excitement. When Gilbert was on leave he wanted to rush about and Dinah was continually dragged in two directions. "Darling,"

Gilbert would say; "darling, for the love of Mike can't you get someone in to look after the children! I want my wife. I want to dance with her for one thing. Darling, let's go to town and have a spree! Do let's! Oh, of course, I think they're simply marvellous, especially Nigel. (You know Nigel is exactly like me when I was small.) I'm terribly proud of them—well, of course I am—but, dash it all, this is my *leave*! I mean, one looks forward to leave for months, so of course one wants to get about and have a good time. You see that, don't you?"

Dinah saw. She managed to arrange matters so that she could go dancing with him, but somehow or other it was not a tremendous success. Dinah had left a little bit of herself at home. The twins were four years old, but not as strong as they should have been; and she found herself wondering if that girl were really reliable. Would she remember Mark's cod liver oil? Would she remember to change their shoes and socks when they came in from the garden? This dancing business was fun, of course, but . . . well, perhaps she had outgrown it a little . . . or perhaps it was because she was tired. But Gilbert had not outgrown it. That was the trouble.

She sought for excuses for Gilbert, and they were easy to find. Gilbert wasn't a father in the same way that Dinah was a mother. How could he be, when his children were comparative strangers to him? He could not be expected to love them as she did. She had carried them in her body for months, suffered their birth, fed them and bathed them, watched for their first smiles, agonised over their small illnesses, rejoiced over their recoveries; she had seen the dawning of their intelligence and encouraged their first attempts to walk; she had punished them and rewarded them and answered their questions. If Gilbert had been at home he would have seen all this happening and played his part, but he wasn't at home. So you could hardly blame him for not being really interested in the children (but only proud of them, which was not enough).

Once or twice in the middle of the night—a time when we are all prone to dismal reflections—Dinah was visited by the dismal reflection that Gilbert's wife was a stranger to him, and that he was a stranger to his wife. It was obvious to Dinah when she went in next door and saw Irene and Henry together that they had something—something nebulous but very important—which she and Gilbert had not. ("These twain shall be one flesh." It was something like that, thought Dinah.)

Irene and Henry had learned to know one another, to live together and to share everyday joys and troubles. She and Gilbert *would* have learned—so Dinah tried to assure herself. If Gilbert had been at home all the time, like Henry, he would have settled down and become a real husband, a real father; the sort of husband to lean upon, the sort of father who would have taken an interest in Polly's teeth and arranged for Mark's adenoids to be removed. Dinah was sure of it . . . or nearly sure.

It was after the not very successful leave (when they had gone dancing and Dinah had left a little bit of herself behind) that Dinah had discovered another baby was coming. She was somewhat dismayed for already she had more than enough to do. How on earth was she going to manage? She could not make up her mind whether to write to Gilbert at once and tell him about it, or to keep it to herself. Gilbert wouldn't like it. He thought three children was a lot. What would he think of four—or would it be five? It was no use blinding oneself to the fact that twins were fairly common in the Bell family.

Dinah put off the evil day as long as possible, but when Gilbert wrote to say he had got a fortnight's leave she could put it off no longer, for it is easier to break unwelcome tidings by letter—or so Dinah felt. She wrote off at once and awaited Gilbert's reply in some trepidation. Strangely enough he was quite nice about it (not pleased, of course, but she had not expected him to be pleased) and he comforted her by saying that she must not worry, she must try to take things easy; couldn't she get a girl to help in the house? *Once I get out of the Navy we shall be much better off*, wrote Gilbert. *I've got that job in London waiting for me. Meanwhile we must just do the best we can. And now for my bit of bad news—my leave has been cancelled. It is absolutely sickening and I am very disappointed. I know you will be disappointed, too, poor darling, and that makes it worse. I asked the Commander and told him the circumstances and he said he would see what he could do, so I might manage to get a couple of nights at home. That's not much, is it? The worst of it is we are off to the Med. next month and no chance of seeing you again until I get out of the Service for good. I will let you know about the two nights when I hear for certain. Take care of yourself, darling. I hate to think of you feeling ill and miserable . . .*

Dinah was terribly disappointed for she had been building all sorts of hopes and dreams upon that fortnight's leave (Gilbert could not drag her about, so they would stay at home and be quiet together and get to know one another; and Gilbert would see the children at their best and learn to love them) but it was no use lamenting; she must be sensible. Gilbert would be free quite soon—in another six months perhaps—and he would be home for good, travelling to London daily like Henry next door. So she wrote a cheerful letter to Gilbert and set her hopes upon the couple of nights at home which was better than nothing.

All would have been well if Dinah had not met Mrs. Starkie in the post office (and she very nearly didn't, because it was only at the last minute she remembered she wanted stamps). Mrs. Starkie had smiled at Dinah and rushed up to her in great excitement, saying, "I'm *so* glad your husband got his leave after all. We saw him in town last night at the Whirlygig Club—he didn't see us, of course."

"Didn't he?" said Dinah.

"He's so marvellously good-looking, isn't he? He seemed in tremendously good form. You weren't there, were you? I looked for you, but didn't see you."

Dinah managed to laugh. "I'm not exactly in dancing form, am I?"

"Well—no—" agreed Mrs. Starkie.

"Gilbert loves dancing—so why shouldn't he enjoy himself when he can?"

"Oh, of course," agreed Mrs. Starkie hastily. "Very sensible—I mean—as you say—why shouldn't he?"

Why shouldn't he? Dinah asked herself as she ploughed her way home, laden with fish and dried milk and potatoes and all the other comestibles which she had managed to obtain that morning to feed her children—and Gilbert's. Why shouldn't he enjoy himself? Why shouldn't he racket about with women? Why shouldn't he lie to her? Even at this moment Gilbert's letter was tucked down the front of her blouse and crackled as she moved. Hateful, lying letter! The first thing she did when she got home was to take it out and drop it into the kitchen fire. The envelope burned first. She watched it burn. She saw the words "ever your own true Gil" before a flame caught the paper and it vanished into ash.

Gilbert came home for two nights, bearing gifts (like the Greeks) for all the family. The gifts were exactly right, for Gilbert was the sort of person who was good at gifts; he liked choosing them and presented them with a joyous grace which made them doubly worth having. There were gifts for every one; there was even a lovely blue woollen pram rug for the member of his family who had not yet arrived. He was in very good form and was particularly sweet and loving and delightful; playing games with the children and helping Dinah in the house . . . and all he did was done easily and happily as if he enjoyed every moment of it.

Dinah had meant to have it out with him of course, for it was her nature to be open and straightforward. She had meant to tell him that she would never grudge him his fun, that she understood his love of a good time and sympathised with it. If she could not go dancing with him he could go with any one he liked . . . but he must not lie to her. All this she had decided, lying awake at night and thinking it out, for she realised that this was dangerous matter and if she didn't handle it carefully it might explode. She must say neither too much nor too little; she must be perfectly calm and friendly but absolutely firm . . . for unless marriage was built upon truth it would fall into ruin. Truth is the rock upon which all human relationships are built.

Dinah had settled this and prepared herself to have it out with him, but when he arrived the children were there, dancing about in wild excitement and tearing open the parcels he had brought (it was impossible to tackle him in front of the children) and when they had gone to bed it was still impossible to tackle him, so Dinah found. She had never been able to decide whether it was sheer cowardice on her part, or whether it was because she felt so awfully ill and wretched (much more so than with the other children) that she simply couldn't begin an argument with Gilbert or raise unpleasantness between them. She comforted herself with the promise (or was it a threat?) that someday she would tell him, someday when he was settled at home and they had begun to get used to one another. She *must* tell him someday so that everything should be fair and square between them—no secrets at all—but Dinah never saw Gilbert again. He was killed in a flying accident on his way home.

These were the miserable, uncomfortable memories which kept Dinah awake.

4

THE evening had belonged to Dan and Dinah, but the morning was definitely the children's. Dan came down to a thoroughly domestic scene: Polly and the twins were busily eating porridge, and Margy was having porridge ladled into her mouth. Dinah seemed a different person in this *milieu*; in fact, Dan had the uncomfortable feeling that his hostess was a complete stranger, years older than himself . . . and not only did she feel older, but she looked older, tired and haggard, in fact definitely ill.

"I slept badly," said Dinah, replying to his inquiry. "It was hot, wasn't it?"

"I didn't go to sleep for ages," announced Nigel, with pride. "I heard you come in your car. Will you take me for a drive?"

"Yes, of course," said Dan.

"What's it called—or hasn't it got a name?"

"His name is Bildad," replied his owner promptly.

Dinah laughed. "Bildad the Shuhite?"

"Yes; you see he's just about the height of a shoe, so—"

"Could you take me?" interrupted Mark. "I mean would it be too much for Bildad—two people?"

"Bildad can take everybody if you don't mind a squash. We might have a picnic this afternoon. What about that?"

It was agreed that a picnic would be fun, and some time was spent discussing where they should go. Dan took no part in the discussion for he did not know the country. His mind wandered as he ate his egg . . . he was amused to see that the twins were drinking milk out of their Burmese mugs.

Dan had been in Burma when the news of their arrival reached him together with the invitation to be their godfather. He had bought two mugs of beaten silver and dispatched them by registered post; mugs for the little mugs! It was fun to see his presents on this very British breakfast-table, to watch the twins drinking from them—their faces disappearing inside—it was fun to look back and remember the stall in the bazaar where the mugs had been bought. Dan remembered it clearly; the blazing sunlight, the vivid colours of silks and brasses and beads, the swarthy face of the Burman, his long thin hands and the gold rings in his ears, all the colours and noises and smells of the East.

"They love their mugs," said Dinah who had an uncanny habit of reading his thoughts.

"I'm glad they use them," replied Dan . . . and he began to tell them about the day he had bought the mugs. The story was a tremendous success.

After breakfast Dan found himself carried off into the garden and realised what Dinah had meant when she said he would see enough of the children to-morrow. They monopolised him completely. He was drowned in children. Dan had vaguely dreaded his introduction to Dinah's brood, for to him children were an unknown quantity. He was afraid they would be shy, that they would not like him; he was afraid he might find nothing to say to them . . . but he need not have worried. Dan was a success from the very start. He was taken to see Mark's rabbits and was introduced to "Mummy's hens." He was invited to climb the tree and his prowess in climbing "almost to the top" was commented on and admired. There were screams of delighted laughter when he rode Polly's fairy-cycle round the lawn with his knees sticking out at an angle of forty-five degrees.

He discovered that they were calling him Dan (it was natural, of course, for they had heard their mother call him Dan) and he was pleased that they should. "Uncle" was such a sober, elderly sort of title.

It was a very hot morning. Dan suggested that a tent would be nice.

"But we haven't one," said Polly regretfully.

"We could make one," Dan told her. "It isn't difficult to make a tent. We could rig up a tent in half no time with a couple of dust-sheets."

The idea was received with acclamation.

"A tent. A tent!" cried Nigel, dancing about like a Dervish.

Dan was used to working with people. He was used to sizing up men and appraising their worth, so it interested him profoundly to watch the reactions of Dinah's children to the job in hand. Polly was on her toes the whole time. "Dust-sheets!" she cried, and was off like an arrow to find her mother and ask for dust-sheets. Mark worked stolidly. He held the poles while Dan hammered them into the sun-baked lawn. He held the ball of string and produced a knife out of his pocket at the right moment. Nigel danced about, lending a hand occasionally and making suggestions, but obviously impatient with the slowness of the work.

By lunch-time Dan had made friends with his young relatives—except Margy who had slept serenely in her pram through all the noise—but he was so tired that the idea of a picnic was less appealing than it had seemed at breakfast-time, and he was relieved when Dinah decided that it was much too hot to go for a picnic to-day.

"You can have tea in the garden—in the tent," said Dinah who knew pretty well how to manage her family. "You can be explorers in Darkest Africa, and drink your milk out of bottles, like real explorers do."

Whether or not real explorers drink their milk out of bottles is open to doubt, but the young Savages did not question it for a moment; they were charmed with the idea. Polly announced that she would take pemmican to eat, and Mark's rabbits could be tigers. Her mother did not object to tigers and pemmican in Darkest Africa, why should she if Polly were pleased?

The explorers agreed to rest until half-past three (which Dan assured them was zero hour) and, this being settled to every one's satisfaction, they retired to bed with books and their elders were left in peace.

Dan and Dinah sat at the window in two deep chairs while Margy played contentedly, sitting on the floor, with a box of coloured bricks.

"I like my young relations," said Dan as he lighted his pipe.

"Oh, Dan!" said Dinah in delight; "but I was afraid they were wearing you to a shadow. There's no need to play with them *all* the time."

"I wanted to make their acquaintance."

"Yes," said Dinah—and waited for more.

"Polly is a darling," declared Dan. "I've fallen in love with Polly head over heels—if only she were a little older and not my niece . . ."

They smiled at one another.

"Mark is grand," continued Dan, drawing at his pipe. "He's the sort of fellow I should like to have beside me in a tight spot."

"Mark would never let you down," agreed his mother softly.

There was a little silence. "And Nigel," said Dan. "Nigel is charming. He's like Gil, of course."

"Yes, that's what I think," said Dinah. She was looking in her basket for some blue wool to darn a very small sock, and did not raise her eyes.

"All different! All interesting!" said Dan, cheerfully. "Lucky woman, aren't you?"

The Barnards' dinner was a very pleasant affair. Dan, after a whole day in the company of children, was ready for a little adult conversation. He was grateful to the Barnards for their kindness to Dinah, and was prepared to like them immensely.

It was not difficult to like them. He found his hostess attractive; she was very forthcoming and inveigled him into a mild flirtation on joking lines. Mr. Barnard was solid. Dan might have thought him a trifle dull—for naturally they had little in common—but nobody who had been so good to Dinah could seem dull to Dan. While the two young women were busy washing up (having chased the men out of the pantry with assurances that they would only hinder matters) Dan tried to thank his host for his interest in Dinah's affairs.

"What she would have done without you and Mrs. Barnard I simply can't imagine," said Dan earnestly.

Henry Barnard smiled. "Well, of course, it would be foolish to say we've done nothing, but you mustn't run away with the idea that it has been one-sided. Dinah is a wonderful person. Our lives would have been a good deal less interesting without her and her nice children. Irene is absolutely devoted to her of course. As you know, I've been managing Dinah's business affairs—I rather wanted to talk to you about that."

"She's all right, isn't she?" Dan inquired, anxiously.

"Yes, in the meantime. Her husband left her enough to live on, and of course she has her pension, but it's going to be difficult for her to educate her family, I'm afraid."

"I might be able to help."

"You might get married," said Henry sensibly. "It isn't wise to saddle yourself with responsibilities—and if I know anything of Dinah, she wouldn't let you do it. No, there's only one thing for it; she'll have to live somewhere near good schools. She could never afford boarding-schools for them. I haven't mentioned this to Dinah—nor to my wife. It won't be well received by Irene."

There was no time to say more for the dishes were finished; but Henry Barnard's words had started a train of thought in his listener's mind.

"Dinah is taking the children to the seaside for August!" cried Irene as they came in.

"Yes," said Dinah. "Dan has fixed it up—I must admit the journey terrifies me."

"They'll love it," declared Irene. "Margy will sleep the whole way and the others will be so interested in everything they see that the time will pass like lightning. You'll be there before you realise you've started. How I envy you!"

Irene was always full of optimism so her assurances did not carry much weight with Dinah but they cheered Dan considerably.

"That's what I tell Di," he said, eagerly. "The children will enjoy every moment. The house can be shut up for a month—it won't come to any harm."

"Oh!" exclaimed Irene. "Oh, here's an idea! You wouldn't think of letting Oakfield, I suppose? My sister, Dora, wants a house in the country for a month. It would be lovely to have her next door."

Dinah was somewhat doubtful. She realised she would have to leave the house in apple-pie order for a tenant—a circumstance which would add to her burdens—but her companions were all enchanted with the plan and would listen to no objections. Before she knew where she was Irene had rushed off to telephone to Dora and the whole thing was being arranged.

"She jumped at it," said Irene, returning to the drawing-room with the self-satisfied expression of one who has done her day's good deed. "Of course I knew she would. She's been looking for a house for ages and could hear of nothing suitable at all. The children need a change; she can't keep them in town all August—"

"Did you say anything about the rent?" asked Henry, who was a practical man.

"Ten guineas a week, I told her," said Irene firmly. "Dora can easily afford it. She'll feed the hens and you can let her keep the eggs. The boys will look after Mark's rabbits. I've thought of everything, haven't I? It's very good of me to fix it up so beautifully, because I hate the idea of your going away. If I wasn't a nice woman—with an unselfish nature—I should put every sort of difficulty in your way instead of smoothing your path."

"Forty guineas!" exclaimed Dinah, who had heard no more than this.

"But such delightful neighbours," Irene reminded her.

"You'll fight," said Henry, smiling at his wife.

"Why, of course!" cried Irene joyfully. "We'll squabble like anything—we always do. What fun that will be! I ought to have charged her twelve guineas a week at least."

5

ON MONDAY morning Dan opened his sleepy eyes to see his sister standing beside his bedside with a tray in her hands.

"Great snakes!" he exclaimed. "What's the time? I meant to get up and help you!"

"You were tired so we let you sleep on," Dinah told him.

Polly now appeared on the scene with a bed-table and Mark with a large fat cushion which he arranged efficiently at his uncle's back, and in a few moments Dan was sitting up and starting his meal. It was extremely pleasant to be pampered and if he had not been a victim to his conscience he would have been as happy as a king.

After breakfast Polly and the twins were packed off to school and Dinah looked in to say she was going to the town on her bicycle.

"You'll be all right, won't you?" she asked. "Shopping takes ages, of course—"

"Can I have Margy?" Dan inquired.

"Margy! You don't want to be bothered with her!"

"I do," declared Margy's uncle. "I want a little female society."

Margy was fetched and dumped upon his bed, and Dinah set off to the town.

Dan surveyed his youngest relative critically. He had made friends with the others yesterday; it was Margy's turn to-day. Her figure was portly—in fact she was definitely stout—but she had her mother's eyes which counted a lot in her favour. She had her mother's dazzling complexion and fair wavy hair—two more points in her favour, thought Dan. He had no idea at all how much intelligence he might expect from this unknown and somewhat alarming creature. It would be amusing to try her out.

Dan held up his watch. It was a large gold watch and had belonged to his father; he used it in preference to his wrist-watch, partly for sentimental reasons and partly because it was a reliable timekeeper and had a stop. The stop was useful for timing races when he was in the Service.

Margy took the watch and held it to her ear. "Tick-tick," she remarked conversationally.

"Yes, it does, doesn't it?" said Dan, nodding. "We'll do it again, shall we?" He took the watch, touched the stop and handed it back.

Margy repeated the performance exactly. She took the watch, held it to her ear and remarked, "Tick-tick." Then a disappointed expression spread itself over her plump features. She shook the watch and listened again.

Dan smiled. This was very amusing.

"No good," said Margy sadly and dropped the watch over the side of the bed.

Fortunately Dan was able to catch it but he was only just in time, for he had not expected such a rapid and violent reaction to his experiment.

"You're no fool, that's clear," said Dan emphatically.

Margy smiled. Her smile was dazzling; it was Dinah's smile.

"I like you quite a lot," continued her uncle in a thoughtful tone. "There's something about you . . . I'm not sure it isn't S.A. . . . Listen again." He held the watch to her ear.

"Tick-tick," said Margy with a pleased expression.

They played with the watch for several minutes. Margy blew upon it and the back miraculously opened. Margy put it to her ear and listened; sometimes it said "tick-tick" and sometimes not. When they were tired of that game they played with Dan's stud-box, rattling it, emptying out the curious assortment of studs and buttons which it contained and putting them back again. Dan was just beginning to think out another experiment when the door opened and Irene Barnard walked in.

"Good Lord!" exclaimed Dan in horror-stricken tones.

"Now don't fuss," said Irene, seating herself upon the end of his bed. "It's so silly to fuss. I wanted to talk to you, so I came. What could be more sensible?"

Conscious of tousled hair and unshaven chin, Dan thought quite a lot of things could be more sensible.

"If you were ill nobody would think twice about it," added Irene, composedly.

"Dinah has gone to the town," said Dan.

"I know," nodded Irene. "That's why I came. I want to talk to you. Margy is all that a chaperone should be."

Margy was still busy opening and shutting the box. They both watched her for a few moments in silence.

"She *is* a pet," declared Irene. "The nicest of all Dinah's children. She almost makes me want to have another myself, but not quite."

"Not the nicest," objected Dan.

"The nicest of all," repeated Irene emphatically. "Now don't say you like Nigel best. Nearly everybody likes Nigel best and of course he's the best-looking, really beautiful with his goldy-red hair and his white skin, but when you get to know them properly—"

"I never said I liked Nigel best," Dan interrupted.

Irene smiled at him. "Don't let's waste time arguing," said Irene sweetly. "Tell me what you think of Dinah."

"What I think of her?"

"Yes. She's wonderfully gay and cheerful, isn't she? But there's a queer sort of tension about her; have you noticed it?"

"Yes, I know what you mean."

"It's something that's worrying her, something she can't forget. She'll never be really normal until she can get it off her chest. Dinah ought to marry again; but she won't marry again until she gets rid of this obsession. She's terribly attractive, you know," continued Irene earnestly. "Or perhaps you *don't* know—brothers are often a bit blind—but of course she doesn't go about at all or meet any one. She can't, because of the children."

"I know," agreed Dan.

"There's a man here, Wilfred Harrington, he's a perfect dear, but unfortunately he hasn't a penny," said Irene regretfully.

"Does Dinah like him?"

"I think she might if she felt free."

"But she is free."

"Technically—yes—but as I said before there's this curious—well, I suppose it's a sort of inhibition. It's to do with Gilbert, of course. Gilbert was an absolute rotter," said Irene with sudden violence.

"Oh, no!" exclaimed Dan.

"He *was*," declared Irene. "He was disloyal for one thing. He tried to say things to me about her; complaining sort of things about how she put the children first, and didn't consider *him*. But I wasn't having any. I told him he wasn't fit to clean her shoes. He didn't like me after that! I know people say one shouldn't speak ill of the dead, but . . ."

Dan's thoughts went back to the gay debonair figure of the man who, at one time, had been his friend. Gilbert had always seemed to be in the sunlight when Dan thought of him like this . . . sunlight in his red-gold, wavy hair, sunlight in his hazel eyes, sunlight shining on his brilliantly white skin which even tropic suns never seemed to tan.

"Oh, I know he was attractive," said Irene, reading Dan's mind. "He was absolutely and utterly charming. When he talked to you he made you believe there was nobody else in the world he wanted to talk to. It's a fatal gift. Women especially can't resist it. Even I, who never liked him, felt his charm."

"He loved Dinah, I know that," declared Dan.

"Queer sort of love!" exclaimed Irene.

"I was there when they met," said Dan. "Gilbert loved her. He raved to me for hours about Di. It was when we were in the *Incomparable* and we shared the same watch . . ." He hesitated, for there were certain things he couldn't tell Irene—had no right to tell her—about Elaine, for instance.

Gilbert's parents had set their hearts upon Gilbert marrying this girl, and she came into Gilbert's ravings a good deal.

"Why should I marry Elaine?" he had demanded. "I love Di and I'm going to marry her. I couldn't go on living without Di."

"Who is Elaine?" Dan had inquired.

"Oh, quite a nice little thing. I mean I quite liked her until I met Di. Her parents have always been tremendous friends of my parents; they live near us at Harrogate. That's absolutely all. Elaine won't mind a hoot (she's probably found someone *she* likes better) and anyhow even if she does mind—I mean this amazing thing that's happened to Di and me doesn't happen every day. It's the most staggering thing! It's quite *extraordinary*."

"You'll go and see them and make it all right, won't you?" suggested Dan who was rather worried about the whole affair. He was Di's only relative except for the aunt in Glasgow who didn't care what happened to either of them.

"Oh, well!" said Gilbert. "Perhaps I might go and see them . . ."

He did go and see them (Dan badgered him so that it was easier to go, and Gilbert always took the easier way). He went to Harrogate and returned the next day in the most outrageous temper. Dan went into his cabin and found him sitting on the edge of his bunk with nothing on but a pair of blue silk pyjama trousers. His eyes were blazing with rage and every hair of his head seemed alive with electricity: Dan almost expected to see sparks flying from that red-gold mop.

"But why?" Dan kept saying, as he tried to piece together what had happened from the scraps of information seeping out in the spate of blood-curdling language. "Why did they take it like that? What was the row *about*?"

"Because they want me to marry Elaine. I told you that."

"Were you engaged to her?"

Gilbert had raised one foot and was examining the sole. "No, of course not," he said.

It was a lie. Dan was sure he had been engaged to Elaine; but, even so, people *did* make mistakes. And if you found you had made a mistake surely it was better to own up to it. Gilbert's people couldn't be so crazy as to want him to marry Elaine when he was deeply in love with another girl.

"They're mad," Gilbert said. "They're old. They were old when I was born. They're utterly selfish and impossible. They're a pair of doddering old fools."

Dan was shocked. His father had been a wise and generous parent (always busy, of course, and therefore debarred from intimacy with his children; but busy, as they knew, making money to keep them clothed and fed). He said quietly: "I expect they're disappointed, that's all. They'll come round."

"They won't get a chance!" interrupted Gilbert, with a mirthless laugh. "You don't suppose I'm going there again? . . . I'm through with them."

"But, Gilbert, surely—"

"We had a blazing row. Father has got the devil's own temper, and he fairly let himself go. I can't think of it *now* without boiling all over—the things he said—unforgivable things—"

"But Gil—"

"I've done with them! I've no parents—"

"But your mother?"

"She's completely batty," Gilbert declared.

"Perhaps if they were to see Di—" began Dan.

"They're not getting the chance. D'you think I'm going to take her there and trot her out like a filly for their inspection? Not likely! I've done with them for good—and I'm not sorry. It was bound to come sooner or later—this row, I mean—they've always carped at me. They're impossible, interfering, narrow-minded. I've done with them . . . and they can keep their blasted money. They can take it with them when they die or give it to a Cats' Home. I've got enough money of my own. We'll be all right, Dinah and I; there's a cracking good job waiting for me when I can get out of the Service. You don't need to worry about that side of it, old boy."

Dan wasn't really worrying about that side of it, for he was one of those people who don't worry about money very much. He and Dinah had a few hundreds between them—no more—but they got along all right and managed to enjoy life in their own way. No, what Dan worried about was this extraordinary row with Gilbert's parents. It seemed all wrong. However, he could do nothing so it was useless to make a fuss.

Dinah was nineteen when she married Gilbert. They were madly in love and blissfully happy. Dan knew that for a fact.

"Queer sort of love," Irene had said. He looked at Irene and saw that she was smiling at him.

"I was thinking," he explained.

"Dan," said Irene; "take my advice. When you marry, choose someone kind. It's kindness that matters in the long run. Marry someone who would love you just as much if you were covered with spots."

They both laughed at this. It was a welcome break in the tension.

"But I mean it—honestly," declared Irene. "Henry is like that. He loved me just the same when I had chicken-pox. Gilbert was quite different. Gilbert couldn't be bothered with Di when she looked ill and unattractive. Did you know that the last leave he had (before Margy was born) he spent in London?"

"You mean he didn't come home!" cried Dan, incredulously.

"Only for two nights."

Dan looked at her.

"Yes," said Irene, nodding. "It's absolutely true. The Starkies saw him in town, dancing. He was with a horrid little tart. Joan Starkie is a most awful fool—she told Dinah!"

"You mean Di didn't know?"

"He had written to say his leave was cancelled." Irene hesitated, and then continued: "Perhaps you would have to be a woman to understand how unutterably caddish it was. Here was Di, slaving away day after day, looking after her children and feeling like nothing on earth . . . but Gilbert preferred to dance in town rather than come home to her. Queer kind of love, wasn't it?"

"It was frightful!" declared Dan. "It was beyond everything. What did he say when she taxed him with it, I wonder."

"How should I know?" Irene replied. "They may have had a row— knowing Gilbert I should think they did. Di never said a word to me about it, not a single word. Perhaps it's because she knew I didn't like Gilbert. It could be that."

Dan was silent. He really was appalled. Di must have been terribly hurt, wounded beyond endurance. No wonder she looked tired and ill.

"She might tell you about it, mightn't she?" continued Irene. "In fact, she *must* tell you. You must make her speak of it, Dan. She's got it on her mind and she can't forget it. She would feel a lot better if she talked it over with someone—and that someone must be you."

"I'll try," said Dan doubtfully.

"That's why I came," added Irene and, so saying, she got up and went away.

6

THE children did not go back to school in the afternoon; they trooped out to the tent and Dan went with them. Christine crept through a gap in the hedge and joined the party. It was too hot for games so Dan was invited to tell them a story.

"Mummy tells us about the Dees," said Mark. "All about how they played on the sands at Seatown and climbed the rocks and paddled and fished and went to see the lighthouse and the old castle on the cliffs."

"The castle of the Red Douglas," nodded Nigel.

"Of course," agreed Dan. "It's a fine old castle. Perhaps you'll see it some day. The cliffs tower up from the sea and the castle is built into the solid rock. We often bicycled over and took our lunch with us. Shall I tell you about that?"

"No," said Polly, firmly. "You see, that's Mummy's story. You must tell us something else."

"Tell us about the mugs," said Nigel.

"But I've told you about them already!"

"Tell us again!" demanded all the children at once.

Dan told his story again, but not so well as before. He found it boring to repeat the same story twice over. He was asked to repeat it a third time, but refused point blank.

"I like my mug best of everything I've got," said Nigel, thoughtfully. "There's something *very* nice about it. Don't you think so, Mark?"

"Yes," agreed Mark. "But I don't like it best of all. I like my rabbits best."

"Silly!" exclaimed Nigel. "Your rabbits aren't *lasting* like a mug. Your rabbits will die and then you won't have them, so it's silly to like them best."

"They know me," explained Mark.

Dan looked at him with interest. It was as good a reason as you could get. The rabbits knew Mark; they watched for his coming; they ate dandelion leaves which he picked for them; they allowed him to handle their young. The rabbits *knew* Mark, so of course he liked them best ... but Nigel did not see it in the same light; he continued to jeer.

"Smelly brutes!" cried Nigel. "Fancy liking them better than your mug!"

"They aren't smelly!" retorted Mark.

The argument was boiling up, and Polly, who was aware that arguments between her brothers usually led to blows, began to look anxious.

"Now, listen, you two!" said Dan, raising his voice to be heard above the turmoil. "Listen to me. Everybody is entitled to his own opinion, which means you can think as you like but you mustn't be rude. I'm going to tell you a story about an old sailor I used to know, and if you don't shut up you won't hear it."

It was the voice of authority and produced instant silence.

"He was called Old Monk," continued Dan. "He was chief carpenter in the *Incomparable*."

"Chips?" asked Mark, who had read a story about a ship in *The Boys' Friend*.

"Yes, but his name was Mr. Monk. He was a funny little man, hairy like a baboon, with twinkling eyes and a heart of gold."

The little Savages settled down to listen, for this was a story after their own hearts.

"Hairy all over?" inquired Mark in awed tones.

"Yes, he even had hairs in his ears."

"In his ears! How could he hear? Or couldn't he?"

"He was slightly deaf," admitted Dan. "Sometimes when you said something to him he took you up wrong."

"What sort of things?" asked Polly. "I mean did he go to port when you said starboard—things like that?"

"Goodness, no!" exclaimed Dan. "Monk never steered the ship, and anyway ships aren't steered like that. I mean," said Dan looking round at the four eager faces in some desperation, "I mean there's a telegraph on the bridge and—"

But the little Savages were more interested in Old Monk than in the manner of steering a ship. "What sort of things?" asked Nigel. "Tell us *one* thing that you said and he thought you said something else."

Dan racked his brains. "Well, one day I said to him, 'That grey cat is a marvellous mouser,' and he yelled back, 'What, scarlet trousers? I never did see a cat with scarlet trousers, Mr. Bell!'"

Every one laughed inordinately at this somewhat feeble jest. The boys rolled over and over in paroxysms of mirth.

"Can't you *see* it?" gasped Polly. "A dear little grey cat with scarlet trousers on!"

"Did he have a parrot?" asked Christine, when she had recovered from the joke.

"A parrot!"

"Yes, *you* know—like John Silver—that said: 'Pieces of eight.'"

Hitherto Dan had stuck to fact in his description of the old seaman, but he realised that facts would never satisfy the appetites of his young companions. The well of truth would soon run dry; he must draw upon his imagination . . . and being somewhat elated by the reception of his story about the little grey cat, he felt quite competent to improvise.

"A parrot? Of course," nodded Dan. "But Old Monk's parrot said 'Splice the main brace,' which is the most popular order in the Navy (all right, Nigel, you'll see why in a minute). Well, one day when we were lying off a coral island in the South Sea, Old Monk brought his parrot on deck. He was a very kind-hearted old man, you see, and he thought the parrot would enjoy the sunshine. The parrot sat on Old Monk's shoulder for a few minutes and then suddenly it gave a loud squawk and spread its wings and flew up into the air. It flew round the ship and then across the water and disappeared amongst the palm trees. Old Monk was dancing about in a frightful state of mind and shouting, 'Man overboard!' and before you could say Jack Robinson backwards some of the matelots had lowered a boat."

"Why?" inquired Nigel.

"Well, they do," replied Dan. "I mean, you always lower a boat if a man falls overboard . . . and of course they thought that's what had happened . . . and seeing the boat there, ready, we decided to row across to the island and try to find Methuselah. All parrots are very old," continued Dan, forestalling the question which was hovering upon Nigel's lips, "so *that* was why Monk called his parrot Methuselah."

"What was it called when it was young?" asked Mark.

"Woodley," replied Dan, without hesitation.

"Oh, do shut up, Mark!" said Polly, forestalling another interruption. "We want to hear what happened to Methuselah on the island."

"Yes—well—" said Dan, racking his brains furiously. "We landed on the lovely, white, sandy beach and walked up to the nearest palm tree, and there we stood in the shade wondering what to do. It was Mr. Monk who suggested we should spread out and search the island thoroughly, calling to Methuselah as we went, and as nobody had a better idea that was what we did. The sailors enjoyed it, of course (sailors like anything different for a change). Off they went, crashing through the tropical undergrowth and shouting 'Methuselah!' at the top of their lungs. After I had searched about a bit I went back to the beach where we had landed, and waited near the boat. It was terribly hot.

"One by one the sailors gave up the search. None of them had seen Methuselah nor heard him, but that was not surprising because the vegetation was so thick that he could have hidden in it very easily. We had to get back to the ship before dark and darkness falls very suddenly in the tropics, but—"

"Why?" asked Mark with interest.

Dan paused to explain the reason, but the remainder of his audience fell upon Mark as one man, telling him to shut up and let the story-teller go on.

"Mr. Monk asked leave to stay the night on the island," continued Dan. "He thought Methuselah might come to him when he was alone, so we left Mr. Monk there and rowed away. I must say I wasn't very happy about it and when I saw him standing there on the beach all by himself I wished I had stayed to keep him company. ''E's all right, sir,' said one of the sailors. 'There's no flies on 'im. I wouldn't mind a night on a coral island myself.'"

Dan paused again. It was rather curious, but he could actually *see* that sailor in his mind's eye, and he could see the lascivi-ous-looking sailor who replied with a reference to the dusky maidens who might (if Mr. Monk were lucky) share his vigil. Yet Dan had made up the whole thing out of his head . . . or out of the hotch potch of memories and stories and scenes and personalities which were stowed away inside his head.

"Go on," said Polly, urging him. "What did the other sailors say? Did they *all* think it would have been nice to spend the night there?"

"Most of them," said Dan, abandoning the idea of dusky maidens as being unsuitable and searching for something in their place. "There was bread-fruit and coconuts and other sorts of fruit—which would be a nice change—but none of them would have liked a *week* alone on a coral island, and that's what Mr. Monk had let himself in for! Yes," said Dan, nodding portentously, "yes; he was marooned there for a whole week. A gale got up in the night and the *Incompar-able* had to stand off until the wind abated and the sea went down. At last we managed to get back to the island and we rowed ashore . . . and *there* was Mr. Monk waiting for us on the beach with Methu-selah sitting on his shoulder. Mr. Monk looked just as usual, quite calm and composed. He had not been in the least worried, and he was not the least excited at seeing us again. He was just as neat and tidy, and his eyes twinkled as brightly as ever. I thought Methuselah looked a bit ashamed of himself—and no wonder!

"Afterwards Mr. Monk told me exactly what had happened. That very first evening when the boat had gone, Mr. Monk made a little fire of driftwood, just to keep him company, and he was sitting near it eating bread and milk (breadfruit and coconut-milk, of course) when suddenly he heard a well-known voice remark; 'Splice the main brace!' Methuselah was sitting on the branch of a tree and watching him. Now, of course, 'Splice the main brace' means a tot of grog all round and Mr. Monk had no grog. The only thing he could do was to split another coconut and offer that instead. Methuselah seemed quite pleased—I expect he liked it better than grog, really. He flew down from the tree and shared Mr. Monk's supper. There was no bother after that. Methuselah stayed with Mr. Monk and didn't fly away again; as far as I could make out they had a very happy time together."

Dan was rather pleased with his effort. He began to think he had mistaken his vocation in life. Perhaps he was a sort of Somerset Maugham and had never known it! Perhaps, even now, it was not too late to develop his latent talent! Dan toyed for a moment with the idea of chucking his new job at the shipping office in Leith and devoting himself to literature . . . however, there was a snag: one had to have money to buy food.

The audience was extremely appreciative and having listened to every word of the story with bated breath it was now anxious to be informed as to the manner of Mr. Monk's life whilst marooned upon the island: had he made a little house for himself and Methuselah? Had he bathed in the lagoon? Had he caught any fish? Had he seen any savages? Were they cannibals or not? Dan answered as best he could, drawing more and more freely on his imagination (which was astonishing its owner by its wide range and fertility) and before Dan had finished with him Mr. Monk had become a legendary figure, large as life but not quite natural.

"That's all," said Dan at last. "It's somebody else's turn now. It isn't fair for one person to do all the entertaining. We have sing-songs in the Navy; they're sort of concerts where everybody does his share."

Nobody else had the slightest wish to entertain the company so they drew lots with little sticks to decide who should be first.

When Mark saw that he had drawn the longest stick he became very red in the face and his eyes bulged. Dan, seeing his dismay, was filled with compunction and would have cancelled the sing-song then and there if he could have done so—but it was too late. Despite his dismay Mark had no intention of shirking.

"It's a poem," said Mark. He rose and, standing with his hands clasped behind his back, said very rapidly and indistinctly: "Go, lovely rose; tell her that she wastes her time (gasp) and me that now she knows when I remember her (gasp) to thee how fair and sweet she seems to be."

"He learnt it at school," said Polly, proudly.

Dan felt his diaphragm tremble with internal laughter. "Splendid!" he cried, and clapped loudly. Everybody followed his example.

"I wonder what it means," said Christine, with a thoughtful air.

"It's poetry, of course," replied Polly, surprised that her friend should be so dense.

Christine had drawn the second longest stick. She was a trifle reluctant to do her part, but the others were insistent.

"Mine isn't *real* poetry," said Christine. "I mean it's quite easy to understand." And having made this apology she recited as follows:

> I wonder if you feel like me
> When aunts and uncles come to tea.
>
> In spite of smiles and friendly looks,
> In spite of toys and picture books
> You wish that they would go away—
> And all because of WHAT THEY SAY.
>
> First Aunt Belinda says, 'Poor Rose!
> I wonder where she got that nose.'
> Aunt Alice adds, 'She's *very* small—
> Not like our family at all.'
> And Uncle Ned says, 'Little girls,
> When I was young, had pretty curls.'
>
> Now Aunt Belinda's nose is blue.
> Just like the mandrill at the Zoo.
> Aunt Alice is extremely fat;
> (I wouldn't like to be like *that*!)

And Uncle Ned, who talks of *hair*
He hasn't any, *anywhere*!

But these are things they'll never know
'Cos you're too nice to tell them so.
(At least, I hope you are.)

Christine sat down amidst satisfactory applause. She smiled her pleasure. "It's funny, isn't it?" she said. "My Aunt Dora is rather like that. I mean, she's always saying she wonders why my hair doesn't curl like Mummy's; one day she said to Mummy, 'My dear, I've *just* seen it! She's got poor old Cousin Eleanor's mouth.'"

Christine had put on a very affected, grown-up accent to mimic her aunt and the result was most entertaining. Perhaps Dan was more amused than the others; he was certainly more surprised, for he had put Christine down as rather a dull little girl, a little white mouse, and here she was blossoming into an actress!

"So then," continued Christine, unsmilingly; "then Mummy said, 'It *can't* be poor old Cousin Eleanor's mouth; she uses it herself five times a day at least!'"

Dan laughed. "Mummy is a match for Aunt Dora!"

"Oh yes; Mummy is a match for *any* one," said Christine proudly.

Dan was hoping for more in the same manner, but the other children were getting restive; especially Mark, who having gone through the ordeal himself, was determined nobody should escape.

"It's Polly's turn now," said Mark. "Polly can say 'We are Seven.'"

"But I'm not going to!" declared Polly. "It's a dreadfully *wet* sort of poem. I'm going to stand on my head; will that do?"

Dan said it would do, admirably.

Polly tucked the skirt of her cotton frock inside her knickers and stood on her head with her long, thin legs straight up in the air. Then she turned two Catherine wheels rapidly and expertly. It was an exceedingly good performance and her uncle was interested to observe that she was not in the least out of breath at the end of it. He was able to applaud with a clear conscience.

Nigel was the last to perform. Unlike the others, he had been awaiting his turn with impatience. He rose as Polly sat down and stood for a few moments looking up at the trees.

Then, without any explanation, he opened his mouth and sang:

There's a Friend for little children
Above the bright, blue sky . . .

Dan found it inexpressibly moving. He was always moved by a boy's voice, and this voice was pure and true, every note as clear as the note of a bird. He was carried away so that when the hymn was finished it was a moment or two before he remembered to join in the applause.

"I sing well, don't I?" said Nigel, looking at him.

"Very well," replied Dan, soberly; he could say no less, but the spell was broken. Dan seemed to see Gilbert—not Nigel—standing there (Gilbert with his red-gold head: Gilbert with his straight back and his long legs) and he seemed to hear Gilbert saying, "Good sing-song, wasn't it? The matelots fairly eat me, don't they? As a matter of fact, they're pretty good judges of singing; they know jolly well when they hear something absolutely first chop, matelots do."

Nigel was not only *like* Gilbert, thought Dan, he was Gilbert in miniature. He had all Gilbert's physical characteristics . . . and Gilbert's vanity. Had he inherited Gilbert's other peculiarities? Dan hoped not. Dan did not want to see another Gilbert, and certainly not in the guise of Dinah's child.

7

DAN left on Tuesday morning. He was going straight to Leith to take up his new job. Dinah had a fortnight to pack up and get ready for the move. A fortnight seemed a long time and Dinah had decided to take it easy, to do a little each day and not get over-tired. She began by going over the house and trying to decide what she should leave out for Dora Powell and what she must put away. There was mumps at the school so she kept the children at home, for she could not risk their getting mumps *now*. They would play in the garden, of course, and would not bother her. Unfortunately the children had other views. They had no wish to play in the garden; they were much too excited about their prospective holiday to settle down to their usual games. Dinah found them under her feet all day, getting in her way and asking silly questions and nearly driving her mad.

"Go out and play," Dinah kept saying. "Why don't you play in the tent?" And she would drive them out with all sorts of suggestions as to what they should play . . . but in ten minutes they would be back again.

"Mummy!" cried Polly, running into the room when Dinah was trying to decide whether it would be better to put up clean, but rather faded curtains in the sitting-room, or to leave the present curtains which were in better condition but slightly soiled . . . or whether to send the good curtains to be cleaned and chance them being back in time. "Mummy, listen!" cried Polly, tugging her skirt. "I've just thought, hadn't I better take my *old* shorts to Seatown and leave my best ones at home."

"But they're too small, and—"

"I can just squeeze into them. I can, really. My new ones might get spoilt playing on the sands . . . and Mummy can I take Rose's pram?"

"No," said Dinah, firmly.

"But Mummy, why?"

Dinah explained why and chased her away, and a few moments later Nigel appeared with a large stamp-album.

"I'd better take this, hadn't I?" Nigel said. "It won't take up much room. If there isn't room for it in the suitcase I could tie it up with string and carry it myself."

"But Nigel, you haven't looked at your stamps for months!"

"I want my stamps. I want to take them."

"There will be lots to do at Seatown. You don't want to sit indoors doing stamps."

"But, Mummy, supposing it's wet?"

"It won't be wet," said Dinah, recklessly.

Mark tried to help and Dinah, most ungratefully, found his attempts to be of service even more annoying than the unhelpfulness of her less conscientious children. He followed her round, saying: "I'll carry that, Mummy. Where shall I put it? Shall I take the ornaments off the mantelpiece for you? Would you like me to start packing my box?"

"I'd rather you went out and played in the garden, Mark!"

"But Dan said you weren't to get tired. Are you sure you aren't tired, Mummy?"

She was extremely tired—all the more tired by Mark's solicitude—but she assured him rather shortly that she was not tired at all.

"I could pack my box," he urged. "I ought to start soon, oughtn't I? We'll never be ready in time if we don't start to pack."

As the days went by the children became more and more annoying; they quarrelled amongst themselves; they were rude and irritable; they refused to do what they were told. Dinah could not think what on earth had happened to them; she tried reasoning with them and, when that failed, she punished them by sending them to bed ... and then quite suddenly she realised the truth: it was she who was cross and irritable. She had so much on her mind that she had no patience to spare for the children! I ought to send myself to bed, thought Dinah remorsefully; but that would be no punishment; in fact I can't think of anything I should like better.

Having discovered the source of the trouble Dinah made an effort to be cheerful and pleasant, and the atmosphere immediately improved. The suitcases were brought out and the children packed assiduously, packed and unpacked several times a day.

"Look, Mummy!" Polly said. "I can pack Rose and her bed and my tea-set—only there isn't room for clothes. I shan't need many clothes at Seatown, shall I?"

"You'll need some," replied Dinah. "As a matter of fact you won't need toys. You'll be playing on the sands all day."

"I'll take it out and try again," said Polly, with a sigh.

Dinah nodded. She found this phase less trying, for packing kept them quiet and busy and left her free to get on with her work.

By this time there were only five days left and Dinah decided that she must turn out the cupboard under the stairs. She intended to take everything out of the cupboard and clean it and then put back the things she wanted to keep. It was a roomy cupboard, so if it were tidied up there would be plenty of space left for things she wanted to stow away while her tenants were in the house. She donned an overall, tied a duster over her head and began the job.

It was years since the cupboard had been properly cleaned and Dinah had forgotten what was in it. She dragged everything out: Gilbert's skis, old badminton rackets, a lamp with a frayed flex, pictures, ornaments, boxes of books, brown paper parcels, a bed-table with a broken leg, golf clubs, a sled, rolls of wall-paper. Some of the things could be sent to the Jumble Sale, and the others . . . but what did she want to keep?

Nothing, thought Dinah, looking at the stuff with loathing.

"Oh, Mummy!" exclaimed Mark, who had approached unobserved and was regarding the accumulated rubbish with awe and wonder. "Oh, Mummy, what *treasures*!"

The exclamation was a signal to the others—or at least it acted as a signal—Polly came running downstairs and Nigel appeared from the garden.

"Oh, Mark, what rubbish!" said Dinah, with a sigh. "Rubbish!" cried Polly. "D'you mean you don't want the things? Could I have this bed-table for Rose?"

"I'll have these!" Nigel declared, seizing the badminton rackets. "What are they for, Mummy?"

"And this picture for my room," added Polly. "Please can I have this picture, Mummy?"

"What are those long wooden things?" asked Nigel.

"Skis," said Dinah. "They're for sliding in the snow—you've seen pictures of people skiing, haven't you?"

"I'll take them to Seatown," said Nigel. "They'll be lovely for sliding in the sand. I can, can't I, Mummy? I'll tie them together and carry them myself."

"No," said Dinah firmly. "No, you can't! You can each choose one thing out of the rubbish and the rest can go to the sale."

"I'll choose this!" cried Mark, holding up a fat album with a red morocco cover. "Can I have this, Mummy? It's got pictures in it."

Dinah recognised the book at once. It was her photograph album. She took it from Mark and, sitting down on the bottom steps of the stairs, began to turn over the pages. The children crowded round, leaning against her shoulder and breathing down her neck; but Dinah was so used to being crowded and breathed upon by children that she did not mind.

"Pictures of children!" said Polly. "Who are they?"

"The Dees, of course—that's Dan with his golf clubs."

"The Dees!" exclaimed Mark. "Oh Mummy, how marvellous! Polly, it's the Dees. That's Dan again, sitting on a rock . . . and there's Mummy!"

"Mummy when she was a little girl!" exclaimed Nigel, in amazement.

They were still looking at the little pictures (some dear as the day when they were printed, some yellow and faded, some half obliterated by streaks of white) when the front door opened and Irene Barnard walked in.

"Goodness! What are you doing?" she exclaimed. "I thought you would be knee-deep in suitcases—"

"I ought to be!" said Dinah ruefully.

"It's photographs," explained Polly. "Look, that's Mummy when she was the same age as me!"

Irene had come to help, but instead of helping she sat down beside Dinah on the stairs and prepared to enjoy herself.

"Packing can wait," she declared. "I love old photographs. Who's that? No, don't tell me. It's Dan and Dinah and three little coal miners having a picnic on the sands."

"They aren't really coal miners," said Mark, seriously. "They're the Hart boys—Mummy said so. It's because the light was bad."

"Who's the young man on the horse?" asked Irene with interest.

"Malcolm Armstrong," replied Dinah. "Dan and I had a secret passion for Malcolm Armstrong. He was a sort of hero and we made up stories about him. We used to go along the links and hide amongst the sandhills and watch him playing golf. We used to see him riding along the sands. He always waved when he saw us, and sometimes stopped and spoke to us but he was much older than we were and, to tell the truth, we preferred to admire him from a distance . . . That's Nannie, of course," added Dinah, pointing to another snapshot. "It's a bit out of focus so you can't see what she's really like . . . And that's Craigie Lodge with Father's car standing at the gate."

"Dan diving," suggested Irene, pointing.

"Yes, he won second prize at a diving competition at the swimming pool," said Dinah proudly, "and those two old ladies are the two Miss Stevens. We used to go to tea with them sometimes. There are the Hart boys again. They lived in a lovely old house with a huge garden . . . and that's Tom."

"Tom who?" inquired Irene.

"Tom Cunningham," said Dinah.

They wasted a good hour over the photograph album, but Irene salved her conscience by staying to help Dinah clean the cupboard and put everything straight.

"Now don't bother about things," said Irene as she went away. "There's no earthly need to clean the house any more—Dora will be quite pleased with it. I wouldn't have suggested Dora taking the house if I'd known you would wear yourself to a shadow with all this cleaning. Dora isn't fussy—and, of course, she's used to London smuts, so your house will seem as clean as a new pin."

Dinah felt that the drawers should be lined with clean paper so she did them when Irene had gone, but she did no more cleaning, partly because Irene had said not to, and partly because she simply hadn't time, for it was on the day following the cleaning of the cupboard that everything began to go wrong.

The first calamity was Dinah's fault and hers alone. She dropped the teapot on the kitchen floor and saw it smash into a dozen pieces before her eyes. It was the only large teapot she had, and naturally Mrs. Powell (with her large family) would require a large teapot! Dinah looked at the débris in horror, for she was aware that she would be very lucky indeed if she could buy another teapot in Nettleham. Dinah was aware that if she had happened to want a statuette of a lady in negligé, or a china dog of a breed unknown and undreamt of in the sacred precincts of Crufts' she could have got it quite easily. If she had wanted a bright blue pottery bowl ornamented with birds of paradise, or a vase of crimson glass with a gilt edge, or even a large glass box—which one imagined must be intended to hold powder since it seemed unsuitable for any other purpose—Dinah could have gone out and bought it without the slightest difficulty (without having to wait in a queue), for these things were in good supply and every china shop in Nettleham was fully stocked with them; but if Dinah happened to require a teapot or a milk jug or a mixing-bowl or cups and saucers or plates or, indeed, anything useful and necessary for an ordinary household she could just go on wanting them, for such things were not to be had for love or money in post-war Britain. Dinah had often wondered why. She had gone the length of asking the woman in the china shop why it was that china dogs could be turned out by the gross and china teapots could not. Wouldn't it be better if factories, at present engaged in making china statuettes, could turn their attention to cups and saucers? But the woman had merely murmured something about the quota and continued to discuss Greta Garbo's hair-do with her fellow assistant. "Quota" was one of those new words, one of those words which excused every shortage, one of those words which every housewife in Britain was having dinned into her ears every hour of every day. If you wanted shoes, or dish cloths, or bowls, or biscuits, you couldn't get them because of this mysterious quota. You just had to do without.

All this passed through Dinah's mind with the speed of an express train as she gathered up the pieces of her teapot and threw them into the rubbish bin. I shan't *try* to get a teapot, she decided. I shall just get out my silver one and clean it for Mrs. Powell.

After that troubles came thick and fast. Polly tore her jumper on a nail in the trellis and it took Dinah the whole evening to darn it. Nigel fell out of the tree and hurt his foot.

Soot came down the chimney in the sitting-room and the electric light fused. Margy was sick—having sucked the paint off a small wooden cart—and the Starkie's cat came in through the kitchen window and ate the fish which had just arrived for the children's dinner. Dinah coped with all these catastrophes as they occurred. She was inured to catastrophes of this sort. They absorbed a good deal of time and energy, but she battled through.

The last day came. Dinah awoke and lay for a few minutes thinking of all she must do—everything must be done by tonight, for they were leaving early to-morrow morning. She began to go through her list but before she had got very far the door opened and the two little boys appeared in their dressing-gowns.

"Look at him!" cried Nigel. "Look at Mark! He's got mumps, hasn't he, Mummy?"

Mark's face was swollen.

"It isn't," said Mark earnestly. "It's only swollen one side, Mummy."

"Of course it's mumps!" jeered Nigel. "You've got mumps, that's what you've got. You won't be able to go to Seatown, now. You'll have to stay here all by yourself—won't he, Mummy? You can't go to Seatown with mumps! Oh, Mark, you *do* look queer!"

Mark burst into loud roars of sorrow and dismay, and Dinah felt inclined to follow suit. It was only now, when she saw her holiday disappearing from view, that she realised how much she had been looking forward to it; so much that the disappointment was almost more than she could bear. Dinah could have cried—but it was no good crying; there was far too much to do. Everything must be put off, thought Dinah, as she rose and flung on her clothes. Wires must be dispatched to Nannie, to Dan, to Mrs. Powell, and all the arrangements she had made must be cancelled . . . But first the doctor, decided Dinah, running downstairs, half-dressed, to the telephone.

Dr. Godden had known Dinah for years and knew what a struggle she had had. He had been more than delighted when he heard she was going to Scotland for a holiday, so the news that Mark had mumps was received by him with exclamations of horror and distress.

"Good heavens!" he exclaimed. "What awful bad luck! Are you sure it's mumps? Look here, Mrs. Savage, hold everything; I'll be up in half an hour. It may not be mumps."

Dinah was certain it was mumps. She was so beside herself with worry, and so angry with Nigel for his unsympathetic attitude that she made no attempt to soften the blow to him or to Polly.

"We shall *all* have to stay at home," said Dinah. "We can't possibly go to Seatown and leave Mark behind—besides you're both certain to get it too."

"Not go!" cried Nigel, aghast.

"No!" said Dinah, and she swept out of the dining-room leaving Polly and Nigel to weep into their porridge.

Dr. Godden arrived within the appointed half-hour and marched into the nursery, unheralded. "What have we here?" he inquired cheerfully. "What has the young villain been doing?"

Mark was sitting up in bed, weeping copiously. His face was streaked with tears.

"Let's have a look at you," said Dr. Godden. "Open your mouth wide . . . No, that's not mumps!"

"Not mumps?" exclaimed Dinah, incredulously.

"Definitely not," declared Dr. Godden. "The swelling is due to the eruption of a molar. In other words Mark is teething!"

Dinah was speechless with amazement.

"He's six years old, isn't he?" continued the doctor. "That's the age children cut their first permanent molars. Usually these teeth appear without much trouble and nobody notices their appearance, but Mark has always had trouble with his teeth, hasn't he, Mrs. Savage?"

"He certainly has," agreed Dinah, laughing a trifle hysterically.

"Can I go to Seatown?" asked the patient, anxiously.

"Of course you can! The tooth is through—I can feel it—and the swelling will probably disappear in a few hours. There's nothing whatever to prevent your going to Seatown."

"What a comfort you are!" said Dinah as she followed Dr. Godden downstairs and showed him out of the door. "I don't know what we should do without doctors. I suppose I was an idiot, but I was *certain* it was mumps."

"The fear was father to the thought," returned Dr. Godden, smiling and taking his hat up. "In my experience it often is—far more often than the wish. Mind you have a good holiday and enjoy yourself; you need it badly."

8

THE old house at Seatown in which the Dees had been born and brought up, and which now belonged to Mrs. Anderson, stood in a terrace of houses along the East Bay. Each house faced the sea and was surrounded by a small garden. In front was a narrow road, a low wall, a few tufts of coarse grass and then the sands. In winter the sea broke over the wall, and the windows of the houses were misted with salt spray. When the tide was out there was a lovely sweep of golden sands, a half-moon stretching from the harbour rocks (thrusting out among the waves like a giant's boot) to another smaller huddle of black rocks to eastward. Beyond these eastward rocks was a smaller bay with a burn running down to the sea; and beyond this, cliffs of crumbling grey stone.

The fashionable part of Seatown lay to westward of the town proper and consisted of a goodly number of large houses (built of grey or red stone or covered with white harling) which were dotted about on the hill and along the edge of the golf course. If you came to Seatown for golf it was better to stay in the West End. The lovely green sweep of the course lay spread out before your windows and you could watch your friends setting forth upon the great adventure of the game and returning elated with their prowess, or bowed by their misfortunes, as the case might be. But many people who came to Seatown for their summer holidays preferred the unfashionable East Bay, for here you were nearer the sea; you could hear the sigh and murmur of the waves as you lay in bed, and the breeze that moved the curtains at your bedroom window was straight off the water.

In the old days all the houses in the East Bay had belonged to private people (most of whom had families of children who played on the sands together), but now nearly all the houses had been turned into small hotels or boarding-houses which let rooms for the summer months. Craigie Lodge was no exception to the rule.

Mrs. Anderson liked to have everything "nice." It was her boast that her house was "run like a gentleman's house." She had had ample experience with the doctor, who knew what was what. She was plump and comfortable, rather stout, with white wavy hair and rosy cheeks. She wore spectacles with tortoiseshell rims and her aprons were always spotless. Mrs. Anderson did all her visitors well, but her preparations for the Savages were princely. The whole house—already clean as a new pin—was cleaned all over again and polished meticulously; curtains, bedspreads and chair-covers were plunged into the wash-tub; carpets were Hoovered within an inch of their lives. Nor was the important matter of food neglected. Meat was easy, of course, for Mrs. Anderson's husband was a butcher, and she was aware that he would not let her down . . . but there were other things besides meat to be thought of and, on the morning before the arrival of the Savages, Mrs. Anderson armed herself with an enormous basket and "took a stroll round the shops."

"Ye'll mind Doctor Bell?" suggested Mrs. Anderson, leaning upon the grocer's counter. "Aye, I was nearly sure ye'd not have forgotten the Doctor. Dinah's coming tae me wi' her four wee mites for August. Aye, it's four she's got. I was wondering if ye'd a wee pat o' butter tae spare—over and above the rations. They've bin living in England of coorse, sae they'll just have got their bare rations—*if* that. An' what's the jam situation, Mister Dobbie? Weel noo, that's reel guid o' ye! Aye, I was sure ye'd mind Doctor Bell. He was a grand man—never spared himsel'. D'you mind when your wee Alec took appendicitis in the middle o' the nicht? Aye, I'm sure. Ye'll not forget yon nicht in a hurry! That's reel nice o' ye, Mister Dobbie; bairns like steam-puddens an' a pound o' treacle is just what I'm needing . . . I'll not say no to sultanas, eether. Hae ye any raisins? That's fine. What about a nice piece o' Dundee? There's five o' them, mind . . . My, I was a'most forgetting biscuits! I'll need plain yins for Dinah and chocklate yins for the bairns. Hoo mony points? Och, away, Mister Dobbie; ye'll get the cairds when they're here."

She stayed to chat with Mr. Dobbie for a few minutes longer—for it was well worth her while—and as she was coming out of the shop she overheard one of the assistants say, "No, madam, I'm sorry we have no evaporated milk at all. It's terribly scarce," so she hurried back to her friend and remarked in confidential tones, "An' I could dae wi' a couple o' tins o' condensed milk if ye could manage it."

The same tactics brought equal success at the other shops. Mrs. Anderson collected oranges, bananas and strawberries.

She ordered fruit cakes and prevailed upon the dairy to deliver extra milk. Like many of her kind Mrs. Anderson was bilingual, speaking to her friends in the Doric, and to her visitors in English which was often better than their own. Neither method of speech was "affected" for both came naturally to her tongue. Indeed it is doubtful whether Mrs. Anderson realised that she could speak two languages with facility.

The train was nearly two hours late. Dinah had never felt so tired in all her life, nor so dirty and crushed. The children were exhausted; their faces and hands were black, their hair tousled and straggly. They got out of the train and stood, grouped round their mother, too tired to speak, too dazed to realise that at last they had arrived at their destination.

Mrs. Anderson saw them at once and rushed forward, closely followed by her tall, burly husband. "Dinah!" she cried (quite forgetting that she had intended to greet her visitor as "Mrs. Savage," and had, in fact, been schooling herself for days in this manner of address). "Dinah, my dear lamb, here you are at last! And the bairns—oh the puir wee things! They'll be tired to death! We've got a taxi waiting. Andrew, you'll see to the luggage. Give me the wee girlie, I'll carry her."

"I'll carry her," said Andrew Anderson, taking Margy from her mother's arms. "Bob's seeing to the luggage. You can bring the laddies, Annie; they're fair dazed."

"Oh, Nannie, dear!" exclaimed Dinah. "Oh, goodness! I thought we would *never* get here! You must have been waiting for ages . . . Come, Polly darling; we're *there*!"

They streamed along the platform; Mr. Anderson carrying Margy (who, having slept most of the way, had survived the ordeal a good deal better than the rest of the family), followed by Mrs. Anderson with a twin by each hand, followed by Dinah and Polly, followed by Bob with the luggage on a truck. Dinah's knees were shaking beneath her as she walked along, her eyes were pricking with tears and there was an enormous lump in her throat. These unpleasant symptoms were not entirely due to strain, but partly to the joy of seeing Nannie and hearing her well-remembered voice, and partly to the sight of the little station which seemed to be altered not at all. The brightly painted pillars, the green benches, the bookstall with its pile of newspapers and rows of books were all exactly the same; so, too, the stationmaster's garden, gay with marigolds, blue delphiniums and nasturtiums. Coming out through the big folding doors Dinah had a view of the sea and the islands and the wide stretch of sky.

She was so upset that it was difficult to speak, and when they got into the taxi and drove through the familiar streets it was almost impossible to answer the Andersons' inquiries' about the journey. Fortunately they had not far to go, just through the town (which was all shut up for the night) and along the front to Craigie Lodge.

"You'll away to your bed straight off, Dinah," remarked Nannie as she bundled them into the house. "I'll see to the children—you can trust me for that—I've a gurrl here, helping me."

"But Nannie, you can't—"

"Away to bed, Dinah," said Nannie firmly.

Dinah gave in. She felt as if she were nine years old and it was not an unpleasant feeling. It was certainly not unpleasant to lie in bed with her legs stretched out to their fullest extent and hear the sounds of Nannie "seeing to the children." There were splashing noises from the bathroom and a well-remembered gurgling as the bath water ran away. There was the sound of children's voices and the patter of slipper-shod feet . . . and then the tinkle of spoons and crockery which meant they were having their supper.

Dinah's supper was brought to her by a young girl with fair reddish hair and fair reddish eyebrows. Her extreme plainness was accentuated by enormous freckles which covered her face and arms; but her eyes were beautiful, large and brown and soft.

"Mistress Anderson is managing them fine," said the girl shyly. "They're having bread and milk for their suppers. She said I was to tell you."

"I thought it would be bread and milk. That's what we always had," said Dinah, smiling.

"She wasn't going to bath them," continued the girl as she arranged Dinah's tray. "She said they'd be too tired—but she had to! You should have seen the water!"

"I'm glad I didn't!" declared Dinah.

Dinah had not felt hungry—in fact, the reverse—but she could not resist the crisply fried sole and the small green peas with which Nannie had sought to tempt her. She finished it all and was eating the stewed raspberries and drinking the glass of creamy milk when the door opened and Nannie came in carrying Margy: a lovely, clean, rosy, smiling Margy with neatly-brushed hair and pink feet peeping from beneath her chilprufe nightie.

"There!" exclaimed Nannie, proudly. "Isn't she beautiful? Isn't she a duck? Isn't she Nannie's own dear wee lamb?"

Quite obviously she was. She allowed herself to be hugged and kissed by her mother, but made no objection when Nannie picked her up again and put her into the cot which stood ready in the corner of the room.

"You're a marvel, Nannie!" said Dinah.

"They're ducks, all of them, and so good. I can see them properly now. They might have been chimney sweeps, for all I could tell, till I got them washed. Are you feeling a wee bit more rested, Dinah?"

"I'm feeling much better, Nannie. It was just tiredness. I was tired when I started. It was an awful business getting everything ready and packing all the clothes. I was so afraid I'd forget something or that something would go wrong. And the journey was a positive nightmare."

"I shouldn't wonder," declared Nannie, nodding. "They're the worst age for travelling—and stirring at that." She took the tray and added: "Now, you'll just get away off to sleep, Dinah. It'll be another day in the morning."

9

THE day foretold by Nannie arrived in due time. It was extraordinarily beautiful. Dinah awoke feeling rested and refreshed and, leaping out of bed, rushed to the window. The tide was far out and the brown sands glistened in the early morning sunshine; there was a faint mist over the milky sea, impalpable as angels' breath. The rocky islands seemed afloat between sea and sky, serene and peaceful. There was no sound save the far-off crowing of a cock and the occasional shriek of a seagull as it wheeled in the air. The smell of the sea (or perhaps of the seaweed, left uncovered by the receding tide) was strong and pungent. Dinah had not smelt that smell for years and it took her straight back to her childhood. She could almost believe she was a child again, could almost believe that Dan was sleeping next door, that if she ran in and woke him he would sit up and rub his eyes and say, "Gosh, what a day! Let's bathe before breakfast!"

Dinah smiled to herself a little sadly. How long ago that was! How much had happened! But she could not feel sad for more than a few moments—who could on a morning like this? She was enjoying the peaceful scene and searching out familiar landmarks and promising herself that she would revisit all her old haunts before she was very much older, when the door burst open and Polly rushed in.

"It's gone!" said Polly in agonised tones. "Mummy, Mummy, it's gone! The sea's gone away . . . and Nannie said we could paddle this morning . . ."

Dinah was so used to the vagaries of the sea that for a moment she could not think what on earth Polly meant and by the time she had pulled herself together Polly's tears were coursing down her cheeks, emulating the emotion of a film star.

"It's gone!" sobbed Polly. "We've come here—to see the sea—and it's gone."

"It will come back! Polly, listen! The sea will come back!" cried Dinah, taking her daughter by the shoulders and shaking her gently to make her attend.

"How do you know?" moaned Polly. "How do you know it will come back?"

"The sea goes out and comes in every day."

"Why?" gulped Polly. "Why does it? I wanted it to be *there*."

"It is there, you silly billy! Look, you can see it in the distance. By the afternoon it will be right in here again, nearly up to the wall."

"But why? And how can it? Where does all the water go?"

"To the other side of the world," replied Dinah, hoping this answer was moderately sound; for the truth was that the incidence of tides had been taken for granted by Dinah (taken for granted in much the same manner as the incidence of night and day) so she was somewhat vague as to the reasons governing the phenomenon of the ebb and flow. She reflected—not for the first time by any means—that children's questions are calculated to show up the ignorance of their elders to a positively alarming extent. You thought you knew, but when you started to explain and to deal with searching inquiries as to why and how, you found yourself stumped. "It's the moon," added Dinah, having just remembered this interesting piece of information.

"The moon!" exclaimed Polly, incredulously. "But Mummy, how can it *possibly* be the moon? The moon is in the sky!"

"The moon draws the water round the world. Dan will tell you all about it to-morrow when he comes. He's a sailor, you know."

"Why do sailors—" began Polly; but Dinah was not having any more.

"Why do sailors?" she echoed. "Well, you can think that one out while you're dressing. Hurry up or you'll be late for breakfast."

Nannie was of the opinion that children required a solid foundation for the day so the breakfast provided for her visitors was a substantial meal, but the little Savages were too excited to eat much, too eager to set forth and find the sea; they gulped down the necessary minimum of food and rushed off to find their spades and pails.

"You'll just leave all the catering to me, Mrs. Savage," said Nannie, as she came into the hall to see them off. "It'll be easier for you—and for me, too—and I know fine what the children should get."

"Oh, yes; that will be marvellous," agreed Dinah. "But why 'Mrs. Savage' all suddenly like this?"

"It's the right thing. I was a wee bit het up last night."

"Well, I don't like it much, Mrs. Anderson," said Dinah, gravely. "But if you say so, of course . . ."

Nannie looked at her—and smiled. "Och, well!" she said. "But the only thing is, it'll not be very good for Mrs. Turtle's Flo."

"Mrs. Turtle's flow?"

"The gurrl," explained Nannie. "It'll not be good for her to hear me calling you 'Dinah.'"

"Well, of course, it's for you to decide."

Nannie hesitated, but only for a moment. "I'll just need to be stricter in other ways," she said.

Having settled this satisfactorily for all concerned (except perhaps "the gurrl") Dinah pursued inquiries regarding this individual's name.

"Florence, her name is," said Nannie. "Mrs. Turtle was reading a book when she was born, and nothing would persuade her but the baby was to be Florence."

"*Dombey and Son*, perhaps," suggested Dinah.

"Well, fancy you knowing!" exclaimed Nannie, as she hitched Mark firmly into his paddling-drawers and tied the strings. "Always reading, you were, and that's the result. If you want a book to take to the beach I've that nice Miss Buchan's book all about when they were children. Dear little things they must have been, though maybe a bit of a handful." At this moment Polly, who was already accoutred for the great adventure and had been dancing about in the front garden for the last ten minutes, came dashing into the hall shouting: "It's Dan! It's Dan!"

"Dan? It *can't* be!"

"He's here in Bildad!" cried Polly. "He's come to help us find the sea!"

"They let me off to-day," explained Dan, entering the crowded hall with a suitcase in his hand. "There was nothing much doing, so I asked Mr. Cray and he said 'Yes.' I intended to ring you up," declared Dan, smiling. "But Bildad wouldn't wait. Bildad was champing like a war-horse and pawing the ground like with his hooves, so . . ."

By this time Dan had a twin hanging on to each leg. Polly was doing a war-dance. The noise was positively astounding—one might have thought there were half a dozen children welcoming their long-lost uncle and rejoicing in his wit—

"Bildad was pawing the ground!" shrieked Nigel at the top of his voice.

"Like this!" yelled Polly, cavorting round the hall.

"Wanting to see the sea!" bellowed Mark.

"How lovely, Dan!" said Dinah, when at last the noise subsided and she could make herself heard. "It's the nicest thing for you to have come sooner than we expected."

"The nastiest thing would be if he had come later than we expected," declared Polly.

"Or not at all," suggested Nigel. "That would be still nastier."

"That would be hellish," said Mark.

Dinah let this pass; partly because she agreed profoundly with the sentiments expressed and partly because this was no time to rebuke her son for his unparliamentary language.

"I don't know *where* they hear it," she murmured to Nannie as she picked up Margy and followed the others.

The sea was still a long way out. Dinah, seated upon a rug with Margy, watched Dan and the other children making their way down the sands. The twins were gambolling round and round him like a couple of puppies but Polly had him fast by the hand. How they adored Dan! How good he was with them, how understanding and wise . . . if only Gilbert had been like that thought Dinah with a sigh. She had made excuses for Gilbert on the grounds that he could not be expected to take a real interest in the children because he did not know them, had not seen them growing up; but Dan had seen even less of them and already loved them dearly. These reflections led to the conclusion that the excuses were no excuses at all, and . . . but I shan't think of that now, decided Dinah, and banished the problem from her mind.

The sun was warm but there was a cooling air from the east, real sea air from the North Sea which tempered the sun's heat. Dinah lay down on the rug and relaxed. Her younger daughter was a peaceful companion, fat and comfortable and undemanding, taking life as she found it. The others had never been like that, thought Dinah, glancing at Margy affectionately. The others had always wanted attention, wanted to know something, wanted to crawl away or to find something unfit to eat and eat it. Was it because Margy had had so little attention—because there was so little time to give her—or was it simply that Margy was that sort of person, content with her lot? And did Margy think of anything much as she sat there on the rug looking round at the world and smiling at it quietly, or was her mind a complete blank like that of a cow, chewing the cud? I've time now, anyway, thought Dinah, abandoning with regret the idea of reading "that nice Miss Buchan's book" and dedicating herself to her daughter's entertainment.

They amused themselves very happily making patterns with shells and stones. Dinah made a sand pie, not a very successful one because the sand was too soft and dry, but Margy was quite pleased with it.

There happened to be an old gentleman sitting on the sands quite near them. He had a grizzled beard and bushy eyebrows and little twinkling eyes. He was reading his paper, off and on, putting it down for a few minutes and looking about him and then taking it up again.

Margy was interested in him. She pointed at him with her spade. "Man?" asked Margy, inquiringly.

Dinah smiled and nodded. She was aware that Margy's doubt was due to the fact that hitherto her acquaintance with the male sex had not included a bearded specimen.

Thus reassured Margy smiled at the man. He smiled back. It was now time for Margy's milk. Dinah poured it out and gave it to her. She took the mug in both hands and drank with obvious enjoyment.

The old gentleman was watching the performance. Margy raising her eyes as she took breath, saw that he was interested.

"Bung ho!" said Margy loudly and clearly.

For a moment the old gentleman was startled and then he began to laugh.

Margy paused. Her blue eyes regarded him with a stare of dewy innocence over the rim of the blue enamel mug. "Bung ho!" she said again.

"The boys teach her things," explained Dinah. "She's a little parrot, I'm afraid."

"A very charming little parrot," said the old gentleman, moving nearer.

Dinah had a feeling that he was lonely and for her part she was quite ready to be friendly with him. She liked the look of him; his eyes were humorous and kind. They spoke of the weather and agreed it was exactly the sort of weather they would have chosen for their holiday. The old gentleman was staying at Miss Brown's, a little further along the front than Craigie Lodge; he and his wife and their nephew had come for two months—the nephew was fond of golf. During this conversation Margy was by no means forgotten; it appeared that the old gentleman was an excellent hand at sand pies.

"We require wet sand," he explained to Margy in a serious tone, as if he were talking to a grown-up person. "The dry sand doesn't stick together well. Fortunately suitable material is close at hand; if we make a hole with your spade we shall find sand to suit our purpose." He made a hole, filled the pail, and turned out an excellent pie.

"Cake!" exclaimed Margy rapturously.

"But not for eating," her new friend hastily declared. "Your mother will tell you that although my cake looks nice it is unfit for human consumption."

"Again," said Margy.

The old gentleman repeated his feat of skill and went on repeating it.

Presently Dinah saw the twins come running across the sands towards her. Nigel was in front, bounding like a deer, his long white legs covering the ground easily and gracefully; Mark was lumbering along behind—he was not built for speed—but it was Mark who arrived first after all for Nigel stopped to look at a sand-castle on the way.

"The hare and the tortoise," murmured the old gentleman, who had paused for a moment in the midst of his labours.

Dinah realised the idea was apt, but Mark's haste to reach her roused her anxiety. "What's the matter?" she asked.

"Nothing," gasped Mark. "It's just—can we go and—fish off the pier—with Dan—?"

"Of course, if he's willing to take you. But remember, you must do exactly as he says or there will be trouble."

"No trouble," said Nigel, strolling up in a leisurely manner. "It's all fixed. We can get lines and hooks from a boy and we can get mussels from one of the fishermen—for bait, you know."

"Polly's coming too," said Mark, wiping his hot face with a grimy handkerchief. "Dan said to tell you we might be late for lunch."

"All right," said Dinah. "But be good. Remember what I said."

They hastened away.

The old gentleman was beginning to get a little tired of making sand pies (it is a form of employment which is apt to pall upon an adult, though seldom upon a child). He rose and shook himself and said he would walk along to the pier and see how the fishermen were doing.

10

THE fishermen were late for lunch. Dinah and Margy had already started when the front gate squeaked open and there was the sound of steps on the gravel outside the window; but there was no sound of chattering voices and Dinah had an uneasy feeling that something had gone wrong.

Mark rushed in first and, opening a small and extremely grubby hand, disclosed a shilling. "It's mine," he announced. "Mr. Monk gave it to me."

Nigel was just behind him. "But I caught a bigger one d'reckly afterwards," declared Nigel, earnestly. "If Mr. Monk had known *that*, he would have given it to me."

"They should share it, shouldn't they?" said Dan, appearing in the doorway with Polly. "It's much nicer to share things."

"Perhaps you could explain," suggested Dinah crisply; for, relieved to see the entire party safe and sound, she was feeling the reaction from her fears.

"We *are* explaining," said Nigel. "It was Mr. Monk. He would have given the prize to me if he had seen me catch that big one."

"Why not share?" asked Dan.

"If Mummy says so," agreed Mark, with reluctance.

"No," cried Nigel, stamping his foot. "No, it's mine! I caught the biggest one, didn't I? Mr. Monk would have given it to me—I know he would."

"Who is Mr. Monk?" inquired Dinah. She was busily, engaged shovelling mince and potatoes into Margy's mouth; but feeding her offspring had become second nature to Dinah.

"Mr. Monk!" said Mark in surprise. "He's a friend of yours, Mummy. He was talking to you and Margy on the beach."

"An old gentleman with a beard," put in Dan. "The children thought he was like an old seaman called Monk. I've been telling them stories about him."

"He *is* Old Monk!" cried Polly excitedly. "He's all hairy with twinkling eyes and a heart of gold. That's what you said Old Monk was like."

"And he's got hairs growing out of his ears," added Mark, as if that clinched the matter.

The last scraps of mince and potatoes had vanished. Dinah laid down the spoon and wiped her daughter's mouth.

"All gone!" remarked Margy, in regretful tones.

"Dan had better explain everything from the beginning," said Dinah firmly.

"Yes, of course," agreed Dan. "Well, what happened was he came down to the pier and watched the boys fishing. He seems an awfully nice old chap. At first they didn't catch anything and Nigel got a bit bored and began fooling about; then Mark caught a fish—it was tremendously exciting—and when it was safely landed the old gentleman took a shilling out of his pocket and gave it to Mark."

"It was a prize," explained Mark.

"He said: 'Well done, young man! There's something to buy ice-cream.'"

"Yes, that's what he said," agreed Mark.

"And then he said he mustn't be late for lunch, and went away. After he had gone Nigel caught a fish—"

"A much bigger one," said Nigel, hastily. "I should think it was almost *twice* as big as Mark's. If Mr. Monk had been there he would have given the prize to me, wouldn't he, Mummy?"

They waited, looking at Dinah.

"I said they should share it," suggested Dan.

"No," said Nigel. "No, it's mine, isn't it, Mummy? My fish was much the biggest."

"It's Mark's shilling," said Dinah, firmly.

"Mark's!" cried Nigel. "But Mummy—"

"The old gentleman gave it to Mark. If Mark likes to share it well and good, but it's definitely his own to do what he likes with."

"We'll share it, then," said Nigel hastily. "That's the best way—Dan said so, didn't he?—Ice-creams are sixpence each."

Mark was frowning. He said: "No, I'll share it with Polly. That's what I'll do."

"But she didn't catch *anything*!" Nigel cried.

"That's why," replied Mark. "It will be a present, not a prize," and with that he put the shilling in his pocket.

Dinah sighed. It was a pity, but it couldn't be helped. "Go and wash," she said. "Wash thoroughly—all of you. Don't just dip your hands in the water and wipe them on Nannie's towel."

They ran off to do as they were told. Dan had noticed before that Dinah's children were obedient (and having been in the Service he knew the value of discipline and appreciated it), but he thought she had handled the matter of the shilling in the wrong way.

"Why didn't you make them share?" asked Dan, after a moment's silence.

"They wanted justice, Dan."

"It's nice to share."

"Yes, if you want to. Sharing is no good unless you do it willingly. That's why communism doesn't work—because it isn't *true* communism. True communism is sharing gladly what you've got with your neighbour. It isn't taking his possessions, it's giving yours."

"All right, I see that," said Dan. "Personally I'd call that true Christianity and not communism at all; but let's get back to Mark and Nigel, shall we? They're up against each other a bit, you know. We always shared everything—you and I—so why not teach them to do the same?"

"I've tried. It isn't any good. *Of course* we shared everything, but Mark and Nigel aren't like us. As I said before you can't *make* people share; they must either do it willingly or not at all."

"If you had persuaded them—" began Dan.

"They asked me for justice, so I gave it to them. It was Mark's shilling, wasn't it?"

"Yes, of course."

"Well, then," said Dinah.

"You worry too much. They're only babies, Di."

"No, they aren't babies, they're people . . . and I don't worry *too* much. It's my job to worry about them. They're my responsibility and nobody else's. Sometimes it terrifies me to think what power I have for good or bad, to help them to grow up straight—or crooked."

"But Di—!"

"Shakespeare helps quite a lot," declared Dinah, smiling at the absurdity of it. "There's a good deal of sense in Shakespeare; he's fundamental and logical and sound. Take Shylock, for instance. Shylock wanted justice, he wouldn't accept mediation; he wouldn't accept an iota less than what he considered his due. He wanted justice. If you refuse to share and continue to demand justice you can't complain when justice is given you."

"A Daniel come to judgment!" said Dan, half laughing, half serious. He saw her point, but he still thought she was making mountains but of molehills. It was natural, of course, for the children were her responsibility and she had nobody to help her bear the strain. Dan had evolved a plan; he had been thinking about it ever since his conversation with Henry Barnard and intended to open the subject with Dinah quite shortly.

The children were quiet at lunch. Nigel was sulking and the others were somewhat subdued. Mark kept feeling in his pocket where the shilling was burning a hole.

"How have you been getting on?" asked Dinah, who had had no opportunity to inquire into her brother's affairs since his arrival.

"All right, really," replied Dan. "Mr. Cray is a nice old spud and he's got rather a nice daughter. I think you'd like her, Di."

"Would I?" asked Dinah with interest. "What is she like?"

"Pretty," said Dan. "She came into the office yesterday and we had a chat—the old man was busy. They've asked me to go in to drinks some evening."

"You'll go, of course?"

"Oh, of course!" nodded Dan. "I mean one's got to keep in with one's boss and all that. I mean it would be silly not to go—"

"And what about the job?"

"Oh, well," said Dan doubtfully; "there's not much scope in it, if you know what I mean. It's all right in a way—I can do it quite easily—but I must say I should like to find something better, something that required intelligence. It seems a pity to let the little grey cells atrophy, if you know what I mean. I shall have to look for better digs, too. The old woman is dirty and disagreeable. Dirt might be bearable without disagreeableness, or disagreeableness without dirt, but the two together are getting me down."

"Oh, Dan!" cried Dinah, in horrified tones. "We must find somewhere nice for you to live. What a pity you couldn't live here and go up every day!"

"Too far, I'm afraid; but I could live in Edinburgh, of course. I wondered whether you and I could set up house together in Edinburgh. What about that, Di?"

There was silence—chiefly because Dinah had no breath to speak.

"It seems to me a very sensible plan," continued Dan, helping himself to pudding with a lavish hand. "Gosh, I'm hungry! It's the sea air, I suppose. We could share a little house which would be cheaper for both of us as well as more pleasant. I should have cleanliness and comfort instead of dirt and disagreeableness; you would have someone to lock the front door at night and spank the children . . . and, talking of the children, there are excellent schools in Edinburgh for both sexes."

"Dan, you've been thinking about this!"

"For ages!" nodded Dan. "Weighing the pros and cons; though as a matter of fact, I can see no cons at all."

"You might want to get married."

"Not likely. Even if I did there's no harm done. I should move into another house, preferably in the same street, so that my children could enjoy the society of their cousins."

"But what about Christine!" cried Polly, in dismay. "Oh, Mummy! I couldn't *live* without Christine next door!"

(It was odd, thought Dan, how often it happened that one forgot the children, assuming they were not listening or would not understand and then suddenly, when one least expected it, they would leap into the conversation with a remark or exclamation which showed they had understood every word.)

"You could easily live without her," Nigel was saying. "You're living without her now."

"But only for a month—that's different—and what will Christine do?"

"She'll get on all right."

"She hasn't got any friends except me," said Polly tearfully.

"But she'll soon get friends when you aren't there," declared Nigel, with conviction.

This assurance did not seem to comfort Polly. Why should it? wondered Dan; there are few people unselfish enough to welcome the prospect of being easily replaced in the affections of their friends.

"Don't worry, darling," Dinah said. "We haven't settled anything. It's just an idea, that's all."

"Are we going or not?" Nigel wanted to know.

"We'll see," said Dinah firmly.

Dan was obliged to hide a smile, for this was one of Nannie's sayings (one which had always irritated the Dees beyond measure) and here was Dinah using it herself. Yes, we'll see, thought Dan. He was pretty certain he would gain his end. What alternative was there? What other plan could be half as good?

"I hope we go to Edinburgh," said Mark, in a thoughtful voice. "We'd have Dan all the time then, wouldn't we? Not just for week-ends."

"Could he bear it? That's the question," said Dinah, seriously.

The shilling which had caused so much trouble and which was burning a hole in Mark's pocket ought to be spent. Dan realised that the sooner it was spent and the incident closed the better it would be for all concerned, so after tea he called the children and they set off together for the café near the pier where ice-creams were to be had for sixpence each. Nigel was nowhere to be found and Dan was sorry for he had intended to stand Nigel an ice-cream. He was not sure whether Portia would approve of this mitigation of sentence, so he did not ask her.

"Nigel's sulking, I expect," said Polly cheerfully as she skipped along clinging to Dan's hand. "He always sulks for ages. We don't care, do we?"

"He isn't sulking," said Mark. "I saw him go out of the gate with his fish directly after tea."

"P'raps he's going to put it back into the sea," suggested Polly.

"Silly, it's dead!" replied Mark. "It wouldn't come alive again, so what would be the use? I'm going to have mine for breakfast— Nannie said so."

Dan listened to their prattle with half an ear. He was busy making plans. The first thing was to find a house that would suit them. Not too big, thought Dan, but of course it must not be too small. Four good-sized bedrooms and a smaller one for a maid. Dinah was to have a maid if he could possibly manage it. Part of his idea was to relieve Dinah of her burden of work and to make it possible for her to go out and enjoy herself occasionally. Dances, thought Dan. It would be fun to dance with Di again.

At this moment his eye fell upon a large notice announcing a dance at the Town Hall to-morrow night, and, following his lucky star which usually led him in the right direction, he went into the little stationer's shop and bought two tickets. He might not be able to persuade Dinah to go but it was worth trying. It would be good for her to have a little fun—good for her to dance. It might even help her to get over the queer obsession about Gilbert (of which Irene Barnard had spoken), for Gilbert and dancing were mixed up together in Dinah's mind. Dan was no psychologist—he would have denied it vehemently—but he had a feeling that there was something in his idea.

The café was almost empty. Dan and Polly and Mark chose a table near a large window which looked out onto the harbour and beyond it to the sea. The sea was never far away in Seatown (wherever you went and whatever you did the sea was always there) for the town was built upon a boot-like promontory with bays sweeping inland on both sides; and the harbour rocks, volcanic in origin, were the toe of the boot.

Dan ordered three ice-creams and they paid for them then and there (Dan paid for his own, and Mark paid for the other two). Mark heaved a sigh as the waitress took the shilling; not a sigh of regret, but a sigh of relief to be rid of it at last. Odd little beggar, thought Dan, looking at him with affection—so determined, so old-fashioned, so conscientious—there was no need to worry about Mark's future; whatever he chose to do in life he would do well and thoroughly.

"There's Nigel!" exclaimed Polly.

"So it is!" exclaimed Mark.

It was Nigel. He strolled into the café as if the place belonged to him and took a seat at an empty table further down the room. He knew they were watching him, of course, and obviously he wanted them to see him, but he took no notice of them at all. When the waitress came he ordered a double ice-cream and, taking a shilling out of his pocket, handed it over with a nonchalant air.

Dan was dismayed. He realised how absurd it was to feel dismayed by the trivial incident, but—but was it trivial? There was something definitely nasty about the whole affair. Nigel's behaviour was a piece of bravado (yes, *bravado*, thought Dan) and where had he got the money? Where had the shilling come from?

The same idea had occurred to Polly. "I expect Mummy gave him the shilling," she whispered.

"Yes, of course," agreed Dan. But he was perfectly certain she hadn't, for that would have made nonsense of the whole affair. No,

Di had not relented. She had too stern a sense of justice to propitiate Shylock with his pound of flesh!

After a few moments Dan decided that frankness was the best course. It was an impossible situation and must be tackled immediately. He rose and went over to Nigel's table.

"Hallo," he said. "What's the idea? Why didn't you speak to us when you came in?"

Nigel was taken aback. He was only a child, after all.

"And where did you get the shilling?" inquired Dan.

Nigel smiled. That was the question he had expected and his answer was ready. "From Mr. Monk, of course!" he replied promptly.

"From Mr. Monk?"

"Yes, I showed him my fish," said Nigel easily. "He saw at once it was twice the size of Mark's."

It was too difficult for Dan. He did not pretend to his namesake's wisdom in judgment. Dinah would have to deal with her son and he had a feeling she would deal with him drastically.

11

FRIDAY dawned grey and cloudy. The sea was grey, a circumstance which astonished Polly, who had been under the impression that the water in the sea was blue. It was too cold to paddle but the conditions were ideal for digging, so Dan drew out a square and set the children to work on building a sand-castle of noble dimensions. Several other children appeared and were invited to join the party and soon there was quite an army of industrious little creatures toiling upon the shore. When the castle was half-finished it was reinforced with a layer of seaweed, then more sand was piled on top and the whole stamped firmly down to make a solid platform.

In the afternoon the sea came in—as Dan had foretold—and the builders stood upon the castle and waited to be surrounded. Gradually the waves crept up, the sea poured into the moat and the castle was an island. But the sea did not stop there of course (even Canute of venerable memory had been unable to halt the encroachments of the tide); it advanced slowly but surely, the waves lapped against the castle and sucked the sand away . . . suddenly an extra big wave approached in majestic strength and swept right over the top, drenching the children's feet. There were screams of excitement and delight. The children splashed across to the shore; they jumped up and down; they rushed backwards and forwards leaping upon the castle and shaking their spades in the air and retreating before the advancing waves. In a few minutes it was all over; the castle had melted away to a sodden heap and the sea rolled over it unchecked.

"It's sad, isn't it?" said Polly, as they walked back to tea.

"Sad? I think it was gorgeous," declared Mark.

"I mean the poor castle has gone. We made it so beautifully, too."

"We made it for that purpose," said Dan, comfortingly. "We made it to be swept away, so it has done its job. That's the main thing."

The children did not understand, but Dan was struck by the symbolism of the vanished castle. It had been well constructed and had provided a whole day's entertainment for its builders. Now it was a memory—no more.

To-night was the night of the dance for which Dan had obtained tickets, and Dinah, after a good deal of persuasion, had consented to go with him. The children were put to bed and Dan was waiting for Dinah in the drawing-room when she came in. He was glad to see she was already dressed for the occasion in an afternoon frock of printed voile, for he had had a feeling that even now, at the eleventh hour, she might change her mind and decide to stay at home.

"Supper in ten minutes," said Dan, cheerfully. "Just time for a glass of sherry and a cigarette."

"I don't know why we're going." said Dinah, sitting down. "I can't think why I said I'd go. Couldn't you get somebody else?"

"I'm going because I like dancing and you're going to please me; and I couldn't possibly get somebody else. I don't know a soul."

"That girl on the shore this afternoon—"

"You mean the one with the sticking-out teeth?" inquired Dan in disgust.

"I thought she seemed rather nice," said Dinah with a sigh.

"It will be fun," wheedled Dan. "There'll be reels and country dances—Dashing White Sergeants and things. You'll enjoy it, Di."

"I know quite well why you took the tickets. I'm not so silly as you think," Dinah told him.

"I think you are a *little* bit silly," declared Dan. "I *do* like dancing and you *are* going to please me. Why not leave it at that?"

"All right," agreed Dinah, without enthusiasm.

"I intend to enjoy myself," added Dan.

"I hope you will," she said listlessly. "I'm pretty certain I shan't. You know, Dan, you've got it all wrong. You think I'm sad because Gilbert isn't here. It's much more complicated than that."

This is it, thought Dan. It's coming now, and he poured himself out another glass of sherry to sharpen up his wits. Aloud he said: "How is it complicated, old thing?"

"It was something that happened," said Dinah slowly. "I wish I could forget about it but I don't seem able to. It comes and goes—like toothache."

"Gilbert was a curious creature."

"He was, wasn't he? This particular thing that happened was very curious indeed—rather horrible, really. I wish I didn't know about it. I wish I could think about him naturally—and sadly—without always remembering this. I wish I could . . ." She hesitated and stopped.

"Tell me," Dan said.

"Well, it sounds so awful. I was going to say I wish I could forgive him. I try to forgive him, and sometimes I think I've succeeded, and then the horrid feeling comes back. If I could *understand* it would be easier. If I could find some excuse!"

"You couldn't judge Gil by ordinary standards, Di. You've got to take people as you find them, haven't you?"

"Yes, and usually I can. Anything but lies."

"Lies are horrible," he agreed.

"Gilbert lied to me," said Dinah, in a low voice. "He wrote and told me his leave was cancelled—and it wasn't. He went to London instead of coming home; he was with a party, I suppose. I wouldn't have grudged him his fun—at least—well, perhaps I would, a little—but it wouldn't have left such a horrid taste."

Dan did not know what to say. He should have been prepared of course (Heaven knows he had been trying to prepare himself and to decide what to say ever since his chat with Irene Barnard), but the fact was Dan was afraid of saying too much and making things worse than before. It was obvious when Dinah said she did not grudge Gilbert his fun she assumed that "his fun" consisted of spending his leave in

London "with a party" and dancing all night. Dan's assumption was different. For a moment Dan wished Gilbert were alive so that he could get hold of him and tell him exactly what he thought of him, and follow his relation with bodily violence (it would have eased Dan's rage and fury considerably if he could have dealt out some shrewd punishment to his one-time friend) but second thoughts reminded him that Gilbert's death was a fortunate eventuality for Di. Imagine if Di had been tied for life to that unspeakable cad!

"It was horrible, wasn't it?" continued Dinah. "It hurt me frightfully, of course, but that isn't the worst of it, Dan, not really. The worst is I lied to Gilbert—acted a lie—pretended I didn't know. That's the worst."

"Pretended you didn't know!"

"Somehow or other I just couldn't—couldn't speak of it."

Dan was silent. This was the most difficult part to understand. It was not difficult to believe that Gilbert had acted like a cad because unfortunately Gilbert was completely selfish and had had no scruples about lying his way out of anything he didn't want to do; but Dan thought he knew Di pretty well and, knowing her as he did, he would have expected her to blurt out the whole thing in the first five minutes. It was out of character for Di to keep things to herself and brood upon them . . . and when people act out of character it means that they are terribly hurt, wounded beyond endurance. Yes, thought Dan, it was because she minded so much.

"It was awful of me, wasn't it?" said Dinah miserably.

"I don't see why," objected Dan.

"You don't see why!"

"What could you have done?"

"Told him the truth. Told him that I knew and was angry about it."

"There would have been a most unholy row," said Dan with conviction.

"I know—that's why I funked it."

"You didn't funk it," he said quietly. "You realised it was no use, which is a very different thing. I knew Gil very well—better than you, perhaps—and I can assure you it would have been no use at all. You would have had an almighty row and been worse off than ever. It was no use trying to have things out with Gil; it never got you anywhere. He couldn't bear criticism—nobody had the right to question what he did."

"I know that."

"Unless you wanted to break with him entirely—"

"No, of course not!" she exclaimed. "I mean I never even thought of it."

"—the only way was to take him as you found him—the good with the bad."

"And I took him for better, for worse," said Dinah, thoughtfully. "I accepted him as he was, so I had no right to criticise him or complain if he acted according to his nature. Is that what you mean?"

It was not what he meant at all but it seemed to comfort her so he let it pass. Women were queer, reflected Dan. Even Di was queer about some things.

Now that the ice was broken Dinah found it easy to tell Dan everything that had happened in detail and Dan encouraged her. They talked about it while they had their supper and were still discussing it when they set off to the dance. Dan was not going to let her off the dance. She had promised to come, and come she must. He felt rather a brute in holding her to her promise but comforted himself with the reflection that it was for her good. Fortunately it was a damp, misty evening so Dinah was not able to say they were wasting fine weather.

The hall was decorated and brilliantly lighted. It was full of people, though not uncomfortably full, and Dan noticed with relief that it was reasonably well-ventilated. The band consisted of a piano and two violins. They were playing a waltz, and playing it with plenty of vigour, when the Dees arrived.

"Come on," said Dan, and putting his arm round his partner's waist he swept her on to the floor.

It was years since Dinah had danced, not since that leave—but she wouldn't think of it. She would stop thinking about Gilbert and think of Dan who was worth half a dozen Gilberts. Dan danced well and after a few moments Dinah's feet became alive and followed of their own accord . . . it was extraordinarily pleasant. I'm enjoying it, thought Dinah with surprise.

The music ended and they found chairs. There was time now to look about; they saw nobody they knew (which seemed funny in dear old Seatown) but for all that it was a cheerful sight. The men were in flannels or lounge suits and the girls in gaily-coloured frocks.

"Not too bad, is it?" Dan inquired.

"Nice," said Dinah smiling.

A reel followed. The Dees got into a good set and acquitted themselves well. They were quite pleased with their performance—though extremely hot—when the reel was over.

It was just after the reel that Dan saw a tall, thin figure making his way across the floor towards them.

"Goodness!" exclaimed Dan. "Here's a fellow I know—Pat Yoker—he was in hospital with me at Colombo. What on earth is he doing here?"

"Hallo, Dan!" exclaimed the man. "What on earth are you doing here?"

"Just what I wondered about you," retorted Dan rising.

"Golf," said his friend. "Golf by day and dancing at night whenever possible. Not a bad spot, is it?"

"Better than Colombo!" Dan said.

At this moment the band started to play with its usual verve, so Dan's introduction of his friend to his sister was practically inaudible. Fortunately he had mentioned his friend's name before, so it did not matter much. Yoker, thought Dinah (as she smiled at her new acquaintance) and obviously a sailor ... Commander Yoker, perhaps.

"May I butt in?" he asked, bending down and shouting to make himself heard.

Dinah was not particularly anxious to dance with him and leave Dan in the lurch, but she could hardly refuse and Dan was no help at all; in fact Dan seemed delighted to surrender her.

"Go on!" said Dan. "Don't waste your time."

They danced.

"Rather mean of me, I'm afraid," said Commander Yoker.

"Dan doesn't mind," she replied.

"And I hope you don't mind either?"

She did not answer that. She was a little breathless; dancing took up all her attention. Commander Yoker was a very good dancer and expected intuition from his partner—and Dinah was more than a little rusty. His dancing reminded her of Gilbert, who was wont to do the most extraordinary things and expect instant co-operation.

"Dan's found someone," said Commander Yoker suddenly. "Quite a nice little bit of fluff in a pink dress . . . that make you feel better or worse?"

"Better," gasped Dinah.

He laughed and swung her round so that her feet almost left the floor. "Fun, isn't it?" he exclaimed. "You're a feather. We'll streak now."

They streaked. It was an eccentric evolution but somehow her feet followed his.

"Great!" he exclaimed. "We'll do that again in a minute."

They did it again with equal success.

The dance ended and they found seats near the door. Dan seemed to have vanished.

"Saw you on the beach with some children," said Commander Yoker, abruptly.

"Yes, I've got four."

"Four?"

"It isn't too many," Dinah assured him.

"No, of course not," agreed her companion hastily. "People like you ought to have dozens of children."

Dinah was somewhat taken aback at this sweeping statement, it was so different from the usual reaction of those who heard for the first time that her family numbered four. What could he mean, she wondered . . . and glanced at him to see if by any chance he had intended it as a joke; but Commander Yoker's face was as solemn as the face of a judge.

"Dozens," he repeated nodding. "We can't have too many—if you see what I mean."

She laughed. This friend of Dan's was a queer card and no mistake.

"I'm staying here with the uncle and aunt," he continued. "You spoke to the uncle, didn't you? He's a little old fellow with a good deal of hair about him. The aunt is a bit of an invalid, doesn't get about much. She's terribly interested in your children, watches them from the window with a glass. You don't mind, do you?"

"Of course I don't mind."

"Good!" said Commander Yoker, nodding. "Very good indeed. You don't mind. She hasn't much to interest her, you see."

"I don't mind a bit. Why should I?"

"I suppose," began Commander Yoker doubtfully, "I suppose you couldn't let them come in and see her. You couldn't let them do that of course, could you?"

"Why not?" asked Dinah, smiling.

"You could?"

"Yes, if she wants them. They're rather wild sometimes."

"No matter," declared her companion. "The aunt understands children and the uncle would be there to keep them in reasonable order. I'll pass on the good news. Tea would be best, wouldn't it?"

"Tea!" exclaimed Dinah, in surprise.

"Oh, definitely tea." said Commander Yoker. "I mean children like cakes and biscuits and Miss Brown provides quite an astonishing spread. We'll fix up the day later. It's terribly good of you to let them come. Shall we dance again?"

They danced again. Then Dan appeared and the Dees took part in Petronella while Commander Yoker looked on.

It was getting hot now, hot and airless, and Commander Yoker suggested that they had had enough.

"You wouldn't like a drink, would you?" he inquired. "I mean I know rather a decent little place just around the corner."

Dan was quite ready for a drink and Dinah was willing to do what the others wanted, so they got their coats and followed their guide to a small pub in a back street. It was a clean, bright little room with a sanded floor and rows of bottles on the shelves behind the counter.

"Trust you to find a good place!" commented Dan as they went in.

"Yes," agreed the Commander. "I've got a nose for this sort of place. I've been coming here for years. You know me well, don't you Sam? Three beers, please."

The bartender, a short, tubby little man in a clean apron, agreed that he knew the Commander very well indeed. "We've cider to-day," he suggested, with a glance at Dinah.

"Cider!" exclaimed the Commander. "Good heavens, I thought you knew me better than that!"

"For the lady, I meant," explained Sam.

The lady said she liked cider much better than beer.

"There's no accounting for tastes," remarked Commander Yoker as he drained his tankard to the dregs.

The three of them sat at the bar-counter on high stools and talked about various matters in a friendly manner. Dinah was somewhat alarmed at the amount of beer her new acquaintance consumed. No sooner was his tankard empty than Sam seized it, refilled it and replaced it. Even Dan began to get a trifle uneasy.

"Go slow, Tapioca!" he said.

"But half of it's water," explained Commander Yoker gravely, "which means you have to drink twice the quantity. It's a mathematical calculation—and I couldn't say *that* if I'd had too much."

"Why does he call you Tapioca?" Dinah inquired.

"It's his prep. school mentality of course. But you can't complain if you're saddled with a name like mine. Pat Yoker—well, there you are! Awful, isn't it?"

"It's better than dinner-bell," said Dinah, who had suffered from this cognomen at school.

"Worse," declared the Commander. "Much worse. Dinner-bell is pleasant in my ears. It promises well. It may not live up to its promise of course, but it has a hopeful sound. Tapioca is just a mess . . . white (or perhaps grey), sodden, claggy, lumpy! Another beer," said the Commander, shuddering. "Bring me another beer for heaven's sake!"

"You'll have the most frightful head to-morrow," objected Dan.

"Not me," he replied. "Beer suits me. I shall be as bright as a bee and as lively as a cricket. You wouldn't like a game of golf to-morrow, Dan?"

"That depends on what Dinah wants to do," said Dan, looking at her.

"Dinah won't mind, will you?" the Commander inquired.

Dinah didn't mind at all. She was a little surprised at being addressed as Dinah by Commander Yoker, but she liked him so she didn't mind that either.

"It's easier," he explained, reading her thoughts. "I mean we're going to see a lot of each other because of the uncle and aunt and the children." He sighed and added: "You can call me Tapioca if you like."

"I shall call you Pat," said Dinah laughing.

Dan and Dinah walked home arm-in-arm. Everybody seemed to be walking home arm-in-arm. It was dark and the lamps were shining. The mist had cleared away and the stars were bright.

"You were right," said Dinah. "I enjoyed myself and it did me good. The mist is clearing—my mist, I mean."

"I'm as good as a bottle," declared Dan, proffering the old joke. "And, talking of bottles, what did you think of Tapioca?"

"Rum," said Dinah, thoughtfully. "Rum, but nice. There's something very innocent about him."

"Poor old Tapioca has lost his heart to you."

"Nonsense! An old woman like me, with four children!"

"Quite senile, of course, but I don't mind betting that he has. I know the signs, my dear," declared Dan, with a little chuckle.

"You're mad!" said Dinah, firmly.

The Dees loitered by the sea front. The air was warm and still and it was such a glorious night that it was a pity to go indoors. Quite a number of people seemed to have the same idea; shadowy couples passed and re-passed, strolling along and talking in lowered voices. It was long after midnight when the Dees said good night to the sea and retired to rest.

Dinah felt happier than she had for a long time, partly because she had been able to tell Dan what was worrying her and partly because the little outing had given her a new perspective. She realised she was too much with the children, too wrapped up in them, but what could she do? I must think of other things, decided Dinah. I must read more and go about and try to be sensible and sane. It will be better for me and better for the children.

Dinah was almost asleep when the door opened very softly and a small, woebegone figure in a blue flannel dressing-gown appeared. The moonlight shining in at the open window filled the room with radiance so that it was almost as bright as day.

"What's the matter, Polly?" whispered Dinah.

"Everything," replied Polly in a voice choked with tears. "Everything's the matter. I can't *bear* it! I was dreaming! Oh, Mummy! I was dreaming all about Christine!" She ran across the room and flung herself into Dinah's arms.

"It's all right," declared Dinah, hugging her. "Just a dream—"

"But it isn't," sobbed Polly. "It isn't *all* a dream. I shan't see her ever again! I'm miserable. I love Dan awfully of course, but I love

Christine too. I want to go to Edinburgh and I want to stay at home. You see I've always had Christine next-door, and she's always had me."

Dinah drew Polly into bed beside her. "Listen," she said. "You're old enough to understand so I'm going to talk to you just like a grown-up person. We can't go on living at Nettleham because there are no schools and we haven't enough money to pay for you and the boys to go to boarding-schools. Christine will go away to a boarding-school when she's bigger because she's an only child. It's different with you."

Polly was quiet now and they discussed the matter reasonably.

"We'll have her to stay with us in the holidays," continued Dinah. "You'll like that, won't you? It's sad to leave Nettleham but it can't be helped. We've got to think of what's best for everybody. You see that, don't you?"

Polly saw that. She was comforted and flattered at being talked to as if she were a grown-up person. She was the eldest. The others were too young to understand. She fell asleep in her mother's arms and slept dreamlessly till the morning.

12

DINAH awoke to find Polly getting out of bed. She sat on the edge for a moment before she slipped down on to the floor and her mother had a view of her back: the narrow shoulders and the two little pigtails tied with white tape. The fragility of the little, white nape of Polly's neck gave Dinah a qualm of compassion. Polly was a woman—feminine, mysterious, vulnerable as boys and men were not. "Oh, God! don't let her get hurt," said Dinah's heart. "Don't let there ever be anything I can't comfort."

Softly Polly crossed the floor, took up her blue dressing-gown (which already was too small for her) and stood gazing out of the window. It was a lovely day. Polly stretched her arms above her head and gave a little chuckle of pleasure before she tiptoed out of the room.

It was still very early as Polly could tell by the pale golden haze which lay over the sands and the sea; but it was too good a day to waste. She dressed hastily and let herself out of the door. How fresh it was! She felt as light as air—she felt as if she had only to spring into the air and she would fly or float or glide like the seagulls with her arms spread out like their wings. She was nearly the only person awake. There were two old fishermen digging for sand-worms and a small, slight figure in a grey suit standing upon a rock and gazing at the sea. Polly's keen eyes told her it was Mr. Monk.

Polly ran down the sands and splashed into the sea. The little waves licked her legs and the sand squelched between her toes. Mr. Monk waved to her, so she paddled across to his rock and he pulled her up beside him.

"Have you got a parrot?" asked Polly. It was a question she had wanted to put to him when she met him on the pier (but there had been no opportunity for questions on the pier). If Mr. Monk thought it an odd question to be shot at him out of the blue, standing upon a rock at six o'clock in the morning, he managed to conceal it.

"Yes," said Mr. Monk. "Not here of course; we left it at home."

"Does it say: 'Splice the main brace!'?"

"Well, no, I'm afraid not. My son was in the Navy so he taught it several nautical expressions, but—"

"But *that* isn't naughty-cal," objected Polly. "That means everybody is to have a glass of grog. The twins say naughty-cal expressions sometimes—like hellish, you know."

"I know," agreed Mr. Monk.

"My real name isn't Polly," continued Polly, following an obvious line of thought. "My real name is Elvina, but the twins called me Veener and Daddy said it was awful. Daddy called me Polly and then everybody did."

"That's the way it happens," said Mr. Monk. He hesitated for a moment and then continued: "Talking of names, Polly, why am I Mr. Monk?"

"Because you are," replied Polly instantly. "I mean you're *exactly* like him. He's *very* nice, so you needn't mind."

"I don't mind in the least. I was interested, that's all."

"He has a heart of gold," said Polly. She had enough social sense to refrain from mentioning Old Monk's less desirable peculiarities. "Old Monk has twinkling eyes and a heart of gold."

"And a parrot that says: 'Splice the main brace!', I suppose," said Mr. Monk, laughing heartily.

"Yes," agreed Polly, nodding. "Dan tells us stories about him—they were shipmates, you see. You're sure you don't mind being called Mr. Monk?"

"Not if he has a heart of gold," said Mr. Monk decisively.

They stood and looked about. It was very pleasant. The golden mist was thinning rapidly and the sun was shining through, warming up the day. It would be hot later, but at the moment it was delightfully cool and fresh.

"We're the only people in the world this morning," said Mr. Monk, smiling at his companion as he spoke.

"Except the fishermen," said Polly, pointing to them.

"But they're just part of the scenery, you know."

"Not real people, like you and me?"

He smiled and replied: "Real to themselves of course, and to their wives and children, but not real to us. To us, just a part of the rocks and the sea."

"And we're just 'visitors' to them," said Polly, showing she had understood.

The day passed quickly and pleasantly. Dan played with the children in the morning, and in the afternoon went off with Tapioca for his game of golf. Dinah renewed her friendship with the old house, going round it by herself and remembering a hundred little incidents which happened when she was a child.

Dinah loved the old house. It was home to her as no other house could be. One could hardly call it a beautiful house but it was well-designed and strongly built of pale-grey stone with a blue-slate roof and squat chimneys. The house had been built close to the sea, exposed to the winter gales, and its designer had taken this into consideration when he planned it. There was no nonsense about the inside of the house either. On the ground floor, facing the sea, was the dining-room and the room which had been the doctor's surgery; the kitchen premises and a small, cosy study were at the back and looked on to the garden. Upstairs was the drawing-room, Dinah's bedroom (which had once been Doctor Bell's) two small rooms and a bathroom. On the top landing there were several rooms which the Andersons used themselves, another bathroom and the nursery. The twins were sleeping in the nursery now, and sleeping in the same small beds in which, long ago, the Dees had slept. Later, of course, the Dees had been promoted to the two small rooms on the drawing-room floor and had used the old nursery as a play-room. Dinah looked out of the window, with its iron bars, and saw the same view: the walled garden, the green sweep of common and the steep green hill. It was all exactly the same.

Nannie had altered the house and furniture very little, for, like Dinah, she had always thought it as nearly perfect as an earthly mansion could be. She had replaced the furniture which Dan and Dinah had taken by furniture of the same Victorian style, good and solid and sensible; but most of the old furniture remained and Dinah recognised the pieces and greeted them as friends. The big, deep sofa in the drawing-room was especially dear to Dinah, for the Dees had sat there every evening and often on wet afternoons. They had sat, one in each corner, reading aloud to each other and discussing what they had read, or conducting exhaustive conversations about all sorts of matters which interested them. The big easy chairs, the cabinet and the table near the window were all the same and stood in the same places; so, too, the music cabinet which, for some reason which the Dees had never understood, was called a Canterbury. (Why Canterbury? they had wondered. Why not Salisbury, or Rochester, or some other cathedral town? They had never asked any one to elucidate the mystery and the matter was still obscure to the grown-up Dinah.) The dining-room had the same mahogany furniture, polished so that you could see your face in it; the same oil paintings, framed in heavy gilt, hung upon the walls. The pictures were of Highland mountains and glens and of Highland cattle standing knee-deep in Highland burns. They had hung there peacefully all these years, thought Dinah, as she looked at them.

The hall was slightly different for the stained-glass windows in the inner front door had been replaced by plain glass. Dinah regretted the change (she would have regretted any change) for the stained glass with the sun shining through had filled the hall with red and blue and yellow shafts of light which had been interesting and unusual. She was obliged to admit the hall was lighter now—perhaps that was why Nannie had done it. The stairs were of dark wood, with carved banisters and a rail from top to bottom. One afternoon—a wet one, of course—Dan, sliding down, had fallen off and landed upon the hall floor with a sickening thud and had lain there for a few moments without moving. Dinah remembered the event as if it had happened last week. She had been petrified with horror. Fortunately he sustained nothing worse than a slight concussion, but that had put an end to the sport of banister-sliding.

There was still the Indian Boy in a corner of the hall. He was made of black wood, and stood upon a small plinth of the same material; his hands were raised above his head and supported a brass bowl with a fern growing in it—not the same fern, Dinah supposed, but one which resembled its predecessor as one pea resembles another. There was still the coat-cupboard of dark oak with its elaborately carved panels depicting the eviction of Adam and Eve from the Garden of Eden. It was a roomy cupboard—an excellent place to hide—and smelt most curiously of apples. There was a chip off one corner of the cupboard; Dan had removed it when practising a mashie shot and had disguised it very cleverly by rubbing in boot polish. The chip could still be felt, though not seen. Dinah's fingers found it.

She was smiling over the chip and the memories it evoked when Nannie appeared from the kitchen premises.

"You've been all round, Dinah," said Nannie, nodding approval. "It's as well kept as it was in the Doctor's day—except, maybe, the carpets. I'm needing new carpets but I'll have to wait for them—and the door, of course. Och, I could have cried over the door! It was the wee Hamilton boy gave it a slam and the window fell out on the floor and smashed to bits. The Hamiltons were quite decent about it and said I was to get a new one, but they're not to be had."

"It makes the hall brighter," said Dinah, comfortingly.

"Och!" exclaimed Nannie in disgust. "The place isn't the same. I tell you, Dinah, I could have cried and that's the truth."

She hesitated for a moment and then continued: "And while we're on the subject I might as well tell you that the house will be yours when I'm gone. It's yours *now* to all intents and purposes—I always meant that, and Andrew agrees."

"But Nannie—"

"I've always meant it and I always will. Who would I leave it to, Dinah? We've no chick or child of our own, Andrew and me, and you're the one that ought to have it. The thing's fixed," said Nannie defiantly, "and there's no need to talk about it."

"Nannie—really! It's most awfully kind of you. I hope it will be a long, long time—" began Dinah.

"I'm not dead yet, nor anything near it," declared Nannie and so saying she disappeared into the kitchen premises and shut the door.

13

DAN returned home to tea slightly crestfallen. "I was hopeless," he declared as he sat down. "Tapioca beat me six and four—I couldn't hit a ball."

"They're such very small balls," remarked Polly comfortingly.

Her uncle laughed and laughing cheered him. He declared that a football would have suited him much better and added that he thought he would go along to the bathing-pool after tea and have a swim.

"Dinah can go too," said Nannie, who had brought in a fresh brew of tea and was lingering in the room as long as possible. "It will be a nice wee outing for Dinah. I'll see to the children. You'll not go in yourself, Dinah—not to-day. Just wait till you get acclimatised," added Nannie firmly.

"Are you sure you can manage?"

"Manage!" exclaimed Nannie. "How would I not manage?"

It was pleasant to be ordered about. Nobody had ordered Dinah about for years and she found it soothing. Quite meekly she put on her swagger coat ("You'll be cold, sitting," said Nannie) and set forth with Dan.

The swimming-pool at Seatown is near the harbour (in fact it is part of the harbour rocks) and is surrounded by tiers of seats and a concrete wall. There is a large open space at one side of the pool where the pierrots give their performance, and Dinah reminded her fellow-Dee of an historic occasion upon which the sea, breaking over the wall, had suddenly and unexpectedly put a stop to the pierrots' entertainment.

"It's just the same," declared Dinah looking round. "I love this part of Seatown. Most seaside places are so artificial, you feel they're only for pleasure, but here you have the harbour and the fisherfolk and the rocks all round you and the pool in the middle."

Dan found her a seat out of the wind and she sat down to enjoy herself and to watch the swimmers. She was surprised at the number of small children in the pool, most of them swam like frogs and, like frogs, seemed amphibious. In the shallow part of the pool there were about twenty little girls having a lesson from the swimming instructor. They belonged to a local school—so Dinah decided. She watched with interest and amusement as the children were made to lie down in the water with their hands on the bottom and strike out with their legs. Some of them seemed to enjoy it immensely; others were less enthusiastic and made no effort to learn.

Dan had engaged a cubicle at the deep end of the pool and presently he emerged ready for his swim. She looked at him with pride as he stood waiting for his turn at the spring-board. Dan stripped well; he was tall and well-made without an ounce of unnecessary weight. Feeling her eyes upon him he looked across the pool and waved to her.

It was at this moment that a man approached him and touched him on the shoulder. Dan turned at once and, after a moment of surprise and explanation, they shook hands cordially.

Who was the man, wondered Dinah? Somehow or other he seemed vaguely familiar yet she could not place him. He was small compared with Dan and lightly built, with a brown face and dark brown hair; he was dressed in well-cut grey flannels, his shirt open at the neck.

They were talking eagerly now, and as Dinah watched them she saw Dan turn and point to her and wave. Dinah waved back. The stranger gave Dan a little push (as if he were saying, Go on and have your swim; don't mind me) and, with that, Dan ran along the board and took a header into the water. The other man climbed over a bench and began to make his way round the pool to where Dinah was sitting. Where have I seen him? wondered Dinah, trying to remember. It was not until he had reached her side and smiled and held out his hand that she realised he was Malcolm Armstrong.

"Goodness!" she exclaimed as she shook hands with him. "Goodness, I was trying to think who it was!"

"You didn't know me?"

"Not at first. To tell you the truth I remembered you as being enormous—more than life-size!"

"How disappointing for you! It must have been because you were quite small in those days," suggested Malcolm, laughing.

"Partly, perhaps, but partly because we admired you tremendously. It was Dan's ambition to do everything as well as you."

His face clouded a little as he replied: "Not a very high ambition!"

"It's astounding that you should remember *us*," continued Dinah. "How *did* you, I wonder? You couldn't have expected to see us here."

"I'll tell you how I knew you. I saw you arriving at the pool; you were swinging along, side by side, and talking earnestly together—you were always swinging along and talking earnestly—that's how I remembered you. I said to myself: 'Golly, it's the Dees!'"

They both laughed. Dinah made room for Malcolm and he sat down.

"We couldn't have been very interesting to other people," Dinah said.

"You were to me; I often saw you about the place—on the sands when I was riding, or fishing off the pier. You always seemed busy about something and so happy, so absolutely wrapped up in each other. I was a lonely sort of creature and I envied you. And then, of course, I was extremely grateful to you for helping me to win my match in the East of Scotland Amateur Championship," added Malcolm with an engaging grin.

"Helping you!"

"Don't you remember, Dinah? You walked round and watched. Quite a lot of people were walking round and watching, but they were all watching Ferguson, all intent upon every stroke he played, all perfectly certain that he would lick me into a cocked hat. I was terribly nervous and playing like a beginner—couldn't see the ball, far less hit it. I lost the first three holes straight off—and then I saw the Dees. They were there, standing together, earnest and intent—watching *me*."

"Of course we were!" cried Dinah. "We were determined that you should win. We held our thumbs and prayed!"

Malcolm smiled at her. "I knew it," he said. "I felt it! Every time I settled down to play a stroke I saw you out of the corner of my eye. You were never too near and never too far away. When I hit my ball into the rough, there you were, standing beside it . . . I remember Ferguson lost a ball at the fourteenth."

Dinah chuckled. She said: "Dan was frightfully good at watching the flight of a ball so he always shut his eyes when Mr. Ferguson was playing."

"An admirable idea," commented Malcolm.

"And it really helped?" asked Dinah, with interest.

"It helped enormously. Golf is a queer game, you know. There's so much psychology in it. If you're in the right state of mind everything goes right, you can't make a mistake; but if you're upset or lose confidence you're done."

"Do you still play as well as ever?" Dinah inquired.

"I don't play at all," he replied.

Dan was diving now. He accomplished a very creditable swallow-dive and disappeared.

"Good!" exclaimed Malcolm involuntarily.

"He dives well, doesn't he?" said his sister proudly. "He does everything well—not brilliantly, but competently."

"You distrust brilliance?" said her companion.

Dinah was surprised, not only by Malcolm's intuition, but also by the discovery that what he said was true. "I—distrust brilliance," agreed Dinah in a low voice.

"I wonder why."

"Because it's too easy. One ought to have to work hard for competence."

"That's an interesting idea. Yes, I think I agree—but don't you think the world would be rather a dull place without our birds of Paradise? And can we be quite certain that we aren't a tiny bit jealous of them?"

He smiled as he spoke and Dinah smiled back but her smile was thoughtful.

"Never mind," he added; "you're thinking of a special person and so am I. Perhaps one day we'll get down to it and discuss the matter thoroughly. There's Dan waving to you—"

Dinah waved back. He was sitting on the raft in the middle of the pool with two mermaids in extremely scanty costumes which displayed their charms to the full.

"Dan is enjoying himself," remarked Malcolm.

Dinah agreed. "What have you been doing?" she inquired.

"Making paper. I made paper before the war and now I'm back at the job again."

She remembered that his father, Sir Andrew Armstrong, owned a paper-mill in Edinburgh. "It must be interesting."

"It is—to me. My father died some years ago and I'm trying to fill his shoes—which isn't easy. We still live at Abbot's End."

"A lovely house!" exclaimed Dinah, envisaging the grey stone-built house (long and low, with the blue-slate roof) which was situated in a clump of fir-trees on the edge of the golf course.

"It's a bit too big for us now, but we manage none too badly. I live with my stepmother and her niece, Edith Grover. I have a man called Clarke, who is rather a wonderful person and can turn his hand to anything, and—actually—we have a cook."

"You're lucky," Dinah said.

He nodded. "Talking of cooks," he continued, "could you and Dan come to supper one evening? Supper is best because I'm away all day."

Dinah was about to refuse but remembering that there was now no need to refuse an invitation since Nannie would look after the children—she accepted instead. "It would be lovely," she declared. "Dan is only here for week-ends, but—"

"To-morrow?" suggested Malcolm. "Sunday night. That would suit him, wouldn't it? What sort of work is he doing?"

Dinah told him about Dan's job (and of Dan's fear that the little grey cells might atrophy) and Malcolm listened, and was interested in all she said. She was wondering whether she should call him Malcolm; he had called her Dinah. In the old days she would not have dreamt of calling him Malcolm to his face, for he had been so much older and bigger (a grown-up young man on vacation from Oxford when she and Dan were children) but now the years had passed and they were almost contemporaries so it seemed silly to stand on ceremony with him. She was wondering whether he was Sir Malcolm now. Had his father been a baronet or a knight? She was wondering what he had done in the war, and whether he were married . . . but no, he couldn't be married if he lived with his stepmother at Abbot's End.

Presently Dan came out of the water and joined them. His hair was wet and his eyes were sparkling. He looked very young compared with Malcolm Armstrong, young and fit. He was delighted at the idea of supper to-morrow night at Abbot's End. As the Dees walked home together, swinging along and talking earnestly as was their wont, their talk was naturally about the man they had left sitting by the pool.

"He was marvellous," declared Dan. "He was cracking at golf, wasn't he? I wonder why he's given up golf—it seems a pity. He seems old—"

"Not old," said Dinah quickly. "Not old to talk to. He's alive and interested in everything. He's only about ten years older than we are, Dan."

"He looks—tired," said Dan. "Tired and sad. When we came away and left him sitting there I thought he looked sort of lonely. I wonder what he's been doing all these years—in the war, I mean."

When Dan and Dinah got home from the swimming-pool the two little boys were in bed and Nannie was brushing Polly's hair. It was the first time for years that Dinah had gone out and left the children at bedtime and she was amused at their reactions and at the warm welcome she received. One would have thought she had left them for days instead of barely an hour.

"Tell us a story," suggested Mark. "We've been *very* good—Nannie said so, didn't you, Nannie? Tell us a story about the Dees."

"Oh, do!" urged Nigel. "It will be *much* more interesting now that we know what Seatown is like."

"Well, just a short one," agreed Dinah. She sat down on the end of Nigel's bed, and Polly, in her blue dressing-gown, curled herself up on Mark's. Six large eyes gazed at Dinah in expectation as she began the story.

"One day when the Dees were about nine years old they went along to the Black Rocks to fish."

"Why didn't they go to the pier?" inquired Nigel.

"Shut up!" exclaimed Mark. "What's the good of interrupting?"

"They took hooks and lines," continued Dinah, "and they dug up a fine lot of sand-worms for bait . . . and then they settled down to a morning's fishing. It was a perfect day for fishing—not too bright, warm and cloudy and quiet. Sometimes they saw a seagull diving. The waves came gurgling into the crevices of the rocks, lifting the seaweed and filling the little pools. The Dees went on fishing and they caught a lot of fish and it was so exciting that they forgot the time and forgot that the tide was coming in. They had no excuse, of course, because they knew all about the tides—"

"Not like Polly," put in Mark with a chuckle.

"Shut up—don't interrupt!" cried Nigel, delighted to get his own back.

"The Black Rocks," said Dinah, hurrying on, "are high rocks in the opposite direction from the harbour—you haven't been there yet. They form a sort of promontory, striking out into the sea, with grass growing on the top. When the tide is out you can walk out onto them quite easily without getting your feet wet, but when the sea comes in it surrounds them so that they are an island. The Dees went on fishing until they began to feel hungry which meant it was time for lunch; but when they had strung their fish together and come round to the landward side of the rocks they found they couldn't get across. There was a wide stretch of water between the rocks and the mainland."

"Couldn't they paddle?" asked Polly.

"It was too deep and the tide was running fast, which made the water very rough and dangerous. There was only one thing to do, and that was to sit and wait until the tide went out and the water became shallow enough for them to wade across. They were rather miserable," said Dinah, thinking back down the years and remembering her feelings very vividly. "They were hungry, for one thing, and they were worried because they knew Nannie would be anxious about them and wonder where they were . . . and they were pretty certain there would be serious trouble when they got home."

"Spanking, perhaps," suggested Mark sympathetically.

"That was what they thought," agreed Dinah. "But you'll hear what happened. They sat and talked and waited. Dan made a mark on the rock to see whether the tide was still coming in, and it was. But after a long, long time it began to go out. The Dees were still sitting there when they saw somebody coming along the shore. It was their father. He had found out from one of the fishermen that the Dees had been seen going along the shore and he had come out to look for them. The Dees were *very* glad to see him—it made them feel a lot better just to *see* him—and they stood up and waved to him with all their might. He came to the water's edge and waved back and shouted: 'Stay where you are until you can come over without wetting your feet.'"

"Why?" asked Mark. "I mean they could have got home sooner if they had paddled."

"It was a sort of punishment, I think. A sort of punishment to teach them to be more careful. Anyhow, it was the only punishment they got. It seemed a long, long time before the sea went out far enough and the Dees were getting hungrier every moment."

Yes, thought Dinah, silent now that the story was finished. Yes, that must have been the reason. It was a good punishment (she saw that now) for it fitted the crime and was a lesson which the Dees did not forget. It had plenty of time to sink in and make a lasting impression. Dinah tried to punish her children in the same way—when punishment was necessary—but it wasn't easy. She saw now, as she looked back, how wise their father had been, how just and sensible in his dealings with his motherless children. The Dees must have been a problem to him (just as her fatherless children were a problem to her) causing him endless anxiety. If only he were still alive what a help he would be, thought Dinah sorrowfully.

14

ABBOT'S End was just as Dinah remembered it; a long, low, grey-stone house with shining windows, set upon a rocky mound and surrounded by tall fir-trees. She had never been inside the house so it was an exciting moment when she and Dan stood upon the doorstep.

"I wish we hadn't come," said Dan hesitating with his hand on the bell.

"But, Dan—"

"Oh, I know it's silly, but Abbot's End has always meant something rather special to me. I couldn't bear it to be full of—of steel-tube furniture."

"It won't be," replied Dinah, with conviction. "And, anyway, it's too late now. You don't really want us to turn tail and go home, do you?"

Dan laughed and rang the bell; and after a very short interval the door was opened by a short, sturdy man in a neat dark-blue suit. (This was obviously Clarke, of whom Malcolm had spoken.) He opened the door wide, with a welcoming gesture, and ushered them into the hall. It was a large square hall with a balcony and a glass dome, and it was panelled in light oak, quite plain and unvarnished; the carpet was deep blue, self-coloured and very thick; there was a refectory table, two large wooden chests and several carved chairs—all of them period pieces—but it was the flowers which took the eye of the beholder. The hall seemed full of flowers. There were tall vases of delphiniums and hollyhocks, pots of hydrangeas in brass bowls and a veritable bank of flowers against the side of the staircase; quite a wonderful sight, but slightly overpowering. The scent was overpowering, too, and Dinah was suddenly reminded of a funeral.

Lady Armstrong and Miss Grover were awaiting their guests in the drawing-room. Lady Armstrong was tall and stout, with a heavy face and lustreless blue eyes. Miss Grover was slim and dark with rather a sallow complexion. They were arrayed in full evening dress, which was an unpleasant surprise to Dinah—for she, having been invited to supper, had put on a blue silk afternoon frock as being suitable to the occasion. However, it could not be helped, so she went forward with her best smile and shook hands.

"How d'you do?" said Lady Armstrong, without cordiality. "This is my niece, Miss Grover . . . Mrs.—er—Bell, isn't it?"

"Savage," said Dinah.

"Oh, yes," said Lady Armstrong. "You used to live here, Malcolm said."

"When we were children," nodded Dinah.

"Won't you sit down?" said Lady Armstrong.

They all sat down.

"What a lovely view!" exclaimed Dinah, looking out through the tall windows which faced west over the gleaming water of the bay.

"People often admire it," said Lady Armstrong.

"And such a lovely house!"

Lady Armstrong was silent.

"So bright and—and spacious," added Dinah.

"Too big," said Lady Armstrong.

"And very cold," put in Miss Grover.

"Inconvenient," said Lady Armstrong.

Dinah sought for something to say but found nothing.

"There's far too much to do," complained Miss Grover. "It takes me two hours every morning to do the flowers."

Dinah was not surprised to hear this for the drawing-room was almost as full of flowers as the hall: flowers were massed in the fire-place and on the mantelpiece and elsewhere in the room upon tables and cabinets and bookcases. There were great bowls full of roses and sweet peas. It was like a flower show. The room itself was beautifully proportioned and all the woodwork was light oak, like the hall. Several large Persian rugs lay upon the parquet floor. The window sills were low, so that one could see out of the windows while sitting in one's chair. The furniture (chairs and sofas and window-seat cushions) was covered in cretonne which looked as fresh and new as if it had been put on that morning. It was this freshness which Dinah found so attractive, for most people's covers and carpets—including her own—were shabby and faded after seven years of wear without the possibility of replacement. Abbot's End was like a show-place; it looked unlived-in, thought Dinah. It was beautiful and peaceful and spotless . . . it was the sort of house you might dream of if you happened to live in a small suburban villa with four stirring children.

"The flowers are beautiful," said Dinah, after a little pause.

"My aunt likes flowers," said Miss Grover.

"I couldn't live without flowers," said Lady Armstrong complacently.

There was another pause—somewhat longer this time. Dinah thought of several things to say, but rejected them as being unsuitable. She might mention the children and say how much they were enjoying their holiday, but she did not think Lady Armstrong would be interested to hear about the children; besides, Dinah was aware that if she began to talk, about the children she was liable to go on talking about them, and people who talked about their children and told anecdotes about their cute remarks were terrible bores. It was difficult not to, of course, but one had to be firm with oneself. Dinah had decided to be firm. In fact she had made a vow that she would not mention the children unless somebody asked for information about them.

"What a lovely place Seatown is!" said Dinah at last.

"Do you think so?" said Miss Grover, with a disagreeable little laugh.

"I never feel well here," added Lady Armstrong complainingly.

"Oh, what a pity!" said Dinah, trying her best to make it sound as if she were exceedingly sorry for this unfortunate circumstance.

"It's so dull," explained Lady Armstrong.

Dinah did not find it dull. She wondered what Lady Armstrong would have thought of Nettleham. She said, doubtfully: "I suppose it depends on what sort of things amuse you."

"My aunt is fond of music," said Miss Grover.

"There are very good concerts in Edinburgh," suggested Dinah.

"In Edinburgh—yes," agreed Lady Armstrong.

"It doesn't take long to go up to Edinburgh," Dinah pointed out.

"But it's such a bore," declared Miss Grover.

"We're quite sick of that long, dull road," said Lady Armstrong. "It would be much more convenient to live in town."

"But you wouldn't leave Abbot's End!" exclaimed Dinah, in surprise.

"No, of course not," agreed Miss Grover hastily, glancing at her aunt as she spoke.

"Certainly not. We wouldn't dream of it," affirmed Lady Armstrong.

There was another silence. Dinah was sure that they had thought of leaving Abbot's End; she was certain that they had discussed it between themselves but had not intended to mention it. Personally she did not care whether they went to Timbuctoo; the farther the better, thought Dinah . . . The whole thing was rather mysterious (for why should they mind talking about their plans) but Dinah had no time to elucidate mysteries; she had to try to make conversation and this was becoming increasingly difficult. Why didn't Dan help? Dan had not uttered one word since their arrival. Dinah glanced at him appealingly, but he was gazing straight in front of him (looking from him, as Nannie would have put it) with an expression of abject misery upon his face. What on earth was the matter with Dan? Could he have been seized with a sudden and violent pain? What had he eaten for lunch? Nothing that could possibly upset him, thought Dinah as she reviewed in detail the plain, excellent fare which Nannie had provided.

"What lovely weather we are having?" said Dinah in desperation. "It's a *real* summer, isn't it?"

"Too dry," said Lady Armstrong.

"Oh, do you think so?" asked Dinah. "I like it dry and warm—and it's so lovely for the—" she stopped.

"It's much too dry for the marrows," said Lady Armstrong.

"The flowers don't last any time at all," added Miss Grover.

"But it's nice for people having their holidays," Dinah pointed out.

"Visitors!" exclaimed Miss Grover, with the disgusted expression of one who rated visitors a little lower than earwigs.

Dinah was annoyed. After all she and her family were visitors to Seatown—in company with many other worthy and hard-working citizens who looked forward to their summer-holiday for months and months—she opened her mouth to defend the rights of visitors and then decided not to defend them. What did it matter, anyhow?

"We need three days' solid rain," said Lady Armstrong.

This was too much. The prospect of three days' solid rain with the children cooped up in the house was more than Dinah could bear. "Oh, *no!*" cried Dinah. "Oh, no, surely not! Not three days—"

"We need it for the marrows," said Lady Armstrong firmly.

"People are more important than marrows," declared Dinah, recklessly abandoning all idea of tact. "We need fine weather—especially for children, so that they can play on the sands and enjoy themselves and lay up a store of health and energy for the winter. We need sunshine even more nowadays when food is so scarce—"

"What a fatuous argument!" exclaimed Miss Grover, with an unpleasant little smile. "I never heard anything so ridiculous. Either the weather will be fine or else it will be wet. It doesn't matter in the least what any one *wants.*"

Dinah felt herself blushing, partly with rage and partly because of course it was perfectly true. It *was* a fatuous argument, but she had been led into it by her hostess who was (Dinah decided) a fatuous person, utterly selfish and smug, and yet at the same time discontented. It was difficult to know what to say without being openly rude but fortunately at this moment the door opened and Malcolm appeared.

Malcolm was wearing a grey flannel suit; he looked cheerful and happy and his friendly manner and cordial greetings changed the atmosphere completely.

"So awfully sorry I'm late," declared Malcolm. "I was going through some papers and never noticed the time. What about drinks?"

"I didn't know you wanted drinks," said Miss Grover.

"Not want drinks?" asked Malcolm in surprise. "Why did you think we had suddenly gone on the water-wagon? Sherry is one of the few nice things left to us in this uncomfortable world."

He went out of the room and returned immediately with a tray of bottles and glasses. "Here, Dan," he said; "give me a hand, will you? I want this table cleared."

Dan was already there, clearing the table. With the advent of his host Dan's mood had changed completely and he was smiling and cheerful. He helped to pour out the drinks and then he went and sat near Lady Armstrong and began to talk to her.

Malcolm brought Dinah a glass of sherry and sat down beside her on the sofa.

"Here's to the old days!" he said, raising his own glass and smiling. "Here's to the days when you were a little girl with pigtails and I was a giant!"

Dinah smiled back at him. She was reminded suddenly—and for no very good reason—of Margy saying "Bung ho!" to Mr. Monk. It would be rather fun to tell Malcolm about it and she was pretty certain Malcolm would appreciate the joke but she resisted the temptation.

"Here's to the old days!" said Dinah. "They were happy, weren't they?"

"In some ways," agreed Malcolm.

"They were very happy for me. I had Dan all the time and no worries."

"Would you go back if you could?"

She hesitated. Would she go back? "Not for good," she said slowly. "I'd like a month of it—a whole month of being eight years old—but after that I think one would miss one's responsibilities."

Talking to Malcolm was pleasant and easy. It would have been even more so if Edith Grover had not been sitting unnecessarily close to them and listening to every word. Miss Grover wore a supercilious expression (she was a little like a camel, thought Dinah unkindly) and the lines round her mouth had been marked by discontent. Now that there was no need to search feverishly for conversation Dinah was able to look at the two women objectively, and even to feel a little sorry for them. They were well-dressed and well-fed; they seemed to have everything they could desire and yet they were discontented with their lot. They created discordant music in this lovely harmonious house.

15

THE dining-room at Abbot's End matched the rest of the house. It was a light, airy room with lovely old furniture and a few good pictures on the panelled walls. There were no flowers here (except a small bowl of roses on the round, polished table) and Dinah was glad, for, although she was fond of flowers, she realised it was possible to have too many.

Conversation was general now, which meant that there was no real conversation at all, for Lady Armstrong seemed to have an uncanny knack of wet-blanketing any interesting subject that happened to crop up and of putting a stop to all attempts at argument or discussion. Her mind was so narrow that nothing interested her except people and she could speak of nothing except people—preferably titled people—of her acquaintance. The Dees knew none of Lady Armstrong's friends, so they were unable to respond. It was noticeable that, while Malcolm did his best to change the subject to one of more general appeal, Miss Grover encouraged her aunt and continually brought the conversation back to the level of Lady Armstrong's intelligence.

"I heard rather a good story the other day," said Malcolm, falling back upon anecdotes as a last resort. "An elder of the Free Kirk happened to be going up to London on business and was asked to order a new sign to be hung outside the kirk. It was to be a large wooden board with a text on it, and the elders had some difficulty in deciding what the text was to be. They all had their own ideas on the subject of course. When the elder arrived in London he lost the sheet of paper upon which he had written the text and the dimensions of the board, so he wired to his wife, 'Please send text and dimensions.' Some time later a girl in the telegraph office was seen to fall off her stool in a dead faint. The elder's wife had complied with her husband's request, and the message read: 'Unto us a child is born six feet long and four feet wide.'"

Malcolm's guests laughed long and loud.

Miss Grover smiled in a tepid manner.

Lady Armstrong looked down her nose.

When they had all recovered a little Miss Grover said: "I expect Mrs. Savage knows Sir Abraham Welshman."

"No," said Dinah.

"But they live in Kent!" exclaimed Miss Grover in surprise.

"Quite a number of people live in Kent," said Malcolm.

"But Lady Welshman is so well-known," explained Miss Grover. "She takes such an active part in social life."

"No, I'm afraid I've never met her," said Dinah, shaking her head. "I don't go out much, of course."

"How strange!" said Lady Armstrong with a sigh. "I suppose you don't know the Whitticombes either?"

"No," said Dinah.

"Commander Bell is sure to know Admiral Frigate," declared Miss Grover, making a brave attempt to find some point of contact with her aunt's guests.

Dan admitted that he had heard of the admiral, but added that he had never seen nor spoken to him in his life.

"Such a *dear*!" exclaimed Miss Grover. "One of my aunt's *oldest* friends."

"His daughter married a Pygge," said Lady Armstrong.

Dinah, by this time, was in such a condition of nerves that she giggled feebly.

"Are you sure it wasn't a swan?" asked Malcolm, with a perfectly grave face.

"No, Malcolm," said Lady Armstrong. "You're thinking of General Gunn's daughter."

"Oh, she was a goose," declared Malcolm.

In spite of Malcolm's efforts to entertain the company, dinner (or supper) was definitely a failure. The food was good and well-served—it was the diners who were at fault. There were moments of uncomfortable silence followed by sudden bursts of speech as everybody started talking at once. Nothing in the nature of conversation was possible and there was no exchange of ideas. The meal seemed to last an extraordinarily long time but at last it came to an end and Dinah received a look from her hostess bidding her rise. She rose at once. Everybody rose. Malcolm opened the door and Lady Armstrong and Miss Grover waited for Dinah to precede them. It was obvious that the conventions were observed at Abbot's End and that the ladies would retire to the drawing-room leaving the gentlemen to their wine. Dinah was appalled at the prospect of half-an-hour—or perhaps longer—in the company of her hostess and Miss Grover. She had not been to a formal dinner party for years and she had almost forgotten that this was the normal procedure in days gone by. She looked back from the door and caught a glance from her brother—a commiserating glance.

The drawing-room was stuffy with the scent of flowers. Lady Armstrong and Miss Grover spent several minutes discussing whether or not to open one of the windows.

"Better not risk it, perhaps," said Miss Grover, turning away from the window and sitting down.

It seemed ridiculous that Dinah could not ask for the window to be opened, but she could not. I shall have to bear it, she decided as she sought for something to say. It was all the more difficult to find something to say because she had made a fool of herself once by saying something "fatuous" and she had no wish to incur Miss Grover's scorn, yet what subject was there of common interest to herself and her hostess? Dinah could find none. Did Lady Armstrong like reading?

"My aunt has very little time for reading," said Miss Grover, before her aunt could reply.

Lady Armstrong had said she was fond of music, suggested Dinah.

"Not modern music," said Lady Armstrong.

"Bach?" asked Dinah, hopefully.

"My aunt finds Bach too heavy," said Miss Grover firmly.

"Perhaps you like Gilbert and Sullivan's operas?"

There was a faint glimmer in Lady Armstrong's fishy eyes. She leant forward and was about to speak, but Miss Grover was before her.

"So hackneyed, aren't they?" said Miss Grover. "One gets dreadfully tired of Sullivan's music, don't you agree?"

Miss Grover was no help at all; in fact, Dinah would have got on so much better without Miss Grover's interference that she began to suspect Miss Grover of interfering on purpose and making conversation as difficult as possible (in that case she was more clever than she looked, thought Dinah, glancing at the camel-face and wondering what sort of person lived within). And why should she bother, wondered Dinah. Why should Miss Grover take pains to prevent any sort of *rapprochement* between her aunt and their guest? Why should she wish the aforesaid guest to make a bad impression?

There was no doubt that a bad impression was being made. Everything that Dinah said was wrong or, if not wrong, absolutely and completely uninteresting. Lady Armstrong was bored to death. She yawned several times without bothering to conceal the spasm; she wondered aloud what Malcolm was doing; she glanced at the clock and commented with surprise that it was earlier than she had thought. Dinah had exactly the same reactions as her hostess. She had been struggling with yawns; she had been wondering if the clock had stopped; she had been wishing—not for the first time, of course—that she was of the sex which remains drinking wine in the dining-room when the ladies withdraw.

It seemed ages before Malcolm and Dan appeared but they came in at last looking very pleased with themselves—looking as if they had enjoyed their conversation enormously.

Malcolm went straight over to the window and opened it. "We must have some air," he said.

"Oh, Malcolm, it's such a draught!" exclaimed Lady Armstrong.

"A draught! There's scarcely a breath of wind," objected Malcolm. "This room is exactly like a greenhouse."

"Aunt Edith's rheumatism," murmured Miss Grover.

Malcolm shut the window at once. "We'll go out, shall we?" he suggested. "You'd like to go out, wouldn't you, Dinah?"

Dinah rose at once saying quite truthfully that there was nothing she would like better.

"It's too cold," objected Miss Grover. "And anyhow it's almost time for the news. I expect Mrs. Savage would like to hear it."

"What do you say, Dinah?" asked Malcolm, smiling at her.

Dinah was about to say she would rather go out, but Lady Armstrong got a word in first.

"It's much too cold for the girls to go out in their evening frocks," declared Lady Armstrong.

"But Dinah isn't wearing an evening frock," said Malcolm, good-humouredly. "I'm not wearing my evening frock, either, and it seems a pity to stay indoors when it's so lovely outside." He crossed the room as he spoke and opened a side door which led on to the terrace. Dinah went out and Dan followed closely—perhaps Dan was afraid he might be expected to remain and chat to his hostess and her niece.

It was not cold—just fresh and clear after the stuffy room. Dinah drew in deep breaths of air. She was a little worried about the way in which she had ignored the wishes of her hostess, but what joy it was to escape . . . and after all she had done what Malcolm wanted and Malcolm was her host, it was he who had asked her to come.

"I hope Lady Armstrong won't be annoyed," said Dinah.

"She is annoyed," replied Malcolm. "But don't worry. So many things annoy Lady Armstrong that the only way is not to worry. Edith will take care of her."

Dinah did not reply. She was surprised at the implication in Malcolm's words for it had seemed to her that Edith Grover was much more likely to fan the flame of Lady Armstrong's annoyance than to damp it. Edith Grover was the villain of the piece—or so Dinah thought.

They strolled along the terrace together and sat down on a wooden seat in the shelter of a wall. In front of them was a wild garden sloping down to the golf course, an undulating carpet of short green turf, smooth as velvet. Beyond the golf course were shaggy sand-dunes and beyond the dunes lay the sea, like a peaceful lake of dull silver. The islands were dark, their shadows from the setting sun spread out upon the water; away in the distance was the faint outline of the coast of Fife.

"How lovely!" said Dinah, softly.

"It is lovely," agreed Malcolm. "I often sit here in the evening and watch the sun go down." He laughed a little, and added: "I said that to the old gardener the other day, and he replied in reproachful tones: 'But Mister Mawlcolm, it's the airth that tips up, ye ken!'"

"Not nearly so poetical," smiled Dinah. She was amused not only at Malcolm's joke, but at Malcolm's accent which was extremely good. Time was when the Dees had prided themselves on their ability to mimic the broad Lowland speech of Seatown folk, but it was so long since Dinah had heard it that she was doubtful if she could do it now.

Dan had not spoken, but now he leaned forward on the seat. "Malcolm," he said eagerly. "Malcolm, I *must* tell Di; you don't mind, do you?"

"Of course I don't mind."

"Malcolm has offered me a job," said Dan, his voice tense with excitement. "Di, isn't it marvellous! That's why we were so long—talking about it—"

"Dan!" exclaimed Dinah in delight.

"Isn't it splendid!" cried Dan. "Isn't it too wonderful for words—a *real* job—something worth doing—something I can get my teeth into—"

Malcolm laughed. "You can get your teeth into it all right," he declared. "As a matter of fact I've been on the lookout for somebody with teeth. It's amazing how few people seem to have any teeth nowadays; they all want to be spoon-fed."

"I'll speak to Mr. Cray to-morrow," said Dan. "He won't mind a bit—I mean anybody could do the job I'm doing now unless he was completely imbecile. I don't want to let him down, of course, but I'll find out how soon he can fill my place."

"Good!" nodded Malcolm. "I'd like you to start as soon as possible."

"Meanwhile I can read up about it, can't I?" said Dan eagerly. "I shall have plenty of time in the evening when I've finished work. That would help, wouldn't it? I mean I shouldn't be so absolutely ignorant if I had read some books on the subject."

Malcolm promised to look out some books. "But don't worry," he said. "You'll soon learn . . ."

They were silent after that; silent, not because their minds were empty, nor because they could find nothing to say, but because their minds were busy with thoughts, peaceful and friendly. Dinah was thinking of the queer way things had worked out and of how they might easily have worked out differently. For instance if she and Dan had not conceived a childish hero-worship for Malcolm Armstrong (and followed him round the golf course to see him win his match) Malcolm would not have remembered the Dees . . . He would not have spoken to Dan yesterday at the swimming-pool and asked them to supper. This job which obviously, was the chance of a lifetime for Dan, was the direct outcome of that childish adventure.

Dinah chuckled involuntarily. "And we got punished for being late for dinner!" she exclaimed.

"I know! I was thinking of that," said Dan with a grin.

Their companion looked at them in bewilderment. "What on earth are you two talking about?" he inquired.

It was natural that the Dees should discuss the evening's entertainment as they walked home together in the dark. Dan was still full of excitement about his prospective job and was anxious to tell Dinah all about it. He explained that he was to help Malcolm, to understudy him as it were, so that eventually he would be able to lighten Malcolm's burden . . . possibly run the business for a few weeks if Malcolm were away; or, alternatively, be sent as a plenipotentiary to America. Dinah exclaimed and commented suitably and said all the right things; she was overjoyed at Dan's improved prospects. They spoke of their hostess and her niece and agreed that they had never met such disagreeable people . . . and wondered how on earth Malcolm could stand it and continue to live with them. Dinah inquired why Dan had been so unhelpful in the drawing-room before their host appeared and learnt that it was because Dan had expected his host to appear in evening-dress.

"*They* were in evening kit," explained Dan; "so of course I thought he was sure to be—and there was I in a flannel suit and a coloured tie!"

"Would it have mattered so frightfully?" Dinah inquired.

"Of course it would have mattered, you ass!" said Dan, affectionately.

Dinah was silent. She had been slightly put out at the discovery that she was inappropriately attired, but her social sense had triumphed; it seemed odd that Dan should have taken the matter so much more seriously.

"But you aren't *interested* in clothes!" said Dinah at last. "You wear the most awful rags; the tweed jacket you were wearing this morning is only fit for a scarecrow."

"That's quite different," said Dan firmly.

16

DAN left early on Monday morning and Dinah, having supervised the children's breakfast, shepherded them to the beach. The tide was not so far out this morning so she was able to sit with Margy and keep an eye on the older ones who were paddling and sailing boats. Mr. Monk appeared at eleven o'clock with his paper and a chocolate biscuit for Margy. She ate it with her milk. For some reason best known to herself she refused to say "Bung-ho" to Mr. Monk, but remained absolutely dumb in spite of every blandishment.

"Don't bother her," said Mr. Monk, smiling and sitting down. "That's the joy of small children—they're completely natural. When they grow' older they discover the necessity to conform to convention and to hide their feelings behind a mask. Why should Margy say 'Bung-ho' if she doesn't feel like it?"

"She might at least say thank you for the chocolate biscuit," objected Dinah, looking at her younger daughter in disgust. "But she won't, and I can't make her."

Mr. Monk chuckled.

"And another thing," continued Dinah. "Another thing I must apologise for—a far worse thing—is Nigel's behaviour on Friday. I haven't seen you since. It was *very* naughty of Nigel to ask you for a shilling. It was dreadful, really! I'm terribly ashamed."

"He didn't ask me!" exclaimed Mr. Monk. "He just . . . and anyhow it was my fault. I shouldn't have given it to one child and not the other."

"Why not?" asked Dinah. "The children must learn to be sensible. I'm trying to teach them. No, honestly, I want you to understand. It was Mark's shilling—you gave it to him—but Nigel was silly about it. They *must* learn."

"I see what you mean," he replied. "I wish we had been as wise with our son. We spoilt him, I'm afraid. But I must repeat that Nigel didn't ask me for a shilling."

"He knew he needn't," said Dinah, with a half-smile.

"Well—perhaps. It was quite a good-sized fish."

Dinah laughed. "You aren't sticking to the point."

"I know. It's one of my weaknesses," said Mr. Monk, regretfully.

This little exchange had taken them a good deal further forward in their acquaintance, so when Mrs. Monk appeared and her husband jumped up to help her down the bank it seemed natural for her to join the party. She was a little, frail old lady, with snow-white hair and very light blue eyes.

"This is a friend of mine, my dear," said Mr. Monk, as he settled her comfortably on the rug. "She is the mother of those delightful children."

"You're staying at Craigie Lodge," declared Mrs. Monk, smiling very sweetly at Dinah. "I've watched you going in and out. You see, I can't go about much so I'm allowed to be inquisitive about my neighbours; it's one of the advantages of getting old. Nobody minds old people being inquisitive . . . And of course Patrick knows Lieutenant-Commander Bell. Patrick is our nephew. They met at Singapore or somewhere—"

"Colombo, my dear," put in her husband.

"Colombo," agreed Mrs. Monk. "They met there in the war. Patrick would like a game of golf with Lieutenant-Commander Bell, so perhaps—"

"They played together on Saturday," Mr. Monk reminded her.

"But they could play again, couldn't they?" said Mrs. Monk.

"Of course," agreed Dinah. "Dan would like to—perhaps next week-end. He's got a job at Leith, so he only comes down for the week-ends."

"He's left the Navy?"

"Yes; so you needn't call him Lieutenant-Commander Bell. Plain Mister will do."

"It's certainly easier," said Mrs. Monk, smiling. "I'm sure you must be glad he's left the Navy. I wish Patrick would, but he says he hasn't got the brains for anything else. It must be lovely to have Mr. Bell at home for good. I suppose you will be looking for a house in Edinburgh."

"Yes, we are," said Dinah. "It won't be very easy to find one, but—"

"Patrick said you would allow the children to come to tea," said Mrs. Monk, interrupting suddenly. "He *did* say so, didn't he, Jack?"

"Yes," said Mr. Monk, nodding.

"If you really want them," said their mother doubtfully.

"Of course we want them!" cried Mr. and Mrs. Monk with one voice.

"Wednesday," suggested Mr. Monk. "How would that do?"

Dinah said it would do admirably.

The day had passed quickly and pleasantly. It was not until the children had gone to bed and Dinah was sitting down to her solitary supper that she began to feel lonely . . . and how silly it was, thought Dinah. She had done without Dan for years, but now, because she had had him with her for a long week-end, she was missing him quite horribly. I shall move, she decided as she helped herself to the succulent dish of macaroni and cheese which Nannie had provided for her. I shall move to Edinburgh—that's settled. Dan and I have nobody in the world except each other, so it's ridiculous to live hundreds of miles apart. Having made this decision she decided that she must write to Irene Barnard and to the House Agent at Nettleham—and perhaps a few lines to Dan just to tell him it was definitely fixed.

After supper she put on her coat and went out. She had been out all day, but still she had not had enough Seatown air. There was no air like it, Dinah thought, no air so fresh and tonic and energising. The sea was right in, almost up to the wall. It was ruffled by the evening breeze and the little wavelets glittered and sparkled in the rays of the sun. They made a gentle splashing sound as they curled over and fell upon the beach, a peaceful sound, monotonous and soothing.

She was leaning on the wall, watching it and enjoying it, when a big car drove up behind her and Malcolm Armstrong got out.

"Hallo!" exclaimed Dinah in surprise.

"Sorry to bother you," he said, smiling at her. "It's a note for Dan, that's all. He forgot to give me his address at Leith." Dinah took the note. She was slightly uneasy; had Malcolm thought better of his offer to give Dan the post?

"It's nothing important," Malcolm assured her. "Just to ask him to look in at the office and see me. I want to give him some papers to read."

"Of course. I'll send it, shall I?" said Dinah, nodding. "I was going to write to him, anyway. Dan and I are going to set up house together in Edinburgh, you know."

"An excellent plan! The Dees should live together."

"That's what the Dees think."

Malcolm leant on the wall beside her; he seemed in no hurry to go. "It's lovely here," he said. "So peaceful and restful after the hustle and bustle of business. I get awfully tired."

"I expect you have a great deal to do."

"It isn't that so much. It's my leg that bothers me. I was wounded rather badly and it still goes on growling," he explained. "But don't let's talk about it."

"Why not?" asked Dinah. "Don't you like talking about it?"

"People don't like listening," replied Malcolm, with a little smile.

"That's nonsense," she said quickly. "Of course people want to know. Tell me about it, Malcolm."

"There isn't much to tell. I've got a little shell splinter in my ankle. They've taken out several other splinters, but apparently this particular splinter is in a difficult place. Sometimes it settles down and doesn't bother me much, and then, for no reason at all, it starts up and gives me hell. They've tried all sorts of treatment, but nothing short of getting the thing out is going to be any good—I'm sure of that." He hesitated, and then added: "It may end in losing my foot, of course."

"Oh, Malcolm!"

"It's all right," declared Malcolm. "I mean, lots of people are much worse off. Look at that fishing-boat in the bay. Isn't it a pretty sight?"

The boat was going out for a night's fishing; it was gliding along with a peaceful but purposeful motion, the gentle breeze from the west filling its widespread sails.

"It's Ben Johnstone's boat," continued Malcolm. "He's a friend of mine—a splendid old chap—I often go out with him. Would you like to come some evening, Dinah? I don't mean all night of course—just for a sail?"

The idea was attractive. Odd, of course, but . . . "I don't see why I shouldn't," said Dinah, thinking aloud.

"No reason at all!" agreed her companion. "In fact, every reason why you should. What about to-morrow night?"

"To-morrow night!" echoed Dinah, somewhat startled. It was one thing to decide that there was no reason why she should not go and another to be pinned down to a definite date in the near future.

"To-morrow," said Malcolm, firmly. "Better to take advantage of the good weather while it lasts. I'll leave a message for Ben at the harbour." He pressed her hand and got into the car. "Eight o'clock to-morrow," he said. "That's all right, isn't it, Dinah?"

"Where?" asked Dinah. "I mean—"

"At the harbour. I'll meet you there," replied Malcolm, and drove off quickly, almost as if he were afraid she might change her mind.

Dinah was afraid Nannie might disapprove, might think it an odd thing to do (she thought it odd herself), but Nannie was not in the least put about at the idea.

"They're nice people," said Nannie. "They're real old Seatown gentry. And of course Dan's going to help him run his business, so naturally he's grateful for that. You'll need to take a warm coat and a scarf for round your head. It's parky on the water, especially at night, and I don't want you getting a chill."

Thus reassured, Dinah went upstairs and wrote her letters and, having sealed them and posted them in the pillarbox (which very conveniently was built into the wall just opposite the gate), she betook herself to bed.

17

DINAH awoke early to find a soft, warm creature snuggling into her back.

"It's me," said Mark's slightly gruff voice. "Nothing's the matter—I mean I haven't been sick or anything—but I just hadn't seen you for such a long, long time."

"You hadn't seen me!" exclaimed his mother in surprise.

"Not properly," Mark explained. "Not just you and me talking."

Dinah took his point. She took it all the more easily because she often felt the same about her children and regretted it, but there was no way to remedy the matter as far as she could see. Living next door to Irene Barnard, who had an only child, she had noticed that Irene was friends with her daughter, that they talked to one another constantly—almost as equals—sharing the same amusements and taking a keen interest in one another's affairs. It was impossible for Dinah to do this with four children. Naturally the children played together, which was good for them and pleasant for them (and incidentally saved her a lot of trouble) but it divided her from them by an impassable barrier. Even if this barrier had not existed, Dinah would not have had time to be friends with each of them separately.

"You see what I mean," urged Mark.

"Yes, of course," said Dinah. "Let's talk now, shall we?"

They talked. It was very pleasant indeed. They talked about what they would do when they went to Edinburgh. Mark was a little anxious as to whether he would be able to have his rabbits there and Dinah did not raise false hopes. If they could get a house with a garden it might be possible but they would have to wait and see.

"It doesn't matter," Mark assured her. "I mean if we can't, we can't. I just wanted to know. I like animals, you . . . see."

Having settled this, as much as it could be settled, Mark went on to talk of another matter near his heart.

"You know Bob, the dustman?" he inquired.

"Bob? No, I'm afraid not."

"Well, he knows you. He came round yesterday with his cart and let me pat his horse—it's an awfully nice horse called Mac. He said he used to know you when you were a little girl. Then he said he supposed I was going to be a doctor like Doctor Bell."

"You're going to be a sailor, aren't you?"

"I think I'd rather be a doctor. Could I be a doctor? It's more use, isn't it? I mean, of course sailors are useful too, but—well, I think I'd *like* to be a doctor."

This was quite a new idea to Dinah, but she welcomed it warmly. If Mark really wanted to be a doctor there was no reason why he should not be. Now that she thought of it, she realised that there was a great deal of her father in Mark; why hadn't she seen it before?

"Mark," she said, solemnly; "it's very hard work to be a doctor and it costs a lot of money; but if you do your part and work very hard I'll do my part and find the money somehow. Your grandfather was a splendid man and a very good doctor. I would rather you were like him than anybody I can think of. If you're as good a doctor as he was I shall be very proud."

"I would try," said Mark, gravely. "As a matter of fact, Bob said that too—that I was like my grandfather."

*

Tuesday morning was Nannie's shopping-time. She suggested that the children might like to go with her and see the shops and, this suggestion being well received, she set off early with her escort. Dinah watched them with an amused smile as they walked down the road; Nannie was not very much taller than the children, her small, plump figure wore a purposeful air, and she waddled rather than walked; the children hopped and skipped round her, talking eagerly about what they intended to buy with the money their mother had given them. Mark was carrying the enormous basket which always accompanied Nannie on her expeditions to the town.

When they had vanished from sight Dinah fetched Margy and they settled down for a quiet morning on the shore. It was astonishing how Margy had "come on" in less than a week. She was beginning to walk and her figure was improving with the exercise; she was talking better, too. Dinah had decided that Margy's backwardness was due to a slight laziness and lack of ambition (to the fact that she was contented with her lot and felt no need to make any effort) so Dinah was beginning to stir her up a little and teach her some nursery rhymes. They were struggling with "Margy had a little lamb" when old Mrs. Monk appeared and, making her way laboriously over the soft sand, sat down beside them.

"Don't mind me, my dear," said Mrs. Monk. "Just go on with what you're doing. 'Margy had a little lamb,'" said old Mrs. Monk, smiling at the pupil. "How delightful! Margy *is* a little lamb, isn't she?"

"Sometimes," said her mother, abandoning all idea of Margy's lesson a trifle reluctantly.

"Don't mind me—please," repealed the old lady. "I'll just sit here quietly and listen. It's just that I'm feeling a little lonely without Jack. He's gone to Edinburgh to-day . . . a little trouble with his plate," said Mrs. Monk, confidentially. "You have such beautiful teeth, my dear, so of course you don't know what it means to have a plate and I hope you never will. The top one is not so bad but the bottom one is a great nuisance to Jack and won't lie down, which seems funny when you think of it. Jack says the law of gravity doesn't work properly with him. He went by the early train and he said he would be back to lunch so he may be here any minute now. I miss Jack terribly when he isn't here; you see we've been married for thirty-five years and have never been separated. We weren't very young when we were married. Jack likes me to get out. It will please him to see me sitting in the sun. You don't mind, do you, Mrs. Anderson?"

"Not Mrs. Anderson," said Dinah, smiling.

"Oh dear—of course not!" said Mrs. Monk, with a worried look. "How silly I am! Mrs. Anderson is that nice fat woman you're staying with. I'm so silly about people's names, especially when Jack isn't here to keep me right."

"He's very kind, isn't he?" said Dinah, who felt annoyed with herself for having drawn attention to the old lady's mistake.

"Oh, *so* kind!" exclaimed Mrs. Monk, smiling proudly. "You can't think how kind he is! I know I'm a bother but he never gets impatient with me, *never*. He *does* get impatient with other people sometimes, you know. Jack has quite a fiery temper . . . Oh, yes; you might not think it but he has *quite* a fiery temper. It's all over very quickly, of course."

"As long as people don't sulk—" began Dinah.

"Yes, but still—still it can do a great deal of damage," said the old lady with a thoughtful air.

Dinah couldn't help smiling. She had a sudden vision of dear little Mr. Monk going berserk and throwing the china about . . . but of course Mrs. Monk hadn't meant that, at all. What had she meant, Dinah wondered.

"Have you met Mr. Barrington?" inquired Mrs. Monk. "Mr. Barrington is a professor, you know. He and his little boy are staying at Miss Brown's—they have the ground floor, of course. Jack talks to him sometimes but he's really too clever for Jack. He doesn't believe in God," added Mrs. Monk, confidentially.

Dinah was about to make a suitable rejoinder, but there was no time.

"So odd," continued Mrs. Monk. "Of course I'm not clever—especially now, when I get muddled—but if you don't believe in God what's left to believe in? Who made the sea, for instance? Who made the trees and the flowers? And, talking of flowers, are you going to the Flower Show?"

It was such a jump, from atheists to Flower Shows, that Dinah was slightly bewildered. She said she didn't think she *was* going.

"Oh, you *should*, Mrs. Bell," declared Mrs. Monk, earnestly. "Really, you should. It was always such a *very* good Show in the old days. Sweet peas do well here—and roses. The best sweet peas I ever saw were in the garden at a place called Abbot's End."

"The Armstrongs!" exclaimed Dinah in surprise.

"Yes; Sir Andrew was a delightful man. Jack knew him quite well, and liked him immensely; and of course Lady Armstrong was charming. She was small and dainty like a piece of Dresden china, and always beautifully dressed. They used to have a garden-party every year—such a beautiful garden it was."

"But Lady Armstrong is tall—" began Dinah.

"Oh, not *this* Lady Armstrong, dear. She's a *very* large woman; rather coarse, isn't she? I'm talking about David's mother, you know. His name *is* David, isn't it?"

"Malcolm," suggested Dinah.

"Of course! Well, it was Malcolm's mother. She died about four years ago—no, long before that, it must have been, because it was before the war started. Oh dear, I do get so *muddled*," declared poor Mrs. Monk. "I never used to get muddled when I was young—before my illness, I mean. Did I ever tell you about my illness, dear?"

Dinah was unkind enough to head her off this fascinating subject, not because she would have minded listening to Mrs. Monk's recital of her misfortunes but because she was anxious to hear more about Lady Armstrong. "The first Lady Armstrong—" began Dinah.

"Was Malcolm's mother," interrupted Mrs. Monk. "She was a beautiful creature, quite small and fairy-like (Malcolm is very like her, not exactly fairy-like but small and well-made). She was very sociable and friendly, and her parties were always delightful. Edith Grover is quite different in every way."

"You mean Lady Armstrong's niece," suggested Dinah.

"No dear; I'm still talking about the second Lady Armstrong— Edith Grover that *was*. Edith Grover is her niece, her brother's child. I knew them very well when I was young. Edith's mother went to school with me."

Dinah was beginning to get a little muddled herself. She decided it must have been the first Edith's mother who went to school with Mrs. Monk.

"So then—" continued the old lady, leaving a gaping void in her story. "So then, when Lady Armstrong died (it really was dreadfully sad because she and Sir Andrew were very happy and suited one another beautifully) Malcolm had to go to Australia on business and while he was away Edith got hold of Sir Andrew and married him. Some men just *have* to have wives, and Sir Andrew was one of them; he was so kind and considerate, you know. I mean it had to have an outlet, hadn't it? But I *was* sorry for Malcolm. It's all very well for men to marry again, but when the second wife is a good deal younger it isn't fair on his family because of course sooner or later *he* dies and his second wife is a nuisance."

"Not always," began Dinah. "I mean I know several cases—"

"If they're like Edith they are," said Mrs. Monk, firmly. "Poor Malcolm would be *much* happier without Edith. I could tell you things about Edith that would make you open your eyes; discontented and underhand, we thought her. Of course, I don't know anything about the niece. Is she a pleasant person?"

"Well—" began Dinah in a doubtful tone.

"I *thought* as much," declared Mrs. Monk. "They're all tarred with the same brush. How dreadful for Malcolm to have two Ediths on his hands! I wonder he doesn't get rid of them. We never see Malcolm nowadays because of course he's very busy and you couldn't expect him to be interested in old people like Jack and me. We used to see him sometimes when he was a little boy—such a dear little boy he was! I never see Edith, either. And I think," added Mrs. Monk, wrinkling her brows, "I rather think there was a little tiff between Edith and me. I can't remember much about it."

"If you mean Edith Armstrong," said Mr. Monk, who had approached noiselessly in the soft sand, "there was a severe disagreement. You told her she had caught Sir Andrew and she objected to the term."

"I was sure you would remember," declared Mrs. Monk, with a satisfied air. "I remember now, myself—*perfectly*. What I said was true, so Edith was very foolish to take exception to it."

"It was because it was true she minded," said Mr. Monk, chuckling.

"So *that* was the reason," said Mrs. Monk, nodding to Dinah. "That was the reason why she stopped inviting us to Abbot's End."

Dinah could not feel they missed much. Her own experience of hospitality at Abbot's End had been exceedingly unpleasant.

"What a delightful gossip we've had!" said Mrs. Monk, as she struggled to her feet and took her husband's arm.

Gossip was the word, thought Dinah, smiling.

18

THE shoppers had a successful morning and returned laden with spoils. Dinah heard full details of the expedition at lunch; everybody had been kind and friendly; everybody had remembered their grandfather and spoken of him with affection.

"They *do* talk a funny language!" Nigel declared.

"Nannie can talk the language," said Polly. "Nannie talks our sort of language and Seatown-language, too."

They discussed Seatown-language, and decided that they must learn it without delay.

It was a friendly language to Dinah of course. She enjoyed hearing it spoken—as one who has been long in exile thrills to the sound of her mother-tongue—and she had discovered that when she was in the bathroom (washing the children's socks and pullovers) she could hear Nannie chattering with people who called or brought messages to the back door. There was the man who brought round vegetables, for instance, and sold them from a cart. Dinah had thoroughly enjoyed his little chat with Nannie.

"Chairley Broon!" Nannie had exclaimed. "D'ye mean tae tell me ye're askin' yon money for a quarter stone o' sproots! It's sproots I'm needin'—no pairls."

"It's awfu', Mistress Anderson, but it's no' me, ye ken. It's the price o' everything that's gone up. I'm no' makin' muckle oot o' it— that's the truth."

"Och, I ken fine ye're daeing it for fun. It's a fine life stravaigling roond the toon wi' a cairt—better nor the mines!"

"I'd no' hae tae worry masel' wi' a wheen o' chattering weemen in the mines—that's ae thing. They'll keep me stannin' for ten meenits an' no' buy a haeporth's worth at the end o' it."

"I'll tak' a haeporth o' sproots, Chairley," said Nannie, dryly. "Ye'll need tae cut yin in hauf, I'm thinking."

Dinah had chuckled. It was all the more amusing because the protagonists were staunch friends. They were like fencers—or, perhaps, more like boxers, who, once their bout is over, are more friendly disposed to one another than before. Shrewd blows are given and taken and each respects the other for his prowess.

No sooner had Chairley gone than the joiner, another friend of Nannie's, had presented himself at the back door.

"My land!" Nannie had exclaimed in well-simulated amazement. "Sakes alive, if it's no' Wullie Ferguson! Ye've no come tae sort the bathroom snib?"

"Ye were speirin' for me—"

"Aye, I was speirin' for ye sax weeks syne, but I wisna' expeckin' ye for anither sax months. Is there nae ither body in Seatown needin' ye, Wullie? . . . Mphm, ye're sure o'that? I wouldna' like tae tak' ye frae some ither job, ye ken."

Unfortunately Dinah had finished her washing by this time so she was obliged to desert her post of vantage, but she was still smiling when she went down with the wet garments and hung them out on the line, for somehow or other this brand of dry, pawky humour was exactly the kind of humour she appreciated. It tickled her deliciously under the ribs.

The afternoon was hot and sultry, there was thunder in the air and Dinah suggested that they should sit in the garden instead of going on the sands.

"Tell us a story," said Polly eagerly. "Another story about the Dees—or tell us again about the day they went to the Black Rocks and got stranded."

"I'll tell you a different kind of story," said Dinah.

"What about?" asked Mark.

"About Tantallon Castle. It's a fine old castle on the cliffs not very far from here. I've told you about the Dees going over there and having picnics and exploring the ruins but this story is about the castle as it was long ago when it was in its pride, when the Great Earl of Douglas lived there with all his family and his servants and his soldiers. It isn't my story," explained Dinah; "it's really part of a long poem called *Marmion* written by a very famous and wonderful man, but the poem would be too difficult for you, I'm afraid."

"Could Flo come?" asked Polly. "Flo knows the castle and she'd be awfully interested to hear about it."

"Yes, if she wants to," Dinah agreed.

They went into the back garden and spread rugs in the shade. Dinah drew up her knees and put her arms round them; she looked thoughtful for she was beginning to wonder whether she had undertaken a task beyond her powers. Marmion was an old favourite; she and Dan had learnt long pieces of it and used to walk along the sands declaiming it in dramatic fashion to the sea-birds. Sometimes they had acted it together, dressing up and playing different scenes. They had liked it all except the last canto which describes the battle of Flodden; it was really the best, of course, and tremendously exciting, but being staunch Scots the Dees had hated to think of the defeat of Scottish arms. Dinah knew the story well; it was like a little series of jewelled pictures in her memory, but it was so rich and varied and so brilliant in colouring that she doubted her ability to render it into simple prose.

"Go on, Mummy," said Nigel eagerly. "How does the story begin?"

"Long ago," said Dinah, "in the days when England and Scotland used to fight against one another, there was a proud English Baron called Marmion. He was very brave and strong and a fine soldier, but he was cruel and wicked and liked to have his own way in everything. Marmion wanted to marry a young girl called Clare; she was good and beautiful and also very rich; it was more for her rich lands than for herself that Marmion wanted to marry her. Clare had no wish to marry Marmion. She had been in love with a fine young man, whose name was Ralph de Wilton, and although he had been killed in a fight she still loved him and was faithful to his memory.

"It happened that Clare was in Edinburgh, staying with the Abbess of Whitby, who was her friend. They wanted to travel south, so it was arranged that they should go to a convent near North Berwick and there take ship to Whitby, but it was so dangerous to travel about the country in those days that they could not go without an escort.

"James the Fourth was King of Scotland. He held his court in Edinburgh, and Lord Marmion had been sent to Edinburgh by the King of England with important letters. As the two countries were at war King James did not want Marmion roving about at large for he was afraid Marmion might play the part of a spy, so he asked the

Earl of Douglas to take Marmion with him to his castle at Tantallon and see him safely over the border. In addition to this King James arranged that the Abbess and Clare should travel with them as far as North Berwick, for they would be safe with Marmion's soldiers as an escort.

"The Abbess and Clare were somewhat alarmed when they heard they were to ride with Marmion for they knew what a traitorous, cruel man he was, but the King's command had to be obeyed so they had no choice in the matter.

"One fine morning they all set off. Marmion rode in front wearing his polished steel armour which flashed like silver in the sunshine; his helmet was embossed with his crest, a golden falcon, and his horse had trappings of blue velvet and gold. Beside him rode the Earl of Douglas, a magnificent old man, and with them was a palmer, or travelling priest, who had joined Marmion's band and come to Scotland with them to act as guide. The palmer wore a long black habit with a red device upon his shoulders and a hood pulled over his face. These three rode in front with the Earl's men-at-arms; behind came Clare and the Abbess and Marmion's soldiers.

"The road which they followed was little more than a track, winding hither and thither up hill and down dale through beautiful wooded country. Clare and the Abbess were glad that Marmion had left them to themselves and had not attempted to speak to them. Soon they would reach the convent and all would be well. But Marmion had arranged otherwise, and when they got to the convent and were about to dismount, one of the soldiers rode forward and said he had orders to bring Clare to Tantallon Castle.

"Poor Clare was very much distressed when she heard this for she hated Marmion and distrusted him. The Abbess did all she could to persuade the soldiers to leave Clare with her, but the soldiers were far too frightened of their master to disobey his orders, so Clare was forced to say good-bye to her good old friend and ride on to Tantallon.

"They had not gone far when they mounted a little rise in the ground, and suddenly in front of them they saw the castle. What an enormous place it was! How massive and imposing, with its high walls and its three great towers outlined against the sky! It had been built on the very edge of the cliff, its foundations welded into the solid rock, and there was a double moat in front of it stretching from side to side of the promontory. The double moat was spanned by two narrow bridges, guarded by bastions or foreworks of enormous strength, for it was only on this side of the castle that the Earl of Douglas need fear an enemy's attack and it was here that he had built all his strong fortifications.

"Clare and her escort rode over the drawbridge, beneath the great portcullis with its iron spikes, through heavy doors studded with iron nails and so into the castle. They found themselves in a wide courtyard with a well in the middle and all round were fine rooms and halls and stately chambers hung with tapestry. The Douglas was so rich and powerful that his castle was more like a small town than a dwelling-place; it was full of all sorts of people. There were the Douglas family and their guests and there were soldiers and armourers and men who worked in leather or sewed clothes or made bows and arrows, and there were other men who looked after the horses—grooms and smiths and huntsmen—and there were servants who cooked the food and waited at table and attended to the fires.

"The Douglases were very kind to Clare, but in spite of their kindness she was unhappy for she had nobody to talk to. Everybody in the castle felt anxious and unsettled because news had come that an English army under the command of the Earl of Surrey was marching through Northumberland and intended to invade Scotland.

"Marmion was anxious, too. He was an Englishman, so he felt he ought to be with the English army instead of sheltering beneath the roof of a Scottish Earl. He had seen the Scottish army camped near Edinburgh; he had seen how large and powerful it was. There were men from all parts of Scotland; men-at-arms in mail armour riding huge horses and carrying battle-axes; spearmen and pikemen, sturdy and strong, and every Highland Chief had brought clansmen from the Scottish hills—wild, fierce men with red beards who carried broadswords and shields of steel and deerskin. Marmion did not think this army would win the day for he had faith in the power of the English archers who were famed all over the world, but he knew it would be a mighty battle and he wanted to be there. Another thing that disturbed Marmion and made him anxious was the fact that the Earl, who had been very friendly with him, had become cold and haughty and unapproachable. Marmion did not like this changed attitude, he could not account for it, and it seemed to him that the sooner he left the castle the better it would be.

"Messengers came galloping into the castle with news about the English army, clattering over the drawbridge and into the court-yard at all hours of the day and night. Some of them brought good news, saying that the English army had been defeated, while others, coming a few hours later, declared that it was still advancing and that a battle was going to be fought. The soldiers were busy mending their armour and the servants were busy preparing the castle for a siege.

"Clare grew more unhappy every day. She was very lonely and she was still frightened of Marmion for she knew she was in his power. Sometimes she went up a narrow stair which led to the battlements of the castle. There were towers and turrets on the battlements and narrow windows from which the soldiers could shoot arrows when the castle was attacked; there were little flights of steps and dark corners and platforms with embrasures which gave wide views of sea and land. On the landward side there were soldiers on guard, but there was no need for sentries on the seaward side. The cliffs were so high and steep that no enemy could approach, so this side of the battlements was deserted and it was here that Clare liked to walk. She walked up and down, gazing out through the narrow windows over the grey waters of the sea and thinking sadly of Ralph de Wilton. She listened to the waves beating on the rocks and to the wild pier-cing cries of the sea-birds.

"One evening when Clare was walking there she saw some armour lying on the stones. It was the armour of a knight. She stood and looked at it, wondering who had put it there, and then she raised her eyes and saw a man standing beside it, a tall slim figure in the gloom . . . it was Ralph de Wilton.

"Clare could not believe her eyes. She had thought he was dead; she had thought she would never see him again. She was so surprised and so overjoyed that she could scarcely speak. De Wilton was surprised, too, for he did not know Clare was here in the castle; he had thought her hundreds of miles away, but here she was, standing before him as beautiful as ever—more beautiful than ever, or so he thought. Her golden curls seemed to glow and shine in the dim light which filtered in through the narrow window-slits and her sweet face was bright with gladness at the sight of her beloved Ralph. She was wearing a rich gown ornamented with gold embroidery, which fell in graceful folds to her feet, and round her neck was a golden chain upon which hung a golden cross with a ruby stone.

"When their first surprise and gladness was over they began to talk and to tell one another all that had happened since they had last met. Ralph de Wilton told Clare that he had been very badly wounded in the fight and left lying on the field, but a faithful old servant had rescued him and had taken him home and looked after him and nursed him back to health. When he recovered de Wilton had disguised himself as a palmer and, joining Marmion's band, had come to Scotland with him. He had done this not because he liked Marmion, but because he knew what a wicked man Marmion was and wanted to find out more about him. He had found out a good deal and had told the Earl of Douglas how cruel and traitorous Marmion was, and this was the reason that the Earl had become less friendly towards his guest. Having listened to the story of de Wilton's adventures and being very much impressed with his courage and his noble air, the Earl had offered to make him a knight and de Wilton had accepted gladly for he wanted to fight in the battle which was about to take place. All this de Wilton told Clare as they walked up and down the deserted battlements together, and he told her that this was the reason he had laid out his armour on the floor—for the ceremony was to take place in the castle chapel at midnight and the Earl had promised to be there.

"Poor Clare did not know whether to be glad or sorry. She was glad that Ralph had won the Earl's favour and was to be made a knight, but she was distressed at the news that he must leave her again. She loved him so dearly that all she wanted was to be his wife and live with him in a humble cottage—that would have been happiness to her—but she knew it was his duty to fight and she must be brave and not try to keep him from going.

"At midnight Clare and Ralph de Wilton went down the winding stair together and across the courtyard to the chapel. It was a beautiful building with finely carved stone pillars and rich moulding. The moonlight streamed in through the arched windows, it gleamed upon Ralph's silver armour and made pools of light upon the floor. Two priests were there, holding blazing torches, and at the altar stood the bishop with the great Earl of Douglas by his side. The Earl was old and grim; his hair was white as snow but his eyebrows were dark and his eyes were proud and melancholy. He was tall and gaunt with broad shoulders and long arms. When he was younger he had been one of the strongest men in the land; his sword was so big and so heavy that nobody but he could use it, but in his hand it was deadly to his enemies and many had fallen before its fierce attack.

"Ralph hesitated for a moment and then he went forward and knelt at the altar and Clare bound his spurs on his heels and fastened on his sword. It was the custom in those days that a knight's chosen lady should prepare him for war and Clare was proud to do Ralph this service. Then the old Earl spoke to Ralph and wished him good fortune, and raising his famous sword struck him on the shoulder and dubbed him Knight.

"Next morning very early Sir Ralph de Wilton set off to join the Scottish army, and later the same day Marmion mustered his men in the courtyard and told them to saddle their horses. Marmion had made up his mind that he could wait no longer but must join the Earl of Surrey without delay. He told his men to ride on and take Clare with them while he, himself, waited in the courtyard to say good-bye to his host.

"When the Earl came down to the courtyard Marmion held out his hand and thanked him for his hospitality, but by this time the Earl knew some of the wicked things that Marmion had done, and wrapping himself in his cloak and looking at Marmion with scorn he declared that he would never take his hand in friendship. Marmion's eyes flashed with anger—he was a proud man and the insult was more than he could bear—and he replied with such fierce cruel words that the Earl was enraged and called to his soldiers to draw up the bridge and let down the portcullis and to hold Lord Marmion prisoner; but it was too late—Lord Marmion heard the order, he turned and spurred his horse so that it gave a great leap and galloped out of the castle doors . . . and the portcullis fell behind him with a crash and shaved off the plume which floated from his helmet. Away he went, galloping over the moor and shouting defiance at the Douglas and all his clan."

Dinah paused. It was very quiet in the little garden.

"Go on, Mummy," said Mark. "That isn't the end, is it?"

"Tell us about the battle," urged Nigel.

Dinah did not want to tell them about the battle. She said slowly, "You can read about it when you're older. It was a terrible battle. Flodden Field was a black day for Scotland—one of the blackest days in all her history—everything went wrong. The Scottish king was killed and hundreds of his knights—the best and bravest in the land. Marmion was killed—"

"But not Ralph!" exclaimed Polly in anxious tones.

"No, not Ralph. He was one of the few who survived. He fought bravely until the Scottish king was dead and all hope of victory had gone, and then he swam across the Tweed and got back to Scotland and made his way to Tantallon Castle to bring the news to the Earl. Later, when things had settled down, he was able to find Clare and they were married."

"And lived happily ever after," nodded Polly.

"It's a lovely story," said Flo, with a sigh. "I'd like to read it, Mrs. Savage."

"Why not?" said Dinah, smiling at her.

19

THE thunder clouds had passed and the sun was shining brilliantly when Dinah walked along to the harbour. She had had some trouble in escaping from Nannie without the comforts which Nannie considered essential for a sea voyage. Nannie had wanted her to take a thermos flask full of coffee and a packet of sandwiches, a cushion to sit on and a warm rug to wrap round her knees. Nannie had offered Mrs. Turtle's Flo as a beast of burden to carry everything down to the harbour. Dinah had refused the offer. She refused the offer of seasickness tablets and Wellington boots and a pair of Nannie's woollen knickers, but agreed to take her mackintosh and a warm scarf to tie round her head. Much as she loved Nannie she could not consent to set out for an evening sail looking as if she expected to be wrecked upon a desert island.

Seatown harbour had changed very little since Dinah was a child. The tall red-stone houses where the fishermen lived were still standing, facing west over the bay—and what a beautiful colour they were in the evening sunshine! Flights of stone steps, worn into hollows by the passage of feet, led up to the open doors. There were still fisher-men in dark-blue jerseys, lounging in the doorways, and women and girls sitting on the steps, mending nets and chattering to one another as they worked. There were still lobster-pots, bleached by salt, piled up into heaps, waiting to be baited and slung into the boats; and a horde of small children were running about playing together—different children, of course, but to Dinah's eyes the same.

The harbour itself was enclosed by breakwaters which had been built to last by people who knew the power of the winter gales; they consisted of huge blocks of stone—red and white and mauve and brown—fitted together like a jigsaw puzzle and weathered into a harmonious whole. These walls sloped inwards from the base and were so thick that one could have driven a coach and four along the top of them. To-night the harbour was full of boats; fishing-boats, rowing-boats, yachts and dinghies lay peacefully within the sheltering walls. The light of the sun, which was beginning to decline towards the west, made a bright shimmer upon the clear water.

Dinah stood upon the quay and looked down. There was Malcolm! He was already seated in a big, solid-looking fishing-boat. He was waving to her. She waved back and walked along to the stone steps near which the boat was lying. The two fishermen who had been sitting in the boat with Malcolm sprang up as she approached. One of them was tall and strong and old with features which looked as if they had been carved out of mahogany; the other was younger and less spectacular in appearance.

"Mind, noo!" said the older man—obviously Ben Johnstone—as he took her hand to help her down the steps. "Jist tak' it easy. They steps is slipp'ry. That's fine. Will ye sit there in the bows wi' Mister Mawlcolm?"

They pushed off, easing the boat along with their hands against the wall. Then the huge oars came out and the boat floated between the great red pillars that guarded the harbour entrance. The sea caught the boat and she lifted to the swell.

"She's alive!" exclaimed Dinah, smiling at Malcolm as she spoke.

He nodded. "It's a grand feeling, isn't it? But wait till the sails go up. Ben has no engine; that's one of the reasons I like to come with him."

"We're auld-fashioned," said Ben. "The engine's a useful contraption, but it tak's the life oot o' a boat."

"Aye," growled his friend. "An' it's dangerous, mind you. There's no telling when it'll conk oot—mebbe when the boat's nigh on the roacks—I've seen that happen. Ye ken whaur ye are wi' sails." He pulled on a rope as he spoke and the sails went up—they were brown and carefully patched—the breeze filled them and the old boat gave a joyous bound.

The tide was in. The water looked green this evening, green like bottle-glass and so clear that one could see shells and stones and seaweed on the sandy bottom. They were making straight out to sea and ahead of them lay the rocky island veiled by faint haze; it looked drowsy and peaceful as though it were resting after the heat of the day. Behind them lay Seatown, its houses stretching all along the bay and rising steeply to the Station Hill . . . the little houses by the harbour were already decreasing in size and looked like a cluster of children's toys.

Dinah felt the breeze on her hot cheeks, she felt the breeze in her hair. Beside her sat Malcolm, wrapped in an Inverness cloak—an ancient garment of lovat tweed—he was hatless and was smoking a pipe with a silver lid.

"It's a lovely motion," Malcolm said. "It knocks flying into a cocked hat. Riding comes nearest to it, perhaps."

"But it's easier than riding," said Dinah, thoughtfully. "Unless you mean a white circus horse with a broad back that goes round and round the ring."

"I didn't," replied Malcolm. "The circus horse isn't getting anywhere; it canters round and round, while the spangled lady jumps on and off, and the ring-master cracks his whip. We're going places, as the Americans say. To-night I feel as if I'd like to go on and on, away to the horizon and beyond. I feel as if I should find freedom there."

He had spoken with such force, though the force was controlled, that Dinah was quite disconcerted. She had not the feeling that she wanted to escape from life.

"It's silly, isn't it?" he continued. "We're supposed to be free agents, but in reality we're bound hand and foot. It's only when I'm on the sea with Ben that I lose the feeling and imagine myself free."

"What binds you?" Dinah asked, for it seemed to her that Malcolm was a free agent. He was a single man and ran his own business and had enough money to live on very comfortably.

"People, possessions, responsibilities, disabilities," he said slowly.

She was silent for a few moments and then she said, "Yes, I see that. One is bound by one's responsibilities to people, but if one loves the people . . ."

"I dare say that would make a lot of difference!" agreed Malcolm. He was smiling at her now—though somewhat ruefully.

Having seen Lady Armstrong and her niece, Dinah understood. She returned the smile and asked; "Why do you let people cramp your style, Malcolm?"

"Heaven knows!" he replied. "I don't wonder you ask *that* after what happened on Sunday night. My stepmother isn't always so—so difficult."

"She didn't like me."

"No, I don't think she did," agreed Malcolm, chuckling. "Her likes and dislikes are somewhat peculiar."

Dinah was silent. It was a little difficult to know how far to go.

"The fact is I've got tangled up," explained Malcolm. "When my father died it seemed natural to go on living with my stepmother at Abbot's End. Incidentally, the house belongs to me and I love it. What can I do? That's the question. I've got tangled up and I don't possess a sharp enough knife to cut myself loose."

"But when Lady Armstrong goes to Edinburgh—"

"Goes to Edinburgh!" echoed Malcolm, in amazement.

"I thought—"

"You thought she was going to Edinburgh?"

"I'm *sure* she's thinking of it," declared Dinah, making up her mind to be frank (for Malcolm was her friend; he had been good to her, whereas Lady Armstrong had not). "Yes, I'm perfectly certain she's thinking of leaving Abbot's End, and going to live in Edinburgh. It was something she said—I forget the exact words—and afterwards she and Miss Grover both denied it vehemently—far too vehemently, I thought. The impression I got was that they had discussed the matter together but hadn't intended to mention it to me."

"Well!" he exclaimed. "Well . . . Good heavens, that takes the cake!"

"You had no idea of it?"

"None whatever. Of course my stepmother often says that Seatown doesn't agree with her, but I had no idea she was thinking of going away. We'll get this cleared up," declared Malcolm thoughtfully. "We'll bring the whole subject into the open and discuss it. I hate underground currents."

Dinah wondered if she should warn Malcolm not to say that he had got wind of Lady Armstrong's intentions through her, but she cared so little what Lady Armstrong thought of her that she decided to leave it alone. If Malcolm wanted to quote her as his authority he could do so. She hated underground currents as much as he did.

They were silent for a few moments, busy with their thoughts. Then Malcolm laughed. "This looks like the sharp knife," he said. "This looks *extremely* like the sharp knife. Thank you for giving it to me, Dinah."

They talked about other things after that, talked or were silent with equal felicity. Dinah had met very few men in her life, for she had had little opportunity of meeting people. There was Dan, but he scarcely counted for he was a part of herself, her alter ego; and then there was Gilbert, of course. Malcolm was different. His manner was different; his approach to herself. Gilbert had treated her as a plaything, as a sort of ornament—amusing, precious and beautiful. Malcolm treated her as an equal, exploring her mind, asking for her opinions upon this or that and considering them carefully before agreeing—or disagreeing and offering his reasons for so doing. He was completely natural and friendly; there was no indication in his manner that he admired her, or that he thought her pretty or charming. There was no gallantry in his attitude, no "man to woman" business at all. She felt as if she were talking to a tried friend, a friend wiser than herself and more experienced, somebody who could be relied upon for sound advice . . . but he was amusing, too, capable of mischievous little turns of phrase and of light-hearted gaiety. She had discovered that he could be indiscreet and this discovery put her at her case with him (for the person who speaks with considered care is the person to be treated with caution).

The sun was setting in a clear sky, a sky of turquoise-blue which blended into palest lemon and orange. The great rocky island towards which they had been sailing was dark with shadows, its reflection stretching out towards them and turning the green water to deep and inky black. Ben pointed to a seal, basking upon a flat rock at the water's edge. He clapped his horny hands with a noise like a pistol shot and it slipped off the rocks into the sea and a cloud of sea-birds rose shrieking from the ledges and swooped about in circles above their heads.

It was getting dark quite quickly now and Malcolm made a sign to Ben. He brought the boat round in a wide sweep and they headed back for the mainland.

As they neared the shore Dinah noticed that they were not making for the harbour where they had embarked, but for the East Bay. There was a natural jetty in the rocks to the westward of Craigie Lodge, and they were landing their passenger there.

"At your door," said Malcolm, smiling. "It will save you walking from the harbour. You'll come to-morrow night, won't you?"

"Not to-morrow, I'm afraid," replied Dinah.

"Thursday, then?"

Somehow it seemed natural to say yes.

Dinah was handed on to the rocks from one fisherman to another and Ben escorted her over the rocks with his hand beneath her elbow as if she were old and frail.

"Ye'll be safe enough noo," declared Ben, as they stepped on to the sand. "We'll see ye on Thursday nicht for sure."

Dinah agreed that they would. She waved to Malcolm and went up to the house. When she had got to the gate she turned and waved again. The boat was pushing off; they had got the oars out; Malcolm was waving his handkerchief to her.

20

A LETTER from Dan was lying upon the breakfast-table next morning, and one from Irene Barnard, bulky with news. Dinah got the children started with their porridge and took up Dan's letter first.

Darling Di,

You can imagine my delight—or can't you?—when I got your letter to say you had definitely decided to take the plunge. I'm sure it is the wise thing to do, besides being the most pleasant. Of course the first thing I did was to dash off hot-foot to a house agent. He was not very helpful nor hopeful. Several large ruins are in the market, but as we should be allowed to spend only ten pounds on repairs I was obliged to turn them down. Umbrellas are all very well, but Nannie always says it is unlucky to open an umbrella in the house, so a watertight roof is essential. I suppose you would be able to come up to Edinburgh and see a house if I could find a possible one? Nannie and Mrs. Turtle's Flo could look after the brats for one day, couldn't they? The second thing I did was to beetle along and see Malcolm at his office (I shall have to call him Mr. Armstrong, of course). He introduced me to some of the staff and explained who I was and what I was going to do. He called it confidential secretary, which sounded very grand, and said I was a very old friend of the family—altogether made everything smooth and easy. It is a good thing I can do type-writing—I shall brush it up a bit—pity I can't do shorthand but Malcolm says it doesn't matter; what he really wants is someone who will use his brains and take responsibility if necessary. I shall have to spend some time going through all the departments and learning the whole business from A to Z. I'm longing to get started. Malcolm gave me some books and papers to study so I'm getting down to it. Before you know where you are your brother will be a "King of Industry." Doubt-ful if I shall be able to get down to Seatown on Friday because I can't very well ask Cray for week-ends when I'm leaving so soon, but I'll be down on Saturday if I can manage it . . .

Oh, Dinah, you faithless creature! [wrote Irene], To think I have cherished you all these years! How could you be so cruel as to desert me! Honestly, my dear, I feel absolutely shattered at the prospect of no Dinah-next-door to rush in and disturb at any hour of the day, to ask advice about jam or hats or Christine's tummy or discuss the affairs of the universe with. What a sentence! You can *see* how shattered I am. Christine wept at the news and then recovered and became fairly cheer-ful. Heartless creatures children are! Of course she will miss Polly frightfully—probably more in the winter when there isn't so much going on. Henry is sorry, too, but he says I am to tell you that you are doing the right thing. He says Dan is sound—which, as you know, is the highest praise Henry can give—and you will be able to educate the children well and cheaply in Edinburgh. I wish it were not quite so far away. We shall come and stay with you of course and you must come to us. Dora likes Oakfield immensely and actually is toying with the idea of buying it (I suppose you will want to sell it), but I'm not encouraging her at all. I don't want to accept any responsibility in the matter. If she buys it and regrets it the mistake won't be mine. Dora is a bit trying in some ways, but I might have a worse neighbour and Christine likes the boys. So there you are! Of course you made my mouth water by your description of the food. How does Mrs. Anderson manage to provide such excellent fare? The queues in Nettleham are longer than ever and supplies shorter. Wilfred Harrington came in to drinks last night and was quite *crushed* by the news that you are leaving Nettleham . . .

Dinah smiled to herself. Irene's matchmaking propensities used to annoy her considerably, but now, for some reason, she was only amused. Crushed, thought Dinah, looking at the heavy underlining of the word in Irene's letter! Wilfred was no more crushed by the news that he was unlikely to see me again than I am by the thought that I shall never see him.

There was great bustle and excitement at Craigie Lodge that afternoon, for the children were going to tea with the Monks, and Dinah and Nannie were determined that they should arrive at the tea-party in a spotless condition. They certainly looked very clean and neat as they started out and their mother had cause to feel proud of them.

"Umph'm, they pay for dressing," remarked Nannie. "It's a pity they don't look like that more often; but you and Dan were just the same—always tearing your clothes and wearing out your shoes at the toes, and usually as dirty as tinkers into the bargain. The doctor never minded; he used to say: 'Better to wear out leather than sheets.'"

It was extraordinarily quiet in the house when they had gone. Dinah and Margy had tea together in the drawing-room. Flo brought it up to them on a tray and lingered to chat with them. She was not shy now, and was very good and helpful with the children; Nannie had suggested tentatively that when Dinah was settled in Edinburgh, she might take Flo as a permanency, but nothing had been said to

Flo about the idea. It would be very pleasant to have Flo, thought Dinah, and she would come (if her mother would let her) for she thought Mrs. Savage was the most wonderful person in the world. Dinah was fully aware of Flo's devotion and very touched; few people are too high and mighty to enjoy hero-worship and Dinah was not one of these. In fact, it seemed incredible to the humble-hearted Dinah that she should have won Flo's heart with so little effort and in so short a time.

The children arrived home about six o'clock full of excitement and the old house which had seemed so quiet came alive again. They arrived home laden with presents and with paper hats and trinkets which had come out of crackers. Mr. Monk had managed to buy a large box of crackers in Edinburgh.

"Look at my gold-fish!" cried Nigel. "It's to swim in the bath—and Mark has a frog. Look at this sailing-boat! I can sail it in the sea to-morrow morning. Polly got a doll. Show Mummy your doll!"

"Her clothes take off and on," said Polly, excitedly. "Look Mummy! Look at her dear little vest. Mrs. Monk made it herself. Mrs. Monk made *all* her clothes, Mummy!"

Dinah was quite overwhelmed by the generosity showered upon her offspring. "Goodness, how kind of them!" she exclaimed. "I hope you all said thank-you?"

"Of course we did!" Polly assured her. "We felt thankish, so it was easy. We said it again and again, didn't we, Mark?"

"Two or three times at least," agreed Mark, gravely. He was already sitting upon the floor, turning over the pages of a book which had been given to him. It was a beautifully illustrated copy of *Treasure Island*.

"You needn't worry. We were *very* good," declared Polly. "They both said so when we came away, so we must have been."

"Mark upset his milk," Nigel reminded her.

"That was an accident—not naughty," said Mark, quickly. "And Mrs. Monk didn't mind a bit. She said accidents happen in the best related families."

"We had plums with sugar," said Polly. "They were great big white plums with red cheeks and flannel skins."

"Peaches?" suggested Dinah.

"And so *juicy*," said Mark, with a faraway look. "*So* juicy. The juice ran up my sleeve. Mr. Monk said we could lick our plates, so we did. We couldn't waste all that sugar."

"I hope you didn't call him Mr. Monk," said Dinah, anxiously; but the children were far too excited to reply.

"We played a game with little balls," said Polly. "You pulled a sort of loop and the ball popped up and ran down a slope into a hole."

"Sometimes it didn't," put in Nigel.

"Mr. Monk was terribly good at it," added Polly. "It nearly always ran into a hole when he was playing."

"And he *is* deaf," declared Mark. "Just a *little* bit deaf, like Old Monk. You don't notice it when you're talking to him, but he can't hear what everybody is saying. He thinks you're saying something when really you're saying something else. Did you notice, Polly?"

"Mrs. Monk told him things once or twice," said Polly, nodding.

"Told him the jokes," agreed Nigel.

"So that he wouldn't miss the fun," explained Mark, in case his mother had not understood.

"And then Patrick came in," said Polly, giggling at the recollection. "Oh, dear, he *was* funny! He put on my hat and crawled about on his hands and knees."

"I jumped on to his back," declared Nigel. "He bucked and bucked, but he couldn't get me off . . ."

Dinah listened and smiled. It was obvious that the party had been an enormous success; she only hoped the host and hostess were not worn out by the hospitality they had given.

21

IT WAS now time for bed. Dinah and Nannie had evolved a most satisfactory arrangement for putting the children to bed. Margy was bathed first and, while she was having her supper, Nannie dealt faithfully with the twins. By the time Margy was safely tucked up the twins were supping and Dinah was free to supervise Polly's ablutions. It all fitted in very neatly and everybody was pleased with the scheme.

Having played her part and said good-night to her family Dinah went downstairs and was surprised to find Pat Yoker sitting at ease in the drawing-room and reading *Treasure Island.*

"Goodness! They never said you were here!" exclaimed Dinah.

"I told them not to bother you," he replied. "That's a jolly nice book, you know. I wouldn't mind reading it *all* through."

"Quite a lot of people have," said Dinah, innocently.

"Well, I don't wonder . . . nice pictures," declared Pat. "I mean pictures make a lot of difference. Look at that one of the old pirate with the wooden leg."

"It's Silver!" exclaimed Dinah, with interest.

"No, it's wooden," said Pat. "I know it looks silver in the picture, but it's made of wood all right. You see I *know*, because there was an old pensioner I used to talk to sometimes. He had a peg leg—and was he nippy on it! You should have seen him scooting about!"

"I dare say Mark would lend you the book," suggested Dinah.

"Well, I don't know," said Pat doubtfully. "Fact is, I'm not much of a reader. I like to have a snoop at *The Times*, just to see who's got married and who's got promoted and so on, and I usually have a glance at the news—though it's a bit depressing. I mean there's nothing except strikes and accidents and some Russian chap saying No to something—depressing, that's what I think."

Dinah said she couldn't agree more, which was one of Dan's sayings and expressed her feelings perfectly.

"But I didn't come to talk about that," said Pat. "I don't know how on earth we got on to the subject . . . Oh, yes, that book! Well, I really just looked in to tell you the party was a terrific success and the aunt and uncle are still alive."

"That's relieved my mind a lot!" said Dinah laughing.

"And to bring you a bottle of gin," added Pat, producing it from behind his back with the air of a conjurer.

"Gin!" exclaimed Dinah, in surprise.

"Real gin," said Pat, nodding. "Pretty rare, isn't it? Anyhow, there it is, and I thought we might have a snifter if you're feeling like it—if you've any lime juice, or—or even if you haven't—" said Pat hopefully.

Dinah laughed again, Tapioca amused her a good deal. She was able to produce a bottle of orange squash and a couple of glasses, so they had a snifter. Tapioca had more than one.

"Good gin that," he declared. "Don't drown it with that yellow stuff. Yes, the party was an absolute wow. I arrived just at the end and had a game with them, and then the presents were given out . . . awfully appreciative little beggars, your children are!"

Dinah said she was glad.

"Oh yes, the uncle and aunt were as pleased as Punch—and Judy!" He chuckled. "Quite a good joke that! You see," he continued, pouring out a liberal helping of gin and waving away Dinah's offer of yellow stuff. "You see, my father and mother were killed in an air raid, so the uncle and aunt are all I've got . . . yes," added Pat when Dinah had endeavoured to commiserate with him. "Yes, it was pretty awful. Seemed wrong, somehow. I went off to do a bit of battling and they stayed at home and got killed! Pretty awful, wasn't it? So the uncle and aunt are all I've got left and they haven't any one except me."

"I thought they had a son."

"Killed," said Pat. "They had a daughter, too, but she died when she was a child. Pretty awful for them, really—not having anybody."

"Frightfully sad!"

"So you see they're very *alone*," explained Pat. "And that's why I feel sort of responsible for them—because they've had such a mouldy time."

Dinah saw. She thought it was nice of Pat. "Was their son married?" she inquired.

"No; that was another blow to them," replied Pat, looking regretfully at his empty glass. "He was engaged to a very nice girl, and had been for ages. The uncle and aunt liked her immensely and were awfully pleased about it. The date of the wedding was fixed and everything laid on and then at the last minute he changed his mind and threw her over. Pretty awful, wasn't it?"

"Frightful!" agreed Dinah.

"It wasn't so much the doing of it as the way he did it . . . Yes, I will have just a suspicion more if you can spare it. He didn't give any *reason*, you see. The uncle tried to argue with him, but he wasn't having any—just walked out and left them sitting. The uncle had to tell the girl it was all off, and cancel everything. Pretty awful, wasn't it?"

"Frightful!" exclaimed Dinah, in horrified tones.

"The uncle has got a bit of a temper, you know. He was simply livid—I don't blame him really—I mean it was pretty awful to have his son behaving like that. It let *him* down, if you see what I mean. He was so fed up that he just left it alone for a bit, thinking that time would put things right—but it didn't. If I'd been here I might have done something, but I was in Australia—and then in Colombo. I wasn't home at all for years, so I couldn't do anything."

"They never made it up?" asked Dinah incredulously.

"No," said Pat, shaking his head. "The uncle left it for a bit, as I told you, and then wrote and said let bygones be bygones—you know the sort of thing—but there was no answer. It worried them no end, especially the uncle because he felt he ought to have been more patient. He blamed himself frightfully, poor old boy; but honestly it wasn't his fault. I mean he's told me about it several times and I don't see what else he could have said or done."

"It's dreadful for him!"

"Yes, and he still worries about it, still goes on wishing he had written again and climbed down even more and got things squared up. Fortunately the aunt seems to have forgotten all about the row. I dare say you've noticed she's a bit forgetful."

"What an extraordinary creature your cousin must have been!"

"You've said it," agreed Pat. "The cousin was a curious bloke. I never had much use for him. He was spoilt, really. They gave in to him too much when he was a kid—gave him everything he wanted. They're so kind, you see, and of course they were oldish—I mean the aunt was about forty when he was born—and their daughter had died. Well, I mean you can see why they spoilt him, can't you? But it wasn't a good thing. He didn't appreciate it."

"It's a lesson," said Dinah, thoughtfully.

"You shouldn't be too unselfish with kids," agreed Pat.

"I try not to be," Dinah told him, taking the point. "It's difficult sometimes. I mean sometimes it's more unselfish to be selfish; you want to give in, you want to make them happy, you want to give them the earth. You have to remind yourself it's kinder to be selfish."

"I'll have to think that out," said Pat. "The old brain's a bit slow on the uptake." He rose as he spoke. "You couldn't come and dance," he added, not as if he were tendering an invitation, but merely as if he were stating a regrettable fact.

"You mean . . . to-night?" inquired Dinah, somewhat taken aback.

"There's another dance to-night. I could get that little bit of fluff out of the tobacconist's, but I'd rather have you."

"I'm afraid it will have to be the little bit of fluff," said Dinah, trying not to laugh.

"I thought so," he said.

She showed him down the stairs, reflecting with some amusement that she was only taking Tapioca's own advice. Oddly enough she would have liked to go to the dance (she had been tempted to accept for she had enjoyed herself on Friday) but it was better for him that she should not go. Tapioca was transparent as plate glass.

Dan will laugh, thought Dinah, as she stood at the door and watched Tapioca walk away. Dan will laugh like anything.

Dinah herself did not feel like laughing. She had her supper and, going upstairs, sat by the drawing-room window and looked out. She felt lonely and dejected; she almost regretted her refusal to go to the dance. Hadn't she been rather silly to refuse? She had refused to go for a sail with Malcolm and she had refused to go to the dance . . . and now she was feeling lonely . . . and dejected.

The sea was very calm this evening; it was about halfway in but everything was so quiet that Dinah could hear the splash of the waves breaking upon the sand. The sun was sinking into a bed of soft grey clouds, tinging their edges with fiery red. Gradually the sun sank and the light faded. The lighthouse on the far-off island began to wink. It was a familiar sight—the winking of that far-off light—and it took her away back down the years. Dinah was a young girl again, wondering about life, dreaming of what life held in store for her. And now, she thought, my life is fixed. My bed is made and I must lie on it. She did not pity herself, nor entertain the foolish idea that at twenty-eight her life was over—but certainly it was fixed. Her work was cut out for her. It was good work and she intended to do it well, to bring up her children to be useful members of society. She did not rebel (indeed, she would have rejected the idea of changing places with any one); but she would not have been human if she had not had moments of regret, moments of longing for the old days when she had been *herself* (not the mother of four children, but belonging to herself alone and complete in herself) looking towards a future full of rosy hopes and dreams: romance, travel, adventure. She had had romance, of course. Gilbert had been her fairy prince and for a little while she had been wildly, madly happy. It had not lasted long but she had had it. Some women did not even have that.

It was nearly dark now. There were footsteps on the road. She could see two shadowy figures strolling past very slowly, with their arms entwined.

"You're wonderful!" a man's voice exclaimed.

Dinah could hear a murmured reply as they passed on and vanished in the gloom.

Lucky woman, thought Dinah. It *was* lucky to have someone who cared like that, someone to lean on. Life was very frightening sometimes. Dinah wanted someone who would make her feel safe; someone who would share her responsibilities and settle things for her—it was a weary business making decisions yourself—she wanted someone to consult and defer to, someone to order her days. Looking forward, she saw herself growing older, the children growing up: she saw herself walking with a stick (like Mrs. Monk) with her hand on Mark's arm—or Polly's. She could not see herself leaning on Nigel's arm.

There were tears on Dinah's cheeks, but she brushed them away impatiently for she was not given to pitying herself. She agreed wholeheartedly with Mrs. Wiggs: people who pitied themselves were despicable creatures.

Dinah was thinking of Mrs. Wiggs and trying to smile when Nannie came in with the usual tray of milk and biscuits.

"All in the dark!" exclaimed Nannie, turning on the light.

"I was thinking," replied Dinah. She hesitated and then continued: "What an odd thing life is, isn't it? So different from what one expected!"

"Maircy me!" exclaimed Nannie. "You're talking as if you were dead."

Dinah laughed. "Not dead, exactly: just settled."

Nannie put down the tray. "Not settled, eether," she declared. "There's a lot of life to be worked out before you're through with it— maybe you're never through. I used to think when the Doctor was alive: This is my life for ever and ever; keeping house and looking after things, answering the telephone, going out Sundays to tea and the Kirk—and, mind you, I liked it. I wasn't complaining. But then, in a moment, it was all changed."

"You like it better?" asked Dinah.

"Better—and worse," said Nannie, doubtfully. "There's more *to* it, having a man of your own, but there's more worries. If the roof leaked I would say to Doctor Bell the roof was leaking and that was all. He'd see the slater came up the very next day. *Now* I've got to go after Will Thomson myself and make sure he comes and pay for it as well. It's the same with everything. There's a deal more work and worry nowadays."

"But you wouldn't go back?"

Nannie smiled.

"I'd miss Andrew—and that's the truth," she admitted.

Nannie had found somebody who cared.

22

THE evening was silver, not golden as Tuesday evening had been. Dinah walked along to the harbour as before and, as before, she found the *Kilt* lying at the steps with Malcolm already aboard. There was more breeze to-night and quite an appreciable swell, but this only made it more pleasant for Dinah was an excellent sailor. They tacked westward along the shore and saw the green stretch of the golf course and people playing. A motor boat, full of people, chugged past them, making for a wreck at the end of the west bay.

"Queer!" said Malcolm, pointing to the boat with his pipe. "It wouldn't amuse me a bit to go out in a boat like that."

"There's lots o' queer things in this wurrld," declared Ben who had come to sit near them. "There's lots o' things that's difficult tae understand."

"What sort o' things are you thinking of?" inquired Malcolm with interest. Malcolm was always interested in the working of other people's minds.

"Weel," said Ben, as he filled his pipe and packed it carefully with his enormous finger. "Weel, Mister Mawlcolm, I wis jis' thinking o' a wee crack I wis having wi' Mister Harvey—he's the meenister, ye ken. I'm no' a verra regular attendant at the Kirk, but I ken ma Bible an' I wis jis' asking him a wee question an' he couldna' answer it." Ben smiled and shook his head. "It fair stumped him," declared Ben.

"Let's have it," suggested Malcolm, with a chuckle.

"Aye, ye can have it. Noo, see here, there wis Adam and Eve, an' they had three sons," said Ben, gravely. "There wis nae ither body in the wurrld but them—Adam an' Eve an' Cain an' Abel an' Seth. That's richt enough, is it no'?"

"Perfectly correct," agreed Malcolm.

"Weel, the Buik says Cain went oot intae the wilderness an' took wives an' his descendants bred an' mustered. Noo then, Mister Mawlcolm, can ye tell me this (an' if ye can tell me ye'll be a deal cleverer nor the meenister) whaur did Cain find wives, eh? Whaur did they come frae? There wis nae ither body in the wurrld—only beasts," declared Ben, nodding gravely. "But Cain got wives. *There's* a puzzle."

Malcolm said he had no idea where Cain's wives had come from.

"God sent them to him," suggested Dinah.

"Weel then, it should of said," objected Ben. "There's naething aboot it in the Buik. It should of *said*, 'An' God sent wives tae Cain,' an' then there'd hae been nae doots aboot it."

Ben's friend who had been listening in silence to the discussion cleared his throat and remarked, "There's things we're no meant to ken. It's Goad's will—that's a' ye can say."

"Na, na; that'll nae dae," retorted Ben. "If we dinna ken we're meant tae find oot. We're no intended tae sit doon an' dream. Puzzles is sent us tae mak' us use oor brains. Thawr wis Newton that saw an aipple fall an' he asked himsel' why; an' there wis Watt that saw the lid o' his mither's kettle lifting wi' the steam. Did Watt say, 'That's unco' queer, but there's things we're no' meant tae ken, sae I'll tak' a wee darder roond the toon an' mebbe hae a game o' bowls'?"

Dinah laughed, but there was no suspicion of a smile upon Ben's mahogany features.

"An' there wis Lister," continued Ben. "Lister saw folks deeing like flees wi' gangrene. Mebbe if you'd been Lister you'd hae said, 'Weel, weel, that's a peety—puir bodies—but it's Goad's will.'"

Ben's friend was silent under this fearful accusation.

"Na, na," continued Ben. "We're no' intended tae sit doon an' dream. We're intended tae use the brains we're given . . . an' mebbe ye'll use what brains ye've bin given," added Ben, in a different tone of voice. "We'll be on the roacks in a wee meenit if ye dinna bring her roond."

Ben's friend used his brain and brought her round skillfully. "Aye, that's a' verra weel," he declared, as he completed the evolution. "That's a' verra weel for folks like Lister an' Watt, but they're special kind o' folks wi' special kind o' brains. The likes o' us isn't intended tae question Goad's will. We've no grand eddication like them. We're just puir ignorant fisherfolk an' naething mair."

Malcolm leant forward. "You've forgotten one thing," he declared. "Christ's chosen companions were poor ignorant fishermen."

"Aye, ye'd forgotten that!" cried Ben, in delight. "Mister Mawlcolm's got ye there. That's one ye canna' answer in a hurry. Tak' Peter, noo. Peter wis forever asking questions. He got a wee set-doon noo an' then, but he wisna' discouraged—not him! He wis up an' at it again, wanting tae ken this an' that an' the ither. It wis aye Peter that asked the questions, it wis Peter had a' the ideas . . . Aye, an' it wis Peter that wis chosen abune a' the ithers tae be their heid."

"Och away!" exclaimed Ben's friend in disgust. "It's a meenister ye should of been. Yer faither should of made a meenister o' ye, Ben."

They had turned now and were running home before the westerly breeze with a lovely free, bounding motion which was most exhilarating. Malcolm had not talked so much to-day, but his silence was friendly and without strain. Dinah had enjoyed every moment of her outing. She wondered if Malcolm would ask her to come again (she was half afraid he would and half afraid he wouldn't) and as they approached the East Bay to land her on the rocks she tried to make up her mind what to do about it. There was no reason why she should not go with him again—if he asked her—but somehow she felt uneasy. Somehow she felt it would be better not to go again. He might not ask her, of course, in which case there would be no difficulty about it. But the idea that Malcolm might not ask her was not wholly pleasant.

"What about Monday evening?" asked Malcolm, as Ben brought the boat skilfully to the landing place. "Would Monday suit you, Dinah?"

"The tide'll be oot, Monday," said Ben's friend.

"An' who asked ye fer an opeenion?" demanded Ben. "Can we no' tak' the boat oot in the efternune an' get Mister Mawlcolm off the pier?"

Ben's friend was suitably crushed.

"Monday?" said Dinah, trying somewhat half-heartedly to look for an excuse . . . but what excuse could she find? Seatown did not offer many evening entertainments.

"Tuesday, then?" suggested Malcolm. "Would Tuesday suit you better?"

Dinah could find no excuse—she had not tried very hard—so she thanked him and agreed to come on Tuesday.

23

BY THIS time Dinah's children had made friends with other children who played on the shore and sometimes they split up and could be seen in widely scattered groups, building castles, or sailing boats, or hunting for crabs in the seaweed. The odd thing was they seemed to have different friends . . . but perhaps it was not really odd for they were all so different from one another. Dinah regretted this splitting up of her family. She and Dan had been enough for one another and had never wanted outside friends.

Nigel was the most popular member of his family; he was tall for his age, and extremely good-looking and he had a charming manner with strangers. It was a pity his manner was not so charming when he was at home in the bosom of his family, but there are quite a number of people in the world with the same peculiarity.

Dinah was thinking about this and wondering what could be done about it when she saw Pat coming towards her across the sands.

"No golf this morning?" she inquired.

"The old heel has let me down," replied Pat.

"The old heel?" repeated Dinah, chuckling. "Who on earth is that?"

"Who?" inquired Pat, in a bewildered manner.

"Yes," nodded Dinah. "Which of your friends?"

"Oh, I see the idea! The old heel! But it isn't a friend, it's a blister, that's all. Better to-morrow," said Pat cheerfully. He sat down on a nearby rock and watched Dinah, who was trying to induce her younger daughter to paddle in a pool.

"Cold," said Margy, trying the temperature of the water with the tip of her toe and withdrawing hastily. "Too cold."

"Lovely," declared Dinah, enticingly. "Lovely water."

"Mummy put hot in," said Margy, making this admirable suggestion with one of her ravishing smiles.

"No," replied Dinah. "Don't be silly, Margy. Mummy can't put hot in—besides, it's *nicer* cold."

"Nastier cold," said Margy, firmly.

Pat laughed. "But why bother?" he inquired. "I mean if she doesn't like paddling, she doesn't. I wouldn't put my big toe into ice-cold water for a good deal."

"The others like it," explained Dinah, tossing back her curls which had fallen over her face during her efforts. "The others simply love it and so would Margy if she would only try it properly. Margy is like—like a cushion," continued her mother, looking at her with a mixture of amusement and vexation. "She's soft and comfortable but you can't squeeze her into another shape."

"You *can* squeeze a cushion," objected Pat . . . and then he stopped. "Hallo! What's up?" he exclaimed.

Polly was running towards them at full speed, dragging a boy by the hand. He was a tall thin boy, a good deal bigger than herself.

"What's up?" repeated Pat. "That's the Barrington boy she's got in tow. They're staying at Miss Brown's."

By this time the pair had arrived; Polly, breathless and obviously distressed, pushed her friend forward.

"Tell him, Mummy!" she cried. "Tell him it's true. *Tell* him."

"It's all right," said the boy disengaging his hand and smiling at Dinah disarmingly. "I shouldn't have said it, really, because she's just a kid—I mean kids believe in fairy stories, don't they? I'm eleven, you see, so *of course* I don't believe in Santa Claus—"

"Tell him!" besought Polly. "Please tell him quickly. It's wicked, isn't it? But he doesn't mean to be."

Dinah hesitated.

"Of course there's a Santa Claus," declared Pat, with conviction. "Who do you think fills your stocking if it isn't Santa Claus?"

"It's your father dressed up," replied the boy.

"But our father wasn't *there*!" cried Polly.

"It's your mother, then," said the boy, smiling at Dinah as he spoke.

Pat shook his head sadly. "Of course if you don't believe in him you can't expect him to come, can you? I'm afraid that's the reason you don't get a Christmas stocking."

"But I do get a stocking," declared the Barrington boy. "I get a marvellous stocking every year. My father fills it for me. My father says it's silly to believe in Santa Claus, but he doesn't want me to miss any of the fun."

"It seems to me you miss *all* the fun," said Pat thoughtfully. "I can remember when I was a kid and Santa Claus came and filled my stocking. Gosh, what a thrill! I mean it wouldn't have been the same at all if my father had done it."

"But it isn't *true!*" cried the boy. "It *must* have been your father!"

"Santa Claus came to me—*always*," declared Pat with the utmost conviction. He rose as he spoke and taking Polly's hand began to walk up the beach.

Dinah picked up Margy and followed. Dinah had not spoken at all; she had left it to Pat, and Pat had done it beautifully. She had not spoken because she could not make up her mind what to say. Was it right to tell children lies—even innocent lies about a time-honoured myth such as Santa Claus? It was such fun for them . . . but lies were horrible.

Pat was in no doubts about the matter and as Dinah followed them up the beach she could hear snatches of his conversation with Polly.

" . . . There was a sort of clatter," Pat was saying earnestly. "And when I opened my eyes, there he was . . . no, it was the fire-irons, I think . . . Yes, an enormous sack, goodness knows how he got it down the chimney . . . Yes, it was red and trimmed with white fur and there was a hood pulled over his head . . . No, not really. I shut my eyes light in case he would see I was awake . . . No, of course he wouldn't come unless you *believed* in him. I mean why *should* he? There are lots of children who *do* believe in him, so naturally . . . No, I wouldn't talk to Philip about it any more . . . Yes, but I wouldn't if I were you . . . No, honestly, it wouldn't be a bit of good . . ."

The afternoon was dull and misty and the sands looked less attractive than usual so when Dinah suggested a walk up the glen the children agreed to come.

"It will be fun to explore," said Polly. "We can pretend we're exploring the jungle. Did the Dees go for walks in the glen?"

Dinah tried to remember but for some reason she could not. "I don't think so," she said slowly. "We liked the sands better; but it will be nice for a change."

They set off after tea, walking along the bay to eastward and turning inland when they came to the burn. The glen was a cleft in the hill through which the burn ran down; it was filled with trees, oaks and hazels and elms, twisted and bent by the winter gales. There was a ruined mill at the bottom of the glen, a small tumbledown house with thick walls, and a steep path led upwards beside the burn, winding this way and that between fallen rocks.

Dinah and the three children crossed the meadow and entered the wood, and as they did so the sun broke through the clouds, touching the trees with gold and throwing dappled patches of light and shade up on the grass and the tangled undergrowth. The children were running about, dabbling in the little burn, climbing on the rocks and calling to one another. It was a splendid place for children to play, thought Dinah, and again she tried to remember why she and Dan had not made it one of their "haunts." She was sure they had not; no, she couldn't remember a single picnic here.

She climbed on, looking about her as she went. There were masses of brambles. Soon the fruit would ripen and she and the children must come and pick the berries; bramble jelly would be lovely, and Nannie made it so well. Suddenly Dinah found a hot little hand thrust into hers and looking down she found it was Polly's.

"I don't like it," said Polly earnestly.

"You don't like it!" exclaimed Dinah, in surprise.

"Let's go home," said Polly and she tugged at Dinah's hand so that Dinah was obliged to stop.

"But, Polly—why?"

"I don't like this walk."

"But it's such a pretty place. Look at the foxgloves, Polly! Look at the funny old trees! They're very old, you know. Why don't you play with the boys?"

"I want to go home."

Dinah hesitated. The boys had run on; they had disappeared round a bend in the path. "We'll go and find the boys," said Dinah.

"No," said Polly, hanging back. "No. Mummy, let's go home!"

"We can't go without the boys," said Dinah, reasonably. "You know that as well as I do. We'll go and find them and then we'll all go home together." She tried to walk on as she spoke, but Polly, clinging to her hand like a limpet, held her back.

"Very well, then," said Dinah. "You can wait here. I'll go on, and—"

"Don't leave me," said Polly, in a low voice. "They'll be all right. It isn't them, it's me."

"I don't know what you mean!" exclaimed Dinah in amazement.

"Let's go home," repeated Polly, urgently. "Please, Mummy, please—I want to go *home*. I don't *like* it here."

It was so unlike Polly to be deaf to reason that Dinah was alarmed.

"All right," she said. "I'll call to the boys, but we must wait for them."

"Don't call," said Polly, earnestly. "*They* might hear you. *They* don't like you to make a noise."

There was silence. There was not a sound in the little wood; not a bird sang, not a leaf moved. The burn ran muted in its pebbly bed. Dinah felt a curious sensation at the back of her neck; she was panic-stricken. She knew suddenly for the first time in her life what panic really meant. If Polly had not been there she would have taken to her heels and run helter-skelter down the stony path.

"Home," whispered Polly, beginning to whimper. "Home, Mummy!"

"Not without the boys."

They stood there together on the path. Polly was trembling; she had pressed her face against Dinah's side.

"It's all right," said Dinah, trying to control her voice. "It's nothing, Polly. Don't be silly! The boys will come."

They waited. It seemed a long time. There wasn't a sound except the uneven beating of Dinah's heart. She moistened her lips and said again, "It's all right; it's nothing—don't be silly—"

The sun had vanished behind a cloud and the little wood was damp and cold. There was an odd sort of mist rising from the burn. There wasn't a sound . . . and then they heard the boys coming back.

"Hallo!" exclaimed Nigel. "We've been to the top! There's nothing to see, really. It's a silly old wood."

"Just a few old trees and a broken-down cottage," added Mark, lightheartedly.

"Lots of nettles and toadstools!" shouted Nigel.

They ran past, scattering the stones and gravel with their feet, jumping over the rocks and whistling cheerfully. Dinah and Polly followed, hand-in-hand.

Nothing was said about the incident and by the time they reached Craigie Lodge Polly's colour had returned and she was chattering away as usual—it was as if she had forgotten all about it. But if Polly had forgotten Dinah had not and later that evening she made some pretext for going into the kitchen.

The Andersons were having their nine o'clock tea and they invited Dinah to sit down and join them. Mr. Anderson was a retiring sort of man; except for an occasional meeting on the stairs when they exchanged polite greetings and commented upon the weather Dinah would not have known that he was in the house, but to-night he seemed more approachable. He brought a chair for Dinah and offered her scones and cakes and seemed pleased to see her.

"Why didn't we ever play in the glen, Nannie?" asked Dinah, as she accepted a large chunk of gingerbread.

"Dear knows," replied Nannie. "There were plenty of cold days when the glen would have been nice and sheltered, but I could never get you to come. There was always some excuse or other."

"Did we ever tell you there was something rather odd about it?"

"Gracious, no!" said Nannie with conviction.

"But there *is* something odd about it, Nannie."

"There's nothing odd that I ever saw."

"But you've heard odd things about it?"

"Folks will say anything," declared Nannie. "There was a lady staying here two summers ago that had some tale about feeling queer in the glen—indigestion, if you ask me!"

"Maybe it was and maybe it wasn't," said Mr. Anderson, impartially.

"Phooh!" exclaimed Nannie, tossing her head.

"And she was not the only one." Mr. Anderson continued. "There was the wee Dobbie girl that went to pick brambles and sprained her ankle running down the path. You'll mind she was funny in the head when they found her, Annie?"

"Funny in the head! She was always a bit daft. I've no patience with yon kind of nonsense. Many a time I've walked in the glen and I've never felt queer."

Dinah could well believe it.

"I've a book about Seatown," said Mr. Anderson, turning to Dinah. "It's an old book—a bit shabby and dirty—but you might care to take a look at it some time."

"Dinah doesn't want to be bothered with your dirty old book!"

"It's interesting," said Mr. Anderson apologetically.

"Is there something about the glen in it?" Dinah inquired.

"There's quite a bit. The Ladies' Glen they called it in the old days."

"Not such *old* days," put in Nannie. "I mind when it was called the Ladies' Glen. It would be because ladies used to walk there, most likely."

"It was because witches used to dance there," said Mr. Anderson, leaning forward and helping himself to a cookie.

"Andrew!" exclaimed Nannie. "I never *haird* such nonsense in all my days! You know as well as I do that it's all nonsense!"

"Well, I wouldn't say that," remarked Mr. Anderson, in his slow deep voice. "I wouldn't go so far as to say it was all nonsense, Annie. There's a good deal of nonsense talked about witches, but there's no doubt they existed and folks believed in them—and what's more they believed in themselves. There's a wee clearing half-way up the glen where they used to meet and dance, it's said that's the reason the sward is so green."

"Maybe you saw witches when you were in the glen this afternoon, Dinah?" suggested Nannie, with dry humour.

"No," said Dinah, gravely.

"Or haird them?" pursued Nannie, pressing home her advantage.

"No," said Dinah. "I heard nothing."

"No," agreed Nannie. "You wouldn't, because it's all nonsense!"

"Maybe Mistress Savage felt something," suggested Mr. Anderson, in his quiet voice.

Dinah hesitated. She was unwilling to speak of her experience, but they were looking at her and waiting.

"Yes," she said at last. "I felt something—Polly felt it, too. In fact, we were both terrified."

"Terrified!" exclaimed Nannie, incredulously.

"Quite suddenly, and for no reason at all," nodded Dinah. "The boys didn't seem to feel anything, but Polly was shaking all over and my hair literally stood on end. The hair at the back of my neck," said Dinah, putting up her hand.

Nannie rose without a word and left the room.

"She isn't—annoyed, is she?" asked Dinah, glancing at Mr. Anderson.

"She'll be away to have a look at the wee girl," replied Mr. Anderson with a smile.

24

DAN came on Saturday as he had promised. The children were having tea on the sand with Flo, so Dan and Dinah were able to chat comfortably in the drawing-room.

"You're looking marvellous," Dan declared. "I do wish you needn't go home at the end of the month."

Dinah smiled. "Nannie suggested we should stay on until we can find a house in Edinburgh. She'll keep us all the winter if necessary."

"Gosh! Of course *that's* the answer to our difficulties! No need to drag the children back to Nettleham. It's by far the best plan. Will your tenants stay on?"

"They may buy Oakfield, but it isn't actually decided. I should have to go south and fix things up, but I could leave the children here. Nannie and I have been talking about it."

"And talking to good purpose," declared Dan. "I wish I were as far forward; I can't hear of a suitable house *anywhere*."

It was impossible to make definite arrangements until Dan had found a house, but it amused them to discuss their plans. Dan was tremendously excited (it was years since he had had a settled home) and his excitement was infectious.

"Nannie must give us the old sofa," said Dan. "We'll buy her another, of course, but we must have the old sofa in our drawing-room."

"It's a very big sofa," said Dinah, looking at it doubtfully. "I mean, unless it's a big room—"

"You must get a house with a big room," said Dan, firmly. "We must, honestly; I've set my heart upon having the old sofa. I can see us sitting in it, one in each corner, in front of a roaring fire . . ."

Dinah smiled. She wondered how many years it was since she had seen a roaring fire, but she let it pass without comment. Dan would realise all too soon that life nowadays was austere and comfortless.

Dan's week had been pretty strenuous. He had worked all day at the shipping office and had studied books and papers when he got back to his rooms at night. "Books about paper," said Dan. "I must know all about it before I can be of any use to Malcolm."

"Is it interesting?" Dinah wanted to know.

"Tremendously interesting," declared Dan; and forthwith he began to discourse upon the subject with fluency and enthusiasm. Dinah heard about the various ingredients which go to the making of paper—rags and hemp and esparto-fibre and sulphate wood-pulp— she heard about sand-tables and calendars and smoothing rolls, and a host of other devices. She was told how to prepare rosin-sizing with carbonate of soda and alum; rosin-sizing was the stuff that made paper ink-proof. It was all far too technical for Dinah's comprehension, but at least it taught her that paper-making was a difficult and complicated business. Having dealt faithfully with the making of paper, Dan proceeded to throw out a few facts about its history and informed Dinah that the first English paper-mill was at Stevenage, in Hertford, and that its owner, John Tate, was Lord Mayor of London in 1476. Scotland had no paper-mill until two hundred years later. Water-marks were fascinating, declared Dan. There were books and books about water-marks, and he intended to read them all. At first water-marks had been made by means of a twisted piece of wire which was fixed to the mould in which the paper was manufactured, but nowadays the process was different . . . And Dan went on to compare the merits of wire-gauze and photo-mechanical processes, touching lightly upon gutta-percha and stencils placed between two sheets of half-finished paper.

"There's quite a lot in it," said Dan at last. "I mean I've only just given you a few of the most interesting facts, but you can see how thrilling it is."

"Yes," agreed Dinah, who was slightly exhausted by her vain endeavor to follow the exposition. "Yes, I can see there's a tremendous lot in it."

"A tremendous lot," nodded Dan.

"And what about Miss Cray?" asked Dinah, who had been thinking about Miss Cray off and on all week and had almost arrived at the stage of expecting to have her as a sister-in-law.

"Miss Cray!" exclaimed Dan, in amazement. "What about her?"

"I thought she was nice."

"Oh, I don't think you'd like her, Di!"

"Wouldn't I?"

"No," said Dan. "No—honestly—I thought at first she was rather nice so I wasn't sorry when old Cray asked me to go in to drinks. As a matter of fact I thought I might get her to come to the flicks with me or something."

"Couldn't she come?"

"I didn't ask her."

"Why not?"

"She had bare feet and holes in her shoes—oogh—frightful!" said Dan, shuddering at the recollection.

"But, Dan, I often wear sandals—everybody does!"

"Oh, I don't mind *sandals*," said Dan. "These were ordinary brown-leather shoes with holes cut in them and naked big toes sticking out—toes with crimson nails! You've no idea how horrible they were! It made me uncomfortable to look at them and yet I couldn't help looking at them. I could hardly speak to the girl. Honestly, Di, there was something quite—quite *indecent* about them," said Dan, earnestly.

Dinah could find nothing to say—or rather, there was so much to say that she could not choose her words—so she said nothing.

"Well, that's that!" said Dan cheerfully. "Now you know what I've been doing. Now it's your turn, Di. What mischief have you been up to?"

Dinah began to tell him. She began rather half-heartedly, for her week's activities seemed somewhat tame in retrospect and she was afraid Dan's head was too full of paper for him to be interested in them, but it was not so. Dan was interested in everything she had to tell. He was interested in all that Mrs. Monk had said about Lady

Armstrong; he laughed heartily at Dinah's rendering of Nannie's conversation with Chairley Broon; he heard about the children's tea-party at the Monks' and about Pat Yoker's spirited defence of Santa Claus. Finally, somewhat to Dinah's surprise, he listened carefully to the story of the adventure in the Ladies' Glen and was not in the least incredulous.

"You always hated the place," said Dan, thoughtfully. "I can't remember that we ever talked about it—which is odd, because we talked about everything, didn't we?"

"Everything," nodded Dinah.

"You hated the place," he repeated. "You avoided it like poison. I just accepted the fact that we never went there. Children are queer, aren't they? I don't think I ever felt anything funny in the glen—I wonder if I would, now."

"You can try if you like," said Dinah. "As long as you don't ask me to go with you—"

Dan smiled and shook his head. "I'll take your word for it," he said.

"Has your hair ever stood on end?" Dinah wanted to know.

"Only once," replied Dan. "It was in Burma. I was out shooting and suddenly I came across a half-ruined temple in the middle of a thick wood and—well—I mean the hair at the back of my neck—"

"I know!"

"I ran for my life," admitted Dan with a rueful smile.

There was no need to say any more for they understood one another. Dan asked whether the children had been for any expeditions.

"You mean by themselves?" asked Dinah in surprise.

"Why not?" asked Dan. "We used to go all over the place by ourselves when we were their age."

"But we were different," objected Dinah. "We were much more independent. The children haven't had the same chance of going about and doing things by themselves. They're *babies* compared with us at the same age."

"In some ways they are—and in other ways they aren't," agreed Dan, thoughtfully.

So far Dinah had not mentioned her evening sails with Malcolm. She was leaving that until the end for she wanted to discuss it thoroughly. She had decided to take Dan's advice in the matter and if he thought she shouldn't go she would find some excuse for next Tuesday. She took a deep breath and began to explain, but she didn't get far with her explanations.

"Malcolm took you!" cried Dan in surprise. "Gosh, how decent of him!"

This reaction was so different from what Dinah had expected that she scarcely knew how to go on. It showed—to say the least of it—a distinct lack of understanding on the part of her fellow-Dee.

"He's like that," continued Dan. "I expect he thought you were feeling a bit lonely. He's tremendously thoughtful and kind."

"I think he likes taking me," said Dinah, trying to express her point of view.

"Oh, of course," agreed Dan. "He likes doing kind things. He's that sort of person."

She tried again. "Do you think I ought to go?"

"Of course you ought to go. I mean if Malcolm is decent enough to ask you it would be ungrateful not to go. Nannie doesn't mind looking after the children, does she?"

Dinah sighed. She decided it was hopeless. For the first time in her life Dan had failed her.

The Dees had arranged to go to the "movies" that night, so they had their supper early and started off. Dan had seen the picture before—it was *Arsenic and Old Lace*—but Dinah had not been to a picture house for years so it was new to her. They arrived in good time and found seats in the middle of a row; Malcolm and Miss Grover were sitting quite near and Mr. and Mrs. Monk were in front of them with Tapioca.

Dan nudged Dinah and whispered; "There are the two Miss Stevens, d'you remember them? They won't know us, of course."

"Goodness! They haven't changed a bit!" exclaimed Dinah.

The two old ladies had been patients of Dr. Bell and had always been extremely kind to the Dees, and the Dees had been fond of them and had often dropped in to see them. Dinah, looking back, remembered that the Misses Stevens had invariably produced a large tin of sugar biscuits and a jug of homemade lemonade; but she was almost certain that she and Dan would have called upon the old ladies just as frequently if no refreshment had been offered them.

Once the film had begun she had no time to think about the Misses Steven. She was enthralled—the humour was exactly the type of humour she appreciated. The two old ladies were admirable; they were so gentle and kind, so sympathetic that they could not bear the idea of any one being lonely and unhappy. A few grains of arsenic in their famous elderberry wine was an unfailing cure for loneliness.

The Dees were still laughing delightedly when they came out of the picture house and Dan was assuring his fellow-Dee that he had enjoyed the film more than the first time he had seen it. Malcolm and Miss Grover were standing in the porch waiting for Clarke to bring the car; the two Miss Stevens were there, but the Monk contingent had vanished.

"Hallo!" exclaimed Malcolm, smiling at Dan and Dinah. "I didn't see you before. How did you like it?"

"I loved it," said Dinah.

"Good fun, wasn't it?" said Malcolm, chuckling.

"I could see nothing *funny* in it," declared Miss Grover. "They were murderers. It's a disgusting film and quite pointless. It was dreadfully stuffy in the picture house, wasn't it?"

Malcolm seemed unmoved by these disagreeable remarks—perhaps he was used to them by this time. He seized the elder Miss Steven by the arm and said, "You know the Dees, don't you? Dr. Bell's horrible little children. Don't you remember them?"

"Of course!" cried Miss Steven. "Dear me, I was wondering why I seemed to know your faces! Clara—look! It's Dan and Dinah!"

"You haven't changed a bit," declared Dan and Dinah with one accord.

There was a babble of talk after that; the Misses Steven exclaiming that it seemed only yesterday, and how glad they were, and Dan and Dinah must come to tea with them—or supper if they could manage it—and Malcolm teasing them and saying they had never asked *him* to supper and he supposed they would sup off veal.

Eventually the party broke up. The Misses Steven were whirled away in Malcolm's car and the Dees walked home. Dinah had enjoyed her evening enormously—every moment of it.

"You should get in touch with people," said Dan. "If you're going to be here all winter it would be nice for you to know some of the old gang—the Cunninghams and the Craddocks, for instance—everybody remembers Father, so it wouldn't be difficult; and it's good for you to go about a bit."

Dinah agreed. She had been thinking the same thing herself.

25

NIGEL had been asked to go for a lunch-picnic with the Barringtons and although Dinah would rather have kept him at home she had no excuse to refuse the invitation. She would rather have kept him at home because she had a feeling that Mr. Barrington and Philip were not the right friends for Nigel. Mr. Barrington was a widower and evidently very well-off. Mrs. Monk had said he was an atheist. Dinah did not think for a moment that Mr. Barrington would endeavour to disturb the faith of her son but all the same she was reluctant to let Nigel go.

Mr. Barrington called for Nigel shortly after ten and Dinah went out to speak to them. It was a very large car and Mr. Barrington was seated at the wheel with Philip in the seat beside him. Nigel was tucked in between them very comfortably.

"Good of you to let him come," said Mr. Barrington. "We'll take great care of him. We'll probably be back about four."

"It's very kind of you to take him," Dinah said. There was no need to tell Nigel to be good and to behave nicely because Nigel always behaved nicely with strangers.

They drove off and Dinah watched them. She distrusted Mr. Barrington even more now that she had seen him. He had light blue eyes, very cold and expressionless. If Dinah had seen him before she would have been even more reluctant to accept the invitation for Nigel.

It was Sunday and Dinah would have liked to go to church and take the children, but the Andersons were going and she could not leave Margy alone with Flo, so they went out on to the sands as usual; Margy had her lesson and the other two played together, near by. They dug a little house for Polly and the dolls. Mark was the doctor, coming to visit the children and prescribing nauseous medicines for their complaints.

"This is Rose," explained Polly. "She's got mumps, I'm afraid. It's a *dreadful* nuisance because we're all going away to the sea-side to-morrow, Doctor Mark."

"*That* isn't mumps," declared Doctor Mark. "That's a tooth coming through. Here's a bottle of medicine for her. You must shake it well, because the sand—I mean the powder—sinks to the bottom. I'll help you give her a dose of it if you like."

There was a good deal of fun over the dose of medicine, for Rose's lips were tightly clenched and the medicine ran down her chin.

"*Isn't* she naughty!" said her mother with an elaborate sigh. "I can't think *why* she's so naughty. I've tried my best to bring her up properly—shall I spank her, Doctor Mark?"

"No," replied Doctor Mark. "Spanking wouldn't be any good. We'll put it on her chest as a poultice. That's the best thing."

Doctor Mark was an expert at poultices—he had had quite a number of them himself—so he folded his handkerchief and the mixture of sand and water was made into a very creditable poultice and placed upon Rose's chest.

"Will she be better to-morrow?" inquired her mother.

"No," said the doctor firmly. "I shouldn't think she'd be better for at least a week. I'll come back to-morrow and make another poultice for her. Perhaps the other children should have poultices too, just in case . . ."

They would not have played like this if Nigel had been here, thought Dinah as she smiled and listened to their prattle. Nigel was the stormy petrel of the family. She had known it before, of course, but today the fact was brought home to her more plainly than ever. She had tried all sorts of different ways of managing Nigel but none of them worked; Nigel needed a man to manage him. Perhaps Dan would be able to do something with him—or perhaps not. Dan had not been very helpful over that business with the shilling.

Presently Mark got tired of playing with Polly and went off to paddle with some other boys and Polly abandoned her little house and came and sat on the rug.

"When will Margy be old enough to play dolls?" she inquired.

Dinah did not know.

"She's too fat," said Polly, looking at Margy critically. "She's like a pudding, isn't she?"

"A very nice pudding," agreed Dinah smiling.

"But not very interesting," objected Polly.

"She is to me," declared Dinah. "You're all interesting to me."

Polly nodded thoughtfully. "I love you best," she said. "I love you frightfully. Mark is going to be a doctor when he grows up and Nigel is going to be a sailor, but I shall stay with you always, Mummy."

Dinah was touched at this sign of devotion on the part of her daughter. She knew it was nonsense of course because Polly was the sort of person who would marry early—Dinah was certain she would—but all the same it was very sweet of her to feel like that.

"I mean it—honestly," said Polly gravely. "I've thought about it a lot. I shall never leave you, Mummy, so you don't need to worry."

"But Polly, you'll get married someday and have children of your own. You'd like that, wouldn't you?" suggested Dinah.

"Oh, yes," agreed Polly. "Oh yes, of course I would, but I'll wait until you're dead."

It was rather a shock, really. So much of a shock that it was a moment or two before Dinah saw the funny side of it.

"Why are you laughing?" Polly inquired.

"It was an idea I had," replied Dinah. "As a matter of fact I think it would be nice to have grandchildren so if you feel like marrying before I'm dead I shan't object."

"Grandchildren! Oh yes, you'd be their grandmother, wouldn't you? Why haven't we got a grandmother?"

Dinah did not reply to that. Polly was far too young to be told of the breach between Gilbert and his parents. For the first time Dinah began to feel a little regretful about that breach and to wonder whether Gilbert's parents had really behaved so very badly, whether the fault was entirely on their side. She had believed Gilbert's version of the quarrel implicitly (his version of it had been fixed in her mind) for it was not until years after the quarrel that she had discovered how unreliable Gilbert was. Now that she thought of it, and could think of it dispassionately, she saw that Gilbert might have been partly to blame . . . but it was no use worrying about it now; the breach was too wide and of too old standing to be mended. Dinah did not even know if Gilbert's parents were still alive. He had always spoken of them as being old.

"Mummy, you aren't listening!" exclaimed Polly.

"No, I'm afraid I wasn't," admitted Dinah. "You'll have to tell me again."

It was a quiet, restful sort of day. Polly and Mark bathed in the afternoon and came in to tea with wet hair and glowing cheeks and enormous appetites. They had just sat down to tea in the dining-room when the Barrington's car drove up to the gate and Nigel got out.

"It's been lovely!" Dinah heard him say. "Thank you so much, Mr. Barrington."

"Swank!" exclaimed Mark, biting savagely into a slice of cake.

"But Mark, what nonsense!" exclaimed Dinah. "It's the right thing to say. I've told you so over and over again."

"I know," said Mark uncomfortably.

"We know but we can't do it," explained Polly. "Nigel *likes* doing it, but Mark and I just *can't*—I don't know why."

"It sort of sticks and won't come out," added Mark.

Dinah could not blame them—not really—for she remembered suddenly and quite distinctly that she and Dan had been afflicted with the same Curious inhibition. They had known quite well that the correct procedure on leaving a party was to thank your hostess for a pleasant time, but the words stuck in their throats and wouldn't come out, just as Mark had said. She remembered that she and Dan used to toss before they went out to tea to determine which of them should have the task . . . and on more than one occasion they had shirked it altogether and crept away like thieves in the night to avoid thanking their hostess for her entertainment. It wasn't ingratitude, thought Dinah, revolving the matter in her mind. It wasn't because we hadn't enjoyed ourselves . . . what was it, then?

By this time Nigel had run up the path and was standing in the doorway smiling at them.

"You had a lovely time?" asked Dinah.

"Grand!" declared Nigel. "Mr. Barrington's car goes like smoke. He let me hold the steering-wheel. We went for miles along the Great North Road and then we came back and had our lunch at Tantallon Castle. We had ham sandwiches with real ham inside them and hard-boiled eggs and little jellies in paper cups. Don't you wish you had been there, Mark?"

"No," said Mark, frowning.

"You do," declared Nigel. "Polly wishes she had been there, too. You both wish you had been there."

"Come and have tea and tell us all about it," said Dinah. Nigel sat down and helped himself to bread and butter. He said, "Mr. Barrington couldn't believe I was only six. He's awfully nice. He makes funny jokes and watches you laughing and doesn't even *smile*. He gives Philip half-a-crown every week for pocket-money . . . and Philip goes to a boarding-school and plays cricket. Could I go to boarding-school, Mummy?"

"Four children can't go to boarding-school," said Polly hastily. "There isn't enough money."

"But perhaps I could go," said Nigel hopefully. "I mean Mr. Barrington said I *ought* to go. It's different for Polly and Mark, isn't it?"

"Why is it different?" asked Dinah.

"Because," said Nigel. "Well, because . . ."

"Because you're you," suggested Dinah. "That isn't a reason, Nigel. That's just selfish."

"I don't want to go to boarding-school," said Mark. "I'd rather stay at home and so would Polly."

"Well, we'll see," said Dinah doubtfully. Her idea had been that it was unfair to send one of the boys to boarding-school and not the other, but perhaps it would be the best thing for every one if she could manage to send Nigel away from home. Nigel would benefit from the discipline and the others would be left in peace. Was she being selfish to consider it? Was she trying to shirk her job?

"I'd like to go to Philip's school," continued Nigel, who seemed to think the thing was settled. "It's near his home and Mr. Barrington comes over on Sundays and takes him out. Philip is going to Eton when he's old enough, he's going to be a scientist like his father—"

"You can't go until you're eight," said Dinah, "And perhaps by that time you'll have changed your mind. Eton is absolutely out of the question, I'm afraid."

Fortunately Nigel did not seem to mind, he was eating ravenously and talking at the same time. "Philip and I climbed right up to the very top of the castle," he was saying. "It was a bit difficult because the huge walls were all crumbly, but it was tremendous fun. You could see for miles and miles over the sea. There was an enormous battleship coming up the firth and we looked at it through Mr. Barrington's field-glasses."

"We saw it," said Mark. "Polly and I saw it."

"But I saw it *much* better," declared Nigel. "I saw it through field-glasses. You haven't ever seen a battleship through field-glasses, Mark."

"I don't want to," replied Mark. "I saw it all right with ray eyes."

"It came quite close in," continued Nigel, helping himself to a slice of cake. "We saw the sailors with their blue collars—some of the sailors waved to us. They didn't wave to you, did they?"

"We bathed," said Polly.

"Oh, bathing!" said Nigel scornfully. "You can bathe any day. You can't go for a drive in a lovely car every day."

"We'll go upstairs and play a game, shall we?" said Dinah, who saw that the other two were becoming very cross . . . to tell the truth she was feeling cross herself and had a sudden and almost uncontrollable desire to shake Nigel. She would have liked to hire a car and go for a picnic to the castle, it was a favourite haunt of the Dees, but to hire a car for a whole afternoon would be far too expensive so she had abandoned the idea. Another matter which was worrying her was Nigel's assertion that the battleship had come "close in" and the sailors had waved. It made a good story but she was almost certain it was untrue. Why should it have approached that wild and rocky coast without any object except, presumably, to greet Philip and Nigel on the castle battlements?

"Mr. Barrington has asked me to go again," continued Nigel as they all trooped upstairs. "Mr. Barrington liked me. He asked what my name was and when I told him he said I was a sophisticated young Savage."

"Goodness, what does that mean?" asked Polly in surprise.

"I asked Philip," admitted Nigel, "and Philip said it meant I knew a lot and had nice manners—not like a savage at all. It was a joke of course," explained Nigel smugly. "That's the sort of joke Mr. Barrington makes."

"I think he's a *horrid* man," said Polly firmly. "Patrick thinks he's horrid, too . . . and I'm very glad I didn't go with you to that horrid old castle, so there."

"Get out the Ludo, Mark," said Dinah hastily. Ludo was the game of the moment and the little Savages played it with enthrallment on every possible occasion.

"Philip plays chess," remarked Nigel as he drew his chair up to the table. "He's eleven, of course, but I expect I could learn. It's my turn to have red . . ."

26

DINAH had finished her supper and was about to go upstairs when the front-door bell rang. She opened the door and found Clarke standing on the doorstep with a basket in one hand and a large bouquet of sweet peas in the other.

"Mr. Malcolm's compliments," said Clarke, "and he thought you might like some flowers and vegetables."

"How lovely!" exclaimed Dinah. "Will you thank him—or wait a moment while I write a note."

"He's in the car," said Clarke.

Dinah ran down the path to thank him, remembering as she did so that this was the night she had refused to go for a sail. Would he think it odd to find her here—obviously free from any engagement? But if Malcolm remembered and thought it odd he showed no signs of it. He seemed just as usual.

"We're going over to Whittington," Malcolm said. "I was wondering if you'd like to come. It will be a nice run and the country is looking so beautiful—we shan't be more than an hour."

Dinah was tempted. Here was her chance to see the country. It seemed a queer coincidence that her chance had come to-night.

"Do come," added Malcolm.

"I'd love to come," said Dinah.

She put on her coat and got in beside Malcolm, who was sitting in the back seat, and soon they were climbing the steep hill and bowling along the road to Whittington. It was beautiful country and Dinah had not seen it for years. She feasted her eyes upon each well-remembered landmark. There were fine trees, and hedges gay with dog roses, there were huge fields with long-stalked, heavy-eared corn. Here and there were big farms, tidy and prosperous, with barns and cattle byres . . . and always in the distance was the silvery-blue gleam of the sea.

"I love it," Dinah said with a little sigh. "Not only because it is beautiful but because it is in my bones. You can never love any place as much as the place where you spent your childhood. I know it all so well. Dan and I used to bicycle a lot, and sometimes if Father happened to be going to an outlying farm he took us with him. We loved that."

"I've been all over the world but I've never seen country that suited me better," said Malcolm gravely. "I love to see mountains and rivers and lochs, I like travelling in foreign lands, but give me this to come home to. It fits me like a well-made suit. I don't want to leave it."

"Why should you?"

"Well, the fact is I've been talking to my stepmother and trying to find out whether she's really thinking of leaving Abbot's End. It's a bit difficult because she won't say definitely one way or the other; she keeps on saying what do I want to do. Supposing she decides to go to Edinburgh could Clarke and I carry on at Abbot's End alone? That's the question."

Dinah was silent.

"You see," said Malcolm, turning his head and smiling at her ruefully. "It wouldn't be easy, would it? The fact is I don't know what to do."

"We could manage," declared Clarke, breaking into the conversation. "We'd be all right at Abbot's End. I could always get a woman in to do a bit of cleaning. Don't you worry about that, Mr. Malcolm."

"Well, we'll see," said Malcolm. "I certainly don't want to leave Abbot's End while the fine weather lasts."

"I'm glad," said Dinah impulsively.

"Are you, Dinah?" he asked. "Well, that settles it."

There was a little silence. It was the first time a silence between them had seemed uncomfortable. "I'm going to see a man called Brett," said Malcolm at last. "He's been with us for years but now he's got a touch of arthritis in his hip and he isn't fit to come into Edinburgh every day. He's quite fit for his work and enjoys it, but the travelling bothers him. We've got some little houses for our workers and one of them is to be vacant next month, so I offered it to Brett and he was delighted. Unfortunately his old mother, who lives with him, refuses to leave Whittington. That's the problem."

"But she must," said Dinah after a moment's thought.

"She's old," explained Malcolm. "She must be about eighty—Brett isn't a chicken himself—and she's lived in Whittington all her life. As far as I can make out she's a bit childish. Brett has got the offer of a job at Whittington but it doesn't appeal to him. He wants to stay with us."

"Difficult!" said Dinah thoughtfully.

"Yes, isn't it? I don't know what to do about Brett. He thinks I might be able to persuade her to move. That's why I'm going."

"But you won't succeed unless you have confidence in your persuasive powers," declared Dinah, smiling.

"Then it's hopeless," replied Malcolm, returning the smile.

They had reached Whittington by this time. It was an old-fashioned market town with cobbled streets and solid, grey stone buildings. Dinah remembered coming here with Dan; she remembered having tea at a little café in a side street. They had ordered bacon and eggs and cake and raspberry jam. It seemed queer to think of those days when you could have such food (as much as you could eat) and when people were only too pleased to serve you.

Clarke drove slowly through the town and pulled up at a tiny cottage with sunflowers in the garden. "This is it," he said.

Malcolm got out and walked up the path, and Clarke, having shut the gate behind him, got into his own seat and began to talk. Dinah had always thought of Clarke as a silent person. He had seemed to her an automaton—scarcely human—but this evening her opinion was completely changed. Perhaps Clarke had weighed her up and was ready to accept her; Dinah had a feeling that this must be the explanation of his change of attitude.

"Brett is lucky," said Clarke. "Whatever happens he doesn't need to worry with Mr. Malcolm behind him. That's freedom from fear."

"Yes," agreed Dinah, interested. "I suppose it *is* one kind of freedom from fear, but it isn't what the charter intended. The Government—"

"No Government on earth can give you freedom from fear," said Clarke with conviction. "Only people like Mr. Malcolm can give you that. When you're ill or in trouble you don't want the Government poking its nose in; you want a friend, a human being who takes the trouble to go and see you and find out what's the matter. I know, because that's what happened to me. It's human beings that count," said Clarke nodding. "And human beings are all different. That's why I think nationalisation is wrong. I think things should be more spread out instead of more centralised."

"I don't quite understand," admitted Dinah.

"Well, if I was the Government I'd make firms and employers look after their own people—if they didn't do it already—instead of trying to run it all from a central office that doesn't know the people it's trying to help. It stands to reason different people need different kinds of help."

"Perhaps some people would dislike that. They might feel it was charity."

"It wouldn't be—not any more than it is now," declared Clarke. "What's unemployment pay but charity? Old Age Pensions are charity but I've never heard of any one refusing them. My idea is exactly the same, only instead of being run by an office in London—or wherever it is—it would be run by your own firm, by somebody who knew you and was humanly interested in your problems. Oh, I dare say there are snags. I mean I don't pretend to have the brains to make plans, but I often think about things."

"What happened to you?" asked Dinah. "You said 'that's what happened to me.'"

"Quite a lot happened to me," replied Clarke, smiling at her. "I went into Armstrong's as a clerk when I was eighteen (it was Sir Andrew who was the boss in those days) and when I was twenty I got married. She was older than me, and—well, she wasn't a good wife. I wouldn't like to tell you," said Clarke with some embarrassment. "I really couldn't tell you what sort of a girl she was. She spent all our money on clothes and drink and we were always in debt and behind with the rent. I was just a kid, as you might say, and I couldn't do anything with her. She wouldn't take any notice of what I said. I was just about the end of my tether—couldn't eat or sleep and worried silly wondering what to do. Then, to make matters worse, I got ill and couldn't go to my work and the doctor said it was a nervous break-down. She looked after me for a bit, complaining all the time about what a nuisance I was, and then she packed up and went off with another fellow, and that was that. I'd known about the other fellow of course but—well, there was nothing I could do. It seemed just about the end of everything. I was ill and in debt—we owed money all round—I couldn't see a bright spot anywhere. Then Mr. Malcolm came to see me and before I knew where I was I'd told him all about it . . . and he just took hold and straightened it out. He took me to his own lawyer and I got a divorce so that she wouldn't be able to come down on me for any more money, and he cleared off all the debts and let me pay so much every week out of my wages; and when I was a bit better he took me off to America. He was going to America on business, you see, and he took me along to do a bit of typing and that. I wasn't much use to him at first but I soon perked up and set to and learnt to be useful. I didn't want to go back to the works, I wanted to stay with Mr. Malcolm. That was natural, wasn't it?"

Dinah thought it was.

"But I had to learn, of course," continued Clarke. "Wherever I went I learnt things. Well, to make a long story short I've been with Mr. Malcolm ever since and I shan't ever leave him—not unless I get the boot." He looked at her and smiled. "I'm not afraid of that either," he added.

"I don't think you need be," Dinah declared. "He was good to you but you're paying him back in full measure. He couldn't do without you now. You said you learnt things. How did you learn?"

"Using my eyes," replied Clarke promptly. "Asking people. There was a chauffeur at one of the houses we stayed at in America and he taught me about cars; and I went to a tailor in London and got them to show me how to look after clothes—folding and pressing and that. I could always cook; I've got a taste for cooking and I like well-cooked food myself. When Mr. Malcolm was ill I watched the nurses and got tips from them: how to lift him and that. I learnt to wait at table from a table-maid that Lady Armstrong had, and she showed me the right way to clean the silver, too. She was a bit of a tartar but she knew her job. You see, I like doing things properly," explained Clarke. "It doesn't matter what you do as long as you do it well."

"If a thing is worth doing it's worth doing well," suggested Dinah.

"No, that's different," said Clarke looking thoughtful. "I think if you do it well it's worth doing, no matter what it is."

Malcolm had come out of the house unperceived and had overheard the last few sentences. "Even painting spots on rocking-horses!" said Malcolm gaily. "Even making wooden pips for raspberry jam!

Well, if you two have quite finished philosophising I'll get in and we'll hit the trail. I can do no good here, that's certain."

"No good?" asked Dinah as Malcolm got in and they drove off.

"No good at all. She's one of the most unpleasant old ladies it has ever been my misfortune to meet." He laughed and added: "Arsenic is the only solution as far as I can see. A spot of arsenic in elderberry wine would settle it all beautifully, of course."

Dinah smiled. "But even without the elderberry wine she can't live for ever."

"Oh, I shall keep my eye on Brett," Malcolm assured her. "Brett knows that."

The expedition had not taken long and it was still quite light when they drove up to the gate of Craigie Lodge. Dinah had enjoyed her drive and said so.

"You aren't forgetting to-morrow," inquired Malcolm anxiously. "You said Tuesday, didn't you?"

"I thought perhaps this was instead of to-morrow—"

"Oh no!" cried Malcolm. "At least—if you would like it. Perhaps you would rather go to the pictures?"

Dinah assured him that she would much rather go for a sail.

"Weather permitting of course," said Malcolm, smiling at her.

27

TUESDAY morning was misty but soon a breeze sprang up and the mist was blown away. Dinah was busy helping Nannie to mix a cake and when it was ready and put into the oven she took Margy and went out. She saw Nigel, afar off, playing with Philip, but there was no sign of the other two. Somehow Dinah felt a trifle uneasy . . . but that was silly of course. What could happen to them here? She sat down and began to darn some socks and tried to entertain Margy as she worked.

At dinner-time there was still no sign of Polly and Mark, and what was even more alarming she discovered their pails and spades hidden behind a bush at the gate.

"Where can they have gone?" she exclaimed.

"To the town, most likely." said Nannie. "Polly had six-pence in her purse, so they'll have gone to Miss Douglas to spend it. They'll have forgotten the time. You and Dan were often late for meals and I used to tear my hair out by the roots—very nearly—but you always turned up safe and sound. Come away in and have your dinner, Dinah. I'll keep theirs hot."

Dinah had her dinner and fed Margy but when two o'clock came and there was still no sign of the children she began to get frightened. She went out and gazed up and down the sands . . . where were they? What on earth could have happened?

"Don't worry," said Nannie, following her out. "There's two of them. What could happen to them in Seatown?"

Dinah was almost sick with anxiety. She felt sure they had been drowned.

Earlier that morning Polly and Mark had come out as usual with their spades and pails but instead of following Nigel on to the sands they lingered at the gate.

"Mark," said Polly. "Do you want to see the castle?"

"No," said Mark firmly.

"I do," said Polly. "I want to see it awfully much. I'll take you if you like."

"How?" inquired Mark.

"In the bus of course. There's a bus that goes from the harbour. Flo told me. Flo has been often—it doesn't take long."

"Mummy wouldn't let us."

"She wouldn't mind. She likes us to be independent. You know she does."

"But Polly—"

"The Dees used to go to all sorts of places by themselves."

"Yes, but—"

"Don't you *want* to come?"

Mark wanted to come, but he was still a little doubtful.

"It won't take long," continued Polly. "We'll be back in time for dinner and then we'll tell them about it. We'll ask them to guess where we've been."

Mark smiled. It would be fun to see Nigel's face when they told him. It would be a tremendous score. He wavered.

"They'll be so surprised," urged Polly. "They'll hardly *believe* it. Nigel went with the Barringtons but we'll go by ourselves. It will be much more fun, Mark."

"An adventure," suggested Mark.

"A terrific adventure," agreed Polly. "Of course if you don't want to come . . ."

"I *do* want to come," said Mark firmly.

They hid their pails and spades behind a bush and set off for the harbour. The bus was just starting when they got there but it waited for them and they climbed in and sat down, side by side, on the back seat. They were silent, looking about . . . it was certainly an adventure. When the conductor came to collect the fares Polly took sixpence out of her purse and handed it to him.

"Two tickets, please," she said. "We want to go to the castle."

"It's sixpence each," said the conductor.

"But that's all I've got," exclaimed Polly in dismay.

There was an old farmer sitting opposite to them, he had a round, red face and little side-whiskers. He took sixpence out of his pocket and put it into the conductor's hand.

"Oh. thank you!" cried Polly, smiling at him. "Are you sure you can spare it?"

"It'll put me back a bit." declared the old farmer gravely. "But I'll get through somehow."

The conductor laughed.

"Aye, ye can laugh," said the farmer.

"It's very kind of you," said Polly earnestly. "You see my brother and I want to go to the castle very, very much."

The farmer nodded and winked. Then he folded his hands across his middle and shut his eyes.

"He's nice, isn't he?" whispered Polly.

"He's like Santa Claus," said Mark.

Polly gazed at him. It was quite true. He hadn't a white beard of course but in every other particular he was exactly like the picture of Santa Claus in the nursery at Craigie Lodge. Perhaps he was Santa Claus—who could tell?

The bus rumbled through the town and up the hill. It stopped several times and people got in.

"It's a long way, isn't it?" said Mark suddenly.

Polly nodded. She had expected to arrive at the castle in a few minutes. Perhaps they shouldn't have come; perhaps they should have told Mummy. Her heart began to beat uncomfortably fast, she wished they were safely at home.

"No, I don't," said Polly firmly.

"What?" asked Mark.

"Nothing," said Polly hastily. "I mean it's lovely, isn't it? Are you enjoying it, Mark? I'm sure the bus is going just as fast as Mr. Barrington's silly old car."

"Faster," said Mark with conviction.

They pulled up with a jerk and the old farmer opened his eyes and rose. He winked at Polly again. "Next stop," he said hoarsely as he got out.

"Next stop," said Polly to Mark. "He means next stop is the castle. I *do* think he's nice."

Several people got out at the next stop. There was a big white farm-house at the corner and a rutty lane which led across a moor. Beyond the moor was the old castle, standing up, outlined against the bright blue sky. The children were so thrilled at the sight that they ran down the rutty track and arrived breathless before the entrance.

"There it is!" exclaimed Polly with the air of a conjurer who has produced a very large rabbit out of a very small hat.

"*That's* Tantallon Castle."

"It's huge," said Mark in awed tones.

"Of course," agreed Polly. "It had to be huge because of all the people who lived there. Hundreds of people, Mummy said . . . it looks awfully sad, doesn't it?" added Polly with a sigh.

The castle stood on the edge of the cliffs which dropped straight down to the rocks and the sea below. The walls were enormously thick and, although they were crumbling, the castle retained a proud air—an air of ruined majesty, of solitary grandeur. As the children stood there a jackdaw flew out through one of the gaping windows and, perching upon a rock quite near them, gave a loud caw. It was as if he, the sole inhabitant of Tantallon, were voicing his displeasure at the invasion of his solitude.

"Come on," said Mark going forward.

Polly followed him and they went in together through the open door.

There was no roof, of course. You looked up and far above your head you saw the jagged edges of the massive walls outlined against the sky. These walls enclosed a courtyard, carpeted with smooth green turf, and in the middle of the courtyard was the well. Polly and Mark leaned upon the stone wall and looked down; the sides of the well were of solid black rock and far below there was a faint glimmer of water, like a winking eye. When they had finished looking at the well they turned and looked round the courtyard.

"This is where the Earl of Douglas stood," said Polly in a hushed voice. "He stood here, wrapped in his cloak, and wouldn't shake hands with Marmion. This was where the messengers came galloping in at all hours of the day with news about the English army . . ."

"Where is the Chapel?" asked Mark. "The Chapel where Ralph was made a Knight."

The Chapel was not to be found for all the buildings on the seaward side had vanished, all except the dungeon which was welded firmly into the solid rock.

"This is where they'd have put Marmion if he hadn't escaped," said Mark looking round the dungeon and shuddering.

"It would have served him right," observed Polly vindictively.

"No," said Mark. "I mean he was brave. It was better for him to be killed in the battle. I'd rather be killed in a battle than be shut up here."

The dungeon was a dank, gloomy place. The huge iron rings to which the Douglas had chained his prisoners were still embedded in the rocky walls. There was one small window with rusted iron bars, it looked out on to the sea. The Bass Rock with its sheer sides, whitened with the droppings of thousands of sea-birds was less than two miles away.

"I wish there was a ship," said Mark suddenly.

"There's one far out," said Polly.

"But it isn't a battleship," said Mark.

"Perhaps Nigel didn't see the dungeon," suggested Polly comfortingly.

Mark sighed. He was pretty certain Nigel had seen the dungeon.

They climbed up to the battlements by a stone stair, which wound round and round inside a tower, and found themselves upon a platform. There was a parapet upon which the explorers could lean.

"This was where Clare came," said Polly.

"No," said Mark. "This was where the sentries kept watch. It was the seaward side that was deserted; *that* was where Clare walked about. The seaward side has all gone now."

"There was a fall of cliff," said a voice behind them.

Polly and Mark swung round and saw that a lady and three girls had come up the stairs behind them. The lady was tall and thin, she had a book in her hand; the three girls were wearing school uniforms.

"Perhaps you would like to hear about the ruin," said the lady, looking at Polly as she spoke. "It is very interesting to know about places that you see. This castle was the residence of the Douglas family, it was built before 1375. The principal rooms were situated in the Mid Tower on the wall, and through its base is the castle entrance which was extended outwards in a fore-work or barbican. There were fine stairways with chambers in the heart of the main wall. Other lodgings occupied the remaining sides overlooking the sea but these have now disappeared owing to a fall of the cliff upon which they stood. The well was sunk with great labour so that in the event of a siege the garrison could depend upon a constant supply of pure water within the fortress walls. The castle was deemed impregnable, and was so before the advent of heavy cannon, it held out against James the Fifth in the sixteenth century but General Monk succeeded in destroying it with cannon in 1651."

The lady paused and looked at Polly.

"I'm afraid I don't understand all that," said Polly shaking her head. "It isn't as interesting as Marmion, is it?"

"Marmion?" asked the lady in surprise.

"Marmion makes you see it," explained Mark. "It tells you about the people who lived here and what they did. It tells you what they looked like. The Earl was tall and strong, his sword was so big that nobody else could use it, and he was so proud that he wouldn't shake hands with Marmion because Marmion was wicked and cruel."

"So they quarrelled," said Polly eagerly. "And the Earl ordered his soldiers to let down the portcullis—but Marmion spurred his horse over the drawbridge and escaped—and the portcullis fell with a crash and cut off the plume in his helmet."

"You should read about it," said Mark kindly. "You should have read it *first*, before you came, I mean. It makes it so much more interesting."

"*Marmion,*" said Polly nodding at the lady. "*Marmion,* by Sir Walter Scott."

The lady did not take this information in good part. She muttered something under her breath and walked along to the other end of the wall. The three girls looked at one another and giggled as they followed her.

"Silly, aren't they?" said Polly turning and leaning her elbows on the parapet.

"General Monk destroyed it," said Mark, who had managed to glean this piece of information from the description he had heard. "How awful, Polly! I mean it must have been dreadfully sad for the Douglas to see his home being battered to bits."

Polly nodded. She could understand the feelings of the Douglas because she had seen quite a number of homes battered to bits. She had seen houses which had been cut in half by bombs, rooms with only two walls left standing and pictures hanging on these tottering walls, and beds and chairs and cupboards and dressing-tables exposed to the public eye.

Quite a number of houses at Nettleham had been rent asunder and others had been reduced to heaps of untidy rubble . . . Yes, Polly could understand only too well.

"It would be nice if we could see it as it was," continued Mark, gazing round. "The rooms all furnished with tapestries on the walls, and soldiers marching up and down and all the men busy, making armour and bows and arrows . . . and the horses."

"I wonder where the kitchen was," said Polly. "I wonder what they had for dinner."

There was a moment's pause and then Mark said, "Polly, I'm hungry."

"You *can't* be!" she exclaimed, looking at him in dismay. "We've only just *come.* It's hours and hours until dinner-time."

"I think it's dinner-time *now,*" declared Mark.

Polly's heart sank. Supposing it really was dinner-time! What would Mummy think when they didn't come in from the sands? She would go and look for them and they wouldn't be there.

Mark had started down the winding stair and Polly followed him. She said, "It's all right, you know. The Dees were *often* late for dinner—and it can't be *very* late because I'm not a bit hungry."

"I am."

"But you can't be, all of a sudden like that."

"I am," he repeated. "It wasn't until you said what did they have for dinner and then I *was*, all of a sudden."

They ran down the corkscrew stairs and through the courtyard and out at the gate. They ran down the rutty track and did not pause until they reached the main road. Somehow or other Polly had been certain that the bus would be there, waiting for them, but there was no bus in sight.

"I suppose it will come soon," said Mark breathlessly.

"Of course it will," declared Polly. "You know what buses are. If you miss one you have to wait ten minutes for the next."

"Yes, at Nettleham," agreed Mark. "But perhaps it's different here."

Polly did not reply. She was beginning to have a dreadful feeling that Mark was right. The road looked so deserted. The whole land seemed deserted; there was not a creature to be seen.

"I mean," said Mark in a voice that trembled a little. "I mean there were such a lot of people in Nettleham that there had to be a lot of buses."

"It can't be terribly long," said Polly without conviction. "And anyhow we've seen the castle, Mark. It was lovely, wasn't it?"

Mark did not reply, and Polly saw two large tears roll down his checks.

"Don't be a baby," she said crossly.

"I'm not."

"You are. Only babies cry when they're hungry."

"It's because of Mummy," he explained, taking out his handkerchief and blowing his nose. "I should think Mummy will *die*."

Polly could find no answer to this frightful prophecy. They sat down on a low wall and waited. Nobody came. Nothing passed.

"We might pray," said Polly after a long silence.

"I've prayed already," said Mark.

They were still sitting on the wall when they heard the sound of a motor in the distance and presently a farm-tractor came down the road with a man driving it. He passed them and then stopped and looked back.

"Are ye waitin' on the bus?" he shouted. "The bus has gone. There's no anither for twa 'oors."

Polly ran after him. "Please, what can we do?" she cried.

"What can ye do?"

"We *must* get home," explained Polly in a trembling voice. "Mummy will be wondering where we are. It's my fault—I brought Mark to see the castle."

"That's a problem," said the man, shaking his head.

"It's frightful! You see I never thought—I mean there were always lots of buses at Nettleham. You see don't you?"

"Aye, but what can I do?"

"Please do something!" said Polly, dissolving into tears. "Please, *please* do something."

"Is it to Seatown?" asked the man.

Polly nodded.

"Well, if it's to Seatown there's the milk lorry. It'll be coming any minute noo—but maybe you'd not like the milk lorry?"

"We'd like anything that took us home," Polly declared.

Dinah had been along to the harbour to see if by any chance the children were there; she was hastening home with the intention of telephoning to the police when she saw a large milk lorry drive up to the gate of Craigie Lodge. She ran after it and arrived at the gate just in time to receive Mark who hurled himself out of the lorry into her arms.

"You're not dead!" he cried, hugging her fiercely.

Dinah was too breathless to reply.

"They couldn't help it," explained the lorryman, who had learnt the ins and outs of the matter during the drive home and was anxious to smooth the path for his passengers.

"We couldn't—honestly," declared Polly earnestly. "We'd have been much later if it hadn't been for Mr. Duncan. In fact if it hadn't been for him we wouldn't have got home at all because I quite forgot I hadn't any more money, you see, and the bus wouldn't have brought us without money—"

"Unless we'd met Santa Claus again," put in Mark. Dinah was completely bewildered. She began to wonder if the children had gone mad—or perhaps she, herself, had gone mad with the strain.

"Anybody might lose a bus," said Mr. Duncan seriously. "I've lost buses myself—not knowing the time. It's against rules to take passengers in the lorry but there's occasions when rules are all the better of being broken."

"But I don't understand!" exclaimed Dinah. "Where were you? What on earth were you doing? D'you know it's nearly three o'clock?"

"We saw the castle," said Mark.

"We meant to be back in lots of time for dinner," said Polly. "Honestly we did; but we forgot the time until Mark felt hungry and then it was too late."

Dinah began to understand (she was used to picking up little bits of information and putting them together). She thanked Mr. Duncan and endeavoured to reward him suitably for his kindness, but Mr. Duncan refused to accept a reward.

"I've two of my own," he said. "It's been a pleasure . . . and you won't be too hard on them, will you? They were in an awful way when they found they were going to be late."

Mr. Duncan drove off and Dinah shepherded the children into the house and sat with them while they ate their dinner.

"If you had only told me you were going!" Dinah said. "I've been terribly worried about you. I looked for you everywhere—"

"You had better spank me," said Polly in a quavering voice. "It was all my fault. Mark never thought of going."

Dinah looked at Mark, but instead of agreeing that the woman had tempted him he heaved a deep sigh and said: "You had better spank us both."

"I shan't spank either of you," declared Dinah, hiding an involuntary smile. "It was a silly thing to do but it wasn't exactly naughty. The only thing I can't understand is why you went without telling me."

Polly hesitated and then she said, "Nigel saw the castle and I wanted to see it too; and I thought it would be fun to make you and Nigel guess where we'd been. You'd never have guessed, would you?"

"The Dees went to places all by themselves," added Mark.

Dinah nodded. The reasons were quite sound.

Once the wanderers had got some food inside them their spirits improved. All was well, their mother was neither dead nor angry, they had seen Tantallon Castle and seen it thoroughly all by themselves. They began to talk about their adventures and to describe all they had seen.

" . . . And there was a lady with three girls," said Polly. "She had a book about it, telling you when it was built and all that. She said it was interesting to know about places, so she read it out to us."

"But it was dull and difficult," put in Mark.

"Not very interesting," Polly agreed.

"So then," said Mark. "So then we told her she ought to read *Marmion*."

"And what did she say to that?" Dinah inquired.

"Nothing," replied Polly. "She just gave a sort of mutter and went away."

"It was more a kind of snort that she gave," said Mark gravely.

Dinah laughed. She wished she had been there.

28

DINAH felt so shattered by the anxiety she had experienced that she had decided to ring up Malcolm and cancel the sail, but by the time she had put the children to bed she had recovered, and the evening was so fine that it seemed a pity not to go. Nannie looked at her a little strangely when she went into the kitchen to announce her plans—or so Dinah thought.

"It will do me good," said Dinah. "It's better for me to go out than to sit at home and think about what might have happened to them."

"M'ph'm," said Nannie doubtfully.

"I shan't be late," added Dinah, hesitating at the door.

Nannie made no comment. She merely remarked that she would leave a glass of milk and some biscuits on the kitchen table as usual.

The tide was out, of course, and when Dinah arrived at the harbour the boats and skiffs and pinnaces were lying on a bed of greenish-black mud. There is nothing so dejected as a boat aground and Dinah cast a compassionate glance towards them as she skirted the harbour and made for the pier according to Ben's directions.

The pier was quite short. It was a wooden platform supported by heavy wooden beams jutting out from the rocks into deep water. There was a concrete foundation for the beams and this was bare to-night, bare of water but covered with seaweed and barnacles, the beams had barnacles round their ankles which gave them a monstrous, unhealthy appearance. There was no doubt about it the harbour was a very much nicer place when the tide was in.

As Dinah approached the pier she saw Malcolm and Ben standing on the wooden platform with another man, and she waited for a few moments to see what they would do. She wondered whether the third man was coming with them for the sail.

While she was still hesitating Ben stooped and taking Malcolm on his back he began to climb down the ladder to the concrete foundation of the pier. The brown, snub-nosed boat was rocking there, tied to an iron ring; a moment later Malcolm had been handed into the boat and was settling himself in his usual position.

The third man, having satisfied himself that all was well, turned and came back over the rocks towards Dinah. It was Clarke.

Clarke greeted her with a friendly smile. "Mr. Malcolm's all right," he said. "I was worried about that ladder but Ben managed it nicely. He's a fine old chap, isn't he? Mr. Malcolm's leg is bothering him but it always does him good to have a sail."

"It's a lovely evening for a sail," Dinah said.

Having chatted to Clarke for a few moments Dinah went forward and met Ben coming up the ladder.

"Guid evening!" said Ben. "I'll carry ye doon; it'll save ye getting yer feet wet on the stanes."

"No, no, I can easily climb down myself," declared Dinah.

"Wait, noo," said Ben, putting his hand on her arm. "We'll need tae wait a wee meenit, here's the Pilot."

The pilot boat with its red and white flag was coming in to the pier and they had to wait until it had picked up the Pilot and put off again. Dinah looked with interest at the Pilot (a fine figure of a man in his navy-blue uniform and peaked cap) for the Dees had always loved the Pilot and at one time Dan had decided that a Pilot's life was the life for him. What better job could there be than to live at Seatown and navigate the big ships which went up the Firth to Leith with their varied cargoes.

While they waited Ben talked. "I could easily carry ye doon," said Ben persuasively. "It's naething tae me—I'm reel guid at carrying folks. When Clarke wis away his holidays I went up tae Abbot's End ilka day tae carry Mister Mawlcolm oot tae the shelter in the gairden. That wis before he wis able tae walk, ye ken. He's reel nippy on his leg noo, but Clarke wis a wee thing anxious aboot the ladder. I'm thinking Mister Mawlcolm's feeling his leg these days, he's no jist quite sae joco as usual. Mind you, he's had an awfu' lot o' trouble wi' yon leg o' his. Fower oaperations he's had. It's a wonder tae me hoo he bears it."

"Four operations!" echoed Dinah in horrified tones.

"Umphm," said Ben nodding gravely.

Dinah was so sorry for Malcolm that, when at last the pilot boat moved off and she was able to climb down the ladder and embark, she was especially nice to Malcolm, especially gay and cheerful and kind . . . and Malcolm, responding to her mood though unaware of its source, was gay and cheerful too. They bandied jokes and teased one another and laughed.

Malcolm informed her that the sharp knife had cut him loose and he was a free man. He made a funny story of it, a story in keeping with the jocund mood of the evening. "What a fool I was," said Malcolm, chuckling. "There was I wondering how on earth I was going to get rid of her ladyship and all the time her ladyship was planning her escape. You were right, Dinah, the plan to go to Edinburgh has been on the *tapis* for quite a long time. In fact it appears that a flat has been found, examined and approved. I can't think why she was not open about it, but that's her nature, I suppose."

"And you're staying on here?"

"Yes, Clarke and I are staying on. He has managed to get a woman who will come in every day so we shall be very comfortable—we shall be as happy as kings. All this has taken some arranging and was not accomplished without unpleasantness. I'm being terribly indiscreet but I've told you so much about it that you may as well know *all*."

"But if she wanted to go—"

"She wanted me to go too," explained Malcolm. "That was the rock upon which the whole scheme was very nearly wrecked. When she found I intended to stay on here alone with Clarke she was very angry. We had words over it," said Malcolm smiling. "Quite a lot of words. When she discovered that no persuasions would avail she decided to cancel the flat and remain at Abbot's End, a martyr to duty; but fortunately she has changed her mind and the flat has been taken. People like my stepmother are difficult to deal with because they will not say straight out what they think. I've been groping about in the dark—that's what it feels like—and even now I'm still in the dark as to *why* she wants me to go to Edinburgh with her. Why on earth does she want me? We have nothing in common at all—absolutely nothing."

Dinah had known this before.

"She doesn't approve of me," continued Malcolm. "She doesn't understand my jokes; we don't meet—I mean our minds don't meet—anywhere. You would have thought she would be delighted to get away from me and lead her own life."

"Are you sure it isn't Miss Grover who wants you to go to Edinburgh?" asked Dinah impulsively.

He was silent for a few moments and Dinah wished her words unsaid, but when she glanced at him to see if he were annoyed she found he was smiling at her.

"Well!" he exclaimed. "What a clever girl you are! Why didn't I think of that myself?"

Nothing more was said on the subject. Malcolm spoke of Dan, praising his keenness and saying that he was looking forward to having Dan in his business; and Dinah, delighted to hear nice things of her fellow-Dee, told Malcolm how interested Dan was in the art of paper-making.

"You know, Dinah, you're rather a mysterious person," said Malcolm suddenly. "I mean you talk so little about yourself and your own affairs. I've talked endlessly about my affairs and bored you with this foolish business of whether or not I shall go to Edinburgh, and we've talked about Dan and his affairs—it's about time we talked about you. What do you do with yourself all day? I suppose you play golf?"

"No," said Dinah, smiling. "No, I'm *far* too busy to play golf."

"You've got a job?"

"Yes, a very important job. I'm trying to bring up my children properly. I've got four, you know."

"Four children!" exclaimed Malcolm in amazement. "You mean—you mean children of your own!"

Dinah chuckled. "Of course, why shouldn't I have children, Malcolm?"

"Four," he repeated incredulously. "Four children! How did you find time? You're only a child yourself . . . and why have I never seen them?"

"Because you only see me at night when they're in bed."

"It's astonishing! I simply can't believe it!"

Dinah was laughing heartily now; she couldn't help it, for his amazement was comical in the extreme.

"I *don't* believe it," declared Malcolm looking at her and smiling. "You're pulling my leg. Come on, now, Dinah—own up. It's a joke, isn't it?"

"It's true—honestly—cross my heart, Malcolm."

"But you never mention them!"

"No," agreed Dinah mopping her eyes. "No, I try not to talk about them because people who talk about their children are such awful bores. Of course if you want to hear about them I can talk about them until the cows come home."

But there was no time to talk about them now, for the boat was nearing the shore and Ben, tiller in hand, was edging his way carefully among the rocks to land Dinah in the usual place.

"You must tell me about them next time," Malcolm said. "You *will* come out with me again, won't you? Or perhaps you're tired of sailing. Don't come if you'd rather not."

Dinah hesitated. She had decided not to go with him again, but he was so eager—and so diffident—that she had not the heart to refuse.

"If you really want me—" she began.

"Of course!" cried Malcolm. "When could you come? Just say what evening would suit you."

"What about Friday?"

"Friday?" said Malcolm. "That's a long way off, isn't it? This is only Tuesday."

"Friday would suit me best," said Dinah firmly.

"Friday, then," agreed Malcolm. "Friday suit you, Ben?"

"Friday'll dae us fine. It'll be the harbour, Mister Mawlcolm."

Dinah landed as usual and, as usual, stood at the gate of Craigie Lodge and waved. It was darker to-night for the sky had clouded over and she could scarcely see the flicker of white which she knew to be Malcolm's handkerchief. She went in and bolted the door and found the milk and biscuits which Nannie had left on the kitchen table.

It had been a memorable evening (the best of all, thought Dinah as she sipped her milk) and she was glad she was going again on Friday. Why shouldn't she go? She enjoyed it and so did Malcolm. Malcolm was a lonely person. He wanted company, that was all. He was sensible and friendly—quite different from poor Tapioca. Malcolm could not spend his leisure playing golf or tennis as other men did, his only recreation was sailing . . . and surely it was right that she should give him what pleasure she could!

Nobody would think it odd if I played golf with him, said Dinah, arguing with an invisible critic. Everybody—even Nannie—would think it quite natural if we went out two or three times a week and had a round of golf, so what's the difference? There's no difference at all, added Dinah firmly, and so put the invisible critic in his place.

29

DINAH had promised to take the children to the Black Rocks, where the Dees had been stranded, and this seemed as good a day as any for the expedition. Margy was too young to go so she was left with Nannie, and the rest of the party set off in good order, the twins carrying the luncheon basket between them. Mr. Monk was sitting on the sands with his paper, he waved to them and they stopped to tell him where they were going.

It was on the tip of Dinah's tongue to say, "Hallo, Mr. Monk!" but fortunately she remembered in time and changed her greeting in mid-air.

"Hallo, what a lovely morning!" Dinah said.

Mr. Monk agreed.

They dallied with him for a few moments and then walked on . . . but as Dinah followed the children across the bay she racked her brains in an effort to remember what his name really was. Had she heard it or not? Surely she must have heard it. Perhaps it was Yoker. If Pat were the son of Mr. Monk's brother it would be Yoker, of course, but (equally of course) he might be the son of Mrs. Monk's brother—or Mr. Monk's sister—so one couldn't be sure.

By this time the "Monks" were friends so it would be difficult to ask them straight out. One can say to an acquaintance, "By the way,

I'm afraid I didn't catch your name," but to say that to dear old Mr. Monk was unthinkable. He would be hurt. He would think her mad. She might say it to Mrs. Monk, of course, because Mrs. Monk got muddled about names herself (she often called Dinah Mrs. Bell and sometimes Mrs. Anderson) so she couldn't really blame other people for having defective memories . . . but perhaps the best way would be to ask Nannie. Yes, Nannie would be sure to know.

"It's a jelly-fish, don't touch it!" exclaimed Dinah, who was so used to keeping a wary eye on the activities of her offspring that her eye did it instinctively even when her thoughts were otherwise engaged.

"Don't touch it? Why not?" asked Nigel.

"Because it stings."

Nigel drew back. "It doesn't look as if it stung," he objected.

"It doesn't look as if it could do anything much," added Mark.

"Why does it sting?" inquired Nigel. "I mean why did God give it a sting? Just to sting people with, or what?"

"Are there baby jelly-fishes?" asked Mark. "I mean how do they get born? How old do you think this jelly-fish would be?"

"Jelly-fish," said Polly thoughtfully. "It's like a jelly, but not like a fish. Isn't it pretty with its purple middle? What does it eat, Mummy?"

Dinah tried to tell them about the peculiarities and the habits of jelly-fish, but once again she found her knowledge insufficient. She knew jelly-fish floated in the sea and could sting you very uncomfortably if you happened to meet them when you were bathing because experience had taught her that this was the case, but she had no idea why they had stings, nor what they ate, nor where they came from, nor how little jelly-fishes were born. Fortunately there were so many things to distract the children's attention that they soon forgot about jelly-fish and the subject was dropped.

They crossed the bay and made their way round the bold headland of crumbling grey rock, scrambling over the stones and boulders which were strewn about its base. The boulders were of all sizes and shapes and (most curiously) of all colours . . . and Dinah as she looked at them wondered what explanation a geologist would give of their presence. She was interested too in the bright yellow lichen which grew upon the rocks which were not covered by water except at high tide. Two oyster-catchers were sitting together upon a ledge of rock, their bright yellow bills and pink legs were most effective with their beautiful black-and-white plumage. Nigel ran towards them and they rose and flew off with graceful sweeping wings.

There was no hurry of course—Dinah and the children had all morning and afternoon before them—so they stopped often, to wade in a tempting pool, to catch a crab hiding beneath the brown ribbon-like seaweed or to watch an anemone folding and unfolding its little red feelers in the clear water (Mark wanted to know if it were a baby octopus but his mother thought not). Presently they came to another bay, carpeted with coarse golden sand, beyond which the Black Rocks jutted out into the sea.

The tide being out it was easy to visit the spot where the Dees had fished so assiduously and Dinah, leading the way, was able to point out the very ledge upon which they had sat. Dinah was flattered and rather touched at the interest shown by the children in the location.

"It makes it real," explained Mark, as he squatted on the ledge. "It's like seeing John Silver's galley in the *Hispaniola*. It's like seeing Nana's kennel or Old Mother Hubbard's cupboard."

Dinah took the point. She was not particularly anxious to see Old Mother Hubbard's cupboard—especially as it was bare—but she would have liked to take a little stroll round Highbury with Emma Woodhouse and visit Mrs. Bates.

There was a swell to-day; the waves came racing in, one after another, gurgling round the base of the hard, black rocks and swooshing into the caves and crevices.

"The waves are stroking the rocks," said Polly thoughtfully. "They're kind, gentle waves, aren't they?"

"They are kind to-day," agreed Dinah. "But you should see them in winter. The wind blows and the waves are rough, they break over the rocks and the white spray flies high in the air."

"I wish it was rough to-day," said Mark regretfully.

"Let's go now," said Polly. "We've seen the ledge and everything. The sea might come in and then we couldn't get back—"

"The sea's going out," objected Nigel.

"But you never know. It might suddenly change its mind," said Polly anxiously.

"It couldn't," Mark assured her. "Dan said the tide was fixed, just like night and day."

"Silly Polly!" jeered Nigel. "You might just as well say we had better go straight home now in case it gets dark all of a sudden."

"But it couldn't because of the sun."

"No, and the sea couldn't either because of the moon."

The boys wanted to have lunch on the rocks and wait until the tide came in, so that they would have to wade across to the mainland. Dinah sympathised with this very natural desire but she saw Polly would be miserable until the whole party was safely ashore. Polly distrusted the tide. It was all very well to say that its comings and goings were unalterably fixed, but how did Dan *know*?

"It isn't only Dan," declared Nigel. "Everybody knows except silly girls like you . . ."

"There's a little spring on the mainland," said Dinah. "The Dees used to fill their kettle and boil the water for tea. I wonder if we could find it."

"Let's try!" cried Mark, beginning to scramble over the rocks.

"Let's try and find it ourselves!" cried Nigel springing up and bounding after Mark like a chamois.

"Wait!" shrieked Polly. "Wait for me. I want to help to find it."

Dinah, following more slowly, marvelled at the ease with which one could manage children if one took the trouble to understand their mentality. Was it wrong to smooth their path? Would it be better for their characters to allow disagreements to boil up and bubble over? The day would come when they would have to go out into the world and stand upon their own feet with nobody to direct and guide them. She and Dan had never been controlled in this way. They had been told to do this, or not to do that and had been expected to comply with orders. In their relationship to one another they had needed no guidance, Dinah could not remember a single quarrel. Her own children were quite different. Unless one watched carefully, directing and controlling, they would spend their days arguing with one another . . . the boys were forever at loggerheads. But perhaps it would be better to let them fight and find their own level, perhaps it was spoiling them to make everything easy and pleasant. Dinah sighed. She tried so hard to do what was best, to bring up the children to be whole and sensible.

By this time she had reached the mainland and the children were busily searching for the spring. Dinah knew exactly where it was; she had not thought of the spring for years but its location was as clear in her memory as if she and Dan had been here yesterday. How odd that was, thought Dinah, how amazing that her brain had held this little piece of knowledge, and held it in secret for over ten years! She sat down upon the warm dry sand and watched the children searching . . . and when they began to tire she helped them by calling out "hot" or "cold."

It was Polly who eventually found it, welling out of a crevice in the overhanging cliff. "Oh, look!" she cried. "Oh, look at it bubbling out of the ground like when Moses hit the rock . . . look, Mark! Look, Nigel!"

They stood and admired the spring for several minutes and on being assured that the water was pure, they cupped their hands and drank.

It was time for lunch now, so they sat down and opened the basket and spread out the ample meal which Nannie had provided . . . and as they ate they subjected their mother to a thorough examination on the subject of springs. Where did springs come from and why did that particular spring come out of the cliff at that particular place? And how was it that if the earth was full of fire—as Mark's geography book had informed him—it was also full of water, and cold water at that?

Here was yet another way in which Dinah's children differed from the Dees. The Dees had never pestered their elders with questions, had never (as far as Dinah could remember) been particularly anxious to know how the tides worked nor where springs came from nor why jelly-fish had stings. Was this because the Dees had been incurious by nature or because they had nobody to ask? For of course we had nobody to ask, thought Dinah as she doled out the sandwiches. Father was much too busy and it would have been no use asking Nannie anything like that. Nannie would have said, "Ask me another," or "That's the way God made it," or something equally unsatisfying to an inquiring mind.

It was four o'clock before Dinah and the children got home. They were all tired with their long day in the open air and nobody wanted to go out after tea. They had settled down quietly to a game of Ludo in the drawing-room when Nannie appeared at the door.

"That's a Miss Grover," said Nannie.

"Miss Grover!" exclaimed Dinah.

"I put her in the dining-room." said Nannie in conspiratorial tones. "I thought, maybe, you'd get rid of her easier."

Nannie seemed to have got the right idea about Miss Grover, thought Dinah as she rose reluctantly and went downstairs to see what her visitor wanted.

"How d'you do," said Miss Grover. "You left your handkerchief the night you came to dinner at Abbot's End, so I've brought it to you." She took a little handkerchief out of her bag as she spoke and handed it to Dinah. It was a green chiffon handkerchief with white spots.

"It's very kind of you, but it isn't mine," said Dinah.

"Not yours!"

"No, I haven't got a handkerchief like that—and even if I had I wouldn't have worn it the night I dined at Abbot's End."

"What *do* you mean!" exclaimed Miss Grover in surprise.

"I was wearing a blue frock," said Dinah, smiling.

Miss Grover folded the handkerchief carefully. "Oh," she said. "I didn't remember what you were wearing."

"Why should you remember?" asked Dinah. She had been watching Miss Grover closely and she felt sure that Miss Grover's surprise was assumed. Miss Grover had known that the handkerchief did not belong to Dinah . . . was it her own? Had she made this an excuse for calling? It was not a very good excuse for it was now ten days since the famous dinner party at Abbot's End. Miss Grover could have posted it. What was the real reason for her call? Dinah was annoyed—she hated subterfuge—she felt inclined to voice her suspicions, but she managed to resist the temptation.

During the pause which followed Miss Grover's eyes roved round the room; they took in the old-fashioned furniture, the worn carpet, the pictures on the walls and finally came to rest on the bowl of sweet peas in the middle of the shining mahogany table. They were Malcolm's flowers, of course, but Miss Grover couldn't know that— or could she? Was it possible for her to recognise Abbot's End sweet peas? The silence was prolonging itself unduly but Dinah was determined not to break it. Miss Grover had come to call with a definite purpose: let her proclaim it.

I'm being horrid, thought Dinah. I feel horrid. Why does this woman have such a queer effect upon me? Is it my fault? If I were nice to her would she be nice to me? We're told to love our neighbours but I can't love her—it's impossible. I can't tolerate the woman, she rubs me the wrong way.

"I've been having tea with Mrs. Murray—along the terrace," said Miss Grover at last. "So I thought I would look in on the way home and bring your handkerchief."

"Good of you," said Dinah.

"Mrs. Murray's husband was a General," continued Miss Grover. "He had a most distinguished career. You don't know Mrs. Murray, do you?"

"No," said Dinah. She smiled mischievously and added "I don't know anybody at all. We discovered that on Sunday night, didn't we?"

"Mrs. Murray knows you—by sight. She says you have several children."

"Four," said Dinah nodding. "Two girls and two boys. Perhaps you'd like to see them."

"My aunt had no idea of it." declared Miss Grover.

"She didn't ask me," Dinah pointed out. "If she had asked me I would have told her. It's quite usual for people to have children. Would you like to see them so that you can tell your aunt all about them?"

"I'm afraid I haven't time," said Miss Grover rising.

Dinah rose too and accompanied her guest to the door.

"It's a pity about the handkerchief," said Miss Grover.

"Not really," replied Dinah. "You should keep it yourself."

"I must try to find the real owner," said Miss Grover self-righteously.

"I think you should keep it—yes, really—it goes so beautifully with that green tweed suit you're wearing. In fact it looks as if it had been bought on purpose."

Miss Grover looked at Dinah and Dinah looked back, smiling.

They were on the doorstep by this time but Miss Grover still lingered. "You like sailing, Mrs. Savage," she said.

"Yes, very much. It's so kind of Malcolm to take me," replied Dinah promptly.

"He offered to take me, of course, but I don't care for it."

"Some people are bad sailors—"

"It isn't that," said Miss Grover hastily. "It's because I have so much to do—so I'm very glad he's found someone with plenty of leisure to go with him."

Dinah nodded. "It *is* lucky, isn't it?" she said.

"Are you going to-morrow?" asked Miss Grover.

"No, on Friday," replied Dinah.

Miss Grover took her bicycle, which was leaning against the wall, and after the usual valedictory remarks she mounted and rode off. Dinah watched her. Miss Grover had come to spy out the land, but Dinah had nothing to hide so it didn't matter.

30

DINAH had received a little note from Miss Steven asking her to come to tea and bring the children. She and Nannie had decided that two children would be enough; Polly must go, of course, and one of the boys.

"You can go, Mark," said Nigel with a self-sacrificing air.

"But you're the eldest so it ought to be you," Mark pointed out.

Dinah was not deceived by this show of altruism, she realised at once that neither of her sons wished to accompany her to Miss Steven's tea-party. "You can toss for it," she said.

"Honestly, Mummy," objected Nigel. "Honestly it isn't a good plan to toss, because I don't mind a bit and Mark would enjoy it awfully. It will be nice for Mark, won't it? You'd like it, wouldn't you, Mark?"

"We'd better toss," said Mark with a sigh.

They tossed and Nigel won. "I shall stay at home," he said quickly.

"But you've won," objected Mark.

"Yes, so I choose what I want to do."

"But Nigel, we tossed to see who was to go!"

"Of course you did," said Nannie firmly. "Nigel is to go with his mother."

Dinah would not have arranged it thus. It seemed to her that Nigel having won the toss had the right of choice, but she was obliged to support Nannie's authority. "Yes," said Dinah nodding. "Yes, Nigel, you had better come in from the sands at three o'clock so that there will be plenty of time to change." There was some doubt in Dinah's mind as to whether Nigel would manage to evade his obligation. Just lately she had noticed an increasing tendency in Nigel to evade duties which did not appeal to him and evade them so gracefully and skilfully that it was difficult to tackle him about it. Dinah was all the more worried because this had been one of Gilbert's habits, Gilbert had always managed to wangle himself out of uncongenial tasks. Thinking about this as she sat at the drawing-room window with a basket of mending beside her on the sofa, Dinah tried to foresee what Nigel would do—or could do—to escape the tea-party. He must come, of course. Much as she regretted the necessity of taking a reluctant child to tea with her old friends the order could not be cancelled or discipline would suffer. Perhaps Nigel would simply vanish . . . but if so Dinah would have to go out and look for him. What a bore it was!

It was nearly three o'clock and Dinah was about to put away her darning when she saw the two boys coming in at the gate.

"Is it three yet, Mummy?" called Nigel, standing on the path and looking up.

"Five minutes to," replied Dinah, leaning out of the window and smiling her relief. "You're in plenty of time. I've put out a clean shirt for you."

"We're both going," said Mark.

"Both going!"

"Yes," said Nigel. "That'll be all right, won't it? Philip Barrington said it would."

"Yes," explained Mark. "Philip says you get an absolutely scrumptious tea at Miss Steven's house and he says she'd *like* us both to go. He's *sure* it'll be all right."

Dinah hesitated and then agreed. She laughed to herself as she went into the bathroom and found her sons scrubbing themselves vigorously—this was an eventuality she had not foreseen.

Polly was ready first. There had never been any doubt in Polly's mind about going or not going to the tea-party, for social occasions were meat and drink to her. She awaited the others, sitting upon the seat in the front garden with her hair neatly brushed and her nice, clean hands folded in her lap. I'm good, thought Polly. It was a delightful sensation.

Miss Steven's house was west of the harbour; it was even nearer the sea than Craigie Lodge for the wall of the house arose from the shore. The house was one of the oldest in Seatown, quite small and compact but extremely solid. In fact it was a miniature fortress, built to withstand the onslaught of the sea. The Dees had often wondered how it withstood this onslaught for wasn't it built on sand? And didn't it say in the Bible that it was the foolish man who built his house upon sand "and the rain descended, and the floods came, and the winds blew and beat upon that house: and it fell: and great, was the fall of it"? But Miss Steven, on being questioned had assured them that, although most assuredly it had an appearance of being built on sand, the foundation of her house had been welded into the solid rock which lay beneath the sand, and Miss Clara had taken them down to the cellar and showed them the rocky floor. The house had been a drinking den for the fishermen in the old days (many a keg of contraband spirit had found its way into the capacious cellar) but later it had been superseded by more comfortable inns and had fallen into disrepair. Miss Steven had bought the place for a song and had spent a good deal of money upon it so that now it was a comfortable home for herself and her sister. The front door was in a lane which led from the High Street but the Dees had always used the back entrance when they visited their two old friends, climbing the old worn steps which led up from the beach, and it never occurred to Dinah to approach the house from any other direction.

Dinah and the children climbed the steps and knocked on the oaken door which was stained and weathered by the salt spray.

Miss Clara opened it immediately. "There you are!" she exclaimed. "We're so delighted to have you. Jean won't be a minute—we saw you coming along the shore so she ran to make the tea."

"You haven't got Phyllis now?" asked Dinah.

"Phyllis left us," replied Miss Clara. "She left us to go into the Wrens—and then she got married—but we manage quite nicely ourselves with a woman coming in two mornings a week. In fact Jean and I were just saying the other day we're really more comfortable than we were before. Phyllis was a little difficult sometimes—just a wee bit touchy, you know. Jean and I divide the work between us and really it's very pleasant indeed. I enjoy housework and Jean is an excellent cook—and so economical—our rations go twice as far and we always seem to have enough for baking—"

"You don't get too tired?" asked Dinah who felt it was about time for her to get a word in.

"Tired? Dear me, no," said Miss Clara shaking her head. "I'll tell you a little secret, Dinah. We have breakfast in bed every morning.

Isn't it lazy? We take it in turns, week about, to get up and make the tea and carry up the tray; and then we settle down comfortably in bed and have our breakfast together, and chat and open our letters and have a look at the papers. So *pleasant*," declared Miss Clara nodding. "Quite delightful, really. Phyllis would never have allowed us to do that, of course—*never*. One couldn't have asked her."

They were in the parlour by this time and Dinah, looking round, was relieved to find it hadn't changed at all. It *was* a long-shaped room, large for the size of the house, and had three windows looking seawards. She remembered that sometimes in winter, when the wind was high and the sea was rough, spray came battering against the windows, battering so fiercely that the two Miss Stevens were obliged to retire to a small sitting-room facing the other way.

"Sit down, dear," said Miss Clara. "Jean won't be a minute. You'd like to sit near the window, I expect."

Dinah sat down in an arm-chair with a straight back. The children were seated in a row upon the sofa, looking as if butter wouldn't melt in their mouths. Tea was already laid upon a round table in the middle of the room—and what a tea! There were plates of thinly-cut bread and butter, and plates of scones and cakes of every size and description, there was jam and honey and chocolate biscuits. Dinah wondered how they had managed it. Had they denied themselves food for a week to provide this sumptuous feast? She hoped not, most sincerely, but even if they had there was nothing she could do about it.

Miss Jean came in with the tea-pot (while her sister was still talking) and welcomed the guests with cordiality.

"Jean!" exclaimed Miss Clara, breaking off in the middle of a sentence. "Jean, aren't they perfectly sweet? So good and quiet. Dinah has brought them up beautifully. The little girl is like Dinah, isn't she? It's her eyes, I think. Her eyes are exactly like Dinah's—and her brow."

Miss Jean agreed and added that Mark was like the doctor.

"I know," said Mark.

"I'm like Daddy," declared Nigel.

"How nice!" declared Miss Clara. "We didn't know your father, of course."

"He was *very* good-looking," Nigel told her with complacency.

There was a moment of slight embarrassment, but only a moment, for the two Miss Stevens were full of social aplomb. They began to inquire after Mrs. Anderson's rheumatism.

Polly was gazing round the room; it was full of interesting things, full of curious old-fashioned furniture . . . and it was all *little*, thought Polly, so it suited the two little old ladies to whom it belonged. There were little chairs with short legs and padded backs, and little tables with boxes and shells and photographs displayed upon them, and there were two little desks and two little cabinets full of fascinating old china. Polly could see figures of shepherds, playing on pipes and shepherdesses with lambs in their arms, and there were dear little china baskets decorated with china flowers and a whole set of strangely-shaped cups and saucers.

The boys were more interested in the tea and when Miss Jean invited them to come and sit at the table "so that they could eat more" they rose with alacrity and took their places.

"Where is Trot?" asked Miss Clara, looking at her sister.

"I shut him up in the dining-room," replied Miss Jean. "I thought the children might be frightened of him."

"Is he a dog?" asked Nigel.

"We aren't afraid of dogs," added Mark.

"Well, if you're quite sure . . ." said Miss Jean and she rose and went to fetch him.

Polly said nothing. She was a trifle nervous, for of course big dogs were apt to be alarming (there had been an Alsatian in the house opposite to them at Nettleham and Polly had not liked him at all) but she need not have worried for there was nothing the least alarming about Trot. Nobody could have been frightened of him. He was a brown and white spaniel, fat and comfortable, with long silky ears and large soft brown eyes and a tail which wagged without ceasing.

"Trot is much too fat, of course," declared Miss Jean, looking at him fondly. "But we can't do anything about it."

"Because he's so greedy," Miss Clara explained. "He's the greediest dog in Seatown. We take him for walks every day but it makes no difference."

Trot had taken up his position between Mark and Nigel, and was watching every mouthful they ate and looking from one to the other with imploring eyes. Every now and then he sat up and begged, waving his front paws in the air. "I'm starving," he assured them. "Don't listen to Miss Clara. I've had no food for a month, for pity's sake have mercy on me and give me something to eat."

"Are you sure he isn't really hungry?" asked Mark anxiously.

"Quite certain," replied Miss Jean. "I gave him his dinner half-an-hour ago, and a very good dinner it was."

"You gave him his dinner!" exclaimed Miss Clara. "But Jean, I gave him his dinner . . ."

They looked at one another in amazement.

"So he's had two dinners," said Miss Jean with a sigh of despair.

Everybody laughed—except Trot of course. Trot went on assuring his new friends that he was in the last stages of death from starvation.

"You can give him a tiny wee piece of scone if you like," said Miss Jean. "It's no use bothering about his figure. If we try to cut down his food he just goes down to the harbour and tells the fishermen that he hasn't had a bite for a month and they feed him until he almost bursts."

Dinah was beginning to be afraid that the same fate would overtake her sons. Bread and butter and jam, scones and honey, cakes and biscuits were all disappearing rapidly. The two Miss Stevens kept on filling their plates and urging them, quite unnecessarily, to make a good tea. Polly had done pretty well but her capacity was limited and she knew it. She refused the offer of a second slice of Miss Jean's almond slab-cake.

"No more!" exclaimed Miss Jean in dismay. "Don't you like it. dear? Try one of these gingerbread cookies . . . or a piece of sponge sandwich."

"I wish I could but I haven't any room," said Polly regretfully.

When tea was over and nobody could eat another crumb Miss Clara produced some picture-books and the children sat down to look at them. It was the best kind of entertainment when you were full to the brim with cake; nobody wanted to run about. The picture-books were fascinating, there was *Shock-headed Peter* and *Kate Greenaway* and *Alice's Adventures in Wonderland* with Tenniel's quaint illustrations. Dinah remembered that she and Dan had loved these books, but they had not appreciated their value.

"They're first editions!" exclaimed Dinah.

"Yes," nodded Miss Jean. "Yes, we know that."

"But they're valuable! You shouldn't let the children have them!"

"Yes, we know they're valuable," nodded Miss Clara. "But the children will do them no harm—no harm at all."

"You must be careful of them, Mark," said Dinah anxiously. "Nigel, put the book on the table. Polly be careful—"

"Don't worry, Dinah," said Miss Jean, smiling. "Books are meant for reading. They like to be read. It's dull for them to lie in a cupboard from year's end to year's end."

Having settled the children comfortably the two old ladies were ready for a good chat with Dinah. They talked about old times and reminded her of a dozen small incidents which she had forgotten (they seemed to remember everything the Dees had said and done). They showed Dinah a plate which she and Dan had bought and presented to them one Christmas, a hideous plate made of cheap pottery with roses and forget-me-nots painted on it.

"How frightful!" Dinah exclaimed. "Yes, I can remember buying it. We thought it would look well in your china cabinet—little idiots that we were!"

"It isn't frightful to us," said Miss Clara as she put it away carefully amongst the Dresden china.

"And you weren't idiots," added Miss Jean. "You bought it to give us pleasure and it gave us pleasure."

"It still gives us pleasure," said Miss Clara, smiling at Dinah affectionately.

It was now nearly six o'clock and nearly bedtime, it was also the hour when Trot had his evening walk, so Miss Jean put on her hat and accompanied her guests as far as the harbour rocks. The children had recovered from their meal and ran about poking their noses into this and that and asking questions about the fishermen's nets and lobster pots. Miss Jean seemed a mine of information and, being unused to children's questions, was delighted to answer them and answer them at length.

"Such bright minds," she whispered to Dinah. "So intelligent and interesting!"

She was so busy answering questions that she failed to keep an eye on Trot and did not discover his absence until they were saying good-bye, but she was in no doubts at all as to where she would find him.

"In one of the cottages, of course," said Miss Jean shaking her head. "This is the hour the fishermen have their tea. Trot knows that as well as I do . . ."

31

THE three "big ones" were playing together this afternoon and Dinah was sitting on the shore with Margy. Dinah was glad they were playing together, and glad to see that they seemed to be getting on so well. They looked sweet, she thought. Polly, slim and dark, with her tanned face and arms and legs; Nigel slim and fair, with his matt white skin which never seemed to burn: and Mark shorter than the others but strong and brown and firmly knit. They were digging a canal from one pool to another and collecting little streams of water into a dam. Philip Barrington had taught them this game—rather a clever game, Dinah thought—and as a rule Philip was here to play the part of chief engineer: but to-day Philip had gone to Edinburgh with his father and the little Savages were playing it by themselves. Mark, as usual, was doing most of the work, digging like a beaver, his face crimson with heat. Polly was digging too. Nigel was heaping up a few spadefuls of sand and standing back to admire the effect or ranging over the rocks to find more pools and streamlets to be led into the waterworks.

"That won't do!" he exclaimed, descending suddenly upon Polly.

"What won't do?" asked Polly, shaking back her hair.

"The way you're digging. It isn't deep enough. Water won't run up-hill."

"But Nigel—"

"Dig deeper," said Nigel.

"Dig yourself!" exclaimed Polly crossly,

"I'm the engineer!" Nigel cried. "I'm the boss—"

"You aren't our boss," declared Mark, throwing down his spade.

"Yes, I am. I'm the man who goes about with a whip and makes the slaves work harder—get a move on, Mark!"

"You aren't," said Mark advancing towards him. "I'll tell you what you are. You're the slacker that gets thrown out for not doing your share."

"Come on, then! Throw me out!" cried Nigel in sudden fury.

"Don't Mark!" said Polly alarmed. "Nigel, it's all right—I'll dig deeper! Look Nigel, I'm digging—"

It was too late for appeasement. Nigel had rushed at Mark, and Mark, having seized him round the waist, was trying to throw him into the pool. They wrestled for a moment and then fell together on the wet sand, rolling over and over and hitting each other as hard as they could.

Dinah was a little way off. She rose and hastened towards them to interfere, but before she could get to them Polly had taken action. Polly grabbed Nigel's pail, filled it with water from the nearest pool, and emptied it over her brothers' heads.

"There!" cried Polly, trembling all over with alarm and excitement. "That's what to do with mad dogs . . ."

Whether or not it was the right thing to do with mad dogs it was most efficacious with angry boys. They let go of one another at once and sat up coughing and spluttering.

"You idiot!" Nigel exclaimed. "What d'you think you're doing!"

"You—nearly—drowned me!" gasped Mark.

Polly made no reply. She had refilled the pail and was ready to give them another dose if necessary; but it was not necessary for there was no fight left in them. Mark was still coughing—he had got the water full in his face—and Nigel had found his handkerchief and was trying to dry his ears.

"You had better go in," said Dinah, trying not to laugh. "It's nearly tea-time anyhow, and you're both soaking wet."

"Did you see what she did, Mummy?" demanded Nigel. "She emptied a whole bucket of dirty water over us. I shouldn't wonder if it has given me water on the brain."

"I had to," said Polly earnestly. "Mummy, I had to—they were killing each other. It's what you do in a dog fight. Dan said so."

Dinah took out her handkerchief and offered it to Mark (whose own handkerchief happened to be doing duty as a bandage round his knee). "Here, Mark," she said. "Dry your face, and get up. You're sitting in a pool."

"There's a funny singing noise in my ear," said Nigel, shaking his head from side to side. "It's water on the brain—that's what it is, Mummy."

"Get up," said his mother. "Get up at once and go home. No, there's no chance of your getting water on the brain. Water can't get into your head through your ears."

The combatants rose slowly and slowly made for home. They were a dejected looking pair. Fortunately Dinah was able to contain her laughter until they were out of hearing, but no longer.

Polly, who was collecting the spades and pails and boats which were lying about on the sands, looked up in surprise. "You're laughing, Mummy!" she exclaimed.

"Yes—I can't help it," admitted Dinah. "They looked so funny— but don't tell them I laughed whatever you do. It's a secret between you and me."

"A girls' secret," said Polly, grinning at her.

Dinah had been looking forward to her sail all day long, looking forward to it with excitement which was difficult to control. She tried to control it, of course, but it showed through the cracks and Nannie had told her she was "fey." She bolted her supper and was all ready to go to the harbour at half-past seven (which was far too early) and then she dawdled about and was suddenly afraid she might be late.

"It's a quarter to," said Nannie. "Or maybe ten to—but I wouldn't worry. No doubt they'll wait if you're not there on the stroke."

Nannie was teasing her, of course . . . and Dinah smiled to herself as she ran down the path and slammed the gate behind her.

She reached the harbour as the town-clock struck eight and, standing upon the quay, looked down. There was a small white sailing yacht drawn up to the steps. The *Kitty*, with her blunt bows, was at the other end of the harbour, near a somewhat perilous-looking iron ladder. Malcolm had not come yet—nor Ben—so Dinah spread her coat on a bench and sat down to wait. The party belonging to the sailing-yacht consisted of two girls and a young man in white flannels; they arrived in a large car, laughing and talking a trifle too loudly. Dinah felt ashamed of them. It was foolish of course for these people were nothing to her; she had never seen them before and it was unlikely she would see them again, but still she felt ashamed . . . all the more ashamed because the fishermen to whom the harbour belonged were behaving with their usual courtesy. They neither gazed at these alien people nor avoided them. When the young man, unable to loosen the painter, called to a bearded patriarch, "Hi, Jock, you might undo this bally rope, will you!" the fisherman immediately came forward with grave dignity and did what was required. ("Hi, Jock!" What a way to address him! Dinah felt hot all over with shame.)

They embarked and departed. By this time it was a quarter past eight. Dinah rose and walked to the end of the jetty; she hung about there for a bit and spoke to a fisherman who was leaning against a stone-bollard smoking his pipe. They agreed that it was a fine evening and promised well for a fine day to-morrow. Having settled this, Dinah walked back to her bench and sat down. Eight-thirty came. She heard the town-clock strike so there was no doubt about it. What could have happened? Should she wait any longer or go home? She rose and hesitated and then sat down again. She would wait another five minutes—no more.

The five minutes were almost gone when Dinah saw Ben approaching; she got up and went to meet him.

"Were ye waiting on Mister Mawlcolm?" asked Ben. "Mister Mawlcolm's no going oot the nicht. I got a message."

"Oh, I didn't know!" exclaimed Dinah in confusion.

"It's queer he'd not send ye a message," said Ben looking at her curiously as he spoke.

"Perhaps he did," said Dinah hastily. "I mean of course he must have—I've been out all the afternoon—so perhaps—"

"That's a peety, noo," declared Ben, commiseratingly. "Thai's a peety, that is—you coming doon here tae no purpose. An' it's a fine evening—aye, couldn't be better. It's a reel peety—"

Dinah escaped as soon as she could. Ben was sorry for her. Every fisherman in the harbour knew that she had come here to meet Malcolm and he had not turned up. It was a hateful sensation— quite unbearable. Dinah realised that it was silly of her to mind; it was illogical; Malcolm had asked her to come (and had asked her in such a way that she could hardly have refused) so she ought to be angry with Malcolm for letting her down like this. But instead of feeling angry with Malcolm she felt angry with herself. She felt a fool.

Of course there was some explanation, thought Dinah as she hurried home. Perhaps he had sent a message and it had gone astray. Perhaps he had been taken ill suddenly . . . but he had sent a message to Ben, so it couldn't be that. Anyhow it didn't matter. It was not worth thinking about. Malcolm was just a casual friend, nothing more.

By this time Dinah had reached the gate of Craigie Lodge, and she was so busy with her thoughts that she almost bumped into a tall figure coming towards her in the opposite direction.

"Hallo! I say you are in a hurry!" exclaimed Pat Yoker, as he stepped aside.

"Yes," said Dinah a trifle breathlessly. "I mean no, not really. I was just thinking—"

"Do you always dash along like that when you're thinking?" he inquired in a serious tone. "I mean it has the opposite effect on me."

"Does it?"

Pat nodded. "I dawdle," he said. "When the old brain gets to work the feet stop. Interesting, isn't it?"

"Interesting?"

"The difference between people," explained Pat.

"Yes," said Dinah.

"There isn't anything wrong, is there?"

"No, of course not. I was just thinking, that's all."

"Because if there *was*—I mean if there was anything I could do—I mean you being here all by yourself without Dan or anybody, if you see what I mean."

"Yes—no—I mean there isn't anything."

"But you would, wouldn't you? You'd tell me. You'd say, 'Look here, Pat, you might do this or that or whatever it was.' I'm not particularly bright, of course, but if you wanted anything *done* . . ."

"Yes," said Dinah smiling at him. "Yes, I would."

"You would!" he exclaimed joyfully—as if she had conferred an inestimable favour upon him—"Gosh, that's splendid! Absolutely first-class!"

They were at the gate. Pat opened it and Dinah went in.

"I say," said Pat. "You wouldn't like to come for a walk, would you?"

"Not just now," said Dinah. He looked so crestfallen that she relented a little. "But perhaps you'd like to come in and talk to me," she added.

He came in at once and they sat down upon the seat in the front garden. "This is the stuff," he said, stretching out his long, thin legs as he spoke. "You know, I saw at once you were feeling a bit blue. That's why I suggested a walk; but this is pots better. You're missing Dan, of course. It's a bit lonely for you in the evenings when the children are in bed."

Dinah nodded. "Yes, I *do* miss Dan. It's rather silly of me because when he was away I got on all right without him, but now I've had him for a bit I miss him dreadfully."

"I knew that was it. I expect he misses you just as much He's lucky to have you," added Pat with a sigh.

"Oh, I'm lucky to have Dan!" exclaimed Dinah.

"I wish I had somebody," continued Pat. "I mean like you and Dan—it must be nice."

"Yes, it is. We've always understood one another awfully well."

"I've got nobody like that," said Pat sadly.

Dinah was silent. It was a curious sort of conversation; she felt as if they were at cross purposes, as if there was some misunderstanding between them. She had decided that Pat was transparent as plate-glass, but she could not see through him to-night.

"I'm not frightfully brainy, of course," continued Pat rather miserably. "Sometimes I go the pace a bit—drink a bit now and then—that sort of thing. Not often, you know, but just sometimes. I could stop it quite easily if I had an object."

"Why don't you stop it?" Dinah said.

"I suppose I should," said Pat doubtfully. "But then again, why should I? It isn't doing anybody any harm. Nobody cares whether I stop it or not—if you see what I mean."

"What about the uncle and aunt?"

"That's different. I mean they're old, aren't they?"

She decided not to say she cared (though as a matter of fact it would have been true, for she was rather fond of Pat).

"I'm not bad, you know," he continued. "Not like some chaps who can't get on without the stuff. I just have a bit of a blind now and then. It's nothing. It's just because I haven't got anybody, that's all. I could cut it out to-morrow if I wanted."

"Of course you could," agreed Dinah, nodding.

Pat was silent for a moment and then he said, "I *will* cut it out if you give the word."

"I've no right to give the word, Pat; but, if you ask me what I think, I think you should."

"O.K.," said Pat.

There was a little silence. It was quiet and peaceful in the garden. The evening breeze rustled through the leaves and, far off, they could hear the splash of the waves on the sandy shore.

"Children all in bed, I suppose," said Pat suddenly.

"Long ago," nodded Dinah. "It wouldn't be so quiet if they weren't in bed—you know how stirring they are. Sometimes," said Dinah smiling, "sometimes when they're all safely in bed I say to myself, 'Peace, perfect peace, with loved ones far away."

It took Pat a moment or two to see it and then he laughed delightedly. "Rather good, that," he declared. "Clever, I call it. Now, how do you think of a thing like that, I wonder. I mean I couldn't—never in this world."

"Perhaps if you had felt it?"

"No," said Pat. "No, the old brain doesn't work like that. I can *understand* it, of course. I mean I like children awfully, but I can see they might be a bit of a trial if you had them milling round all day long. You'd be glad of a little peace. I like children," continued Pat. "Awfully nice little beggars they are. They take you as they find you and they enjoy jokes like anything—even my jokes. They aren't a bit critical. I mean if you let yourself go and clown about with them they never think what an awful fool you are, do they? Dan likes them too, doesn't he? I've seen Dan playing about with them and having jolly good fun. I suppose Dan didn't see much of them in the war?"

"No. he was away for years."

"Pity that! You know, Dinah, I think that's the worst of being in the Navy. It's a fine life and you meet an awfully nice set of fellows but you see so little of your own family. I've thought about that side of it quite a lot," said Pat confidentially. "I dare say you wouldn't believe I was the sort of chap who *thought* much, would you? But I've often been sorry for married officers who were away for years and never saw their families."

Dinah thought of Gilbert. "Yes, you're quite right to be sorry for them," she said. "It makes things very difficult, sometimes. Personally I'm even more sorry for their wives."

Pat nodded and rose. He said, "I expect you want to get off to bed, Dinah, so I'll mooch along. It's been nice talking to you like this. Don't forget what I said about telling me if you want anything, will you? Or if you're feeling a bit blue and want a chat, just—well. I'm always here, you know. And you needn't worry, if you know what I mean."

Oddly enough she knew exactly what he meant. "Thank you, Pat. I like having you as a friend," said Dinah gravely.

They shook hands as if they were sealing a bargain—which of course they were—but after he had gone and Dinah went up to bed she thought over the conversation and was slightly puzzled. She still had the feeling that there was some misunderstanding.

32

IT HAD been a peaceful holiday for Dinah. She had lazed on the beach with Margy most of the time and had wanted nothing more, but this morning—it was Saturday of course—she felt restless and edgy so she volunteered to do the shopping.

Nannie was pleased. "There's lots of folks wanting to see you," said Nannie. "They've been spoiling for you but I just told them you were tired and you'd had enough shopping in England, standing in queues and that, but if you're feeling like a wee stroll round so much the better. There's Miss Douglas—you'll remember her, Dinah—and Mrs. Dunlop at the fish-monger's—and old Mrs. Weir. She's gey old now and not often in the shop but you'll ask the gurrl and she'll take you ben . . . and for maircy's sake have a wee crack with Mr. Dobbie at the grocer's. You could shake him by the hand for he's given the children double butter this week."

"Of course," agreed Dinah. "I shall shake hands with everybody— and especially Mr. Dobbie. Dan and I always liked him. What about Mrs. Small at the baker's?"

"Dead," said Nannie. "It was fatty digestion of the heart and who could wonder? She was always eating. Her grandson has the shop now, a nice lad. He's married on a Douglas and they've a wee boy and another on the way if I know anything about it. There's old Miss Macready at the sweet-shop, too. Don't forget *her*, Dinah, or I'll be hearing about it."

"No, of course not."

"It'll take you the whole morning, I doubt, but you'd better do the thing properly while you're at it."

"Yes, of course," agreed Dinah. "I want to see them all. It isn't just—"

"Och, away!" exclaimed Nannie. "I know that fine. And they'll all want to see you. There's not a doubt of that. But you'll take the big basket, Dinah. You'll not say no to anything they like to offer, I hope."

Dinah took the big basket and set out. The High Street was narrow and winding, it ran parallel to the shore, so that whenever there was a gap between the closely parked houses and shops you got a glimpse of the sea and a whiff of sea air to cheer you on your way. Most of the houses were old (some of them very old indeed); they had been converted into shops with plate-glass windows to display their merchandise. Here and there a small house, wedged between its neighbours, had retained its old-time form, and disdaining any alteration displayed its merchandise as best it could in ordinary windows or hanging from hooks at the door. This was so at the shop where Miss Douglas held sway. It was a cottage—no more—and you stepped down into the front room from the street. The room was small but that only added to its enchantment, for it was literally packed with toys. Toys were packed on the shelves, toys hung from the ceiling, toys blocked the windows so that the room was shadowy and dim. It had not changed a whit, thought Dinah as she stepped down into this Aladdin's Cave and greeted its ancient owner.

"There now!" exclaimed Miss Douglas, bustling forward. "I was just saying to Aggie this very morning I wondered if you'd be coming— and here you are! It's a pleasure to see you—and you looking so fresh and well. We'll not say how many years it is since you and Dan were coming in with your pennies and rouking round the shop. Such nice wee things, you were! And now you've bairns of your own! Annie Anderson was here with them the other day—three of them and as nice as could be, and the wee boy the dead image of the doctor! I was sorry I'd no decent toys for them—nothing but rubbish and that's the truth. Sometimes I'm fair ashamed of selling the things," declared Miss Douglas looking round her shop in disgust.

"You seem to have quite a lot of nice toys," objected Dinah, peering round in the gloom. "What about that little cart and horse?"

"It's rubbish," declared Miss Douglas. "It's not worth the money—just glued together. If you left it out in a wee shower of rain it would fall to pieces, and where would you be then? As for yon doll," she continued, as Dinah lifted a doll from the shelf, "I just wouldn't sell it to you. It's put together with a hot needle and a burnt thread. The wig is crooked, see that? You'd have thought they could have taken the trouble to put it on straight, wouldn't you? And did you ever see such an ugly face as it's got—enough to give a wee child the nightmare."

"Have you anything that would be nice for a small child?" asked Dinah, hiding an involuntary smile.

"Not a thing." replied Miss Douglas emphatically. "Everything I've got is shoddy and expensive. Dear knows why people buy them. But the fact is it's the same with the people that come to Seatown now—shoddy and expensive is what they are—not like the old days. They may look right enough but they come to pieces in your hand."

Dinah had intended to buy something from Miss Douglas but she saw it was going to be difficult if not impossible, so they had a chat instead. Miss Douglas reminded Dinah of the day she and Dan had come in to buy something for the doctor's birthday and had chosen a glass ball with a little house inside. When you shook the ball it created a very realistic snowstorm which raged about the little house for minutes on end. Dinah remembered it distinctly, she and Dan had been fascinated with the toy and their father had liked it too, it had stood on his desk in the surgery for years and had amused some of his younger patients.

"I suppose you haven't another?" Dinah inquired in the unhopeful accents which post-war austerity has engendered.

"Well now, I wonder," said Miss Douglas thoughtfully. "I've got a sort of feeling I saw one of those wee balls. Just you wait a wee minute and I'll see ..."

Miss Douglas vanished behind the counter and after rummaging about for some time she reappeared in triumph with the ball in her hand. "There," she said, as she dusted it carefully. "There it is and I'm real glad I haven't sold it."

Dinah was delighted. She inquired how much it was but Miss Douglas waved her away. "You'll just take it, Mrs. Savage," said Miss Douglas. "It's a wee present to keep you in mind of old times."

"But, Miss Douglas, really—"

"It's pre-war and good," declared Miss Douglas. "I'd not give you anything that wasn't good. I'm real glad I had it to give you."

Dinah emerged from the shop and stood for a moment blinking in the sunlight, but there was no time to lose—she had spent far too long havering with dear old Miss Douglas—so she crossed the street and diving into the fishmonger's began to buy whitings and herrings in accordance with Nannie's list. There was a young girl serving in the shop, but before they had got very far Mrs. Dunlop suddenly appeared (clad, as Dinah remembered her, in a butcher's apron and a man's tweed cap) and swept the girl aside.

"Weel noo, Miss Dinah—Mistress Savage I *should* say—it's reel nice tae see ye. Is it ten years? Aye, I wouldna' wonder. You're luikin' a wee bit the worrse o' the wear but that's tae be expeckit—we're all gettin' on. Maybe Seatown'll set you up. Annie Anderson's a reel nice cook, they say. Umphm, that's fine. And you've three bairns? Four? That's fine. Och, you'll not be wantin' those whitings, they're yesterday's. I'll gie ye haddocks. Away an' get the haddocks cleaned, Maggie. Eh, I mind yer feyther weel—a man fine, he was! It was crab he liked. I mind him sayin' 'I tell ma patients no tae eat crab but I dinna tak' ma ain advice, Mistress Dunlop.' He was aye ready for a joke, was the doctor—an' sae serious aboot it. Whiles it was difficult tae ken whether he was joking or no."

It was ten minutes or more before Dinah could tear herself away—she had a crab in her basket in addition to the haddocks and the herrings—and time was marching on. She drew a deep breath and made for the grocer's.

Mr. Dobbie's business had expanded considerably and he had moved with the times. His was a large shop with plate-glass windows; it was full of people wrestling with ration books; there was an air of bustle here. Mr. Dobbie espied Dinah from afar and bore down upon her with a beaming smile, he looked much the same as ever—a little balder, a little stouter, a little less active on his feet. Dinah shook hands with him cordially.

"So you're back!" he exclaimed. "Everybody comes back to Seatown sooner or later . . . but it's changed days, Mrs. Savage."

"You've enlarged your shop, Mr. Dobbie."

"It wouldn't be so bad if I could get the stuff to fill it," said Mr. Dobbie sadly.

Dinah thought the shop looked well-stocked compared with the grocer's at Nettleham. "I suppose you haven't any bull's eyes?" she inquired.

"Not the old sort of bull's eyes," said Mr. Dobbie shaking his head. "Not the lovely, big, striped bull's eyes that you and Mr. Dan used to come and buy. They're not made nowadays—or if they're made they don't come my way. Maybe they're exported. We've a few little peppermint balls if they're any use."

"Calves eyes, perhaps," suggested Dinah as she handed over her card of personal points.

Having completed this purchase and given in Nannie's order and accepted with due gratitude Mr. Dobbie's offer of slab cake, chocolate biscuits and various other delicacies which were in short supply, Dinah was conducted upstairs and saw Mrs. Dobbie who was engaged in making a batch of jam tarts. She talked to Mrs. Dobbie for some time and admired the photographs of the three young Dobbies and learned their histories. The eldest had gone to America. He had been offered a job by a young American officer who had been billeted on the Dobbies during the war, and seemed to have settled down happily in his new surroundings.

Dinah's visit to old Mrs. Weir at the fruiter's was entirely different. Mrs. Weir did not remember Dinah and it took a little explaining.

"Eh, you're the doctor's lassie!" cried old Mrs. Weir, when at last it dawned. "Noo, why did ye no say so at the start? My, you've grown! It was only last year you came in here wi' pigtails doon yer back."

"I'm afraid it wasn't last year," said Dinah.

"Och, weel, it wasna' verra lang syne. I'm getting auld an' ma memory's no what it was. I'm eighty-siven, ye ken."

"Not really!"

"Aye, it's the truth . . . and I'm fine except for my legs. Ma legs is a wee bit stiff, ye ken. Yon new doctor's nae guid at a'. He's no like Doctor Bell. He canna gie me onything tae cure ma legs. If Doctor Bell was here he'd gie me a bottle and I'd be fine in a few weeks. Na, na, he's nae guid at a', the new doctor. There's naebody like Doctor Bell. 'Here's a bottle,' he'd say. 'Ye can drink it or pour it doon the sink, it'll dae ye a' the guid in the wurrld eether way.'"

Dinah laughed but Mrs. Weir remained as grave as a judge. "Aye, he was daft," she declared. "But his daftness did ye guid. Just tae see the doctor did ye guid. Gin ye were feeling a wee bit blue he was as guid as a bottle, himsel'."

They chatted for a few minutes about the old days which were much clearer to old Mrs. Weir than the events of yesterday. She gave Dinah a peach and insisted that Dinah should eat it then and there.

"It's local," she said, watching Dinah and enjoying Dinah's enjoyment. "There's nae peaches sae guid as the peaches frae Whittington Hoose that's grown on the sooth wa'. I'll ha'e no truck wi' foreign peaches—"

There was just young Small to do now—and Miss Macready at the sweetie-shop. Dinah dealt with them faithfully and they with her. She smiled and talked and listened; she answered questions about her children; she sympathised with their difficulties and joined with them in hoping for better times ahead. At last she was "through" (as Nannie would have put it) and feeling more than a little jaded with her morning's work she sought out a small cafe and sat down to rest.

Shopping was quite different here, thought Dinah, as she ordered a cup of coffee and a buttered scone. It was less of a business and more of a social occasion . . . and it wasn't only because she was Dr. Bell's daughter and they all remembered him, it was the people themselves. The people here had time to talk, they loved talking, and how interesting they were! Each one of them was an individual, a real personality with a peculiar and quite unmistakable flavour (like spices, thought Dinah, as she sipped her coffee and thought about her Seatown friends, like peppermint and almond and nutmeg, like clove and ginger and cinnamon) tickling up the palate with their pungency.

33

IT WAS peaceful in the café for the morning rush was over. Dinah needed peace. Her head was buzzing with talk (she had enjoyed it immensely but it had been a strain) so she was not pleased when she saw Edith Grover open the door of the café and walk in. She was even less pleased when she saw Edith Grover coming towards her between the little tables.

Miss Grover greeted her casually and sat down beside her. It was quite unnecessary because the café was empty. Miss Grover had the choice of half a dozen tables so why choose this one?

"I wanted to speak to you," said Miss Grover, answering her thought.

Dinah did not want to speak to Miss Grover. She did not want to speak to any one and Miss Grover least of all.

"I've been chasing you about all morning," Miss Grover complained.

Dinah said nothing. She had nothing polite to say. She had disliked Miss Grover from the beginning and further acquaintance with the lady had served to augment her dislike.

"I've left my purse at home so you'll have to pay for my coffee," remarked Miss Grover.

The request was quite a natural one but the manner in which it was made annoyed Dinah considerably. "Certainly," said Dinah without cordiality. "Would you like a scone as well?"

Miss Grover accepted the offer. "I wanted to speak to you," she repeated. "That's why I've been chasing you about. It's wasted my whole morning."

"What a pity," commented Dinah.

There was a short silence. Miss Grover was looking out of the window so Dinah could study her unobserved. She looked better to-day, Dinah decided. She looked younger. She was in grey tweeds to-day with a crimson beret set jauntily on her dark hair, and the colour in her cheeks was becoming. If it had not been for the super-cilious expression, which seemed habitual, one would have said she was a handsome girl.

"I had to see you to-day," said Miss Grover, turning her head and looking at Dinah. "We're going to Edinburgh on Monday. Abbot's End is to be shut."

"Is Malcolm going too? I thought—"

"Of course. He couldn't possibly stay here alone. It will be very much easier for him in Edinburgh; the long drive every day is far too tiring."

So they had persuaded him to go, thought Dinah. He hadn't been able to cut himself free after all!

"He was a little reluctant at first," continued Miss Grover. "He's very much attached to Abbot's End, but when he saw that we were really going he began to consider it, and of course he saw the advantages of the plan—not only the advantages for my aunt but also for himself and me. We shall all be much happier and more comfortable in the Edinburgh flat. Theatres, concerts, friends." said Miss Grover, ticking off the advantages on her fingers. "And doctors, of course."

"Is Malcolm ill?" asked Dinah in sudden anxiety.

"Dear me, no. Why should he be ill? Oh, I suppose you thought *that* was the reason he didn't turn up last night?"

Dinah said nothing.

"It wasn't that at all," added Miss Grover after a little pause.

"I'm glad of that," said Dinah.

"Awful coffee, isn't it?" Miss Grover remarked. "These people have no idea how to make coffee and the scone is stale. We should have had tea and biscuits."

"If one could have been sure that the tea was made with boiling water and the biscuits fresh," nodded Dinah.

Miss Grover looked at her with suspicion, but Dinah remained perfectly grave.

"About Malcolm," said Miss Grover. "It's always better to be frank and above board, isn't it? I just wondered if Malcolm had told you we're engaged."

Dinah said nothing.

"No," said Miss Grover in a low voice. "I thought perhaps he hadn't told you. The reason is that just lately we've had a little—a little misunderstanding, you see; but everything is all right again now. I thought it better to tell you the whole thing." She took off her gloves as she spoke and displayed a ring on her engagement finger; it was an opal set in platinum. "Malcolm wanted to give me diamonds," she added, "but I love opals and they're lucky for me because my birthday is in October."

"It's a beautiful stone," said Dinah quietly.

"Yes," agreed Miss Grover, looking at it with pleasure. "It has all the colours of the rainbow in it. Malcolm chose the stone and had it set for me, he took a lot of trouble over it. Of course we've been engaged for years—since the beginning of the war—but the wedding had to be put off when Malcolm was wounded. We've decided to put it off no longer and we're going to be married in October—on my birthday."

"How nice!" said Dinah.

"There isn't anything to wait for, really. Malcolm's leg still bothers him now and then but the doctors can't do much about it."

"I'm so sorry," said Dinah in a low voice. "It's terribly sad for him not to be able to do things like other men—and he's so good about it."

"Not always," said Miss Grover quickly. "Sometimes he's very difficult, but I understand him and can make allowances. I intend to dedicate my life to making him happy."

It sounded a noble aim but somehow Dinah was not impressed. She felt she would hate any one to dedicate their life to making her happy—and especially Edith Grover.

"He's very touchy," continued Miss Grover confidentially. "You may not have noticed it of course but he takes offence very easily."

Dinah had not noticed it.

"Oh yes," continued Miss Grover after a short pause. "You said something that annoyed him. That's the reason he let you down last night. I suggested he should ring you up and tell you he wasn't going. I hope he did that?"

Dinah did not reply.

Miss Grover laughed. "Malcolm really is a most extraordinary creature!" she declared.

"I would rather not discuss Malcolm," said Dinah finding her voice with difficulty.

"Just as you like," nodded Miss Grover, as she pulled on her gloves. "I thought it was kinder to tell you about it, that's all. It seemed a pity for you to waste your time pursuing Malcolm up hill and down dale." She rose and departed without another word.

Dinah was speechless. For a few moments she remained sitting in her chair frozen with rage and dismay . . . at last she got up and taking her heavy basket she started to walk home. It was horrible, thought Dinah, hurrying along the street with only a vague idea of where she was going. It was awful. She shouldn't have gone with Malcolm (Nannie had been right, why hadn't she taken notice of Nannie's disapproval?) she should have found some excuse, any excuse would have done. She had known all the time it was a silly thing to do—to go with Malcolm every time he asked her. ("Yes.

thank you, Malcolm. Yes, Friday will suit me best.") Why on earth had she been such a fool? She had made herself so cheap that at last Malcolm had got sick of her and failed to turn up at the appointed time . . . but no, thought Dinah. No, honestly, that wasn't true. There was no need for him to ask her. and not only ask her but persuade her to name an evening—any evening that suited her! And another thing, thought Dinah as she hastened along. Why hadn't Malcolm told her he was engaged? It would have been natural to tell her. He had talked so much about his private affairs and talked so openly that it almost looked as if he had deceived her on purpose . . . not that it mattered, thought Dinah, not that it mattered a pin one way or the other. If Malcolm was *that* sort of person he wasn't much good as a friend. It was disappointing to find he was that sort of person, so of course she was disappointed . . . but it didn't matter, really. How lucky it was that Dan was coming this afternoon! How lucky that you could always depend on Dan!

34

LAST week Dan had been delighted with Dinah, and had congratulated himself on the success of this holiday, but today he was not so pleased with her. She looked tired and she showed signs of the feverish gaiety which he had noticed when he saw her at Nettleham.

He had arrived late for lunch, the children were resting, and Dinah had sat with him while he ate his belated meal. She gave him a detailed and most entertaining account of her shopping expedition and showed him the glass ball with the imprisoned snowstorm. Dan remembered the original one, of course, and was much intrigued.

"You must have had a rare old time," said Dan, agitating the ball and watching the results. "It was decent of old Miss Douglas to give it to you, wasn't it? But perhaps it's all been a bit too much for you."

"Too much for me!" cried Dinah. "Goodness, no, I loved it."

"I mean perhaps that's why you're tired."

"But I'm not in the least tired!"

Dan hesitated a moment; but he was so worried that he simply had to know. "Is anything wrong?" he asked.

"Of course not," declared Dinah. "We're having a splendid time. We're all as brown as berries. We're all loving every minute of every day."

This answer ought to have satisfied him but instead of satisfying him it increased his anxiety. Dinah was not given to exaggeration and this was almost gush. "You'd tell me if anything were wrong, wouldn't you?" said Dan.

Dinah laughed. "How funny! That's what Pat said."

"Pat?"

"Your friend Tapioca. You were quite right in your diagnosis—he thinks I'm rather nice, but we've made a pact of platonic friendship so all is well."

"He's an awfully decent fellow," said Dan. "You mustn't run away with the idea that he drinks or—or anything like that."

"Oh, we discussed that," replied Dinah lightly.

"You discussed it?"

"Yes, he's going to reform."

Dan said no more but this did not mean he thought no more about the matter. Dinah had told him too much—or too little. She might have meant that Tapioca had proposed and she had turned him down. If so it seemed a pity. Dan did not know Tapioca well but he knew a good deal about him (one gets to know a good deal about one's fellow N.O.'s in the Senior Service). Everybody liked Tapioca. The fellow was thoroughly sound . . . and he had plenty of money, a circumstance which in Dinah's case especially was one to be viewed with favour. Dinah was young and attractive, why shouldn't she marry again? Dan thought she should if possible. It would be a bit of a blow to him, of course, because he had been looking forward tremendously to setting-up house together, but he wasn't so selfish as to wish her to remain single for his sake. If Dinah *had* refused Tapioca why had she, that was the question. Was it because she was thinking of Gilbert, blast him, or could it be that she didn't want to upset the Edinburgh plan? It *could* be because she didn't like poor old Tapioca of course, thought Dan, puzzling it out. Tapioca's part in the affair was equally puzzling, for platonic friendship with a pretty woman was definitely not in his line . . . and why swear off strong drink for the sake of a woman who has turned you down? It seemed unnecessary to say the least of it.

The children found their uncle less interesting than usual that afternoon. He went out with them after tea but instead of playing with them and joining in the fun he sat on a rock and gazed at the sea. It was the more disappointing because they had been looking forward all the week to Dan's visit and to-morrow was Sunday.

"Perhaps he'll play with us to-morrow afternoon," said Polly hopefully.

"No," said Mark. "He's going to play golf to-morrow afternoon. I heard Mummy arranging it. Let's all shout at him as loud as we can. There isn't long before bedtime."

They all shouted and Dan came back and played with them but it was not the same as usual, for Dan was not in the mood.

"About Tapioca," said Dan when the children had been packed off to bed and he and Dinah were alone.

"Yes," said Dinah brightly. "You're playing golf with him to-morrow afternoon."

"Am I?" said Dan in surprise.

Dinah laughed. She said, "Yes, it's all fixed. He said you wouldn't like to go over to Muirfield and have a round of golf and I said you would. Was that right?"

"Quite right. In fact excellent; I want a bit of exercise . . . but that isn't what I meant, exactly. I meant—well—Tapioca is an awfully decent fellow. Everybody likes him. I haven't heard anybody say a word against him—ever—and he's got lots of money."

"You mean you want me to marry him?" inquired Dinah, smiling.

"Yes, if you want to."

"He hasn't asked me."

"He hasn't?"

"No."

"But he would?"

"Well—perhaps," she replied. "I mean—yes, he would—at least I think so."

"What *do* you mean?" inquired Dan.

Dinah laughed a little. She said, "Pat likes me quite a lot but I'm not sure that he wants to marry me. At first I thought he did, but now I'm doubtful. There's something a little odd about it all. Fortunately it doesn't matter because I haven't the slightest intention of marrying anybody. Does that satisfy you?"

"No," said Dan quickly. "At least of course it satisfies me in a way, but we *must* have every thing perfectly straight between us. If either of us wants to get married the Edinburgh plan goes by the board. Neither of us is to be tied down in any way whatever."

"Of course. That was part of the bargain, wasn't it? You might want to get married; I said that from the first."

"Or you," urged Dan. "Either it works both ways or not at all."

Dinah saw the point. Unless she agreed Dan would feel tied. "All right," she said. "It works both ways, but there isn't the slightest chance of it working my way."

"Why not?" inquired Dan, teasing her. "You're still fairly young and not bad looking. Some misguided man might take a fancy to you."

"And relieve you of the necessity of looking after me," nodded Dinah. "Yes, I see the idea."

"I'm glad you see it," declared Dan. "The prospect of having you on my hands for the rest of my life has been worrying me a lot."

They laughed. It was good to have finished on a light note. It was good to find they still understood one another so well.

They had understood one another so well that Dinah was tempted to go on from there and tell Dan about Malcolm—not all of it, of course—just a little. The whole affair was bubbling and boiling in her mind so that she seemed full of it and could think of nothing else.

"I've been out sailing with Malcolm several times," said Dinah casually.

"Yes, you told me."

"He asked me," continued Dinah. "He kept on asking me so that it was difficult to refuse."

"Why should you refuse?" asked Dan. "I mean if you liked going—"

"Yes," said Dinah. "Yes, I liked going, but perhaps I shouldn't have gone so often. Only it was difficult. I mean I had no excuse."

Dan was completely at sea. "I don't understand," he declared. "If Malcolm asked you and you liked going why shouldn't you go?"

"That's what I thought," agreed Dinah with a relieved air.

"I suppose somebody has been getting at you, have they?" said Dan after a few moments of furious thought. "Gosh, how awful people are! People will say *anything*. Gosh, you don't need to worry about that—not with Malcolm. I mean, Malcolm isn't that sort at all."

"Isn't what sort?"

"The sort that thinks about women. Malcolm doesn't know women *exist*. He's absolutely wrapped up in his business—and books, of course. He's a tremendous reader. He isn't the marrying type."

"He's engaged to be married to Edith Grover."

"What!" exclaimed Dan in amazement. "Malcolm? Malcolm engaged to that awful woman?"

"Yes."

"But she's hideous! She's an absolute hag!"

"Not really, Dan. She's rather—rather handsome in a way."

"She's frightful," declared Dan. "And as a matter of fact I don't believe it—not for one moment. Who told you, Di?"

"She told me herself and showed me her engagement ring. They're going to be married in October."

Dan was silenced, but not for long. "I don't understand it," he declared. "I thought he hated the sight of her and I didn't blame him."

"You were wrong for once," said Dinah with an attempt at a smile.

This conversation comforted Dinah a little for she had faith in her fellow-Dee. He was a little obtuse in some directions of course, but his judgment was sound. Lying in bed and thinking it over she decided she had been a fool to be so upset at Edith Grover's accusation. She knew she had not pursued Malcolm so the accusation was false—why be upset over it? And if the accusation were false, as she knew it to be, perhaps the rest of it was false too . . . but how could you account for the hard and fast fact that Malcolm had not turned up last night? He hadn't turned up last night and he was going to Edinburgh on Monday. Don't think about it any more said Dinah to herself. Don't think about him.

35

ON SUNDAY morning Dan and Dinah took the children to church and in the afternoon Dan went over to Muirfield with Tapioca. It was Flo's afternoon off and the children were going for a picnic with the Andersons so Dinah would be alone in the house. She had been invited to the picnic but she had an idea that she was not really wanted, so she had refused, saying she would enjoy a quiet afternoon and would get some letters written.

"Nannie," said Dinah, going into the kitchen where Nannie was busy cutting sandwiches for the picnic-tea. "Nannie, I think I shall go and call on Mrs. Monk this afternoon, it'll be a good opportunity."

"Yes, you'd better," agreed Nannie. "It's the right thing after them having the children to tea and all. They're at Miss Brown's along the front."

"I know where they're staying but I don't know their name. What is it, Nannie?"

"Monk, of course," said Nannie without looking up. "Pass me over the strawberry jam, Dinah."

"It isn't," said Dinah, passing the jam. "That's just what the children call them—I hope they don't call them that to their face—Monk isn't their real name."

"It's good enough."

"Do you mean you don't know? Goodness, what a nuisance! It's all very well for the children to speak of them as Mr. and Mrs. Monk, but I can't ask at the door for Mrs. Monk, can I?"

"You'll not ask at the door," said Nannie. "The front-door bell has been broken for months. The postie was complaining about it. Miss Brown is a nice enough creature—I'm not saying anything against her, mind that—but she doesn't keep her house like I keep mine. I'll say no more," added Nannie darkly.

"Do you mean I should just walk in?" asked Dinah, who was more interested in her own project than in Miss Brown's shortcomings.

"You'll walk in or you'll stay out," retorted Nannie in her usual downright fashion.

Dinah waited until after tea to make her call. She was reluctant to go and her reluctance was intensified by the fact that she did not know their name . . . but the old people had been so kind and Pat had assured her that the aunt would appreciate the somewhat old-fashioned attention. Why didn't I ask Pat, thought Dinah. I could have asked Pat quite easily what their name was.

She went along the front and in at Miss Brown's gate. The bell was hanging from its plate in a dejected manner. Dinah pushed open the glass door and, after a moment's hesitation, proceeded up the stairs.

She knew the Monk's sitting-room, of course, for she had often seen Mrs. Monk looking out of the window. Dinah knocked on the door and, on being told to enter, walked in.

Mrs. Monk was alone; she was reading but she rose at once and welcomed Dinah cordially. "This is very nice of you," she declared.

"It's a proper call," explained Dinah, smiling. "Or at least as proper as I could make it."

"I hope you didn't stand on the doorstep trying to ring the bell! Come and sit down dear, and talk to me. I like being talked to."

Dinah was amused. She was aware that Mrs. Monk liked to do all the talking herself. It was a listener she liked: but Dinah did not mind: she had come to entertain the old lady for half an hour and it did not matter to her whether she talked or listened.

"I saw the children going off with Mrs. Anderson for a picnic," said the old lady, settling down comfortably. "She seems a very nice woman by all accounts. I was just saying to Patrick yesterday that next year we might try to get rooms *there*. Patrick likes Seatown better than anywhere because of the golf. He likes golf, you know, that's why we always come to Seatown for his leave. Patrick lives with us—perhaps he told you—his parents were killed in an air-raid."

"Yes, he said—" began Dinah.

"Yes," said Mrs. Monk nodding. "Patrick's father was my only brother, they lived in London. It was that dreadful raid quite near the beginning of the war. Patrick was in Australia at the time. He's a dear good boy—you like him, don't you?"

"Nobody could help liking him," said Dinah.

"He lives with us you know," continued Mrs. Monk. Like most old ladies who talk a great deal, she was apt to repeat herself. "Or at least his home is with us. Sailors can hardly be said to live anywhere, but of course you know that as well as anybody, dear."

Dinah said she thought she *did* know that as well as most people.

"Our son was in the Navy too," said Mrs. Monk. "He always wanted to be a sailor from the time when he was quite a little boy. He was killed, you know."

"Yes, Pat told me, I'm awfully sorry," said Dinah.

They were silent for a moment. "It was a terrible blow," said the old lady rather shakily. "Of course other people . . . but that didn't seem to make it any less terrible . . . he was such a strong boy. That's a silly thing to say, I know, but he was so strong and full of life that somehow . . . somehow it was difficult to believe."

"I know." said Dinah sympathetically.

"So big and strong and full of life. So gay and handsome. I'd like to show you his photograph," said Mrs. Monk, rising and going over to the desk which stood in the corner of the room.

Dinah got up and followed her. "Yes, I should like to see it," she said.

"It's very good of him," declared the old lady, taking up a photograph in a silver frame and looking at it sadly. "Very, very like him. I'm always so glad I made him have it done. Yes, that's Gilbert," she added, handing it to Dinah as she spoke.

It was Gilbert. For a moment Dinah did not understand . . . and then, quite suddenly she understood the whole thing. It was like a flash of lightning across her brain. All that she knew, all that Pat had told her fell into place.

She put the silver frame back on the desk very carefully. It seemed important that it should be in exactly the right place; and, as the desk was slightly dusty on the top, Dinah could see exactly where the frame had stood.

"My dear, you look rather pale!" exclaimed the old lady in sudden anxiety.

"Yes," said Dinah. "I mean—I don't feel very well. I think I'll just go home. I'm so sorry."

"I'll get you a little brandy—"

"It's nothing," Dinah declared. "Nothing to worry about. I'll—I'll just go home."

"Perhaps if you were to lie down. I've got a bottle of smelling salts in my room. Sal-volatile—"

Dinah refused them all. What she wanted was to get home. Somehow or other she managed to escape, to get down the stairs and along the road and in at her own gate. She pulled herself up the stairs, step by step (hanging on to the banisters like an old woman) and sat down in a corner of the sofa in the drawing-room. The sofa was an old friend, shabby, kindly, safe. Dinah knew every patch upon the worn cover. She sat there for a few minutes trying to recover herself, trying to think. It had been such a shock. It was as if someone had hit her a blow on the heart, paralysing her. Gilbert's face, smiling at her from the photograph—it was so utterly unexpected—*Gilbert's face!*

So they were Gilbert's parents! It was incredible. These people she liked so much had behaved to Gilbert badly . . . but of course they hadn't! It was impossible that the Monks could have behaved like that.

She was only just beginning to recover and to get things sorted out when the door opened and Mr. Monk appeared (but he wasn't Mr. Monk, of course; he was . . . Mr. Savage). He came in looking somewhat scared, with a glass in one hand a large bottle of smelling-salts in the other.

"Mary sent me," he said. "She was very much distressed—especially as she knew you were alone in the house. It's sal-volatile."

Dinah drank it. The fiery stuff ran down her throat and helped her to pull herself together.

"That's right," he said, sitting down beside her on the sofa and taking her hand in his. "You'll feel better in a minute or two. Would you like me to ring up the doctor? Mary thought I should."

"No—please—I shall be all right."

"Well, then, let me ring up your husband. I could easily—"

"My husband!" exclaimed Dinah in horrified tones.

"They'll have finished their golf," he explained. "I could get Patrick on the phone and tell him to come straight back. You'd like that, wouldn't you?"

"You mean Dan!" she exclaimed. "You thought Dan was my husband!"

"Mr. Bell—" he began, looking at her strangely.

"He's my brother." Dinah said. She was beginning to see light, but she felt quite unable to explain. How on earth was she to explain the whole chapter of mistakes and misunderstandings.

"The children call him Dad," said the old gentleman in a puzzled tone. "Patrick told us you were Mrs. Bell."

"The children call him Dan. He's my twin brother."

"Then your husband—"

"My husband's name was Gilbert Savage," said Dinah in a faint voice.

Gilbert's father was still holding her hand. Perhaps that was why he understood. His grasp tightened. "Gilbert!" he exclaimed. "Not our Gilbert!"

"I didn't know," continued Dinah. "I never heard your name. I never thought for a moment—how could I? It wasn't until I saw the photograph . . ."

36

AFTERWARDS when Dinah looked back at that Sunday evening it seemed odd to her that Gilbert's father had understood the whole affair so quickly and accepted it so naturally. She wondered whether he was upset below the surface—as she was—and had concealed his real feelings or whether he was really as calm as he seemed. Mr. Savage was old; he had suffered many things and suffered them in silence, perhaps this had helped to make him a stoic. Dinah did not think all this at the time. She was too dazed. It was all a sort of dream. He had sat beside her on the sofa, not talking much, until Dan came home and then he had got up and gone downstairs to talk to Dan.

They talked for a long time. Dinah could hear the murmur of their voices through the open window. She wondered what they were saying for it seemed to her there was nothing much to say.

Presently the Andersons came home with the children, they disappeared into the house and there was more talk . . . but still Dinah sat on and did not move. What would the children say? How could one explain? What would Nannie think of it all? Dinah felt utterly unable to cope with the situation so it was no use trying.

Presently the door opened and Dan came in. "Are you all right?" he inquired, looking at her anxiously.

"Yes," said Dinah. "I'm all right, but I can't—I mean I don't know what to do."

"There's nothing to be done," said Dan, sitting down and taking her hand. "Everything's fixed up. Nannie is putting the children to bed so you don't need to worry."

"What did he say?" asked Dinah.

"He told me the whole thing. Don't worry about it, Di."

"And the children?"

"Nannie will tell them in the morning."

She sighed. "I can't—think of it properly," she said.

"I know," agreed Dan. "It's a bit of a shock for you—but a nice shock. He's a dear. isn't he? He wants to make everything easy and pleasant—no fuss, he said—then he said he was very fond of you and went home."

Dinah smiled a trifle wanly. "He's pleased?"

"Of course, he's pleased. You know that already. Mrs. Savage will be pleased too."

"Did he say so?"

Dan nodded. "Yes, he said so."

"But Dan, you were talking to him for ages. What else did he say?"

Dan told her . . . but of course Dinah had known it all before, she had heard about it from Pat and the story was the same in every detail.

"Gilbert deceived me about it," said Dinah. "I never knew he was engaged to that girl."

"I was sure of it at the time," Dan told her. "And if you could forgive him for deceiving you about his leave you can forgive him for this quite easily."

Dinah hesitated. It seemed to her almost worse. What misery he had caused his parents—and all for no object! Why couldn't he have explained?

"Don't think about it," urged Dan. "Try to take the whole thing in your stride. It all happened so long ago, didn't it?"

"But Dan—"

"And it makes no difference to our plans," continued Dan earnestly. "We still go on looking for a house in Edinburgh, don't we?"

"Of course," agreed Dinah, smiling at him.

"Well, then," said Dan giving her hand a little squeeze. "If it makes no difference to our plans what's all the fuss about?"

"It makes a difference to my inside feelings. We were so comfortable before. I hate the idea of meeting them—what on earth can I say?"

"Say nothing. They won't want to talk about it any more than you do."

"And the children!" said Dinah. "How can I explain it to them? I just feel I can't cope with it."

"I'll cope with the children," promised Dan.

Dan had intended to go back to Edinburgh that night but he rang up Mr. Cray and obtained permission to be late at the office the following morning. He spent some time trying to decide what to say to the children, how to explain the matter to them, and exactly how much to explain; but he need not have worried for Nannie had told them the news while they were dressing and being a placid, matter-of-fact person she had told them in a placid, matter-of-fact way. They were not even very surprised about it.

Dinah had dreaded breakfast-time. She was sure they would ask scores of unanswerable questions, but they asked none.

"I think it's nice," said Polly as she sat down and began to eat her porridge. "I like Mr. Monk awfully. He understands things."

Mark and Nigel were equally calm. They discussed the matter for a few minutes and then abandoned the topic in favour of their day's plans. The Barringtons had arranged to have rounders on the sands and the point was should they bathe first or wait until after the game was over.

"You see!" said Dan, as Dinah went out to see him off in his car. "You see, Di, you needn't have worried about the children, and it will be just as easy with the Monks—I mean the Savages, of course."

Dan was right. The old people did not want to talk about Gilbert. They could not talk about him with pleasure or profit so it was better to avoid the subject and talk of other things. Meeting Mr. Savage on the sands Dinah discovered that his attitude towards her was almost unchanged. They had been friends before and they were still friends. He greeted her with his usual kindness and asked how she had slept.

"Chocky-bick," said Margy hopefully.

Mr. Savage had not forgotten. He produced the usual little paper-bag and handed it to his grand-daughter.

"You shouldn't," objected Dinah. "Not *every* day. It's making her greedy—or perhaps I should say greedier! The moment she sees you she thinks of a chocolate biscuit."

Mr. Savage chuckled. He said, "There are many worse things with which she might connect me."

"But really—" began Dinah.

"I know, I know," agreed Mr. Savage. "But it *is* so nice to see people happy."

There was no doubt about Margy's happiness. She had taken the biscuit out of the bag and was munching with quiet enjoyment.

"Happiness personified." remarked Mr. Savage, watching her.

Dinah was obliged to smile.

"Yes," he continued nodding. "Yes, Margy is a sensible person, she knows exactly what she likes. The pleasures of the table are the first pleasures to be enjoyed and the last to pall. Very few people are too young and nobody is too old to enjoy good food . . ." and he proceeded to enlarge upon this theme in his usual amusing manner.

Mrs. Savage's reaction was different. She had no wish to rake up the past, but was exceedingly anxious to discuss the future. She wanted Dinah to bring the children to Harrogate for Christmas, (Linden Hall was amply large enough to accommodate the whole family.) They would have a Christmas tree: the children would hang up their stockings; Dinah would let her know beforehand what each child wanted so that they would not be disappointed with their presents. She would write to her sister who lived in South Africa and ask her to send sweets.

"You'll spoil them," Dinah told her.

"No, dear," said Mrs. Savage earnestly. "No. we won't do that. Jack says we mustn't spoil them; but it wouldn't spoil them to have a little fun at Christmas, would it? I wonder if we could get a Punch and Judy show or would they like a conjurer better? You *will* come, won't you, dear? It would be such a very great pleasure to Jack and me."

"Of course we'll come," Dinah said. It was something to be able to do this for them. She would have done a good deal to make up for all they had endured. "If you're sure you want us," said Dinah, smiling at the old lady. "If you're sure it won't be too much for you . . ."

Mrs. Savage was quite sure. Her thoughts flowed on; perhaps Dinah would like Harrogate (it really was a delightful place and so healthy for children), perhaps she would like Harrogate so much that she might think of settling down and living there. Mrs. Savage felt certain they could find a house that would suit Dinah admirably.

Dinah was touched, "It's very sweet of you," she said, "but Dan and I are going to live in Edinburgh."

"Well, we'll see," said Mrs. Savage. "You'll come for Christmas, anyhow. I can't help thinking you would like Harrogate and there is a splendid school for Polly. The boys must go to Eton, of course. Jack, you must write at once and—"

"Only if their mother approves," said Mr. Savage, interrupting her in a manner which was unusual if not unprecedented. "If their mother would like them to go to Eton well and good; but, remember Mary, we decided we had no right to interfere."

"Perhaps we could ask Dan," murmured Dinah who was feeling somewhat overwhelmed by all this.

"An excellent plan," agreed Mr. Savage promptly.

37

THE flower show had always been a "very special" occasion in Seatown; it had paled in glory during the war years, but *this* year— so Nannie declared—it would be as good as ever.

"You should go, Dinah," said Nannie persuasively. "It would be a nice jaunt for you and Polly—wee girls like flowers. The others will be happier at home."

Dinah did not want to go (she was still feeling all adrift) but when Nannie got it into her head that it would be "nice" for you to do this or that or the other, it was easier to do it than to argue.

"They're having it at King's Lodge," added Nannie. "You'll remember the place, Dinah?"

Of course Dinah remembered it. When she was a child the house (which belonged to the laird) had been occupied by Sir William and Lady Hart who had a large family of boys, and the Dees had sometimes gone to tea with them; but it was too big for any modern family so it was empty now, and the laird had given the garden and the park to the town. It was a very old house, parts of it were even older than the cottages at the harbour, and it was said in Seatown that it got its name from a visit paid to it by James IV before the battle of Flodden. The Dees had been tremendously interested in this legend and had done their best to substantiate it. but unfortunately the deeper they delved into the affairs of the misguided monarch the more improbable it seemed that he had graced the neighbourhood with his presence on the occasion in question.

King's Lodge was situated in the midst of the town (the town had grown up round it). A wide street shaded by fine old trees led inland from the harbour, and, walking down the street, one saw in front of one the great gates with their stone gate-posts and the gravel sweep, and the old white house, sleeping in the sunshine. It was a sprawling house with steps leading up and down in unexpected places, and a grey slate roof which sloped this way and that at a dozen different levels. The windows were of all sizes and shapes, most of them mullioned and with small diamond-panes of wavy glass. The garden was at the back and could be entered by a stone passage which ran through the centre of the house. It was in this passage that the Hart children had played when it rained: they had evolved a sort of fives with a tennis ball and exceedingly complicated rules—rules which, Dinah remembered, had often led to war.

Dinah and Polly approached the house in silence. Dinah's mind was full of memories and Polly was so interested in all she saw that for once she was speechless. Polly was feeling very grown-up to-day. The children had been left at home, but she, Polly, was old enough to go to the flower show with Mummy—Mummy all dressed in her best, wearing a black-and-white frock and a black straw hat with a little cluster of pink roses under the brim. You would never have known it was an old hat which Mummy had taken to pieces and arranged in a different way, unless, like Polly, you had seen her doing it.

She looked awfully nice, Polly thought . . . and Polly was aware that she, too, looked nice. Nannie had washed and ironed her pink cotton frock so that it felt just like a new one.

Coming out into the garden from the dim passage was like coming into fairyland. The golden sunshine shone down upon the green lawns and the fine old trees. Surrounding the lawns was a high hedge of rhododendron bushes; they had finished flowering of course, but their dark foliage made a perfect background for the stalls with their masses of flowers and fruit and vegetables, and for the gaily-coloured dresses of the company.

"Oh," whispered Polly, standing quite still.

Dinah smiled down at her. It was good that Polly appreciated the beauty of the scene. Dinah had not wanted to come, but she was beginning to feel glad she had given in to Nannie's persuasions. They walked along together, admiring the exhibits and looking at the people. Dinah had hoped to see the two Miss Stevens, or failing them, the Craddocks, but for a time she saw nobody she knew. The people of Seatown had changed a lot in the last ten years and not many of the old residents were left. Presently, however, she caught sight of Mrs. Cunningham and made her way towards her through the crowd. Dinah had always admired Mrs. Cunningham and thought her beautiful beyond compare, so it was a shock to discover she was no longer beautiful. Ten years had changed Mrs. Cunningham from a slim and beautiful woman into a woman who was fat, middle-aged and somewhat dowdy.

Mrs. Cunningham did not remember Dinah at first, but when Dinah went up and spoke to her she was interested and cordial. "Of course," she said. "I'm so glad you introduced yourself. It's always nice to see old friends. How is Dan?"

Dinah had been afraid she would ask after Gilbert but she didn't, so it was obvious that she knew. "Dan is in tremendous form," replied his sister.

"These are our sweet peas. Second prize," said Mrs. Cunningham. "I grew them myself so I'm very proud of them, Lady Armstrong got the first prize—she always does. She and Edith have come down from Edinburgh for the day. They've taken a flat in Edinburgh, you know."

"Yes," said Dinah nodding.

"Fancy leaving Abbot's End," exclaimed Mrs. Cunningham.

"Your sweet peas are lovely," declared Polly, to whom shyness was an unknown sensation. "They're so big and so frilly. They're like my frock, aren't they—newly ironed? I think they're the best of all the sweet peas in the show."

"Dear little girl," said Mrs. Cunningham who agreed profoundly with Polly's verdict. "Have you any other children, Dinah?"

"Lots," replied Dinah smiling. "Two boys and a girl."

"They're just babies," said Polly grandly. "*Much* too young to go to Flower Shows."

Mrs. Cunningham was pleased with Dinah and Polly. She took them under her wing and introduced them to her friends. Dinah had become a really beautiful young woman—it was amazing what a difference ten years could make—and little Polly was charming. Yes, Dinah was delightful. Everybody was looking at her and wondering who she was.

Mrs. Cunningham's own son was no exception to the rule. He was home on leave and had been dragged to the Flower Show much against his will . . . but now . . . who on earth was she? Where on earth had Mother got hold of her? Tom Cunningham emerged from his lair in the shade and placed himself in a strategic position.

"Oh—Tom!" exclaimed Mrs. Cunningham. "There you are! I couldn't think where you had gone. You're too late to see the judging, I'm afraid."

"Good heavens, what a nuisance!" said Tom with feigned dismay. "Why didn't you shout for me? I wouldn't have missed the judging for anything."

"This is my son, Tom," said his mother. "You remember Mrs. Savage, don't you, Tom? Dr. Bell's daughter."

"Goodness—if it isn't Dinner-Bell!" exclaimed Tom, grinning and holding out his hand. "Come and eat an ice-cream for the sake of auld lang syne."

"They're coming to look at the marrows," objected Mrs. Cunningham.

"Oh, Mother, who wants to look at marrows? If you've seen one you've seen the lot. They're all the same shape—"

"We're showing some very fine ones," urged Mrs. Cunningham, who felt it would be *much* better if Dinah came with her and looked at the marrows. She had seen that glint in Tom's eyes before and knew exactly what it meant . . . poor Tom was so susceptible and Dinah was so pretty. What a pity she had four children! Four! "I really think you should see the marrows, Dinah," said Mrs. Cunningham earnestly.

"Mother!" exclaimed Tom. "You don't realise the significance of this meeting. It simply must be celebrated properly. Dinner-Bell and I ran about the braes and pulled gowans together."

"We'll do both," said Dinah smiling. "We'll go and look at the marrows and then have ice-cream."

It was fun to see Tom again after all these years; she remembered him as a round-faced boy with freckles and sticking-out ears; now he was a good-looking young man—though unfortunately his ears still stuck out. That was his mother's fault, thought Dinah as she admired the marrows and endeavoured to guess their weight. Mark's ears had been inclined to stick out but she had made him a little net cap to wear at night and they were perfectly flat now. Was it too late to do anything about Tom's, wondered Dinah.

Having done her duty by the marrows, Dinah allowed herself to be taken in tow by Tom and presently found herself sitting in a shady corner of the garden. Tom was doing his best to entertain her and succeeding fairly well; she found his admiration pleasant and soothing. Polly was there too, of course, sitting on a rug and eating ice-cream at Tom's expense. Tom didn't mind how many she ate ("as many as you like," he told her) for as long as Polly sat there and ate ice-cream so long would Dinah sit and talk to Tom, and Tom's idea of bliss was to sit in the shade and talk to a pretty woman. Mrs. Cunningham, standing beside her runner-beans, was not so happy and presently she called Tom and beckoned him to come and help her to move a large box.

"Bother!" exclaimed her unnatural son. "Mother wants me to move that box. I've moved it twice already. I'll be back in a minute, Dinah."

But Mrs. Cunningham kept him for several minutes and while he was away Dinah saw Lady Armstrong and Edith Grover approaching her shady retreat. Seizing her bag Dinah rose hastily and taking Polly's hand withdrew down a path which led through the rhododendron bushes.

"But Mummy!" objected Polly. "I was going to have another ice-cream, and we haven't said good-bye to that nice man. He'll be very sad when he comes back and finds we haven't waited for him, Mummy."

It was true, of course. Dinah knew she had been rude and stupid but she could not have faced Edith Grover. The very idea of talking to the woman made her feel quite hot. She would see Tom later and explain. Tom would understand for there was no love lost between the Armstrongs and the Cunninghams.

Dinah had chosen the path at random, it was the nearest by which she could escape from those dreadful women, but now that she had time to look round she remembered it well; for it was here, amongst this maze of paths which led hither and thither between trees and overgrown bushes, that the Dees had played hide-and-seek with the Hart boys.

"What a jungle!" exclaimed Polly, skipping along the path at Dinah's side. "I wonder where we're going, don't you? Perhaps we'll find the Sleeping Beauty in the middle of the wood."

"I know where we're going," replied Dinah. "We shan't find the Sleeping Beauty but I hope we'll find something else."

This mysterious utterance roused Polly's curiosity and she was about to ask what her mother hoped to find when suddenly they came to a little clearing amongst the trees and her unasked question was answered. In the middle of the clearing was a lily-pool, and in the middle of the pool a large toad, carved in stone, sat upon a stone toadstool. There was a low wall round the pool with a flat top upon which the children used to sit or lean while they watched the gold-fish. Dinah remembered the pool as a large pool and was a trifle disappointed to find it so small but Polly was enchanted with it.

"Oh lovely!" she cried, clasping her hands together in delight. "Oh lovely!"

There was a seat at the other side of the pool and, raising her eyes, Dinah saw that somebody was sitting there . . . it was Malcolm.

Dinah had not expected to find any one here and certainly not Malcolm, for she had thought of him as being in Edinburgh. She had thought of Malcolm a great deal in the last few days (in spite of her decision not to think of him at all) and had decided that if she met him she would behave as if nothing had happened, she would be gay and friendly and casual, she would show him she didn't care a pin. That was the best way. But here was Malcolm and she could say nothing, she was speechless with surprise and confusion.

"Hallo Dinah!" exclaimed Malcolm, rising and coming forward to meet them. "How amazing seeing you here. When did you get back?"

"Isn't it a lovely pool!" cried Polly who wanted every one—even this strange man—to share in her delight.

"It is indeed," agreed Malcolm. "I've been sitting here admiring it. I got so tired and hot walking about and looking at bloated marrows and gigantic cabbages."

"So did we," nodded Polly.

"Is this one of your mystery children?" asked Malcolm smiling at Dinah as he spoke. "But I needn't ask. It's rude to make personal remarks so I shan't go into details as to how I know."

"It's my eyes," said Polly seriously. "That's what Miss Steven said." Malcolm laughed.

So far Dinah had not spoken. His greeting had increased her confusion for she could not understand what he meant, but now she must say something and she said the first thing that came into her head. "I suppose you came down from Edinburgh with Lady Armstrong," said Dinah.

"Oh no," he replied. "We're still at Abbot's End, Clarke and I. We're getting on quite nicely, thank you."

Dinah tried to return his friendly smile. "Good," she said.

"And you—" continued Malcolm. "You've come back from London. I thought you had gone for a long visit."

"But—I don't understand—"

"That was the message I got."

"What message?"

"The telephone message of course."

Dinah looked at him blankly.

"Do you mean you never sent a message?" asked Malcolm in surprise.

"No, why should I?"

"To say you were going to London and couldn't come out in the boat on Friday night."

"But I didn't, Malcolm. I never had any intention of going to London."

"Dinah, how amazing! I don't understand it at all."

"It does seem—odd."

"There's been some muddle," said Malcolm in bewilderment. "You must think I'm crazy—"

"It's quite all right," said Dinah interrupting him. "Honestly, Malcolm, it doesn't matter a bit. I just thought you had forgotten—or something."

"Forgotten!" he cried. "You don't mean you went down to the harbour and waited!"

"Well—yes—we had arranged to go, hadn't we? So—"

"But this is awful!" he exclaimed in horrified tones. "You went down to the harbour—"

"Don't worry—"

"Worry! Of course I'm worrying. Worry is a mild word. What *can* you have thought of me! Good heavens!" exclaimed Malcolm. "Good heavens, I don't know *what* to say!"

"It's all right, Malcolm—"

"It's all wrong," he declared. "I would not have had this happen for anything. You went down to the harbour!"

"Yes, but—"

"How could it have happened!" he exclaimed. "How on earth could I have got a message? You sent no message at all?"

"No," said Dinah.

"So it couldn't have been taken up wrongly? I mean if you had phoned and said you were coming later, or something—"

"But I didn't," she assured him.

They had strolled over to the seat and now they sat down. Polly was playing quite happily near the pool.

"We must get to the bottom of this," Malcolm declared.

"We must find out exactly what happened. Let me think, for a minute."

She let him think and while he was thinking she began to puzzle it out for herself. How could the muddle have occurred. Who could have given Malcolm the mysterious message?

"Yes," said Malcolm after a little silence. "Yes, I'm beginning to see light. It was Edith who said you had phoned. She had written the message on the telephone pad and she showed it to me when I got home from Edinburgh on Friday afternoon. She handed it to me and said you had rung up at lunch-time; you were very sorry but you had to go to London unexpectedly and you wouldn't be back for some time. Clever, wasn't it?"

"But it wasn't true!" cried Dinah.

"Of course it wasn't true," he agreed.

"She—she made it up!" exclaimed Dinah incredulously.

Malcolm nodded. "It isn't the first time Edith has lied to me. I ought to have been on my guard but somehow—somehow it sounded true. I wonder how on earth she knew we were going for a sail on Friday night."

"I told her," said Dinah in a low voice. "She came to see me—I wondered why she had come."

"That clears up every thing, doesn't it?" said Malcolm bitterly.

Dinah was silent. As Malcolm said it cleared up everything. Everything was perfectly clear. Edith Grover had been out to make mischief and had succeeded rather well.

"She's a nice woman, isn't she?" said Malcolm at last.

"It's frightful!" declared Dinah. "The more I think about it . . . I mean how could any one think it all out and—and—"

"Yes, it's almost incredible."

"How unhappy she must be!"

"Unhappy?" asked Malcolm in surprise.

"Only a terribly unhappy person would want to make trouble," said Dinah with conviction. "It's when people are utterly and completely miserable that they want to hurt other people and make them unhappy too."

"How do you know?" he asked.

"Because of the children. If they're happy they're good." said Dinah simply.

Malcolm smiled, "And if they're unhappy they're bad? That may be so, but I can tell you this: Edith will be even more unhappy when I've done with her."

"Don't," said Dinah impulsively. "Don't be too hard on her, Malcolm."

"I couldn't be too hard. She—when I think of it—"

"Don't think of it," Dinah said quickly. "Leave it, Malcolm. It's all over and no harm has come of it."

"You'll forgive me, Dinah?"

"There isn't anything to forgive, is there?"

"I was a fool. I shouldn't have believed her."

"Why shouldn't we believe people? Surely it's natural to believe what people say. It would be a queer sort of world if we had to verify everything before we accepted it."

"It's necessary with some people—obviously," returned Malcolm.

There was a little silence. Dinah knew now, without a shadow of doubt that everything Edith Grover had told her was untrue. She could not blame Malcolm for being deceived when she had been so easily deceived herself.

"Let's clear up everything," said Malcolm, as if he had read her thoughts. "I hate lies and people who tell lies. Let's get everything square, shall we?"

Dinah did not agree nor disagree. It seemed to her that there was no point in telling Malcolm everything. He was upset already—why upset him more? She said, "I wonder why Miss Grover hates me. It's an uncomfortable feeling."

"She's jealous," replied Malcolm promptly. "Edith has no friends herself and she doesn't like other people to have friends. She has a most extraordinary nature. She's twisted in some strange way—twisted out of the true. She can be charming if she likes, and then again, she can be positively devilish. Edith and I were engaged at one time. It was at the very beginning of the war when every one was getting engaged. Edith came to stay at Abbot's End and she seemed—I mean I liked her quite a lot. Then, when I was wounded, she broke it off. I didn't blame her."

"Malcolm, how dreadful of her!"

"Now," said Malcolm, taking no notice of the interruption. "*Now* I have a sort of feeling she regrets it, but I know her too well to be taken in by her again. That's the whole story, Dinah."

"Yes," said Dinah. "Well, of course—"

"And anyhow," added Malcolm firmly. "Anyhow, I've given up all idea of marriage."

"Why?" asked Dinah in a low voice.

He laughed rather mirthlessly. "Why? Surely it's obvious. What woman would want to tie herself for life to a useless hulk?"

Dinah was too taken aback to make any adequate reply. She was still struggling for words when Polly approached.

"Shall we go back now and find that nice gentleman, Mummy?" inquired Polly with an engaging smile. "I think I could eat some more ice-cream."

The conversation was over and Dinah was glad. She rose at once remarking that Polly had had enough ice-cream to last her a week, and anyhow it was time to go home.

"I shall stay here a bit longer," said Malcolm. "I don't want to run into Miss Edith Grover until I've thought out exactly what I'm going to say."

Dinah looked back as she and Polly walked away together.

Malcolm had risen to say good-bye but he had sat down again. He looked lonely sitting there by himself. He was a lonely sort of person. He had been very friendly and kind and everything was cleared up satisfactorily but he had said nothing about another meeting.

38

THE afternoon was grey, with low clouds. The sea was very calm. There was a thundery feeling in the air. Dinah left the children with Flo and walked along the shore by herself. She had decided that a solitary walk to the Black Rocks might help her to clear her brain; her brain needed tidying. Her brain, thought Dinah, was like a work-basket in which bits and pieces have got scrummaged up with reels of silk and balls of wool, partly unrolled and inextricably tangled.

She had come out to think seriously about Gilbert's parents and the difference it was going to make in her life and in the lives of her children. Dan had said, don't worry, nobody wants a fuss. She had no intention of making a fuss but she must get it all straight in her own mind before she could stop worrying. Pat had told her the facts. He had told her the whole story long before he knew—or she knew—that he was telling it to his cousin's widow, and Dinah did not doubt a word of it. Gilbert had been engaged to that other girl and the date of the wedding was already fixed when he went to Harrogate—no wonder his father had been angry. Mr. Savage who seemed meek and gentle, was reputed to have a hasty temper, and Gilbert's nature had been proud and intolerant. What Gilbert chose to do or not to do was his own affair and nobody had any right to question his actions. . . . the slightest hint of adverse criticism and Gilbert was up in the air. It was easy to see how the quarrel had arisen; and it was easy (when you knew Gilbert) to see how he had twisted the whole thing out of the straight to make it appear that he was the injured party. He *had* to do it, thought Dinah as she walked along. He had to twist it because he could never admit himself at fault. She was not angry with him now. She could think of him without pain, in fact without any feeling at all except a vague pity. It seemed to her that the girl who had loved Gilbert and had suffered such misery over him had been another girl altogether—not Dinah but somebody else, somebody Dinah knew and liked and was sorry for. Looking back and thinking about that girl Dinah began to wonder how she had borne it. What an appalling time that girl had had! What loneliness she had endured, what disappointments, anxieties and responsibilities! How that poor girl had toiled and slaved day after day for years on end without a single holiday or any prospect of a holiday—without an hour off duty! How tired she had been, tired all the time, so tired that nothing was any pleasure!

But all that was over now, thanks to Dan. Dan had rescued her.

The Savages were anxious to do things for the children, to give them pleasure and help with their education; Dinah had no intention of refusing their offers—why should she? It would be an excellent thing for Nigel to go to a good boarding-school and now that there was no need for economy she could send him with an easy mind. Mark could go too, or he could go to a school in Edinburgh; whichever seemed best. There would be no difficulty if Mark decided definitely that he wanted to study medicine. This was all to the good; it was all to the good that she had made it up with Gilbert's parents and that they were behind her. Mr. Savage was wise and kind, it gave Dinah a safe feeling to know he was there. She was not going to live at Harrogate, of course. It was nice of Mrs. Savage to want her but Dinah's future was settled. She was going to live with Dan. Her future was settled and she ought to be thinking of it with delight . . .

How silly I am, thought Dinah, as she paused and gazed at the sea. I'm terribly ungrateful. If I had had this chance three months ago I would have jumped with joy . . . to live with Dan in a little house of our own! To have Flo to help with the cooking! To have enough money to give the children the best of everything! I ought to be jumping with joy instead of crying for the moon . . .

She stood there for a little, trying to reason with herself but it wasn't much good. She couldn't reason herself into a proper frame of mind. She felt restless.

Presently she took up some flat stones and began to spin them along the surface of the water (it was an ideal day for the game because the sea was so calm and still) and as she did so she remembered that Dan had beaten her at this game, as he had beaten her at every game they played. She remembered getting up early one morning and coming out by herself and practising, so that the next time they played "ducks and drakes" she had been able to beat Dan. It was a low-down thing to do. Dinah had known this at the time and had felt slightly ashamed of herself; she had not intended to tell Dan what she had done, but she had told him, of course. She had never been able to keep a secret from Dan . . . *never until now*, thought Dinah as she watched her flat stone give three—four—five hops before it sank to the bottom.

"Pretty good, I call that!" exclaimed an admiring voice.

Dinah swung round and saw Pat. She wondered how long he had been standing there, watching her.

"Pretty good," he repeated, nodding. "I didn't think girls *could*. I always thought it took a strong wrist."

"It's knack, not strength," said Dinah, smiling at him.

She had not seen Pat since Sunday night and had been wondering how he would take it. Apparently he was taking it in his stride like the uncle and aunt, and Dinah was glad. She held out her hand, intending to shake hands with him, but Pat misunderstand. He look her hand and examined her wrist.

"Tiny, isn't it?" he said, showing how his long finger and thumb could overlap it easily. "Delicate-looking and tiny, but strong. I like that little gold bracelet—sets it off, if you know what I mean."

Dinah retrieved her hand and picked up another stone. "We'll have a competition," she suggested.

"No good," he declared. "I couldn't give you a game. We'll talk if you don't mind. There's one or two things to be cleared up."

"It's all quite clear," objected Dinah.

Pat was not to be put off. "The uncle and aunt are tickled to death. It's amazing. Really, it is."

"Yes, isn't it? But—"

"You don't seem surprised!"

"I've got over it," said Dinah.

"I haven't," he replied. "I mean when I think of Gilbert . . . Gilbert was always so sure of himself, you know."

"I know'," agreed Dinah, slightly puzzled.

"I wish I was," said Pat with a sigh. "I'm never sure of myself—except when I'm doing my job. I'm all right there, of course, but in other things I'm a bit of a fool. I play quite a good game of golf and I'm not so dusty at squash but that doesn't help much, does it?"

"Three hops," said Dinah, who was playing ducks and drakes by herself.

"It wasn't a good stone," said Pat. "You want a thin flat one with rounded edges. Dinah, do listen to me."

"Yes, of course," said Dinah, pausing to smile at him. "What is it, Pat?"

"It's just this," said Pat earnestly. "I thought you were married to Dan. We all thought so. It was absolutely batty."

"It wasn't batty. It was a natural mistake."

"So that's why I said I wanted to be friends with you, of course. You see that, don't you?"

"No," said Dinah shaking her head. "I mean it makes no difference. I hope you'll go on being friends with me."

"It isn't the same at all."

"It is to me," Dinah pointed out. "Nothing is altered between us from my point of view."

He digested this thoughtfully. "It *is* altered," he said at last. "The point is I thought you were married and you aren't. That makes everything different."

"But not different to me; you *must* realise that. It's exactly the same as it always was. I told you I needed a friend."

"Yes, but—"

"We shook hands on it, didn't we?"

"But, Dinah—"

"I still need a friend as much as ever," said Dinah firmly.

"Just a friend?" inquired Pat in a doubtful tone. "I mean you wouldn't think of—of needing—anything else?"

"Just a friend."

"You couldn't—well—leave it for a bit, I suppose? I mean you don't think that perhaps some day—I mean I wouldn't mind waiting—"

"No," said Dinah shaking her head. "No, Pat, I like you most awfully as a friend."

"I suppose there's some other fellow," said Pat wretchedly. "I might have known, of course. I mean a marvellous girl like you . . . well, you know what I mean."

Dinah did not answer that, and by her silence Pat was answered.

"I might have known," he repeated. "'Well, don't worry about it. I mean it doesn't matter a hoot. I wish I hadn't bothered you."

"Oh Pat, I do like you awfully!" exclaimed Dinah.

"Good," said Pat. "That's grand, Dinah. I'm frightfully glad you like me—and of course it still stands—if you want anything done you ask me straight off."

"Yes, of course," said Dinah. She hesitated and then went on, "I'd tell you about it if there was anything to tell, but there isn't. In fact I don't really know whether he—whether he likes me or not. I thought he did—a little—and then something happened. I'm not sure, now. I haven't told any one—not any one at all—just you because we're friends."

"It'll be all right," said Pat earnestly. "Why, of course it will! You'll see. I mean you're so absolutely marvellous. I expect he's just—just wondering whether you could possibly—I expect he's a bit shy. People *are*, you know. I mean it takes a frightful lot of courage to—to—I mean I had to pull up my socks like anything. So you see he may be like me, mayn't he? I expect that's it, Dinah."

"Pat—" began Dinah, and then found she couldn't go on.

"So perhaps," continued Pat, "perhaps you might just—just help him out a bit, if you see what I mean. You might just sort of show him you like him. I mean if he's anything like me . . ."

He picked up a stone and set it spinning. "One, two," he said. "Two hops! Pretty rotten, what? I told you I was no good at it, didn't I?"

As they walked back round the point and over the rocks, Dinah began to tell Pat about the morning she had got up early and practised spinning stones so as to be up sides with Dan.

39

IT HAD become a recognised thing that unless Dinah happened to be going out in the evening she should go downstairs at nine o'clock and partake of tea and cakes with the Andersons. To-night Nannie was alone, for Mr. Anderson had gone to a Town Council Meeting. He was an active and conscientious member of the Seatown Town Council.

"Come away in, Dinah," said Nannie, who was sitting before the kitchen fire with her skirt turned back warming her knees. "Andrew's away to the Council. He wouldn't miss a meeting for the world. There's talk he may be made a baillie in November—that's between ourselves." She put down the *People's Friend* as she spoke and motioned Dinah to draw her chair in nearer the fire.

"It's damp and cold to-night," said Dinah as she sat down.

Dinah was glad Mr. Anderson was out; not because she did not like him, but because Nannie was so much more like her old self when her husband was not there, so much more amusing and unconstrained. With Dinah, who was neither a Seatown crony nor (strictly speaking) a visitor, Nannie's speech was a mixture of her two languages, a sort of half-way house.

"You've not been out sailing lately," Nannie remarked.

"No," replied Dinah. "It isn't exactly the weather for a sail to-night."

This was not a proper answer, of course, for although to-night was damp and cold there had been several extremely beautiful evenings when a sail would have been pleasant, but Nannie was the last person to press for a confidence so she changed the subject.

"Pride's an awful thing," said Nannie thoughtfully.

"Pride?" asked Dinah.

"Mh'm, there's a girl in the story that wrecks her whole life with pride—and loses her man forebye."

"I shouldn't worry," said Dinah, smiling. "She'll get him in the end—or else someone better—stories always end happily in the *People's Friend*."

"I wouldn't read them if they didn't," Nannie declared. "There's enough trouble in this wurrld without stories ending badly. Och, no, I'm not worrying about *hurr*. It's myself I was thinking of. Pride's my besetting sin, Dinah."

"Your besetting sin!" exclaimed Dinah in surprise.

"Just that," said Nannie, nodding gravely. "The wickedest thing I ever did in my life was because of pride. Mh'm, it's true. I let yon wumman take you away to Glasgow. That was the wickedest thing I ever did."

"But Nannie, you couldn't help it. Aunt Teena insisted."

"I should have stood up to her. I should have talked to you and Dan. If the three of us had stood together we'd have gained the day. I was too proud—that's the truth of it. I wouldn't demean myself arguing. I said to myself, if Dinah wants to go she can go, and maybe her aunt can give her a more suitable kind of life."

"But I *didn't* want to go! It just never occurred to me that I could refuse. I mean I had always done what grown-up people told me—"

"Och, I knew that fine! I knew it in my heart of hearts. You were nothing but a child," declared Nannie. "It was my blame entirely, the whole thing. The doctor had left you in my charge, and I let you go. Many's the time I've regretted it."

"She was difficult to stand up to," comforted Dinah.

"Aye, she had a bosom like a battleship," agreed Nannie in reminiscent tones. "Maybe I was a wee bit frightened of her, too—but it was mostly pride. You had a sore time of it with her, Dinah?"

"Yes, it was an unhappy time. She was a queer woman, you know. She had dozens of friends and was always going out to bridge-parties or meetings. Everybody liked her—but at home she was moody and difficult to get on with, just like a different person."

"A causey doo,"* said Nannie with infinite scorn. "There's plenty like that."

"Yes," agreed Dinah, smiling at the term, which she had not heard for many years. "Yes, Aunt Teena was a causey doo. She couldn't keep a maid; they were always leaving at a moment's notice. I often envied them. But don't let's talk about it, Nannie. It's all over long ago and perhaps it was good for me."

They talked about other things and Dinah felt happier when she went up to bed. She decided that she must not let pride wreck her life—like the girl in Nannie's story—and if Malcolm made no move to arrange another meeting she would ring him up. She would wait another day—two more days—and then ring up and ask him to come to tea on Sunday when Dan would be here.

The twins were being scrubbed in the bath. Dinah looked into the bathroom, which was full of steam, and said gaily, "Nannie, you're behind schedule to-night. Margy's in bed."

"They're so dirty," explained Nannie, looking up from her labours with a very red face.

"We're like chimbley sweeps!" cried Nigel. "Nannie says we're like chimbley sweeps—look, Mummy!" He held up a pair of very black hands.

"Goodness!" exclaimed Dinah.

Suddenly Nigel leant forward and drew a large black M on Mark's chest. "M for Mark," he said, chuckling delightedly.

"There—and I've just washed him all over!" cried Nannie, giving the culprit a light smack on his bare back. "Did you ever see such a boy in all your life!"

Dinah smiled. Nannie had mellowed considerably since the Dees were children. If they had behaved like this they would have received a proper spanking, not a gentle, friendly slap.

---

* For the benefit of those born south of Tweed it may be explained that a causey doo is one who coos like a dove on the causeway but shows undovelike qualities at home.

"You spoil them, Nannie," said Dinah. "How do you think I'm going to manage them, myself?"

"Look at my frog!" cried Mark. "It's my frog that I got at the party. It swims beautifully."

"My gold-fish is going to eat your frog!" yelled Nigel, making a dive at the frog with the celluloid fish in his band.

"My frog is biting your toes!" retorted Mark, suiting action to word.

Dinah went forward and picked Mark out of the bath and set him on the mat. "That was a seagull," she declared as she enveloped his pink body in the towel. "The seagull dived into the water and swallowed you whole."

"Swallow me, too!" cried Nigel eagerly.

Dinah had just swallowed Nigel when the door opened and Flo's face appeared. "It's a gentleman to see Mrs. Savage," she explained.

"Who?" asked Nannie. "Why didn't you ask his name? How often have I told you to ask people's names? And you left him standing on the doorstep, I suppose!"

"He wouldn't come in," said Flo apologetically, "He said he'd wait. He just wants to speak to Mrs. Savage for a wee minute."

Dinah was trying to tidy her hair. "Tell him I'm coming," she said.

"Tell him Mummy's a seagull!" shouted Mark.

"Tell him she's swallowed us whole!" yelled Nigel.

"It'll be that nice Mr. Yoker," said Nannie. "You go and talk to him, Dinah. I'll see Polly into bed."

Dinah had the same idea but her visitor was not Pat; it was Clarke who was standing upon the doorstep.

"I'm sorry to bother you," he said. "It's just that Mr. Malcolm would like to see you. He wondered if you could possibly come up to Abbot's End. He's ill, you see, and—"

"Ill!" exclaimed Dinah.

"Yes, they're taking him to Edinburgh to-morrow for another operation. If you could just come up and see him for a few minutes . . ." Clarke stopped and looked at her beseechingly.

"I'll get my coat," said Dinah.

She ran upstairs and got her coat and explained to Nannie where she was going.

Clarke had brought the car. He helped her in and arranged a rug over her knees. As he did so he said, "The ladies are away. Mr.

Malcolm said I was to remind you they wouldn't be there in case you would rather not come."

"Of course I'm coming." she replied.

Clarke made no comment. She realised, now that she saw him properly, that he was very upset. His round healthy face looked haggard and drawn.

"Is Mr. Malcolm very ill?"

"He's very—low," said Clarke unhappily. "I've never seen him so low. That's what's worrying me. He's been through a lot and it was his spirit brought him through. The doctors said so. Now he doesn't seem to care."

"Has he been suffering much?" Dinah asked.

Clarke nodded. "He doesn't complain of course, but I always know. He hasn't been sleeping the last few nights."

Dinah said nothing. There was nothing to say. Clarke shut the door and went round to the driving-seat.

Abbot's End seemed much the same from the outside, except that some of the blinds were down, but inside the house there was quite a different feeling. The banks of flowers had gone and the hall looked larger. It felt cool and airy. There was a dignity about it, a feeling of lightness and space.

"Mr. Malcolm doesn't like a lot of flowers," explained Clarke. "The first thing I have to do when the ladies go away is to take out all the flowers. But ladies always like flowers."

"I like it best without them," Dinah said. "The hall is so beautiful."

"Yes," agreed Clarke. "It's nice wood, isn't it. I like that light oak. Mr. Malcolm likes it. He likes to see it bare. He said to me one day, 'I can't see the wood for the flowers.'"

Dinah smiled. She could imagine Malcolm saying it. She followed Clarke up the wide, shallow stair-case. The landing was square and ran all round the house like an open balcony so that you could look down into the hall below. The woodwork was all light oak, unvarnished, which made the house very bright and cheerful. The sun streamed in through the tall windows on to the dark-blue carpets. The feeling in the house was a feeling of peace and harmony, the smell was of bees-wax and turpentine with a faint flavour of pine and a tang of the sea. Dinah stood upon the landing and savoured it appreciatively while Clarke went into his master's room to tell him his visitor had come.

40

DINAH had expected to find Malcolm in bed, but he was lying, on the sofa attired in a dark-blue silk dressing-gown. His hair was neatly brushed and, although he looked pale and thin, his smile when he saw her was Malcolm's own cheery smile.

"How good of you, Dinah!" he said, stretching out his hand.

Dinah took it. "Not a bit good of me," she declared.

The room was large and airy, it looked all the larger because there was not much furniture in it. The blinds were half-drawn and the sunshine poured in below them making pools of light on the floor.

"Sit down," said Malcolm, pointing to a low chair. "Clarke and I are alone in the house. We like it. There's a peaceful feeling about it. Clarke understands things without being told."

"Yes," said Dinah nodding. Her heart was beating rather fast. She wondered why Malcolm had sent for her—not to talk about Clarke!

"I hope it wasn't terribly inconvenient," continued Malcolm. "It was awful cheek of me asking you to come. I was sorry the moment Clarke had gone, but there was no way of stopping him."

"I wanted to come, Malcolm."

"Visiting the sick," he said, smiling at her.

"How are you?" she asked. "Clarke told me you've got to have another operation. I'm terribly sorry."

"Yes, it's a bore, isn't it? But don't let's talk about that."

"Not talk about it?"

"Much better to talk about something else."

"About the weather?" she asked, trying to smile.

"About the weather," he agreed. "What do you think of the prospects? To-morrow will be fine and dry unless it rains . . ."

"Malcolm—please—" said Dinah earnestly. "I *do* want to know how you are. You were so much better, weren't you?"

He moved his head restlessly on the cushion. "Yes, it's disappointing," he said. "It's such a bore—the whole thing. I wish they would leave me alone."

"It's wretched for you!"

"I ought not to mind, I suppose. I mean I ought to be used to operations by this time but somehow it's the other way about. In fact I dislike it more every time," said Malcolm carefully. "More, not less. I suppose I've lost my nerve or something. Lying here and thinking about it . . . suddenly I couldn't bear it any longer. That's why I sent Clarke to ask you to come and see me."

Dinah repeated that she had been glad to come.

"But I didn't mean to start whining," said Malcolm, turning his head and smiling at her. "That wasn't the idea at all. I hate people who whine."

"It isn't whining to tell a friend how you are!"

"Sounds like it to me," he declared. "But now you know all about it so we can change the subject."

"I know nothing about it," she objected. "You haven't told me anything. Is it a serious operation?"

"Pretty serious," he replied, giving in to her. "It's the same old splinter of course, but the doctors don't seem very happy about it this time. They don't show quite the same cheerful optimism. It isn't so much what they say as what they leave unsaid. I've a good deal to do with doctors, one way and another, and I can read between the lines."

"You mean—" began Dinah in a low voice. "You mean you may have to lose your foot?"

"Well—yes—possibly. They don't know for certain. Dr. Brabazon doesn't want to amputate if he can avoid it because I'm not in a very sound condition. That's the truth of the matter."

"Malcolm!"

"Don't look like that, Dinah," said Malcolm smiling. "Don't look so sad. It's all in the day's work. I hate the idea of the operation but, to be quite honest, I don't mind about the—the outcome. Why should I? Life isn't as wonderful as all that. Why should I go on fighting just to stay alive? It isn't worth the trouble."

Dinah could say nothing, and after a moment's pause he added, "But this is just what I wanted to avoid; bothering you and upsetting you. I didn't intend to say a word about it, not a word. Let's turn over the page and think about something cheerful, shall we? Let's forget it."

There was a cold feeling in Dinah's heart. She was a doctor's daughter and she knew enough about illness to realise the danger.

She could remember her father saying: "He's making a good fight for it, we'll pull him through" or, alternatively, "He'd have pulled through if he had put up a fight." If Malcolm went into the battle half-heartedly feeling that "life wasn't as wonderful as all that," he was not giving himself a chance.

"Malcolm," she said, trying to control her voice. "Malcolm we can't forget it. We can't leave it like that. You mustn't give up the struggle."

"Oh, I'm not giving up," he replied with a little sigh. "It's just that it doesn't seem to matter, that's all."

"All battles matter," urged Dinah, trying desperately to rouse him. "You didn't give up the Championship. You fought for every hole—every putt—and you won through."

He smiled at her. "You were there, willing me to win."

"I shall be willing you to win this battle," she told him seriously. There was a little silence.

"I wonder why you wanted to see me," said Dinah at last.

"I've told you Dinah. I was lonely and I wanted a little sympathy, that was all. It was terribly selfish of me. but you see I've become that sort of person," said Malcolm bitterly. "The sort of person I've always despised, the sort of person who can't take it. You thought I was a hero, 'more than life-size' (I remember you saying that), but now you can see for yourself that I'm not a hero, not within a hundred miles. It's better for you to know the truth."

"It isn't the truth!" cried Dinah. "You're safe and sure and strong!"

"Dinah!" he exclaimed in surprise.

Dinah looked away. She had not meant to say it . . . but of course it was true. Even in his physical weakness his strength of character was apparent and what was more important his honesty matched her own. One would never have to shut one's eyes to anything Malcolm did or thought—Dinah knew that.

"What do you mean?" Malcolm asked.

"You're strong inside," said Dinah a trifle breathlessly. "That's what matters. That's the important kind of strength. You would never let any one down."

Malcolm was silent.

"Listen, Malcolm," continued Dinah in a low voice. "There's something I want to know. Will you answer me honestly and truthfully? Will you promise to answer?"

"Of course, Dinah," he replied.

"I *must* know," she told him. "It's—well it's rather difficult. You said you were lonely and wanted someone to talk to, didn't you? Any friend would have done."

"Any friend?" repeated Malcolm in surprise. "But Dinah, I don't know what you mean."

Dinah hesitated, but only for a moment. She remembered her conversation with Pat. She remembered Pat had said "Show him that you like him." Perhaps she wouldn't have another chance of showing him . . .

"You wanted to see *me*, didn't you?" she said. "Tell me why, Malcolm. You promised to tell me honestly and truthfully, didn't you?"

"You're so nice to look at," Malcolm told her.

His eyes were on her face. She could feel the hot blush rising as he looked at her. "I know now," she said in a very low voice. "I know the real reason."

He didn't speak.

She leant forward and took his hand, it was hot and dry. She held it tightly. "Malcolm," she said breathlessly. "Malcolm, I know why you wanted to see me."

"I don't want you to pity me," he said. He had turned his head aside and was looking out of the window.

"Nor to love you?" she asked. "Don't you want me to love you?"

His hand tightened on hers. "But that's impossible! I can't believe it—a crotchety old cripple—it's just that you're sorry for me. You're sorry. You want to comfort me."

"I want us to comfort one another."

"Listen," he said. "It isn't fair to you—"

"No, I won't listen until you tell me the truth. Do you—like me, Malcolm?"

"Oh Dinah!"

"Please," she said desperately. "Please Malcolm, I must know." There was no other way. "You like me a little, don't you?"

"I love you dearly—who wouldn't love you!" he exclaimed.

"Really and truly?"

He pulled her towards him, "You darling," he said gently. "Of course—really and truly—I wanted you and only you. Just once, I thought, just to see her once . . . to see her dear, lovely face and hear her voice . . . once more . . ."

She knelt down beside him and kissed him very gently. He put his arms round her.

"But this is all wrong," he said, kissing her hair. "This is the last thing I meant to do. I meant to be so—careful. I meant to be cool and cheerful and talk about—about—"

"The weather," she suggested, smiling at him through tears.

"Darling!" said Malcolm softly. "Darling girl!"

They stayed like that for a few minutes very quietly. Then suddenly Dinah drew away. "The children!" she exclaimed. "Perhaps you had forgotten about the children!"

"What children?" he asked in bewilderment.

"Mine, of course."

He smiled. "Yes," he admitted. "I had forgotten all about them. Somehow or other they don't seem very real to me. They won't mind, will they?"

She looked at him doubtfully. "Do you mean *you* don't mind?"

"The only thing I mind is that they aren't my children. Did you love him very much, Dinah?"

She sat back on her heels and thought about it seriously for she knew Malcolm wanted the truth. "I loved him madly," she said at last. "I was nineteen and Gilbert was a sort of fairy prince. We were blissfully happy for a little while, and then gradually I began to realise that he was—not—not quite as wonderful as I had thought. There were things about him that I couldn't . . ." she hesitated.

"Was he brilliant?" Malcolm asked.

She nodded. "Fancy your remembering," she said. "It was that first day we met at the bathing pool, wasn't it? We talked about brilliant people and suddenly you asked me why I distrusted brilliance—or something like that. Yes, it was because of Gilbert; he could do everything superlatively well without effort, without taking any trouble. I believe that was the reason, or one of the reasons, why he was so intolerant of other people's failings, and why he could never own himself in the wrong. He wasn't—straight," continued Dinah in a low voice. "I shut my eyes to it at first. I wouldn't let myself see any flaws . . . and it wasn't difficult to shut my eyes because he was away so much (he only came home now and then for a wild ten days leave), but in my heart of hearts I knew—even before I had solid proof—that he wasn't—wasn't—straight. So you see, Malcolm, you needn't be jealous of poor Gilbert. You aren't jealous, are you?"

"Of course I am," he said.

After a little they began to talk about plans.

"I must ring up and put off the operation," said Malcolm thoughtfully. "There are all sorts of things to be settled."

"What things?" she asked. "No, Malcolm, let's get it over quickly. I'll come to Edinburgh with you. I want to be there."

"Yes, of course," said Malcolm with a little sigh. "Yes, of course I want you to be there, darling; but we *must* put it off for a day or two. I must see my lawyer for one thing. I shall have to tell him about this, of course, but nobody else must know."

"Everybody must know."

"No," said Malcolm firmly. "Nobody is to be told until I'm better. It's bad enough as it is—I mean it's so unfair to you. Don't you understand?"

"It's you who doesn't understand!" cried Dinah. "Everybody must know, because I want to be there, with you. I want to have the right to be there."

"Oh well," he said, smiling at her. "I suppose you had better have your own way. I had no idea you were such a strong-minded person."

"But I'm not," said Dinah earnestly. "I'm not in the least strong-minded. I want everything arranged for me, always. I want to be ordered about and taken care of for the rest of my life. This is the first and last time I shall want to have my own way—honestly Malcolm."

Malcolm was laughing now and laughing quite heartily.

"But it's true—really true," she told him.

At this juncture there was a discreet tap on the door and after a moment's pause Clarke came in with the sherry and biscuits on a silver tray. Dinah was standing at the window, looking out, and Malcolm was still laughing.

"It's done you a lot of good having a visitor," said Clarke looking at him.

"All the good in the world," agreed Malcolm. "I'm a new man. In fact I'm thinking of getting married."

"I was just hoping that," declared Clarke with a beaming smile.

"You were hoping that!" echoed Malcolm in amazement.

"Yes," said Clarke, looking from one to the other and beaming more brightly than ever. "I've been hoping it for some time. I was beginning to be afraid you'd miss the boat, Mr. Malcolm."

"Well, of all the cheek!" cried Malcolm, seizing a small cushion and throwing it at Clarke with all his might.

Clarke caught it neatly in mid-air. "But you mustn't get too excited, Mr. Malcolm," he said in sudden anxiety. "We don't want your temperature going up."

"Oh damn!" exclaimed Malcolm. "First you fuss over me like an old hen because I'm depressed and then you tell me not to get excited. There's no pleasing you, Clarke."

"But I am pleased," objected Clarke. "I couldn't be more pleased, Mr. Malcolm. She's just the right lady for you if you don't mind me saying so."

Malcolm did not mind in the least. "What a good thing our opinions coincide!" he said chuckling. "Clarke, you must drink our health. Bring the table nearer so that I can pour out the sherry."

When the healths had been drunk with due solemnity Dinah took up her bag and said she must go.

"Need you?" asked Malcolm.

"I thought Mrs. Savage would be staying to supper," said Clarke. "I've a duck in the oven and there are peas, of course, and—"

"You see!" exclaimed Malcolm. "Clarke has prepared for a party. You wouldn't like to disappoint him, would you?"

"But you're tired."

"You can't get out of it like that—it's an order," said Malcolm, smiling at her with a mischievous twinkle in his eye. "It's the First Order, Dinah. You must stay and have supper with me."

Dinah had no wish to get out of it. She hesitated and looked at Clarke.

"It's done Mr. Malcolm good," said Clarke nodding. "As long as I can get him off to bed by nine or thereabouts it will be all right. I'll go and telephone to Mrs. Anderson, shall I?"

When Clarke had gone Dinah sat down on a stool beside the sofa; she leant her head against Malcolm's shoulder and for a little while neither of them spoke. Dinah was looking back and wondering about things; she loved Malcolm dearly and she felt as if she had loved him for a long time. It was a different sort of love from the wild, mad passion which Gilbert had inspired, it was peaceful and friendly. She had begun by admiring Malcolm and liking him and these feelings had grown gradually and imperceptibly into love.

"When did you begin to like me a little?" she asked him.

"I've loved you for years," said Malcolm softly. "I didn't realise it at the time, but I realise it now. I've loved you ever since you were a little girl with barley-sugar pigtails. When I saw you at the swimming-pool I knew I had been waiting for you all my life. That's why I was lonely, because there was a hole in my heart that nobody else could fill, it was just the right size for you—neither too big nor too small."

"But what about Edith? You were engaged to her."

"We all make mistakes. We all stray from the path now and then; we shouldn't be human if we never strayed from the path. You aren't jealous of Edith by any chance?"

"Not a bit," replied Dinah, turning her head and smiling at him.

"That's a pity," said Malcolm with an elaborate sigh. "When did you begin to think you would like to marry me?" Dinah wanted to know.

"Never," said Malcolm seriously. "I never thought there was any hope of that. I had given up the idea of marriage long ago. Why should any woman want to marry a crock?"

"She might love you," suggested Dinah. "She might love you so much that she couldn't bear the idea of going on living without you; she might haven hole in her heart that fitted you." They were silent for a little while.

"Dinah," said Malcolm at last. "Just supposing I don't come through—"

She leant over and put her finger on his lips. "I shall be there, willing you to win," she whispered.

"So I can't lose," he agreed, taking the finger and kissing it. He hesitated and then added, "I shan't lose—I feel quite different already—so don't worry."

"I'm not worrying," Dinah replied.

It was not quite true, of course, but it was one of those lies that the Recording Angel overlooks.

THE END

AN AUTOBIOGRAPHICAL SKETCH
by D.E. Stevenson

EDINBURGH was my birthplace and I lived there until I was married in 1916. My father was the grandson of Robert Stevenson who designed the Bell Rock Lighthouse and also a great many other lighthouses and harbours and other notable engineering works. My father was a first cousin of Robert Louis Stevenson and they often played together when they were boys.

So it was that from my earliest days I heard a good deal about "Louis", and, like Oliver Twist, I was always asking for more, teasing my father and my aunts for stories about him. He must have been a strange child, a dreamy unpredictable creature with a curious fascination about him which his cousins felt but did not understand. How could ordinary healthy, noisy children understand that solitary, sensitive soul! And as they grew up they understood him even less for Louis was not of their world. He was born too late or too early. The narrow conventional ideas of mid-Victorian Edinburgh were anathema to him. Louis would have been happy in a romantic age, striding the world in cloak and doublet with a sword at his side, he would have sold his life dearly for a Lost Cause—he was ever on the side of the under-dog. He might have been happy in the world of today when every man is entitled to his own opinions and the Four Freedoms is the goal of Democracy.

My father was old-fashioned in his ideas so my sister and I were not sent to school but were brought up at home and educated by a governess. I was always very fond of reading and read everything I could get hold of including Scott, Dickens, Jane Austen and all sorts of boys' books by Jules Verne and Ballantyne and Henty.

When I was eight years old I began to write stories and poems myself. It was most exciting to discover that I could. At first my family was amused and interested in my efforts but very soon they became bored beyond measure and told me it must stop. They said it was ruining my handwriting and wasting my time. I argued with them. What was handwriting for, if not to write? "For writing letters when you're older," they said. But I could not stop. My head was full of stories and they got lost if I did not write them down, so I found a place in the box-room between two large black trunks with a skylight overhead and I made a little nest where I would not be disturbed. There I sat for hours—and wrote and wrote.

Our house was in a broad street in Edinburgh—45 Melville Street—and at the top of the street was St. Mary's Cathedral. The bells used to echo and re-echo down the man-made canyon. My sister and I used to sit on the window-seat in the nursery (which was at the top of the house) and look down at the people passing by. I told her stories about them. Some of the memories of my childhood can be found in my novel, *Listening Valley*, in which Louise and Antonia had much the same lonely childhood.

Every summer we went to North Berwick for several months and here we were more free to do as we wanted, to go out by ourselves and play on the shore and meet other children. When we were at North Berwick we sometimes drove over to a big farm, close to the sea. We enjoyed these visits tremendously for there were so many things to do and see. We rode the pony and saw the farmyard animals and walked along the lovely sands. There were rocks there too, and many ships were wrecked upon the jagged reefs until a lighthouse was erected upon the Bass Rock—designed by my father. Years afterwards I wrote a novel about this farm, about the fine old house and the beautiful garden, and I called it *The Story of Rosabelle Shaw*.

As we grew older we made more friends. We had bathing picnics and tennis parties and fancy dress dances, and of course we played golf. I was in the team of the North Berwick Ladies' Golf Club and I played in the Scottish Ladies' Championship at Muirfield and survived until the semi-finals. I was asked to play in the Scottish Team but by that time I was married and expecting my first baby so I was obliged to refuse the honour.

Every Spring my father and mother took us abroad, to France or Switzerland or Italy. We had a French maid so we spoke French easily and fluently—if not very correctly—and it was very pleasant to be able to converse with the people we met. I liked Italy best, and especially Lake Como which seemed to me so beautiful as to be almost unreal. Paris came second in my affections. There was such a gay feeling in Paris; I see it always in sunshine with the white buildings and broad streets and the crowds of brightly clad people strolling in the Boulevards or sitting in the cafés eating and drinking and chattering cheerfully. Quite often we hired a carriage and drove through the Bois de Boulogne. My sister and I were never allowed to go out alone, of course, nor would our parents take us to a play—as I have said before they were old-fashioned and strict in their ideas and considered a "French Play" an unsuitable form of entertainment for their daughters—but in spite of these annoying prejudices we managed to have quite an amusing time and we always enjoyed our visits to foreign countries.

In 1913 I "came out" and had a gay winter in Edinburgh. There were brilliant "Balls" in those far off days, the old Assembly Rooms glittered with lights and the long gilt mirrors reflected girls in beautiful frocks and men in uniform or kilts. The older women sat round the ballroom attired in velvet or satin and diamonds watching the dancers—and especially watching their own offspring—with eyes like hawks, and talking scandal to one another. We danced waltzes and Scottish country dances and Reels—the Reels were usually made up beforehand by the Scottish Regiment which was quartered at Edinburgh Castle. It was a coveted honour to be asked to dance in these Reels and one had to be on one's toes all the time. Woe betide the unfortunate girl who put a foot wrong or failed to set to her partner at exactly the right moment!

The First Great War put an end to all these gaieties—certainly nobody felt inclined to dance when every day the long lists of casualties were published and the gay young men who had been one's partners were reported dead or missing or returned wounded from the ghastly battlefields.

In 1916 I married Major James Reid Peploe. His family was an Edinburgh family, as mine was. Curiously enough I knew his mother and father and his brothers but had never met him until he returned to Edinburgh from the war, wounded in the head. When he recovered we were married and then began the busiest time of my life. We moved about from place to place (as soldiers and their wives and families must do) and, what with the struggle to get houses and the arrival—at reasonable intervals—of two sons and a daughter I had very little time for writing. I managed to write some short stories and some children's poems but it was not until we were settled for some years in Glasgow that I began my literary career in earnest.

Mrs. Tim was my first successful novel. In it I wrote an account of the life of an Officer's wife and many of the incidents in the story are true—or only very slightly touched up. Unfortunately people in Glasgow were not very pleased with their portraits and became somewhat chilly in consequence. After that I wrote *Miss Buncle's Book* which has been one of my most popular books. It sold in thousands and is still selling. It is about a woman who wrote a book about the small town in which she lived and about the reactions of the community.

All the time my children were growing up I continued to write: *Miss Buncle Married, Miss Dean's Dilemma, Smouldering Fire, The Story of Rosabelle Shaw, The Baker's Daughter, Green Money, Rochester's Wife, A World in Spell* followed in due succession—and then came the Second Great War.

Hitherto I had written to please myself, to amuse myself and others, but now I realised that I could do good work. *The English Air* was my first novel to be written with a purpose. In this novel I tried to give an artistically true picture of how English people thought and felt about the war so that other countries might understand us better, and, judging by the hundreds of letters I received from people all over the world, I succeeded in my object—succeeded beyond my wildest hopes. My wartime books are *Mrs. Tim Carries On, Spring Magic, Celia's House, Listening Valley, The Two Mrs. Abbotts, Crooked Adam* and *The Four Graces*. In these books I have pictured every-day life in Britain during the war and have tried to show how ordinary people stood up to the frightfulness and what they thought and did during those awful years of anxiety. One of my American readers wrote to me and said, "You make us understand what it must be like to have a tiger in the backyard." I appreciated that letter.

Wartime brought terrible anxieties to me, for my elder son was in Malta during the worst of the Siege of that island and then came home and landed in France on D-Day and went through the whole campaign with the Guards Armoured Division. He was wounded in ten places and was decorated with the Military Cross for outstanding bravery. My daughter was an officer in the Women's Royal Naval Service and was commended for her valuable work.

In addition to my writing I organised the collection of Sphagnum Moss for the Red Cross and together with others went out on the moors in all weathers, wading deep in bog, to collect the moss for surgical dressings. This particular form of war-work is described in detail in *Listening Valley*.

After the long weary years of war came victory for the Allies, but my job of writing stories went on. I wrote *Mrs. Tim Gets a Job, Kate Hardy, Young Mrs. Savage* and *Vittoria Cottage*. All these books were quite as successful as their predescessors and *Young Mrs. Savage* was chosen by the American Family Reading Club as their Book of the Month. My new novel *Music in the Hills* is in the same genre and all those who have read it think it is one of my best. A businessman, who lives in London, wrote to me saying '*Music in the Hills* is as good as a holiday and, although I have read several other books since reading it, the peaceful atmosphere lingers in my mind. I hope your next book will tell us more about James and Rhoda and the other characters for they are so real to me and have become my friends." The scene of this book is laid in the hills and valleys of the Scottish Borders and the people are the rugged individualistic race who inhabit this beautiful country. For a long time it has been in my mind to write a story with this setting and to try to describe the atmosphere, to paint an artistically true picture of life in this district. Now it is finished and I hope my large and faithful public will enjoy reading it as much as I have enjoyed writing it.

Sometimes I have been accused of making my characters "too nice". I have been told that my stories are "too pleasant", but the fact is I write of people as I find them and am fond of my fellow human beings. Perhaps I have been fortunate but in all my wanderings I have met very few thoroughly unpleasant people, so I find it difficult to write about them.

We live in Moffat now. Moffat is a small but very interesting old town which lies in a valley between round rolling hills. Some of the buildings are very old indeed but outside the town there are pleasant residential houses with gardens and fine trees of oak and beech and elm. From my window as I write I can see the lovely sweep of moorland where the small, lively, black-faced sheep live and move and have their being. Every day the hills look different: sometimes grey and cold, sometimes green and smiling; in winter they are often white with snow or hidden in soft grey mist, in September they are purple with heather, like a royal robe. Although Moffat is isolated there is plenty of society and many interesting people to talk to and entertain and it is only fifty miles from Edinburgh so, if I feel dull, I can go and stay there at my comfortable club and see a good play or a film and do some shopping.

There are several questions which recur again and again in letters from friends and acquaintances. Perhaps I should try to answer them. The first is, why do you write? I write because I enjoy writing more than anything. It is fascinating to think out a story and to feel it taking shape in my mind. Of course I like making money by my books—who would not?—but the money is a secondary consideration, a by-product as it were. The story is the thing. Writing a book is the most exciting adventure under the sun.

The second question is, how do you write? I write all my books in longhand, lying on a sofa near the window in my drawing room. I begin by thinking it all out and then I take a pencil and jot it all down in a notebook. When that stage is over I begin at the beginning and go on like mad until I get to the end. After that I have a little rest and then polish it up and rewrite bits of it. When I can do no more to it I pack it up, smother the parcel with sealing wax, and despatch it to be typed. I am now free as air and somewhat dazed, so I ring up all my friends (who have been neglected for months) and say, "Come and have a party."

Another question is, do you draw your characters from real life? The answer is definitely NO. The characters in a novel are the most interesting part of it and the most mysterious. They must come from Somewhere, I suppose, but they certainly do not come from "real life". They begin by taking shape in a nebulous form and then, as I think about them and live with them, they become more solid and individualistic with definite ideas of their own. Sometimes I get rather annoyed with them; they are so unmanageable, they flatly refuse to do as I want and take their own way in an arbitrary fashion.

All the people in my books are real to me. They are more real than the people I meet every day for I know them better and understand them more deeply. It is difficult to say which is my favourite character, for I am fond of them all, but the most extraordinary character I ever had to deal with was Sophonisba Marks (in my novel *The Two Mrs. Abbotts*.) I intended her to be a subsidiary character, an unimportant person in the story, but Miss Marks had other ideas. In spite of the fact that she was plain and elderly and somewhat deaf and suffered severely from rheumatism, Miss Marks walked straight into the middle of the stage and stayed there. She just wouldn't take a back seat. She is so real to me that I simply cannot believe she does not exist. Somewhere or other she must exist—perhaps I shall meet her one day! Perhaps I shall see her in the street, coming towards me clad in her black cloth coat and the round toque with the white flowers in it and carrying her umbrella in her hand. I shall stop her and say loudly (because of course she is deaf) "Miss Marks, I presume!"

It will be seen from the foregoing sketch that my life has not been a very eventful one. I have had no hair-raising adventures nor travelled in little-known parts of the world, but wherever I have been I have made interesting friends and I still retain them. Friends are like windows in a house, and what a terribly dull house it would be that had no windows! They open vistas, they show one new and lovely views of the countryside. Friends give one new ideas, new values, new interests.

Thank God for friends!

Someday I mean to write a book of reminiscences; to delve into the cupboard of memory and sort out all the junk. There is so much to write about, so many little pictures grave and gay, so many ideas to think about and disentangle and arrange. Looking back is a fascinating pastime; looking back and wondering what one's life would have been if one had done this instead of that, if one had turned to the left at the crossroads instead of to the right, if one had stayed at home instead of going out or had gone out five minutes later. Jane Welsh Carlyle says in one of her letters, "One can never be too much alive to the consideration that one's every slightest action does not end when it has acted itself but propagates itself on and on, in one shape or another, through all time and away into eternity."

FICTION BY D.E. STEVENSON

Miss Buncle Married (1936)
The Empty World (1936, aka *A World in Spell*)
The Story of Rosabelle Shaw (1937)
The Baker's Daughter (1938, aka *Miss Bun the Baker's Daughter*)
Rochester's Wife (1940)
Crooked Adam (1942)
Celia's House (1943)
The Two Mrs Abbotts (1943)
Listening Valley (1944)
The Four Graces (1946)
Amberwell (1955)
Summerhills (1956)
Still Glides the Stream (1959)
The Musgraves (1960)
Bel Lamington (1961)
Fletcher's End (1962)
Katherine Wentworth (1964)
Katherine's Marriage (1965, aka *The Marriage of Katherine*)
The House on the Cliff (1966)
Sarah Morris Remembers (1967)
Sarah's Cottage (1968)
Gerald and Elizabeth (1969)
House of the Deer (1970)
Portrait of Saskia (collection of early writings, published 2011)
Found in the Attic (collection of early writings, published 2013)

* see Explanatory Notes

EXPLANATORY NOTES

Mrs. Tim

Mrs. Tim of the Regiment, the first appearance of Mrs. Tim in the literary world, was published by Jonathan Cape in 1932. That edition, however, contained only the first half of the book currently available from Bloomsbury under the same title. The second half was originally published, as *Golden Days*, by Herbert Jenkins in 1934. Together, those two books contain Mrs. Tim's diaries for the first six months of the same year.

Subsequently, D.E. Stevenson regained the rights to the two books, and her new publisher, Collins, reissued them in the U.K. as a single volume under the title *Mrs. Tim* (1941), reprinted several times as late as 1992. In the U.S., however, the combined book appeared as *Mrs. Tim of the Regiment*, and has generally retained that title, though a 1973 reprint used the title *Mrs. Tim Christie*. Adding to the confusion, large print and audiobook editions of *Golden Days* have also appeared in recent years.

Fortunately no such title confusions exist with the subsequent Mrs. Tim titles—*Mrs. Tim Carries On* (1941), *Mrs. Tim Gets a Job* (1947), and *Mrs. Tim Flies Home* (1952)—and Dean Street Press is delighted to make these long-out-of-print volumes of the series available again, along with two more of Stevenson's most loved novels, *Smouldering Fire* (1935) and *Spring Magic* (1942).

SMOULDERING FIRE

Smouldering Fire was first published in the U.K. in 1935 and in the U.S. in 1938. Until now, those were the only complete editions of the book. All later reprints, both hardcover and paperback, have been heavily abridged, with entire chapters as well as occasional passages throughout the novel cut from the text. For our new edition, Dean Street Press has followed the text of the first U.K. edition, and we are proud to be producing the first complete, unabridged edition of *Smouldering Fire* in eighty years.

FURROWED MIDDLEBROW

*titles available in paperback only

Made in the USA
Middletown, DE
25 September 2023

39323097R00146